RENEGADE

By
Justine Sparks

CONTENTS

PART I:

THE OBARION

PROLOGUE

D im, grey light filtered into the little stone shack, and the air was still cold when Talikoth awoke. It must have only been five or six in the morning.

The chains that attached to the rigid metal cuffs encircling his ankles and wrists clinked noisily as he straightened in his splintering wooden chair, and the Vedas' soldiers that stood on either side of his cell simultaneously stiffened, alerted to his state of consciousness.

One of the guards, bolder than the other, glanced over his shoulder. He was a curious fellow—Talikoth knew, for he often caught the boy staring at him, as though observing some foreign species.

"Bathroom," Talikoth muttered, his voice cracked and hoarse from disuse. The boy jumped, then scrambled for the keys hooked onto his belt.

The other guard—a stocky young man in his mid-thirties—kept his rifle trained on Talikoth as the boy led him over to the latrine that occupied the corner of the prison shack.

When he'd relieved himself, the younger guard re-did the restraints around his limbs. As he was locking the wrist cuffs, Talikoth suddenly jerked his arm—as though to make a grab for the boy's rifle, slung over his shoulder.

In a split second, the young soldier had grasped the gun and trained it between Talikoth's eyes. His breath came quickly, but his aim was steady.

Talikoth let out a huff of laughter. "Admirable instincts," he murmured, so low that the other guard would not hear him.

The young guard blinked, his blond brows furrowing. After a moment, he seemed to shake himself, and he closed the final cuff with a *click.*

"And left-dominant, too?" Talikoth continued.

The boy glanced over his shoulder at the older guard, as though he wasn't sure whether he was breaking the rules, before he cleared his throat and answered, "Yes, sir." His face flushed—presumably because he had not meant to refer to the General of his enemy clan as "sir"—and his mouth snapped shut.

Talikoth gave him an approving nod. "That's very useful."

The blond boy shot him one more baffled look before he retreated from behind the bars and resumed his station outside of the cell.

Talikoth watched idly as the sliver of sunlight on the wall opposite him widened and shifted across the stone, climbing higher, towards the ceiling, until the shack was bathed in a faint golden glow.

The air grew warmer. The stone walls trapped in a thick, sticky heat that had his hair clinging to his forehead, but Talikoth could not reach up to push it away.

It was just past eight in the morning when a knock sounded against the heavy metal door that led outside.

The stocky guard went to answer it. He stepped

out, and Talikoth heard the murmur of voices on the other side. There was a pause, and then the door creaked open again.

"You've got half an hour," the stocky guard grunted over his shoulder. Dak came through the door after him, still in his uniform, his black hair cropped short as ever, and his dark face somber. His wife, Alvi, shuffled in his shadow. She wore a long cloak, the hood drawn over her head, and her slate grey eyes narrowed as she surveyed the guards in front of them.

"It's really rather impromptu, Moonstone giving us no notice," the stocky guard continued, his mouth curled into a scowl. He lifted a piece of paper clutched in his hand—Talikoth was almost certain he'd not been holding it when he left—and gave it a suspicious once-over.

"We are beholden to you for the accommodation," Dak said smoothly, bowing his head. The guard strode from the shack, and after casting a perplexed glance between the three of them, his young comrade scrambled after him.

As soon as the door closed behind them, Alvi strode forward, slipping a hand beneath her cloak and withdrawing a rusted silver key.

"Still employing that aptitude for forgery, I see," Talikoth drawled, as she unlocked his cell and slipped inside. "How long did it take you to copy her handwriting?"

"Believe it or not, the note was genuine," Dak piped up, leaning against the wall just outside of Talikoth's cell. "Moonstone seems to trust me a great deal more than the other officers." He glanced sideways at Talikoth and added, in a tone too off-hand to be accidental, "I'm sure Atlas having vouched for me didn't hurt."

Talikoth said nothing, but instead turned his gaze to Alvi, who had withdrawn a bag from beneath her cloak and set it down beside his rickety chair as she lowered her hood. Her dark curls were pulled back in a braid, and her almond-brown skin looked more ashen than usual, but she appeared otherwise unharmed.

"They've done nothing to you," Talikoth confirmed, his eyes raking over her face, before he glanced over at Dak. "To any of you?"

"Nothing at all," Dak confirmed, sliding his hands into his pockets. "They've been perfectly amicable hosts."

It was only because he knew Dak so well that Talikoth could detect the faintest note of bitterness beneath his otherwise indifferent tone.

"You'll inform me if anything changes," Talikoth said immediately. "Ensure that we're positioned to strike should Moonstone show even the slightest inclination towards malintent—and send Chitali here posthaste to release me—"

"I thought you were crazy, giving us spare keys to the prison shack all those years ago," Alvi murmured, rolling her eyes. She had withdrawn a comb from her bag and ran it through Talikoth's hair with painstaking delicacy as she glanced down at him with an amused smile. "Now I see you were just being absurdly proactive, as always."

"You can never be too careful," Talikoth said distractedly. The woman had withdrawn a razor from that bag of hers and started to move it towards his face, but he quickly jerked his head away. "Better not—

they're bound to notice."

She arched a brow, absently scratching the thick beard that carpeted his lower jaw. "I'm surprised you can stand it."

"I hardly can," Talikoth muttered.

"You should have heard her fussing, when they took you into custody," Dak remarked with a wry smile.

"And rightly so!" Alvi retorted, scowling as she gestured around them. "Look at this hovel they're keeping him in!"

Talikoth caught Dak's eye, and they both shared an amused smirk. "Once a rich girl, always a rich girl," Talikoth drawled.

Alvi smacked him on the shoulder, before her hand cupped his cheek, her dark brows knitting together. "How are you really?" she asked with a frown. "They're not treating you too horribly, are they?"

"Garagleen's been having a proper fit," Dak intoned with a snort. "Cursing out any of the Vedas that have the misfortune of coming too near to his quarters —"

"We could sneak you out of here now, rather than later," Alvi insisted. "Dak brought a handgun—you know he could take both of the guards out in a heartbeat —"

"No," Talikoth said sharply. Alvi's face fell, and the harsh edge in his voice softened, ever so slightly. "No. As long as Moonstone continues to conduct herself as she has, I see no reason to disrupt her mode of operation, for the time being."

"Talikoth's been through much worse, Al," Dak reminded her quietly from where he leaned against the wall.

She pouted a little, but nodded, leaning down to press a kiss to Talikoth's cheek before she collected her bag from the floor and made her way out of the cell, locking it behind her.

Dak's eyes met Talikoth's, before he turned to Alvi and said, "Wait for me outside, will you, sweetheart?"

Her eyes narrowed. "Oh, *I* see, now only the *men* can speak, hmm?"

Talikoth's lips twitched, and Dak gave her an apologetic look. "Go on, now. I'll only be a few minutes."

"You two are so aggravating," Alvi mumbled, spinning on her heel and stomping—like a teenager half her age, rather than a grown woman with children of her own—out of the little stone shanty.

"Where is the boy?" Talikoth asked, as soon as the door snapped shut.

"As far as I've heard Moonstone is keeping him away from Headquarters," Dak said. "If everything I've been told is true, he's been isolated from any of our clanspeople—"

"So she's still planning on using him," Talikoth muttered. "That could change at any moment—as soon as she sees fit, she may discard of him. He's a threat to her if she plans on making a grab for power."

Dak hesitated, before he tentatively said, "She appears to have some level of...affection for the boy—"

"That could be fabricated," Talikoth dismissed immediately. "She's been manipulating him—"

"As did you," Dak interjected in a cold voice.

Talikoth glanced at him sharply. It looked as though the words had left Dak's mouth before he'd intended, for his posture grew stiff.

"Ah, so we've arrived here, have we?" Talikoth

said, straightening up taller in his chair. "I wondered what you must have thought, after the trial."

"I just don't understand why you didn't tell me," Dak said curtly, his hands clenched into fists at his sides.

Talikoth lifted a shoulder lazily. "I saw no reason to. The Council only cared that retribution was served—they had no qualms about who served it—"

"Yes, but you'd think you would have told *me*, at the very least," Dak hissed, letting out a harsh breath as he ran a hand over his short hair. "What, you think I would have condemned you? After what she did—after what she took from me?"

"The boy was too young to have understood," Talikoth said dispassionately. "You and Alvi were close to him—Delurah had already found out by mistake—the less people who knew the truth, the better." His brows furrowed, and he gave Dak a piercing look. "Have you spoken to the Council?"

"There hasn't been so much as a whisper of doubt," Dak said. His tone had leveled once more, though his dark eyes still glittered with residual anger. "According to them, you fulfilled your obligation to at least attempt to settle the score for his treason. They were perfectly convinced." He hesitated, before adding, "As was the boy."

Talikoth's eyes remained trained firmly on a spot of wall above Dak's shoulder. "Yes, well...a small sacrifice." Suddenly, anger thrummed beneath his skin, scalding hot like a fire. "He would have deserved it," Talikoth said in a low, fierce voice. "After everything that I gave him—after all that I sacrificed—"

"You cannot deny that, for all your frustration, you admire the boy's gall," Dak said, smirking.

Talikoth's lips twitched again, but he only shook his head, his eyes affixed on the ceiling above him.

Dak turned to leave, but Talikoth cleared his throat and said, "There was...one other thing. There was...a girl. On the battlefield that day."

The dark-skinned man turned back to face him, his hands folded behind his back. "The girl that launched the missile," he said expressionlessly. "You almost killed her. The Council regaled me."

Talikoth nodded. "The girl was—" His jaw flexed, and he pressed on, "She looked just like—just like Olympion. It was—well, it's most likely a coincidence— I was certain my mind was playing tricks on me..."

Dak's gaze was shrewd. "She's here, at Headquarters," he said, his tone carefully neutral. "Moonstone has her working in the lab, according to Ilquir. Clever little thing, they say."

"Probably just a coincidence," Talikoth repeated, shaking his head.

Dak's brows furrowed. "Should I—"

"No," Talikoth said quickly. "Don't say anything to Alvi—not until we're sure. No sense in getting her hopes up—god knows she's lost enough, to have another dream dashed."

Dak bowed his head, and Talikoth continued. "No, we'll bide our time. And when the moment comes, everything will unfold in our people's favor. Just as fate has written for us."

CHAPTER ONE

When Atlas' eyes opened, he could tell that it was too early. The soldiers in the barracks around him were still fast asleep, and outside the campsite was quiet. His mind felt calmer than it had in a long while as he lay there, his body sinking into the cot, his eyelids weighty—

But then Raider's lifeless gaze flashed across his mind.

Atlas' jaw flexed, and he tried to push his thoughts in a different direction—*Jereis, skin blistering and burnt as he seized against the fence.*

His stomach lurched, and he sat up quickly. *Colonel Caddo crumpled to the floor, his wrinkled face twisted with pain and shock.* He swung his legs to the ground, gripping the edge of his cot as his breathing grew labored. *The blood gurgled from the tank soldier's throat and his body sunk back into the hatch.*

Atlas sprang to his feet, bolting out of the tent before he was fully cognizant of what he was doing, his steps carrying him across the clearing as he attempted to calm the race of his pulse, his heart pounding against his rib cage.

The nightmares had plagued him for weeks now, and not only had they been growing in frequency and intensity, but they now appeared to be seeping into Atlas' waking hours.

He saw visions of *all* of the dead, too. Not just Raider, or Koda, or the Obarion that he had killed, but everyone that had died, lined up in long rows before their bodies were covered and transported for burial. He saw Vaddicus, a boy that had been a year behind him in Academy, his shirt tattered with bullet holes. He saw Kendo, blond hair matted with blood, and his blue eyes wide and eerily lifeless. He saw Moabi, and Piston, and Alclavir. Jameson and Dart and Amarillo and Goose and so many others—boys he had grown up with, young men he had laughed with at the Fringe the evening before the attack. And now they were dead, the life snatched from their bodies in the blink of an eye.

Atlas ran a hand through his hair, leaning against a tree and taking in great gulps of fresh, salty air.

He was fairly confident that he would feel better, that he would no longer be tormented by these nighttime terrors, once he had something to *do*. The last month had been painfully uneventful, especially after the weeks of planning and subterfuge.

He knew intellectually he should be grateful for the end of the war, but there was a part of him that itched, that *longed* for another fight—anything to break up the tedium and distract him from the constant images circulating in his head.

Five hundred Vedas had been assigned to Obarion headquarters, where their soldiers were detained and civilians kept under close watch in case of any attempt at revolt. Atlas volunteered, but Moonstone quickly shut him down, insisting that he needed respite after everything that he had been through in the last few months. Instead, Atlas had been sent back to the campsite on the Fringe.

The other soldiers staying on the Fringe took turns patrolling the area and switching off with the guards assigned to Obarion headquarters, but when they were not on duty, many of them had spent the last few weeks celebrating. The Fringe was constantly swelling with the sounds of their merriment and inebriation, but Atlas felt no inclination to join them, and often found himself annoyed with all of the commotion.

For he had *gotten* his respite—he had taken six whole days of rest, full of nothing but pranks with Whitsom, Delurah's cooking, long conversations with her about all that had changed in the time he'd been gone, and stolen hours with Gaiomere in the woods around Headquarters with very little conversation at all.

That had been before Moonstone insisted he leave Headquarters, and now Atlas could hardly take it. He didn't *want* this respite—he wanted something that would keep him from thinking about everything that he had seen.

Every death he'd witnessed, every life he had needed to take, or perhaps most prominently, the cold glint of hatred in Talikoth's eyes as Moonstone's soldiers dragged him away. Ice settled over Atlas every time he thought of it.

One of the perimeter guards was giving him a strange look, so he made his way down the long slope towards the ocean.

Today, at least, would offer potential distraction, no matter how stale the last month had been. Moonstone was finally, *finally* allowing him back at Headquarters, though only temporarily. Still, it was certainly better than nothing, and if all went well...

He contemplated, for perhaps the hundredth time since Moonstone had come to him a few days ago, what he was going to say when he came face-to-face with his clansmen. If he only had some idea of what to expect—but he had none. He had no idea how many of them had been stewing in fury during their detainment, how many of them had taken the words of the trial to heart, and how many were plotting, even now, to enact revenge against the Vedas and the tribes that had helped them. Would they still see him as a criminal who had betrayed his own people? Or would they understand, given what they knew, why he had done the things he had?

The sounds of the other soldiers stirring carried down to the shore, and Atlas made his way back up to the campsite to help with breakfast.

Moonstone arrived a quarter to nine to escort him to Headquarters. As they wound their way through the broken, debris-ridden streets of the Ramshackle and into the wood surrounding the Obarion base, the tension simmering beneath Atlas' skin mounted. Even Moonstone, ever collected and impassive, seemed on-edge. When they arrived at the gate, she was curt with the guards, and a vein twitched in her temple that wasn't normally present.

"Have you determined who will be your first targets?" she asked as they strode across the long front lawn. Two soldiers broke off from the group guarding the gate and walked on either side of them, their guns hitched high on their shoulders and eyes sweeping carefully across the grounds in every direction. One was olive-skinned and dark-haired, the other, gangly and blond.

"I'll be speaking with Colonel Dak, in the officers' lodgings," Atlas told Moonstone. "And after that, a soldier in unit 12B." She nodded.

Far too quickly for Atlas' liking, they reached the officers' lodgings. "It's okay," he said, when one of the soldiers started to follow him in. "I think it's better if you stay out here."

Moonstone frowned. "Atlas, I'm not sure—"

"You promised I could do this my way," Atlas reminded her. "None of my clanspeople will respond well to anyone barging into their homes with guns pointing in their faces. Would you?"

Her brows were still furrowed. "You've got your transmitter," she said finally, her tone reluctant. She nodded her head towards the blond soldier, adding, "Kamar and I will be posted just outside the building— do not hesitate to notify us if there is any trouble."

Atlas nodded shortly, turning to face the door as their heavy footfall retreated back outside. He took a deep breath and knocked.

It was a few moments before the door swung open, and Dak's wife, Alvi, blinked up at him, surprise evident in her expression. She was a tall woman, perhaps in her thirties, with curly dark hair and almond brown skin. Sutti and Quill, she and Dak's twin toddlers, peeked out at him from behind the sofa.

"Atlas," she said after a moment.

"Hello," he mumbled, rubbing the back of his neck awkwardly. Another moment passed, and then Alvi enfolded him in a hug.

"It's good to see you," she said earnestly, pulling back to hold him at arm's length. "How are you?"

A wave of relief washed over him, for her gaze was not accusing, and her tone was welcoming. There was a sliver of hope, then, that *some* of his people, at least, might not regard him as traitorous scum like his father did.

"I'm—" He started to say that he was fine, but the familiar warmth of Alvi's gaze pulled the truth from his lips before he could stop it. "I've been better," he admitted.

Alvi patted his cheek sympathetically. "I'm sure you have."

"Is—I was wondering—is your husband in?" Atlas immediately registered the idiocy of his question; the soldiers and civilians were confined between their quarters and the dining hall during mealtimes and did not have the freedom to roam the grounds.

"Yes, of course. Why don't you come in?"

Dak was sitting in an armchair, a newspaper between his hands, and a pair of glasses perched on his nose. He was dark-skinned and black-haired, tall, broad-shouldered, and muscular. Even seated, he had an imposing presence.

"Moonstone has made you her messenger boy, I see," the Colonel said in his deep voice. He got to his feet and offered Atlas a hand.

Atlas snorted, shaking the offered hand as he wryly remarked, "Well, I suppose after everything I deserve a demotion, don't I?"

Dak gave him a piercing look, his dark eyes flitting over Atlas' face. "I think you have been very brave," he said finally, gesturing towards the sofa and sinking back into his own chair. "I'm sorry that you found out about your mother that way. You probably won't believe me when I say that I had no idea—"

"I believe you," Atlas said quickly, as he sat down. "Let's not pretend that Talikoth was exactly forthcoming unless he had to be."

Dak tilted his head in acknowledgement, carefully folding his newspaper and setting it on the end table.

Atlas hesitated. "Did you know? What was going on at the rigs, I mean?" He tried to keep the note of indictment from his voice, but the older man must have heard it, for he glanced sideways at Atlas, arching a black brow.

"I knew that the Inner Ring soldiers were organizing executions, yes. Though I never witnessed them carried out. Talikoth assured us it was for the safety of our people. The Renegades have demonstrated tendencies towards violence."

"But—but there were children being sent to the rigs," Atlas said. His gaze unconsciously wandered over towards Sutti and Quill, who were playing quietly on the floor together, building a tower of wooden blocks.

Dak followed his gaze and, it seemed, his train of thought. "Understand, Atlas, that I—one never feels *right* about such things—but this is the nature of war. I was sure that in the end, it would be worth it—for the sake of *our* families—our children's futures. Talikoth saw the future all of our people envisioned—and he was willing to make the difficult choices to bring about that future."

Dak leaned forward, resting his elbows on his legs and running his hands tiredly over his face. "You have to understand, Atlas, that we—for those of us that grew up before the Obarion came west—before we amassed power and weapons and before we were able to hold our own—the survival of our clan hung by a thread. We were on the brink of demise. Food was scarce and sickness rampaged our people. We survived, but only just—and each day looked bleaker than the last. It was only when Talikoth took the helm of our clan—it was only then that fate shifted in our favor."

Atlas couldn't help but interrupt, "Fate didn't *shift* in our favor—Talikoth knew that we'd have more food and water if there were less tribes competing for it—so he killed them all. Then, when he realized there were more resources in the West, he killed every tribe in that direction, too!" Atlas let out a harsh exhale. "Look, Talikoth's justification for killing the Ren was that they were a danger to us, but if we work with them they can help us grow more food, make more medicine, detoxify more water. They wouldn't be in competition with us for resources, they'd be helping us to amplify them—"

Dak shook his head. The look he gave Atlas was a mixture of amusement and exasperation, practically dripping with patronization, and Atlas ran a hand through his hair in frustration.

"Look, all I'm saying is this: our clan can't subsist on the murder of innocent people. If the Ren don't stand against us, and the Vedas are willing to work *with* us, wouldn't you be inclined to stop the fighting? To reach a —a compromise, of sorts?"

Dak slid his glasses off, massaging the bridge of his nose. "In theory? Sure. But Atlas, it's never so easy—"

"You believe that Talikoth killed my mother, don't you?"

The dark-skinned man frowned. "Yes. I do. But he's not incorrect—the Renegades *are* dangerous—"

"I know they are," Atlas said impatiently. "Or I know they *can* be. But not all of them are like that. Just like not all of the Vedas are bad. Just like not all of the Obarion are good." Dak looked as though he were going to interrupt, and Atlas pressed on, "The Vedas were only protecting themselves from the Obarion—I was in their base, I *saw* their strategy sessions. General Moonstone wanted to keep her people alive and safe—Talikoth only saw a threat in their numbers. And the Ren?" He let out a huff of humorless laughter. "Colonel, they're only trying to survive. The gangs may have been striking against the Obarion, but the rest of the Ren just wanted to be able to roam the Westland in peace, without having to fear for their lives."

Dak shook his head, but there was a glimpse of doubt in his eyes, and Atlas clung to it. "You believe Talikoth lied about my mother—you admitted that— that he was wrong. Would it be so hard to believe that he was wrong about the Ren and Vedas, too? There's no possibility in your mind that we might actually be able to work together?"

The Colonel didn't answer. Atlas straightened, his gaze boring into the older man's as he said, "Talikoth told our people that he wanted to restore the Westland —but all he ever did for sixteen years was destroy things. The Vedas have kept their promise, haven't they? Since you declared your surrender, they haven't harmed a single soldier or civilian."

"They have not," Dak agreed, tapping his fingers contemplatively on the arms of his chair. "Which, admittedly, has surprised me."

"The Vedas have learned to preserve what resources they have—and they learned *that* from the

Ren. Turn against them and I can promise you, our people will die out. But there's an alternative. What have we got to lose?"

The older man gazed at him, silent for so long that Atlas shifted uncomfortably. But just as he was about to get to his feet, to find Moonstone and report that his conference had been a wash, Dak said, "Only our pride."

Atlas tilted his head to the side, waiting for him to continue.

"We will never be Vedas."

"No," Atlas agreed quietly. "Obarion is in our blood. But working with other clans and tribes doesn't mean renouncing our ways and traditions. We don't have to be like them, and we don't have to try to make them like us. Quite the contrary, our strengths lie in our differences. As long as I have any say in the matter, the Obarion flag will always fly over the South. I just think that—" He hesitated, his hands curling and uncurling in his lap as he tried to find the right words. "I just think I want it to mean something different than it has for the last sixteen years. I don't want to stand under a flag that only inspires fear. I'd rather inspire hope. For something better, I guess. That's what Talikoth was aiming for at the beginning, wasn't it?"

Dak had gotten to his feet, so Atlas did too, gripping the hand offered to him. "It was," he agreed. "Perhaps it is time for a change. You've given me much to think on."

Atlas nodded and started towards the door. Alvi stood at the sink washing dishes, and she gave his shoulder a squeeze as he passed.

"Atlas," the Colonel called.

He stopped and turned back. Dak was still on his feet, and though his expression was impassive, his eyes flickered with something akin to anger. "I do believe that your father lied about killing your mother—and that he was wrong to have lied." He hesitated, and then continued, "But I do not for a second believe that the actions he took were wrong."

Atlas' mouth opened, and then closed again. "How—how can you say that?"

Dak shook his head slowly, his eyes shifting over to Alvi, who had returned to her washing, though her brows were knitted into a frown. "You didn't know her like we did," he muttered.

He said nothing else, but simply sank back into his armchair and disappeared behind his newspaper once more. Atlas stood there for several seconds, flabbergasted, a thousand questions racing through his mind, but when it became clear that Dak would say nothing else, he strode towards the door, yanking it open and letting it slam shut behind him.

Outside of the officers' lodgings, Moonstone waited with Kamar, her fingers drumming impatiently on the folder clasped in her hand. When she spotted Atlas, some of the tension melted from her face.

"Was your conference satisfactory?" she asked.

Atlas' mind was still spinning with Dak's last remark, and it took him a few moments to register her words. "What? Oh. Yeah, I suppose."

"Kamar will escort you to unit 12B, and I shall meet you back at the campsite for a full report after."

Atlas nodded and followed Kamar around the Main to the soldiers' quarters.

The dark haired Vedas soldier was already

waiting outside of unit 12B. He stood stiffly, tapping his foot, and Atlas got the impression that he did not like being inside of Obarion headquarters any more than Atlas had initially liked being at the Vedas' base.

"You guys don't have to stay," Atlas told the pair of them. "Honestly, he won't be any trouble. And even if he was, I could take him easy."

Kamar looked as though he might have been considering it, but the olive-skinned soldier shook his head. "Moonstone wanted you escorted directly back to the Fringe. We'll wait outside."

Atlas shrugged, turning away from them, but a pulse of annoyance throbbed in his chest.

He started to knock, but on second thought, decided against it, and instead pushed the door open and walked inside.

Bettoni sat at the dining room table, his hands folded in front of him. His long hair was pulled back at the nape of his neck, and he was still in his sleep clothes. The door had barely snapped shut behind Atlas when he said, "Since when can you take me *easy*?"

Atlas' mouth curled into a smirk. "Since always, don't be stupid."

It looked, for a moment, as though Bettoni's lips twitched, but then he shook his head, scowling down at the tabletop. Atlas crossed the room and sat in the chair opposite him.

"You lied to me," Bettoni began, his eyes, so dark they looked black, pinning Atlas with a glare. "That night, back in the North."

Atlas frowned, but answered truthfully. "Yes."

The older boy arched a brow. "I didn't know you could lie so well."

Atlas leaned back in his chair, shrugging half-heartedly as he admitted, "I've never had a reason to lie to you before, so I imagine you wouldn't."

Bettoni let out a humorless laugh. "Yeah, I kind of thought that's how friendships worked. That we didn't lie to each other."

Atlas flinched, but his tone was resolute as he said, "I won't apologize for doing what I had to. There were more lives at stake than just yours. If you're too selfish to see that—after everything that you heard at the trial—all the pain those people suffered at Talikoth's hands—then you're half the man I thought you were."

Bettoni's brown cheeks flushed pink. "They could have been lying—" he mumbled, but Atlas interrupted him.

"Oh yeah, *all* those people from different tribes all over the Westland colluded, makes sense," he snapped, rolling his eyes.

Bettoni stayed silent for a few moments, his eyes affixed on the table. Finally, he looked up at Atlas, and quietly said, "Coral never doubted you for a second, you know. When you got captured, he was so sure you'd escape, and even—even when we *saw* you fighting with the Vedas and the Ren...Coral said there had to be an explanation."

A flood of warmth swelled in Atlas' chest, and Bettoni continued, "He said that if it was any other soldier, he would have just written them off as a scummy traitor, but that...that you'd never betray our clan for anything but the truth."

"Is that what you believe?" Atlas pressed.

Bettoni sighed. "Coral's an idiot. But I—I reckon he's right in this case."

Atlas grinned, and Bettoni chucked a coaster at his head. "Don't look so smug—if Moonstone turns out to be dangerous to our civilians—"

"If Moonstone endangers our civilians, I'll kill her myself," Atlas said immediately.

Bettoni gave him a penetrating look. Eventually, though, he seemed satisfied that Atlas was telling the truth and nodded.

Atlas looked him over very seriously. "How are you really, though?"

Bettoni shrugged, tilting back in his chair. "It's strange. Like being a prisoner in my own home."

"It won't be for much longer, if Dak is willing to comply," Atlas told him. "Moonstone just—she doesn't want any of the soldiers or civilians defying the terms of surrender. She doesn't want anyone else getting hurt."

"What exactly is she planning on doing with us?" Bettoni asked.

Atlas hesitated. "Moonstone wants to integrate the clans. Not like assimilating the Obarion," he added quickly, when he saw Bettoni's expression of horror. "Just—an end to the fighting. Mutual utilization of the resources. She thinks we can help each other."

"What about the Ren?"

"What about them?"

"Well, they were willing enough to comply when it came to fighting against the Obarion, but do you *really* think they're going to fall in line and take orders now that Talikoth has been shunted?"

Atlas' eyes roved contemplatively towards the ceiling. "I don't think they'll just 'fall in line,' no. But we don't necessarily need them to. They've got an incomparable understanding of the land and how to use the resources, and Moonstone thinks that if we can get them to share their knowledge, it will benefit everybody —both clans, and all the tribes."

Bettoni looked thoughtful now. "What'd you need me to do?"

Another tide of warmth flooded Atlas' chest. "We need the Obarion to trust the Vedas—*and* the Ren— since we'll all be working so closely. I need you to cast out feelers. See if you can scope out any potential rebellion, pick as many brains as you can. Then I need you to plant seeds. The trial was the first step—and a definitive step at that, from what Delurah's told me. A lot of the Obarion aren't happy with all the secrets that were kept from them—but they're just as afraid of the Vedas, and what they might do. They need to see that there's nothing to fear."

Bettoni looked rather uncertain. "I don't know, At. You're better at all this schmoozing. Why can't you do it?"

Atlas frowned. "Our clanspeople don't trust me right now. Some of them may never trust me again. But they trust you, and Coral. And I trust you guys more than anybody."

Bettoni nodded slowly. "Alright. We'll do our best." He hesitated, and then said, "You should talk to him. Coral, I mean."

"I know. I will. As soon as I—" Atlas broke off, running a hand through his hair. "Believe it or not, I don't have any more freedom to move around here than you do."

"You'd think Moonstone would let you do whatever you wanted," Bettoni pointed out. "She wouldn't have been able to pull any of this off without you. All the intel you must have given her..." He did not speak accusingly, only as a matter of fact, and his confidence reignited the anger in Atlas' mind anew.

"You'd think that, wouldn't you?" he muttered bitterly. "I haven't seen Delurah in weeks—Moonstone won't even let me *near* my unit—"

Bettoni arched a brow. "Why is it you have to listen to her? I mean, it's not as though she's *your* general."

Atlas shifted. "Moonstone means well," he insisted. Maybe it had been a mistake to confide in Bettoni when he was working so hard to assure his clansmen of the Vedas' trustworthiness.

Bettoni shrugged. "I meant what I said. I've got your back here. Coral and I will do what we can within the clan, but just don't—don't think that because Talikoth was the wrong pick—don't think that automatically makes Moonstone any better. If it turns out that we need to, I don't know, stage a coup and take out both of them...well, we've got your back there, too."

Atlas swallowed, his gratitude for his friend's loyalty dampened only by his apprehension for the bloodbath that would surely transpire, should it come to that.

◆ ◆ ◆

When he arrived back at the campsite, Moonstone was waiting for a briefing, and he recounted everything discussed during each of his conversations—though he was careful to leave out the bit where Bettoni offered to help him stage in insurrection.

"Colonel Dak's open to working with us, I can tell," Atlas said. "He'll take more persuading, certainly, but once he's assured that the Vedas only want what's best for the Obarion people, his loyalty won't waver."

"I'm glad to hear he was receptive, with how much resistance Lieutenant General Crowley has given us," Moonstone muttered. She tapped her pencil against her thick notebook as she continued, "I would like to set up a meeting with him as soon as possible. There are some logistics that we need to address—"

"I'd be happy to meet with him again, General—" Atlas offered, but Moonstone quickly interrupted.

"No, Atlas, that won't be necessary." She looked up from her notes, her brow furrowed as her shrewd, dark eyes flickered over his face. "To be perfectly frank, I was hesitant to ask you to act as a liaison in the first place, but the Council insisted that it would be for the best."

"Why not?" Atlas demanded. "I'm perfectly capable of conferring with any of the Obarion officers —"

"That is not your *duty*, Atlas," Moonstone said sharply, and his mouth snapped shut. "You are a *soldier*. We gave you more responsibility preceding the battle because it was necessary, and your efforts have not gone unappreciated." She sighed, her face softening. Her arm lifted for a moment, as though she were going to put a hand on his shoulder, but then she seemed to decide against it. "I don't doubt your capability, Atlas, not for a second. But you've already had more pressure put on you than you deserve." She glanced over towards the firepit, where the Vedas and Ramshacklers were preparing lunch, laughing and cavorting noisily. "You should join the celebrations. Take a rest—"

"I've *had* a rest!" he burst out before he could stop himself. "I've had an entire month of rest and you *finally* give me any opportunity to actually do something useful only to just—just rip it away again!" He took a deep breath, but it did nothing to steady the thrum of anger coursing through him. "Whitsom and the other soldiers are helping to guard the base, you and Vailhelm are consulting with the officers, Gaiomere is helping my clan to utilize her solar conversions. I just want—I just want to do *something*."

Moonstone looked at him with a strangely knowing expression, and he wanted to rip it off her face. It made him feel like a child throwing a tantrum—but he wasn't a child. Didn't she understand all he had done?

"Your time will come, Atlas, I promise you that," she said quietly. "If you'll excuse me, I need to speak with Harcliff."

Atlas didn't bother answering her. He turned on his heel and wound his way around a tall, teetering building and down the broken street. Blood pounded in his ears as he stormed through the Ramshackle, kicking aside blocks of upheaved asphalt and shoving past overgrown foliage carelessly. He had not felt this angry at Moonstone since she had shown him the photograph of his mother, all those months ago, at the Vedas base.

Bettoni was right. What right did Moonstone have, keeping him cooped up like some caged animal? It wasn't as though she actually had any authority over him—she *wasn't* his general. In fact, since he had defected from the Obarion army, by all accounts he didn't *have* a general.

He felt the urge, suddenly, to do something reckless. He could sneak back into Headquarters, stake out in Coral's unit—she'd never think to look for him there. Or perhaps he could sneak back into his *own* unit —Delurah would keep his silence for him, and it wasn't as though Talikoth were there any longer—

His feet stuttered to a halt, and he stared blankly at the crumbling stretch of wall in front of him.

No, Atlas knew exactly what he was going to do.

CHAPTER TWO

Without another second of hesitation, Atlas veered to the right and hurried down the sloping hillside until he reached the point where the concrete met jagged rock. He walked along the Fringe for nearly thirty minutes, adrenaline coursing through him, until he found the old, tilting sign that read *No Diving* in faded red paint.

He half-walked, half-slid down the cliffside, the jagged rock catching on his pants and the skin of his back, but he ignored the discomfort, skimming the rock-face till his boots hit the sand.

Atlas trudged along the narrow beach until he reached the water's edge. In the distance, towering two hundred feet above the ocean, he could see the Gap. It was nearly a half mile swim.

He reached down to unlace his boots and tied them around the belt loop of his pants. Atlas wasn't, by any means, a particularly good swimmer, but his determination outweighed any trepidation he felt about the deep, cold water and brutal waves.

The ocean was icy and as he swam his fingers pruned and began to tremble. Atlas worked his way steadily along the Fringe; he was grateful to see that it was low tide, for he could just make out a sliver of shoreline beneath the cliff that led up to the Gap. It wasn't until he was about a hundred feet away that the intensity of the waves picked up, and they pushed him precariously towards the cliff wall. He took a deep breath and dove beneath the surface, his eyes straining to stay open against the salty sting of the water.

His lungs burned, and the muscles in his legs ached as he kicked with all of his strength. Just as he was sure he was going to run out of oxygen, his fingertips met smooth sand, and he pulled himself onto the shore, gasping in great lungfuls of air.

Atlas lay there for a few moments, his chest heaving as he gazed up at the cerulean sky, and he wondered, for the first time, if he was making a mistake. Beneath his fury and frustration, a small bubble of apprehension had surfaced.

But no, he had come this far already. Atlas lugged himself to his feet, peering up the tall cliff, and began to climb. It had been years since he endeavored up the steep overhang, so it took him some time to rediscover the natural footholds that jutted from the rock—but he was taller now too, so his limbs extended more easily up the mountainside.

Higher and higher he climbed. He made the mistake, about halfway up, of looking down towards the sea, and his stomach lurched into his throat. The further he climbed, the more this seemed like a stupid idea.

But then he could see the top of the cliff, could begin to make out the shape of live oaks and junipers as he drew nearer, and it gave him the burst of courage that he needed. He heaved himself over the clifftop and pushed himself to his feet, looking around.

There was not a soldier in sight. As he knelt to tug on his boots, Atlas wondered if this was a testament to Moonstone's arrogance—that the very pathway which the Vedas had exploited to defeat the Obarion remained unguarded in the wake of their victory.

The woods were quiet as he headed east, the same direction that he had guided Jacoby when the young man snuck into Headquarters, but when Atlas was about two hundred feet from the edge of the front lawn, he took a sharp left and continued north, ducking beneath low-hanging branches and climbing over felled trees and several blackened, jagged stumps that looked as though they'd been struck by lightning.

He'd walked perhaps a mile when he came to it: deep in the woods, surrounded by trees in every direction—a small, stone shack, no bigger than three hundred square feet. It had no windows, and the ivy growing up the side might have camouflaged it against the rest of the wood if Atlas hadn't already known what to look for.

A heavy metal door was the only entrance point, and Atlas pulled it open. The sparse light inside the shack came from the cracks between the stones, but it was late enough in the day that he had no trouble seeing.

There were two guards inside, and they both hastily straightened, hitching their guns onto their shoulders. "What are you doing here?" one of them asked. Atlas immediately recognized him as Mabury, a plump brown-haired young man who was a friend of Whitsom's, but the other guard, pale, gangly, and blond, was unfamiliar.

Behind them, Atlas saw a slumped figure seated in a rickety wooden chair. His hair was disheveled, and a scruffy beard obscured the lower half of his face.

"Mind giving me a minute?" Atlas asked the guards. His eyes were intent on the figure behind them, whose head tilted at the sound of Atlas' voice.

"Uh—yeah, see, we're not supposed to do that," the blond boy said, glancing sideways at Mabury for confirmation. "Moonstone's orders."

Atlas held his hands out at his sides. "You can search me. Five minutes. That's all I'm asking." Mabury's eyes flickered over his damp shirt and his water-logged pants. "There's only one door," Atlas pointed out. "You two can wait right outside—it's not as though I could get him out, even if I wanted to." The blond guard looked as though he were actually considering it, but Mabury appeared more uncertain. Atlas needed to seal the deal. "Can you blame me for wanting a heart-to-heart with my dear old dad?" Behind the soldiers, he thought he saw Talikoth's mouth lift into a smirk, ever so briefly.

"Five minutes," Mabury conceded. "That's all you get."

Atlas saluted him as the two of them made their way out. "Forever in your service, gentlemen."

The heavy door slammed shut behind them, and Atlas turned back to look at his father, who had straightened in his chair, his hands bound behind his back.

"You're really working the beard," Atlas said finally, wandering towards the end of the little stone shack and idly examining the clipboard hooked on the wall. Attached to it was a list of guards assigned to monitor the Obarion General. Whitsom's name was nowhere to be found.

Talikoth just watched him, his head tilted to the

side and dark eyes glittering. "Come to gloat?" he asked quietly.

Atlas snorted, moving back towards his father's cell and stopping in front of it. "That'd be a bit cowardly, wouldn't it? With you locked behind bars?"

"But not necessarily out of character."

The gibe was delivered with no venom, no malice, nothing but indifference in his tone. It was the art of derision that Talikoth had mastered. He knew how to cut a person down without ever raising his voice.

Atlas wished it didn't punch him in the gut still. He wished he had grown out of that, but anger and defensiveness swelled up in him like a tidal wave. "I fought you man to man," Atlas reminded him.

"And you would have lost if you hadn't had your backup to help you. I would have killed you, just like I killed your friend—" Atlas slammed his hands against the bars of the cell, and Talikoth leaned forward, his eyes glinting eagerly, as though he were waiting, waiting for a fight, waiting for Atlas to snap—

Atlas cursed and strode away from his father, running a hand through his hair as he paced in front of the cell. This was *not* how he planned for this to go. He just wanted something—someone—to take his anger out on. Someone who deserved it. Someone he *knew* was to blame for all of this.

But Talikoth had always known how to get under his skin, and he should have known. He should have seen it—

"Oh."

His father's quiet voice broke through his internal tirade, and Atlas looked up sharply. Talikoth had leaned back in his chair, his expression smug, even as he sat with his hands bound in a prison cell so small he could scarcely have stretched his arms out in either direction.

"It's driving you crazy, isn't it."

It wasn't a question, and Atlas knew instantly what his father meant, but he didn't want to give him the satisfaction. "I don't know what you're talking about," he spat, resuming his pacing.

Talikoth laughed. "Yes, you do. Moonstone used you for what she needed, and then she discarded you. It's driving you out of your mind."

"You don't know anything," Atlas argued, but even to his own ears his voice sounded shaky and uncertain.

The door banged open, and Atlas gave his father one more glare before he turned to leave. He was nearly outside when Talikoth called, "See you soon."

Atlas turned, his eyes narrowing. "No, you won't."

Talikoth paid no mind to the soldiers as they posted themselves once more on either side of his cell. "Oh, you'll be back," Talikoth assured him. "I'll bet my life on that."

Atlas scowled, shaking his head and striding out of the building without a glance back.

His mind churned as he made his way through the woods. The anger still pulsed through him, though more muted now than before. His thoughts broke through the haze of rage, and Atlas found himself dissecting every word, every last syllable, that had been exchanged between him and Talikoth.

The disdain he expected. It wasn't surprising that

Talikoth could manage to look so condescending, even from the confines of a prison cell. No, what bothered Atlas was how nonplussed his father had been, and even more so, how certain he was that Atlas would return. Was Talikoth just trying to sew discord between Atlas and Moonstone? Or was he merely a good judge of character, who had seen that once Moonstone had gotten what she'd needed from Atlas, she would cast him aside like a dirty rag?

He was so lost in his thoughts that he forgot he wasn't technically supposed to be on the grounds and was already halfway down to the main gate before he came to his senses. A handful of Vedas soldiers were strolling towards him, and he wracked his brain to come up with an excuse.

Fate, though, appeared to be on his side, for as the soldiers drew nearer, Atlas recognized Whitsom among them.

When the older boy spotted Atlas, he did a double take, and jogged towards him. His dark eyes flitted over Atlas' clothes, which were still damp, and his brows lifted to his hairline. "Do I even wanna know?"

"Probably not," Atlas admitted, his lips pulling upwards, despite his foul mood. He glanced over towards the other soldiers and lowered his voice. "You won't mention this to Moonstone, will you?"

"Don't be stupid," Whitsom said immediately. He nodded his head towards the main gate, a hundred yards from where they stood, and added, "I'd steer clear of there a while, though. Saw Vailhelm and Axe hanging around just a few minutes ago."

Atlas nodded, and took a few steps towards the forest again, dread seeping into his limbs at the thought of mustering the climb back down the Gap, before he stopped, an idea striking him.

He doubled back towards the Main, peering ahead to determine if he'd encounter any Vedas guards, but they were posted mostly around the soldiers' quarters, what was left of the artillery warehouse, and the officers' lodgings. Groups of soldiers and Renegades here and there moseyed about, but none of them looked twice at Atlas.

It crossed his mind that it was only the higher-ups that were even aware that he was not allowed to be at Headquarters—well, the higher-ups and Atlas' closest friends, since it was they who he complained to most frequently about it.

This tidbit of information cheered him up ever so slightly. It would be much easier to get around Moonstone's dictates if it was only she and the Vedas Council he needed to avoid, rather than the entirety of the Vedas' army.

The sun overhead was just past its peak in the sky, which meant, if his estimations were correct, the cooks should still have been cleaning up from lunch in the kitchens and would not yet have been escorted back to their quarters.

The hallways of the Main were empty, and it took Atlas only a few minutes to reach the dining hall. He trudged down the steps that led into the basement and pushed open the doors to the kitchen.

A fragrant, spicy aroma wafted over to him, and the noisy clatter of pots, pans, and running water met his ears. Two Vedas soldiers stood posted on either side of the door, but they only gave him a quick once over— to ensure he didn't have weapons, most likely—before they resumed their stances.

Atlas spotted Delurah at the opposite end of the kitchen, her gaze intent on the loaf of bread in front of her, which she was carefully wrapping in linen. A platter of biscuits lay beside her that had not yet been put away.

The last remnants of his bad mood dissipated like vapor at the sight of her, and Atlas grinned as he made his way across the basement.

"Hey, Delurah," he said brightly when he was right behind her. Predictably, she jumped, and Atlas snickered.

"You *irksome* boy!" she chided in her lilting accent, though without any real malice. Atlas plopped down on the counter next to her, snatching a biscuit off the platter, and he was reminded almost jarringly of all the times he'd done exactly this as a child.

"How was lunch?" he asked around a mouthful.

"Oh, same as ever," Delurah said, rolling her eyes. "Coral tried to start a food fight, and he was given latrine duty. Third time this week."

Atlas chuckled, though his chest gave a pang. Almost as though she had read his mind, Delurah glanced sideways at him and remarked, "He's asked about you almost every day."

Atlas sighed, running a hand through his hair. "Yeah, well it's a lot easier to sneak in here to see you than it is to get into the soldiers' quarters to talk to him...though I suppose it wouldn't hurt to try."

"No, you'd best keep your head down, laddie," Delurah said, suddenly stern. "As a matter of fact, are you even supposed to be here? I've heard Moonstone's been keeping a close eye on you."

Atlas snorted. "That's an understatement." He contemplated, for a moment, airing all his frustrations to her—but Delurah would only worry, and that was the last thing he wanted.

"She just thinks I need a rest," Atlas muttered, scowling. "Which is *stupid*. I'm fine."

"Still, it's better you don't get on her bad side," Delurah advised. Her gaze grew heavy, and she mumbled, almost to herself, "You're too young to remember how dangerous that can be." She faintly shook herself, and finished wrapping her bread before she slid it into a cupboard.

Atlas frowned. "What do you mean by that?"

"Never you mind," Delurah said firmly. She moved across the room to the sink and started to scrub at a heavy cooking pot, as though that settled the matter, and Atlas' eyes narrowed on the back of her head. He wanted to press the issue, but a few of the other cooks shuffled over to their side of the kitchen, and he decided his curiosity would have to wait.

Atlas followed Delurah over to the sink, watching her closely. "You've been alright, though?" he asked quietly. "I would have come and visited sooner, if I could have—"

Delurah clicked her tongue, drying her hands before she pressed a palm to his cheek. "It is *not* your job to look after me, young man—"

"I'm just making sure you're alright," Atlas insisted.

"Besides," Delurah continued, as though he hadn't spoken, "From what I hear, you've been keeping plenty busy." Her eyes raked over his face shrewdly, and her mouth twisted with a smirk.

Atlas straightened, his brows furrowing at the teasing note in her voice. "What...does that mean?"

Delurah only shrugged and turned back to her scrubbing, though her smirk broadened.

"What—no—tell me what you're talking about!" Atlas demanded.

Finally, Delurah admitted, "Major Alekea *may* have mentioned that he walked in on you necking with some pretty little thing in the library nearly a month ago—"

"What, he *told* you about that?" Atlas spluttered, his cheeks flushing. "Why would he just go around *telling* people that?"

"Oh, he only mentioned it to me and a couple of the officers," Delurah said, in what Atlas supposed was meant to be reassurance. "Dak and Alvi, too, I'm sure—they're all good friends."

Atlas groaned. "That's so humiliating."

Delurah set her freshly scrubbed pot on the counter to dry, and remarked off-handedly, "Alekea said she was very pretty."

"She is," Atlas mumbled, keeping his gaze trained firmly on his boots. "She's super smart, too, and very nice. You'll really like her."

Delurah's brows shot up. "Oh, I get to meet her, do I? So this isn't just some floozy that you meet in the library to—what do the kids say? Hook up?"

"Jeez-o-Pete, *no*," Atlas said quickly. He glared at a couple of nearby cooks, who were tittering. "Gaiomere's not a floozy, honest."

"So are you courting her, then?"

Atlas groaned. "Nobody even *says* that anymore."

Delurah wagged a pruned finger at him. "I did *not*

raise you to be the sort of young man that goes *toying* with girls for the fun of it."

"I'm *not*," Atlas said quickly. "We—well, we haven't exactly had a conversation about it... " Delurah gave him a stern look, and he hastily amended, "Yet. But I will. I'll bring it up." He hesitated, before admitting, "I —I really like her, and she's—she's special to me, so I would like you to meet her. Just *promise* when you do you won't mention the library thing." He thought for a moment, and added, "Or my bug collecting phase. *Please* don't mention my bug collecting phase."

Delurah chuckled, shuffling around him. "Fine, I promise." She grabbed a couple of biscuits and thrust them into his hands. "Now you'd best get out of here, sweet boy, before Moonstone realizes you've gone."

By the time Atlas returned to the campsite on the Fringe, it was almost dinnertime. After his visit with Delurah, his spirits were much higher than when he'd left the prison shack, so it only took a few minutes for Zarr and Clancy to talk him into playing a few rounds of rat slap.

Whitsom turned up just after six, declared that he was going to eat a hundred and fifty slices of bacon, and challenged each of them to try to beat him.

"You'll tap out at twenty-five, check me," Clancy wagered.

"I don't think we even have that much bacon," Atlas pointed out.

"Yellow bellies, all of you!" Whitsom shouted,

plopping down on a log. Atlas marveled, not for the first time, at how much the older boy reminded him of Coral, and how well they'd get along. Once, of course, they got past the small detail of Coral having tried to kill him.

As the sun began to set, Atlas found his thoughts drifting further and further away from Moonstone, his conversation with Talikoth, and even from wondering if Dak and the other officers were going to be receptive to the Vedas. Tension seeped from his shoulders, and laughter came more easily than it had in weeks.

"Does Whitsom ever stop showing off?" Zarr asked Atlas, when he sank down on an adjacent log after returning from the latrine.

The young man in question was juggling a black-and-white patterned ball between his knees, while a couple of younger Ramshackle boys counted, "Forty-six, forty-seven, forty-eight…"

"Never. There's no off switch," Atlas said with a snort, though his eyes were intent upon the sandwiches Zarr was preparing.

"Hey, I heard that you punk!" Whitsom called.

Atlas stealthily snatched one of the sandwiches from the younger boy's plate, though he must not have been as smooth as he'd thought, for Zarr turned and glared at him as he took a large bite.

"Make your own sandwich."

"That's too much work—besides, it's the least you can do. You should respect your elders."

"I like you better when you're sulking," Zarr muttered, though the corners of his mouth twitched.

Gaiomere and Jacoby came ambling down the hillside from the direction of Headquarters. Jacoby was listening intently as Gaiomere explained something to him, her voice carrying down to the fireside. She wore a yellow dress, her wild curls pulled back into a pair of braids, and her bare feet moved nimbly over blocks of concrete and overgrown roots, though her eyes were intent upon her notebook.

"Ugh, Gai, shut up, you're breaking my concentration!" Whitsom yelled, as the Ramshackler boys chanted, "Eighty-seven, eighty-eight, eighty-nine..."

Gaiomere shot her brother a glare before she caught sight of Atlas. He waved, and her lips split into a wide smile as she made her way over to him.

"Hey," Atlas said.

"Hey," she returned, sinking down onto the log beside him.

"Hey," Zarr piped up. "I'm here, too. You know, if anyone cared."

"Want a sandwich?" Atlas asked her. "Zarr made *that* one especially for you—"

"If you touch my other sandwich, I will cut off your hand, Obarion," the black-haired boy drawled, and Atlas sniggered.

He scarfed down three baked potatoes, and then he and Gaiomere went for a walk along the beach as she told him all about the work she'd been doing in the lab at Headquarters.

"Moonstone's using the solar power as something of a peace offering to the Obarion researchers. Ilquir's not stupid, he knows exactly what she's doing, but he's *also* not dumb enough to say no to brand-new tech. We've only got one solar station fully-operational now, but he's already over the moon—sun? Doesn't matter, either way, I'm pretty sure she's won him over—"

"That was probably more you than her," Atlas said with a smirk.

Gaiomere gave a bashful little shrug, but her cheeks darkened with color nonetheless. "Ilquir certainly appreciates my input. He's even stopped calling me 'that little Ren girl,' so that's a win I suppose."

They had come to the end of the beach. Gaiomere hopped up to sit on a low wall, and Atlas leaned against the concrete next to her. He hesitated, before tentatively asking, "How's everybody else?"

Gaiomere sighed, leaning back on her arms as she blew a loose curl from her face. "They're just—they're fine, really. No, honestly," she added, when she caught his disbelieving look. "Some of the girls in the lab make...comments..."

Atlas frowned. "What kind of comments?"

"Oh, you know..." Gaiomere gazed determinedly out at the ocean, clearly trying very hard to appear unaffected, but he could still hear the tremor in her voice. "Calling me 'primitive,' saying I'm a 'savage'...telling me to go back to where I came from. And a couple boys shoved me into a wall the other day on my way back from the bathroom—but honestly, Atlas, it's *fine*." His fists had unconsciously curled at his sides, and she placed a soothing hand on his arm. "I've been through much worse. Ilquir shuts them up whenever he catches them at it. Plus, Jem looks out for me too—she's lovely."

"Yeah, Jem's cool," Atlas agreed distractedly. "Listen, I don't know that Moonstone should even have you up there—it's safer down here at the Fringe—"

"Oh, honestly, Atlas, I'm not in any danger there," Gaiomere insisted, rolling her eyes. "There's nothing too bad they can do to me with all the Vedas soldiers around." She hesitated, glancing up at him, and then added, almost nonchalantly, "And besides, not all of them are so bad. Okulus is very nice to me."

Atlas' eyes narrowed. He remembered the tall blond boy the year ahead of him at Academy. Most of the girls thought he was handsome.

"He's got small hands," Atlas observed.

Gaiomere blinked. "That's a really random observation."

"Well, you know what they say," Atlas pointed out petulantly.

Gaiomere arched a brow, tilting her head to the side as she looked up at him, her eyes twinkling with obvious mirth. "No, I don't. Please tell me, Atlas, what do they say?"

His cheeks flushed. "It's—never mind, not important."

Gaiomere smiled, shaking her head. "He asked me if I had a boyfriend."

"Well, what'd you say?" Atlas demanded.

"I told him that I didn't know. He was a little confused by that."

Atlas rolled his eyes. "I can't imagine why," he drawled.

"Then I explained to him that there's this boy that I sometimes kiss in the woods, and on the beach, and in the library, but that I wasn't sure whether or not he was my boyfriend."

"Wood-beach-and-library-kissing-partner does seem like a bit of a mouthful," Atlas said reasonably.

"I mentioned that it was you, and then Okulus got sort of frightened, and he stopped talking to me as much after that," Gaiomere continued, as though he hadn't spoken. She glanced sideways at him, and asked, "Did you know that most of your former Academy peers are *terrified* of you?"

Atlas kept his gaze forward, though he could not help the smirk that tugged at the corners of his mouth. "I may have a bit of a reputation," he divulged. Gaiomere laughed, and he pulled her closer to his side. "You should tell Okulus—and any other guy that's asking, for that matter—that you have a boyfriend."

Gaiomere hummed, nestling into his side, but he could still feel a smile lift her cheeks against his shoulder.

Atlas affixed his eyes on the waves swelling and crashing in the distance, and he heard the words leave his mouth before he made the conscious decision to speak them. "I went to see Talikoth today."

Gaiomere turned her head to look up at him, but she said nothing, waiting for him to continue.

Before he knew it, all his frustrations poured out, and it was not until he had recounted everything—his restlessness, these past few weeks, his argument with Moonstone, and how he had snuck into Headquarters and spoken with Talikoth—that he realized how long he had been ranting.

"I know you probably don't want to hear this," Gaiomere began gently, once he finally finished, "but I do think that Moonstone really is just looking out for you."

He let out a heavy exhale, glaring at the sand beneath his feet. "I'm not a kid. I don't need a babysitter."

She didn't respond, but instead slipped her hand

into his, drawing small circles against his skin, and her touch momentarily soothed the severity of his anger. "What did your dad have to say?"

He hesitated, before telling her honestly, "Nothing important. Just his usual mind games."

Saying the words aloud did little to convince him that was all it had truly been, but Atlas didn't want to waste any more time agonizing over it. Talikoth was locked away in a cell and there was nothing he could do to harm Gaiomere, or Whitsom, or any of them ever again, so worrying about it only played right into his hands.

But when Atlas laid down on his cot that night, he could not help the pervading sense of apprehension that set his nerves on edge. He mulled the day's events over in his mind, again and again, until it made him dizzy. He tossed and turned, his body strangely energized even though his eyes drooped.

And when Atlas finally did fall asleep, his dreams were haunted by corpses that gazed at him with wide, accusing eyes and reached for him with bone-like, bloodless fingers, calling his name, first in Gaiomere's voice, like a whisper of wind, then Raider's, and finally, in his father's voice, so loud that the man could have been in the tent beside him.

CHAPTER THREE

Hardly three weeks passed before all of Atlas' mounting agitation came to breaking point.

It was lunch time at the campsite on the Fringe, and he and Gaiomere had just returned from collecting firewood—which was their code for hastily gathering a few measly branches and then spending the rest of the time kissing until someone called for one of them—when Atlas spotted Moonstone and Vailhelm near the perimeter of the campsite, engrossed in a whispered argument. Atlas wasn't going to concern himself with it until Vailhelm mention his name.

"He doesn't need to be involved—" Moonstone insisted.

"There's no one else we can ask, General, and people's *lives* are at stake," Vailhelm said gruffly. "He's not a child."

Atlas' respect for Vailhelm surged then, and before he even registered what he was doing, he crossed the clearing and stopped in front of them, arching a brow expectantly.

Moonstone sighed, looking more agitated than Atlas had ever seen her. "Fine," she said curtly. She pulled a thick folder from her bag and passed it to him, and Atlas immediately began to flip through it. "The Colonel has been working with me to distribute food and other necessities to the Obarion people—

since we destroyed all of their crop fields—but we've encountered a problem." She tapped a finger against the page Atlas had just turned to—a thorough diagram of the Obarion headquarters, with the large tank that held the water supply circled in bright red. "The water stores are almost gone."

Atlas blinked, looking between she and Vailhelm doubtfully. "What? How—how can that be?"

"I've spoken to Colonel Dak, as well as the officers beneath him, and they've all told me the same thing: Talikoth and the Inner Ring were the ones that handled obtaining the clan's water. How and where they obtained it was never disclosed to any of them."

Atlas cursed, running a hand through his hair as he thought. "What about the Inner Ring members that survived the explosion and the grenades? Have you interrogated any of them?"

"All of them," Moonstone said, her frown deepening. "Only a dozen of them survived, but they all assured me that they were ready to face torture and death before they disclosed any information that they had not been given permission to share."

Atlas began to pace in front of them, his mind racing. All the water surrounding Headquarters was colossally polluted—even Gaiomere's detoxifiers weren't enough to make it drinkable. It might have been fine to swim in, or even for the clanspeople to bathe and wash their clothes, but once the clean drinking water ran out...

"How much is left?" Atlas asked.

Vailhelm grimaced. "About six weeks' worth."

Moonstone peered at Atlas inquisitively. "I presume, then, that this means you also have no idea where Talikoth acquired the water?"

Atlas didn't answer. Talikoth's words were echoing through his mind on a loop.

You'll be back. You'll be back. You'll be back.

"The Ramshacklers have offered to transport water from the North," Moonstone said. "But that's only a temporary solution—"

"What about Harcliff's tribe?" Atlas asked. "How do they get water?"

"They travel for it—once a month, they trek up North—but they only have a hundred or so in their tribe. The Obarion clan is eighty times larger than Harcliff's—"

"We have to go to Talikoth," Atlas interrupted.

Moonstone and Vailhelm both looked at him. He was facing away from them, but he could feel their gazes boring into the back of his head. His hands clenched and unclenched at his sides, and he had the bizarre urge to laugh.

Of course Talikoth would have foreseen this, would have planned, would have *ensured* a failsafe for himself—so that if he somehow was removed from power, his people would still be dependent on him.

"How do you know that, Atlas?" Moonstone asked.

"Because he knew this was going to happen." He turned back to face her, his eyes narrowed. "I snuck into Headquarters a few weeks ago and spoke to him. And he knew—he knew we'd be back to ask for his help."

Atlas lifted his chin defiantly as he met Moonstone's gaze. Suddenly, he was unafraid of the consequences, of what she could do to him, of what would happen if she learned he broke the rules.

Moonstone's face was impassive, even as her shrewd eyes flickered over his obstinate posture. "Very well," she said finally. "Thank you for the information. We shall discuss your misconduct at a later time." Atlas opened his mouth to fire off a retort, but before he could, she turned away, effectively dismissing him, and called, "Gaiomere?"

The curly-haired girl came over, looking between the three of them curiously. "I understand that you have a potential strengthening solution for the detoxifiers?"

Gaiomere frowned, her fingers toying distractedly with the pendant around her neck. "It's not much of a solution at this point," she admitted. "Just some ideas in my notebook—and my detoxifiers don't work on the water in the South, so there's no telling a strengthener would either..."

"I'd like you and Ilquir's team to refocus your efforts on supplying an effective strengthening solution," Moonstone instructed. "The sooner, the better—"

"We have six weeks, that could take *months!*" Atlas interrupted loudly. Moonstone cast him an annoyed look, and several of the Vedas and Ramshacklers gathered around the firepit glanced nervously in their direction, but Atlas didn't care. "Look, we can get the information from Talikoth—we don't have time to bank on technology that hasn't even been developed—"

"Atlas is right, General," Gaiomere said tentatively. "My equations aren't even finished, and that time isn't even accounting for experimentation—"

"*Atlas* has already been dismissed," Moonstone said firmly, but Atlas only scowled, rooting his feet even more firmly to the spot, and she continued, "We need a solution ready in case Talikoth isn't willing to talk. Our interrogators will do the best they can with him, and in the meantime—"

"I think the boy should talk to him."

Atlas looked sharply at Vailhelm, his brows lifting in surprise. Moonstone's mouth was pursed disapprovingly, and she said, "I don't think that will be necessary—"

"Talikoth won't bat an eye at our interrogators— if how his Inner Ring responded is anything to go by," Vailhelm pointed out brusquely. "The boy has to do it. He can get him to talk better than any of the rest of us could. You saw how quickly Talikoth became unhinged that morning on the battlefield."

Beneath her calm exterior, Atlas could tell that Moonstone was fuming. "We will consult the rest of the Council this afternoon," she said tersely. "In the meantime, Atlas, I wish for you to stay at the campsite with the rest of the soldiers." She strode away, and after a moment, Vailhelm followed her.

"What was that about?" Gaiomere asked quietly as soon as they'd gone.

"Let's go for a walk," he said, grasping her hand and pulling her away from the fire pit.

As soon as the laughter and commotion from the clearing died away behind them, Atlas told her everything Moonstone and Vailhelm had said.

"How can you not have known where the *water* came from?" Gaiomere demanded, once he'd finished speaking.

His cheeks prickled with heat. "I don't know, I just —it was always there, we never had to worry about it, so it didn't really matter where it came from."

Gaiomere shook her head, her teeth worrying her lip. "The clan will have to leave Headquarters. They could go north—the water is cleaner up there—"

"What? No!" Atlas turned to glare at her. "We can't —we can't just *leave*. This is our home—"

"Atlas, if the clanspeople don't leave, they'll die—"

White hot anger exploded through his chest, and he ripped his hand out of hers, shouting, "Why is it that no one here seems to have even a *shred* of faith in me?" He was breathing heavily, and he glared down at her so viciously that she took a step back, her eyes widening.

"I—it's not that I don't have faith in *you*—it's just —Talikoth is—"

He shook his head. "Whatever. Look, I'll—I'll see you later."

"Atlas—" she began, reaching for his hand again, but he turned and stormed away.

The Ramshackle was quiet as he stalked through the abandoned streets, picking his way over debris and winding around buildings until he didn't know where he was anymore.

Atlas had tried so hard, the last few weeks, to distract himself from what was, as he could see clearly now, nothing more than a demotion. He no longer attended council meetings, nor did he provide any intel. He was ordinary...just like the rest of the soldiers.

He knew, rationally speaking, Gaiomere hadn't *meant* to cast aspersions over his character or capabilities. Even as he thought back on it, guilt bubbled up in his stomach, but he was just *tired*—tired of being treated like he was a child, tired of being ignored and spoken down to, tired of knowing that he had more to offer, that he could do more to help, and not being allowed to.

His steps slowed as his thoughts became less angry and more pensive. Perhaps he *was* being unreasonable. He never heard Whitsom or Yacielle complain about *only* being assigned to guard Headquarters, or never attending council meetings.

But the truth was, Atlas had gotten used to playing a bigger role—even before he had been captured by the Vedas, when he was only captain—he had known what he was being groomed for. Even then, he had never felt so insignificant as he did now.

Perhaps that was why he found his feet carrying him, once more, down the slope to the Fringe and across the half-mile stretch of sea to the base of the cliff.

He was tired of standing by while Moonstone decided his fate for him. He couldn't wait for the Council to confer, and he certainly couldn't sit around waiting for Moonstone's permission—not when his people were in danger.

He was Obarion, after all. Fate was his to bend.

Atlas' steps were unhesitating as he stalked through the forest, and he must have pushed open the door to the shack with more force than he'd intended, for it slammed against the wall behind it, and both of the guards jumped. He didn't recognize either of them, so he made a split-second decision.

"What do you think you're—"

He lunged towards the first guard, delivering a kick to his stomach and bringing his hands down atop the barrel of the rifle to wrench it from the soldier's grasp. He spun the muzzle towards the other guard, who had started to lift his own rifle, his fingers trembling.

"Out."

The two guards looked at each other, neither of them moving. Atlas' finger tightened around the trigger, and the armed guard flinched. "I've got no doubt in my mind about which of us is a better shot, but if you'd like to find out..."

"What the hell are you—"

"I want you out of this building by the count of five. Stand outside, make sure he doesn't escape, I don't care, but *get out.*"

After a second of hesitation, the two soldiers scrambled towards the door.

As soon as they were alone, Talikoth let out a snort, remarking sardonically, "Such admirable valiance."

Atlas tossed the gun to the floor, wasting no time as he gripped the bars of Talikoth's cell and leaned towards him. "Where is the water?" he demanded.

Talikoth smirked. "That's classified."

Atlas let out a harsh exhale. His eyes flickered down, for just a split second, to the gun he had discarded on the floor, and he contemplated turning it on his father—but as though he'd read Atlas' mind, the smirk on Talikoth's lips broadened, and Atlas knew in an instant that his father would never be persuaded to talk under the pressure of violence—not when Atlas hadn't had the gall to pull the trigger that morning on the battlefield.

"You do understand that your people will die without it, don't you? The Obarion have been here for almost twenty years—some of them have spent their entire lives here. You have to—"

"I don't *have* to do anything," Talikoth drawled.

"And I'm certainly not *inclined* to do anything for Moonstone's messenger boy."

"Moonstone doesn't even know I'm here," Atlas said. He pointed a finger in the direction of the door, where he presumed the guards were waiting outside. "Do you think I would have had to do that if she did?"

His father arched a brow. "I'll confess, I'm surprised. I didn't think you had it in you."

"Yeah, you never have," Atlas retorted before he could stop himself. "Now tell me where the water is."

Talikoth sighed in a burdened sort of way, his eyes disinterestedly roving to the ceiling, and frustration mounted beneath the surface of Atlas' skin.

"Look, the Vedas will do what they can to provide water for the Obarion when it runs out, but—"

"That's only a temporary solution," Talikoth droned. "You're talking about providing water for eight thousand people—"

"Okay, so what do we do? What's the long-term solution?"

Talikoth seemed to have been waiting for these words to leave Atlas' mouth. He straightened, smirking so wide that a dimple appeared in his cheek. "*Ah*, so after all this time—after everything you've done—you've come to ask for your dear dad's advice?"

Atlas rolled his eyes. "I've always respected your advice. And anyway, that's not—I'm not—that isn't the point." His cheeks flushed. "The Inner Ring—or what's left of it anyway—they won't speak without your express permission. So, either you release them from their vow of silence, or you tell us yourself."

"*Or* I do neither."

Atlas growled, pacing in front of the cell. Talikoth

watched him with a maddeningly calm expression, his dark eyes glittering.

"How can you just stand by while your people die out?" Atlas exploded, stopping once more in front of where his father sat.

Talikoth did not answer. Instead, he tilted his head, observing Atlas curiously. "Why do you care? You turned your back on your people—"

"I turned my back on *you*—not my people—because of the slaughter, because you—you killed your own wife—"

For the first time in either of his visits, Atlas saw something other than amusement or smugness in Talikoth's expression His face flashed with fury. "I did what I *needed* to. I made decisions no one else had the guts to in order to protect my people—I took my personal life out of the equation." His mouth contorted into a sneer. "You don't care about our clan, or the water. You're just a boy trying to prove himself."

Atlas' hand wrapped around the cell entrance—as though he could wrench it open by the sheer force of his anger—but it was at that moment that the shack door swung open and Moonstone strode in, accompanied by two soldiers with firearms.

"Indi, please ensure the prisoner is secure. Rya, escort Atlas out. I shall join the two of you shortly."

Atlas didn't even wait for the soldier in question to approach him. He turned on his heel and stalked from the stone shack, running a hand through his hair.

"He *absolutely* knows where the water is!" he burst out, as soon as Moonstone rejoined them. "I know that I can—"

"Atlas, that is *enough!*" Her voice was the closest

to shouting he'd ever heard, and the skin around her mouth was taut.

His jaw clenched and unclenched. "General, I—"

"No."

He stared at her for several moments in confusion. "No?"

"No," she repeated. "Do *not* call me General, Atlas, not when you've treated me with nothing but disrespect in the time following the battle." He opened his mouth to speak, but she held up her hand. "You have disobeyed direct orders *twice* in the span of a few weeks, and you act as though you're above authority."

His cheeks burned. "General, I—"

"No, Atlas." She took a steadying breath, her gaze unwavering. "Since you are operating as though you are not subject to my directives, I will hereby treat you as an Obarion citizen. As such, you will be limited to travel between your unit and the dining hall, and you will be under guard at all times to ensure that *this* mandate, at least, is obeyed."

Atlas' jaw had gone slack, and he stared at her with dread. "General, you can't—"

"I can, and I will," she said firmly. "I will do whatever I need to do in order to keep my people safe, and your actions as of late have been reckless and negligent." Before he could get in another word, she turned to the soldier standing dutifully beside the door. "Rya, please escort Atlas to his residential unit and ensure the guards posted at the officers' lodgings are aware that he is not to leave under any circumstances without escort."

Atlas continued to gape after her, even as she reentered the stone shack. He glanced sideways at his guard and contemplated running for it—but the soldier was a muscular fellow with a stern face, and Atlas had little doubt the man would shoot, if the occasion to do so arose.

Atlas followed the soldier back through the woods, across the grounds, and into the officers' lodgings. Atlas heaved open the door and found his unit empty—his guard rather smugly informed him that Delurah had been moved back to her unit in the civilians' quarters months ago. When Rya exited the unit and Atlas was left alone, he sank down onto the couch, burying his face in his hands as he contemplated how, in a matter of hours, everything had gone so wrong.

◆ ◆ ◆

Atlas' days became a monotonous blend of eating, sleeping, and trying to distract himself from the near-constant torrent of angry thoughts tearing through his mind. He did not attend any of the meals in the dining hall and instead sulked inside of his unit, taking up permanent residence on his couch and grouchily munching on stale crackers and overripe fruit, which were all that was left in his pantry.

The first couple of days, he fumed at Moonstone. How she could do this, after all he had done before and during the battle? Sure, he may have gotten a little overzealous to help, but could he really be blamed for that?

Then his anger shifted toward Talikoth. If he had given Atlas the information needed—if he cared about his people enough to divulge where they'd gotten the water—Atlas wouldn't even be *in* this situation. If Atlas had been able to give Moonstone an answer, she would have praised him as a hero. Instead, he was locked away like a criminal.

But after two weeks of brooding, Atlas could only really be angry at himself. Moonstone had done nothing but protect him since the very first night he arrived at the Vedas base. Talikoth may have been wrong to withhold information about the water, but *he* hadn't forced Atlas to sneak into Headquarters to visit him. All the things he'd done, every choice he'd made, and subsequently, their consequences, had been his own doing.

On his fifteenth day of confinement, Atlas ran out of crackers and mushy fruit, so at lunch time he got dressed, combed his hair for the first time in longer than he could remember, and trudged to the dining hall with his guard in tow.

When he entered, his guard posted up beside the door, and Atlas' eyes, almost instinctively, flitted over towards the furthest corner of the dining hall.

Coral and Bettoni sat at the same table they'd always sat at for almost six years. Bettoni leaned over and muttered something to Coral, who was shoveling food into his mouth so fast it looked almost unnatural.

Atlas' feet dragged as he walked over to them, and with every step he took his pulse seemed to run a little faster.

Bettoni noticed him at ten feet away. He nudged Coral, who had just risen from his seat—presumably to retrieve a second (or perhaps a third) refill on a platter. The blond boy looked up as Atlas stopped in front of their table.

"Uh...hey," Atlas settled on finally, lifting an arm in an attempt at a friendly wave.

Coral stared at him for almost five seconds, before he leaned down to Bettoni, who was still seated, and remarked in an exaggerated whisper, "Wow, he's even uglier than I remembered."

Atlas grinned, and Coral wrapped him in a tight hug. "I'm glad you're not dead," the blond boy mumbled. Atlas clapped him on the back and knuckled his hair, allowing him two seconds longer before he shoved the shorter boy off him.

"Alright, alright, that's enough—you still smell like the latrines—"

"I reckon the scent is stuck on me by now," Coral said, sniggering. Atlas plopped down in a seat between the pair of them, immediately reaching for a ladle to spoon himself a heaping serving of beans, and Coral continued, "We were worried about you, Attie-kins—"

"He cried a couple times," Bettoni informed Atlas.

"Dammit, Bet, I *told* you it was allergies!"

Atlas chuckled as the two boys bickered beside him, and a huge weight lifted off his chest. It returned, though, only moments later, when his eyes fell on a pitcher of water a few feet down the table.

He eyed the pitcher pensively. If Vailhelm was correct, they only had four more weeks of clean drinking water, and it didn't appear as though Talikoth were going to be any help in the matter. Had Gaiomere made any more progress on the amplified detoxifiers, or would they have to rely on whatever water the Ramshacklers could haul down from the North?

His stomach twisted when he thought of

the curly-haired girl. He had not even gotten an opportunity to apologize to her after their argument, and he wondered (in between his bouts of self-pity) if she was still angry at him.

Atlas scanned the dining hall, but he could not spot Gaiomere anywhere. He did, however, see Whitsom winding through the crowd, and when Atlas caught his eye, he waved the older boy over.

"All this time, you been up here!" Whitsom said in a faintly chiding tone as he plopped down in the seat across from Atlas. "I was looking for you around the campsite day before yesterday so you could finally teach us how to play that bruiseball game you're always goin' on about—"

He broke off, and it was not until Atlas glanced up that he realized why.

Coral's eyes had fallen on Whitsom, and widened to saucers, his cheeks red as a tomato. Atlas cleared his throat and spoke up. "Oh, right. Cor, this is Whitsom. Whit, this is Coral—since you two haven't been uh...formally introduced."

Coral gave an embarrassed cough, offering a hand to the dark-skinned boy, as he mumbled, rather abashedly, "Sorry about—about stabbing you 'n all."

Whitsom waved him off, grinning lopsidedly. "Don't be stupid, man. It's all water under the road—"

"Bridge, Whit," Atlas corrected.

"That's what I said. Anyway, you fight good."

Coral puffed up his chest a bit, shrugging. "Yeah, I'm alright." He nudged Atlas, remarking, "You know, every time Atlas and I spar, I keep trying to teach him how to get better, but he's just so scared of me—"

Bettoni let out a guffaw of laughter, and Atlas

knocked the blond boy over the head. "Get out of here, Cor."

Try as he might to keep his mind present, Atlas' thoughts kept circling back to the water dilemma. He thought about it all afternoon, momentarily ceased his obsession at dinner in favor of compulsively glancing at the dining hall doors every few minutes to keep an eye out for Gaiomere, and then returned to his deliberations almost as soon as his guard deposited him back into his unit.

Atlas tried to distract himself by reading *Lord of the Flies* (for the seventeenth time), but his eyes kept lifting to the faucet in the kitchen.

A sudden rapping noise made him jump. He glanced towards the front door, before he realized that the sound was coming from the opposite direction.

Gaiomere stood outside the window, beaming widely and waving at him.

He crossed the room in a few steps. "Moonstone's got the windows bolted," he said loudly, though he wasn't entirely sure she could hear him.

But in a matter of seconds, she had withdrawn a strange device from her bag, and aimed it at the giant metal clamps that kept the window from opening. A bright green beam of light emanated from the device and, to Atlas' astonishment, it began to burn through the metal.

Gaiomere glanced over her shoulder nervously as she worked, but it took only seconds before both the clamps were off. She stuffed the device back into her bag as Atlas pulled open the window and popped the screen out. She clambered inside, dropping to the floor in front of him.

"What are you *doing*?" he whispered, though he wasn't really sure why.

She rolled her eyes, pulling the window closed behind her. "Visiting you, of course."

"But I mean—how did you—how are you—"

She stood on her tiptoes and kissed him, and he was momentarily distracted from his line of questioning. "I'm sorry I made you feel like I didn't have faith in you," she said softly, once they'd broken apart.

Atlas shook his head. "No, don't—I was being stupid. I'm sorry." He glanced at the melted clamps on the ground. "What was that?"

"Oh, a laser. I've been working on it for a few weeks—to sneak into the library when it's closed, you know? I didn't realize it would come in handy for more."

He arched a brow, smirking. "Only you would use your genius to help you sneak into the library after hours."

"Not true, you'd do it, too."

Atlas chuckled, giving her a conciliatory nod, and she set her bag down on the sofa, continuing, "I didn't even know you where you were until an hour ago—Whit mentioned Moonstone had you holed up here. If I'd known, I'd have come to the dining hall for dinner—Jem and I usually just have Jacoby bring us food so we don't have to quit working."

"I was wondering where you were," Atlas remarked. He'd withdrawn the laser from her bag once more, and studied it curiously, contemplating, for perhaps the thousandth time, how it was possible that Gaiomere could so mind-bogglingly clever when she had essentially grown up in the wild.

"Have you always lived here?" came Gaiomere's

voice, slightly muffled.

"Yeah," he responded distractedly, as he peered into the little hole where the laser beam emitted from. "We moved into this unit when I was four, I think." He glanced up suddenly, realizing that Gaiomere was no longer beside him.

She had wandered across the room and peered curiously at the photographs hung along the wall opposite the bookcase. Talikoth had never cared much for preserving memories, but Delurah was diligent about documenting Atlas' childhood, no matter how vehemently he hated having his picture taken.

Atlas' hand came self-consciously to the back of his neck as he surveyed the unit. His bedroom door was open, and his dirty clothes from the previous two weeks were strewn about the floor. Perhaps he could shove them under the bed without her noticing...

She turned to peruse the bookshelf. Atlas was still trying to determine if he could inconspicuously scour his room when she asked, "Which one's your favorite?"

He blinked, his brows furrowing before he realized what she meant. "Oh, my favorite's not in there." He strode past her, hoping rather half-heartedly that she'd simply wait in the living room, but she instead followed him, leaning against the doorway.

"This is your bedroom?" she asked, as his eyes scanned over his personal bookcase.

Atlas finally located *Animal Farm* near the top shelf, its cover faded and pages crinkled and yellow. "When I was fourteen, Talikoth let me play him in chess for the larger room," he told her, smirking as he admitted, "That's the only time I've ever beaten him."

Gaiomere's gaze wandered curiously around his

room, her fingers skimming along the edge of his desk. She did not seem disgusted, at the very least, by the clothes littering his floor. "Your bed's huge," she observed.

Atlas glanced at it, his cheeks flushing. "Yeah, well I'm...tall," he finished rather lamely.

Gaiomere plopped down on his bed, sitting cross-legged and leaning back on her arms. "Is it exciting?" she asked.

Atlas stared at her. "My—my bed?"

She gave him an impish grin, nodding her head towards *Animal Farm*, still clutched in his hand. "The book."

"Oh," he said quickly, and the color in his cheeks deepened to crimson. "Oh, that—it's, uh...I don't think you'd like it, to be honest. It's sort of depressing."

"Your favorite book *would* be depressing," Gaiomere said, laughing as she took it from him and began to flip through.

Atlas spent the next half an hour asking Gaiomere about everything that had been going on at the campsite in his absence. Moonstone had evidently dispatched her interrogators to Talikoth's cell every day the past week with no headway. She'd sent four cars north to begin collecting water and, perhaps the most surprising scrap of news: the Vedas would be lifting restrictions at Headquarters within the next week. The Obarion citizens would be allowed to roam the grounds and utilize the rec room and the sparring gym, without being confined, any longer, between their own units and the dining hall.

"But Moonstone said she's quadrupling security— she's going to have soldiers stationed in every corner of every building," Gaiomere assured him, when she saw Atlas' apprehensive expression. "And they're going to do weapons checks periodically throughout the day—"

"I just think it's too soon," he maintained, shaking his head. "I only spoke to Dak five weeks ago—moving too quickly could put people in danger—the Obarion *have* still got the numbers, even without weapons—"

"Yeah, but not all of them want to go picking another fight, especially so soon after the last one— not when so many lives were lost," Gaiomere said. Her voice, though, sounded increasingly uncertain. She bit her lip, hesitating, before she admitted, "Niko took a car northeast, near where the Vedas' base is, to get water, and I asked him if he could pick up Maggi and Rasta on the way, but...if I bring them back here, only to have something awful happen—"

The apprehension that had been bubbling in Atlas' stomach settled into resolve, and he reached over to squeeze her hand. "I won't let that happen," he said firmly. "They can stay down at the Fringe until we're absolutely certain things are safe here. And I know you've been talking your way out of it, but you need to let me teach you to fight, once and for all."

Gaiomere's brows knitted apprehensively. "I can protect myself just fine—" she began, but Atlas cut her off.

"If you're going to be up here working in a lab with fifty other Obarion researchers that could turn on you any minute, that's the least you can do." He gazed at her earnestly, pressing his lips to the back of her hand. "Please? It will put me at ease."

She sighed. "*Fine*. Whatever. Butthead."

Atlas sniggered, winding an arm around her

waist, and she continued, almost as though she were talking to herself, "At least Moonstone loosening the restrictions will hopefully keep any more resentment from brewing. It's bound to be bad once the water situation gets out."

Her words reminded Atlas rather jarringly of the issue that he'd been working so hard to stop thinking about. "I don't know what Moonstone expects," he muttered. "Talikoth isn't going to budge without incentive."

Gaiomere pulled one of his pillows against her chest. "Maybe that's what she's got in mind—some kind of incentive?"

Atlas couldn't think of what. Perhaps it was just that Moonstone was unconcerned with the fate of the Obarion people.

But then he caught himself. "I don't know. I'm sure she'll figure it out, though. She is General for a reason, isn't she?"

Gaiomere stared at him strangely.

"I've made a resolution to stop meddling," he declared, as he tugged her onto his lap. "It's not my job to worry about it—so I won't."

He leaned in to kiss her, but stopped when he saw her smirk. "What?"

Gaiomere laughed. "I give it a week."

Atlas scowled. "What, you think I'm meddlesome?"

She shrugged, leaning against his shoulder. "I think you can't help but try to fix things. Especially when you believe that you can do a better job than anyone else."

Moonstone's words from all those months ago

flashed through his mind, and he grimaced. *He saw a problem and he believed that he knew how to fix it.*

"I think it's a good thing," she added when she saw his disgruntled face. "It just makes adhering to authority a little difficult—"

"I don't want to think about it anymore," he said quietly, pulling her even closer. She obligingly kissed him, coaxing his mind far away from the water, and Talikoth, and his obsessive speculation about whether or not Moonstone would ever have any confidence in him again.

CHAPTER FOUR

tlas' resolve to stop meddling, as Gaiomere predicted, lasted only a few days. His final week of confinement was not nearly so miserable as his first two with visits from Gaiomere to look forward to, plus meals with Coral and Bettoni.

More frequent trips to the dining hall also meant being thrust into the company of the Obarion soldiers and his former Academy mates, many of whom had once felt something like family to him. Now they seemed little more than strangers.

Atlas watched his peers carefully at mealtimes and as they traversed the halls when the Vedas soldiers escorted them to and from their rooms. A great number of the soldiers avoided his gaze, but many welcomed him back as though scarcely anything had changed.

Ando—a dark-haired, pale, brooding young man that had been three years ahead of him in Academy —greeted him cordially when the two of them ran into each other near the water fountains, and during one meal, Eaton—a strawberry-blond beanpole a year younger than Atlas—sat with he, Coral, and Bettoni and asked him all about what the North had been like, and whether or not it was true that Moonstone had a pet wolf she set on people who angered her.

He could only conclude that the majority of the Obarion in his year either were not aware of the extent of his involvement in the battle, or, after witnessing the trial, bore him no ill will. Though it also could have been that they *did* begrudge him for his actions but, as Gaiomere had pointed out, were terrified of him and thought it better not to pick a fight.

In the back of his mind, he considered that perhaps it was just that Talikoth did not have his soldiers' loyalty so firmly clenched in hand as Atlas might have thought. Perhaps they, like Atlas, were only playing the role assigned to them.

But no, if *that* were true, there would not be such visible malice between Talikoth's soldiers and Moonstone's, for however amicably many of his comrades interacted with *him*, their exchanges with the Vedas and the Ren were another matter entirely. Atlas witnessed four different fights break out in the dining hall over the span of two days before Moonstone's soldiers managed to intervene, and on Wednesday, he'd had to step in himself when a bulky Obarion boy slammed Jacoby's face into a window, breaking his nose before the guards could get to them.

"This is *exactly* why Moonstone shouldn't be opening up the grounds so quickly," Atlas said in a low voice to Whitsom as the two of them made their way into the dining hall one afternoon. Another fight had just broken out near the entrance of the Main, and two Vedas soldiers were being carted away on stretchers. "It's already bad—imagine how much worse it's going to get—"

Whitsom, who was technically supposed to be on dining hall patrol, glanced discretely at the Major posted at the door before he snatched an apple off one of the food carts that lined the wall and followed Atlas towards their table. "Maybe that's exactly why she needs to," he pointed out. "Your boys are getting antsy—they can burn off some of that anger in the sparring gym—"

Atlas started to reply, but broke off, for Gaiomere had entered the dining hall with perhaps a dozen other researchers. She walked arm-in-arm with Jem, a tall, freckle-faced girl a year ahead of Atlas in Academy, whom he'd always gotten along with. Jacoby trailed after them, a huge backpack hitched over his shoulders, and a bright blue splint over the bridge of his nose.

"I'll meet you at the table," Atlas said to Whitsom.

Gaiomere and Jem were whispering, their heads bent together conspiratorially, so Atlas circled around and crept up behind them, narrating in an exaggerated whisper, "And so the ever-elusive, wild creatures of the laboratories of lore descend from their dark and treacherous cave to mingle with the lowly plebeians—"

"Seriously, *how* do you put up with him?" Jem said dryly, arching an unimpressed brow.

Atlas chuckled, and Gaiomere looped her arms around his middle, setting her chin on his chest and smiling up at him. "He's an acquired taste." He leaned down to kiss her, and beside them, the brunette girl mimed retching into her bag.

"*Ew*, please, guys, not before lunch."

"She told me you were 'lovely,' did you know?" Atlas informed Jem over Gaiomere's head. "I couldn't bring myself to tell her about all the worms you've dissected, just for the fun of it—"

"All in the name of science!" Jem shouted.

"She *is* lovely, even if she pretends not to be," Gaiomere insisted, shooting the freckled girl a frown. She held her fingers in front of Atlas' face and wiggled them. "Look, she painted my nails! I didn't know what it meant when she asked me if she could. I thought it would hurt, but it didn't!"

Jem grinned wickedly. "I tried to pierce her belly button, too, but her brother walked in."

"She's letting me crash in the extra room in her unit," Gaiomere explained. "We just figured it was more sensible, so I didn't have to walk back to the Fringe every night after we're done in the lab—"

"Plus, it's way easier for me to teach her how to do tequila shots when I don't have to worry about her stumbling home drunk by herself in the dark—I'm *kidding*, At, stop making that face."

Next to him, Gaiomere muffled laughter into her hands, but Atlas ignored her, glaring at Jem. "You're a bad influence."

"Nah, you're just a prude."

Gaiomere had withdrawn her notebook from her bag and flipped through it, her eyebrows knitted together. "I'll join you guys in a second—I need to go find Marbella real quick and run some ideas by her."

Atlas started towards the table, Jem trudging after him, but stopped short. Jacoby, he noticed, was still standing in the same spot near the door, shuffling his weight rather nervously between his feet. "Come sit with us, Cobes," Atlas called, and the red-haired boy smiled gratefully and shuffled after the two of them.

"You finally got these tyrants to stop making you bring them food, I see," Atlas said to him.

Jacoby chuckled. "It really wasn't any trouble." He lowered his voice, adding, "It's probably better we ran into you, actually. Gaiomere said she was going to hunt down the guy that broke my nose and return the favor."

Atlas glanced over his shoulder for the curly-haired girl, but thankfully, she was only talking to Marbella, a plump, blonde girl five or six years older than Atlas, at a table near the door.

Whitsom was chomping down on a couple of baked potatoes, and across from him, Coral looked as though he had been ranting to Bettoni about something, but he broke off mid-sentence as the trio approached.

"Who's that chick?" he demanded, before Atlas had even managed to sit down.

"I'm Jem, you come here often?" the freckle-faced girl said dryly as she plopped down next to Whitsom.

"Not *you*," Coral said, chucking a boiled egg at Jem's head, which she swiftly dodged. "That girl with the flowers in her hair—"

Bettoni, who was leaning against the table, smirked at Atlas. "You two didn't seem so cozy back in the North—"

"Back in the good old days," Whitsom lamented. "When they were still trying to rip each other's throats out, and Attie didn't ditch me so they could go make out in the woods—"

"I don't...do that," Atlas mumbled, though his tone sounded unconvincing even to his own ears, and the look Whitsom gave him corroborated that.

"That's Gaiomere," Jem told Coral. "She's a Renegade. Freaky smart. Ilquir worships the ground she walks on. It's awesome, it's gotten me out of having to clean the lab like three weeks in a row now, just by association—"

"You *kissed* her," Coral said to Atlas, flabbergasted. "A girl. *You.* Were kissing a *girl*—"

"Well, who else should I be kissing?" Atlas demanded, his cheeks flushing.

"Look, dude, I'm not gonna lie and say I didn't have my doubts—you know I love you either way—"

"Is she your girlfriend?" Bettoni interrupted, his dark brows furrowed curiously.

Coral snorted. "Don't be stupid, Attie-kins isn't allowed to have girlfriends—"

"Well, I'm also *technically* not allowed to betray intel to our enemy clan and help them facilitate an insurrection," Atlas pointed out, shrugging.

"So, she *is* your girlfriend," Bettoni concluded.

"Can't be, she's super hot," Coral reasoned.

Whitsom had been taking a large bite of beans, but he let out a strangled noise, spluttering, "Bro, that's my sister—"

"Oh, my bad," Coral said, correcting, "She's—respectfully—super hot." Whitsom launched a spoonful of beans at Coral, and they hit him in the dead center of his face.

"Wait a minute, what's *that* supposed to mean, 'can't be?'" Atlas demanded.

"Oh, he's saying you have no game," Jacoby supplied matter-of-factly.

"Who has no game?" Gaiomere asked, as she slipped into the seat next to Atlas.

"Oh great, *you're* here," Whitsom muttered, shooting a glare down the table at his sister. Gaiomere re turned his glare, and he added, "Well, he never pays attention to us when you're around!"

"Maybe that's because it's physically painful to look at your face, Whit," Gaiomere retorted.

The other five cracked up, and Whitsom glowered

at them, muttering, "Y'all are the worst."

"I'm Coral, by the way," the blond boy said, holding out a hand across the table to Gaiomere. "Don't be intimidated by my good looks, I'm really quite down to earth." She laughed and shook his hand.

"I hope there's no hard feelings, after everything in the North," Bettoni said to her, with a tentative smile.

Gaiomere sniffed loftily, stabbing at a sweet potato as she said, "I suppose if my brother isn't holding a grudge, I shouldn't either." She hesitated, before admitting, with a furtive grin, "Objectively speaking— that was a really awesome throw—"

"Hey!" Whitsom interjected, with a disgruntled scowl.

"Well, it *was*." Gaiomere suddenly straightened up, her eyes brightening. "Oh, I have news!" They all looked at her. "I overheard Vailelm talking to Axe, and Moonstone apparently is scheduled to lift restrictions tomorrow night, at exactly six o'clock."

"Sweet, *sweet* fates," Jem crooned. "If I had to spend *one* more day staring at my bedroom wall, I was going to scream—"

"You did scream," Gaiomere pointed out. "Every other night. I heard you. I thought you were being murdered in there—"

"It's my *stress* relief, you charlatan," Jem said, sticking out her tongue.

"We'll finally be able to play bruiseball in the Stadium again!" Coral said brightly.

"I'm not sure we will," Bettoni argued. "I heard the bridge to the Stadium is totally destroyed—I guess somebody wrecked it with a bunch of grenades during the battle—"

Gaiomere, Atlas couldn't help but notice, suddenly became very enthralled with her fork.

Coral waved him off. "We'll just play across the grounds, then, I don't care."

That next day, however, the sky was black, and the air was thick and heavy. Mid-afternoon brought an icy, torrential downpour, and by dinnertime, it had not relented.

The clock scarcely read five minutes past six in the evening when Atlas' door sprang open, and Coral came hustling into his unit.

"Oh, I *missed* this couch!" the blond boy moaned, dropping down onto the sofa with a satisfied grunt. He sprang up moments later, though, and bounded into the kitchen, pulling open the pantry. "Got any food, Attie-kins?"

"Dude, don't you have food in your unit?" Atlas asked exasperatedly, as he sank down into the armchair.

"Yours is better—besides, my parents have been fighting for like two hours, I wanted an excuse to leave."

Atlas shifted, guilt stabbing at his stomach. "I nabbed a whole bowl of cherries from the dining hall yesterday," he told Coral. "They're in the back, there."

Bettoni and Whitsom came ambling into Atlas' unit seconds later, the latter clutching a large deck of cards.

"Is Gaiomere coming?" Atlas asked Whitsom.

The dark-skinned boy stopped in his tracks. "What, I'm not good enough for you?"

"I was just curious—"

Whitsom dropped his deck of cards onto the table and turned on Atlas with a wrathful sort of determination. "You listen here, Attie," he said. "Here's what's gonna happen. You're gonna sit here in this unit, and have a game night with your boys, and you're gonna be *happy* about it. No asking where Gaiomere is every five minutes—"

"I don't even do that!" Atlas protested, flushing.

"No dipping out early so y'all can go play tonsil hockey in the library—"

"But—"

"And Attie I *swear* on all things holy, if you *argue* with me, I will revoke my blessing and won't let you date my sister anymore."

"*Ooooooh*," Coral and Bettoni intoned simultaneously from the dining room table.

"Fine," Atlas griped, scowling as he lugged himself to his feet. "Are we going to play cards or not?"

Within the span of four rounds of rat slap, Coral and Whitsom were fighting like brothers, and Bettoni was trying to act as the objective voice of reason, though this more often than not resulted in the two of them ganging up on him instead. Atlas momentarily marveled at how easily his two worlds were beginning to meld together, though perhaps he should have expected it, for Whitsom had a proclivity for getting along with just about anyone, and he had known Coral and Bettoni since he was a child.

At nine o'clock, Gaiomere came trudging into the unit, her eyes tired, and her curls sticking up at odd angles. She stopped beside Atlas' chair and draped her arms across his shoulders, leaning against him sleepily. "Ilquir had us run fifteen rounds of tests on my panels," she mumbled, her voice muffled against his shirt.

Whitsom had evidently been too focused on their game to have heard her enter, but at the sound of her voice, he looked up sharply, and let out an indignant sound of protest.

"Dudes only! Get lost, Geek-omere—"

"Since when are you in charge of me?" Gaiomere snapped.

"Since always, now scram!"

She crossed her arms over her chest. "It's Atlas' unit. I'll only leave if he tells me to." The curly-haired girl turned to look at Atlas, raising her eyebrows expectantly, with an expression that very much said she knew exactly what the outcome of this interaction would look like.

Atlas shot Whitsom a brief, though wholly insincere, apologetic glance before he said, "Oh come on, dude, what harm's she causing here?"

Whitsom threw his hands up in the air, and Bettoni snickered. Coral buried his face in his arms, hacking out a cough that sounded suspiciously like, "*Whipped.*"

"Fine, you can stay," Whitsom conceded. "But go sit in the bathroom."

"She doesn't have to sit in the bathroom," Atlas argued. He slapped his hand on the table, drawing Whitsom's attention back to the game. "Look, dude, I'm focused —you're the one distracted, that's why I'm beating you so bad."

Whitsom was not, however, entirely incorrect. Atlas did find himself more easily distracted when Gaiomere was around. His gaze, even amidst their game, kept wandering back to her as she perused his bookshelf, her fingers skimming over the titles.

Out of all of the lies Talikoth had told him, out of every word that had come from his father's mouth, it was these Atlas knew to be true: girls *were* distracting. Well, this one girl in particular. It was as though his thoughts and gaze were magnetized whenever she was around, and when she kissed him, his brain shut off entirely. However enjoyable it was —it was also moderately disturbing. He didn't *like* it— someone having so much of a sway over his actions. It had crossed his mind, a time or two, that he should do something about it—break things off before he got any more invested than he already was.

But no, Atlas had concluded that wouldn't be beneficial. Even if they weren't kissing or holding hands, even if they weren't *together*, he would still worry about her. He couldn't shut off the part of his brain that so often wondered what she was doing, or if she was safe. No, a much better course of action was to refuse to allow anything happen to her.

The boys had just finished their second round of switch when Coral clambered to his feet to rustle, once again, through the pantry. Bettoni was shuffling the cards, and Atlas leaned back in his seat to stretch his legs beneath the table, a yawn pulling itself unwittingly from his lips.

He glanced up at Gaiomere, and found that she still stood near the bookshelf, but she was no longer surveying its contents. She gazed blankly at the opposite stretch of wall, her hand frozen over *Catch 22*, her brows knitted.

"What is it?" Atlas asked quietly. She did not answer, but merely continued to gnaw at her lip. He could practically see the cogs in her brain turning. Bettoni and Whitsom looked between the two of them in befuddlement. Coral was scarfing down an entire bowl of blueberries in the kitchen, completely oblivious to the happenings a few feet away from him.

"Gai?" Whitsom called. She jumped, turning to face them quickly.

"Have you been in there?" she demanded.

Atlas, Whitsom, and Bettoni looked at each other, each of them pointing at the other.

"Is she—"

"Are you talking to—"

She rolled her eyes, snapping her fingers in front of her face impatiently. "*Atlas.* Have you been in there?" She jerked her head towards Talikoth's room.

Atlas blinked. "Uh—I mean I have...you know...in my lifetime—*what*?"

She had let out a frustrated growl and marched over to where she'd left her bag by the coffee table. Atlas clambered up and peered around the couch to try to see what she was searching for.

"This is why we don't invite her places," Whitsom mumbled to Bettoni. "She's nutso—"

Gaiomere withdrew her laser from her bag, whirled around on her brother, and brandished it at him rather like a sword. "Did anybody—anybody at all— think to look in Talikoth's room for any clues about the water?" They all stared at her blankly, and she smirked in a self-satisfied sort of way. "No. I thought not. You guys can call me 'nutso' all you want, but I'm the only one who *thinks* around this place."

"I never called you nutso," Bettoni piped up, eyeing Gaiomere's laser nervously.

"I definitely thought it," came Coral's voice from the kitchen, muffled around a mouthful of blueberries.

Atlas' mind was already whirring, and he gazed

at her pensively. "Moonstone said they searched his room," he said slowly. "But they might not have known what to look for. Talikoth is stealthy when it comes to keeping secrets."

Gaiomere nodded, her eyes bright. "And if this was information so classified that the other officers weren't even privy to it, it only makes sense to me that he'd take better care to hide it."

She started towards Talikoth's door, but Atlas hesitated. "Wait, you're not—you're just going to burn through it?"

She glanced over her shoulder at him, arching a brow. "Have you got a better idea?"

Atlas sighed and joined her.

"You know," called Whitsom, "I really just came here to play cards—isn't this Moonstone's job? I thought we weren't meddling anymore!"

Gaiomere and Atlas both shushed him.

In a matter of seconds, Gaiomere melted through the doorknob, and pushed the door open easily.

A strange wave of foreboding washed over Atlas as the two of them stepped across the threshold, and he instinctively scanned the room for any kind of trip wires. He wouldn't put it past Talikoth to have his room protected with lethal defenses.

"It just looks...like a bedroom," Gaiomere said quietly.

Atlas snorted. "What did you expect? A dungeon with chains on the walls?"

Gaiomere didn't answer. She had already lifted a folder off Talikoth's desk and was flipping through it, her eyes narrowed.

Atlas strode across the room and pulled open the

end table drawer, rifling through it.

Bettoni, Whitsom, and Coral gathered in the doorway, peering between the two of them with mirrored expressions of trepidation. "Are you guys out of your minds?" Coral asked. "I mean, do you *actually* have a death wish?"

"He's in prison, what's he gonna do?" Gaiomere reasoned. She sat cross-legged on the floor, with a giant stack of papers from Talikoth's desk in her lap.

"Besides," Atlas added, a little distractedly, as he picked up a small grey box and shook it, "If this is the only way to figure out the whole water situation, isn't it worth the risk?"

Whitsom and Coral were sharing an exasperated look, and it was Bettoni that pointed out, "But Atlas...Talikoth wouldn't have just left super classified information in his room for anybody to find— otherwise Moonstone would have seen it. Wouldn't he have it—"

"Locked away," Atlas agreed, straightening up. His eyes roved over the room. "Maybe..." He moved around the bed and pulled open the closet door.

At first, he only saw Obarion uniforms, and the leather jacket that his father was exceptionally fond of —but then he spotted a glimpse of black metal, tucked away behind Talikoth's boots. He dropped to his knees, pushing the boots aside.

His eyes had not been playing tricks on him. It was a metal box, only about a foot in either direction, with a keypad on the front. Atlas grasped the sides and lugged it out of the closet, setting it in the middle of the room.

Bettoni, Coral, and Whitsom scrambled across the threshold now, peering over Atlas' shoulder curiously, and Gaiomere froze in her spot on the floor, her hickory brown eyes wide.

"Do you think that's it?" she asked.

"I'm almost positive," Atlas said, grimacing as he studied the keypad.

"Couldn't you just melt through it with your laser thing again?" Coral asked Gaiomere.

She shook her head. "Those types of safes are designed to be impenetrable—even a bomb wouldn't break the exterior."

Atlas stared at the little black box for another minute before deciding that he wasn't going to get anywhere by just sitting there wondering what it could be—he needed to try *something*, at least.

He was just stretching a finger towards the keypad when Gaiomere said, "Wait! If you're just guessing, I think I know a better way." She sprang to her feet, tossing her stack of papers back on top of the desk. "I'll be back in like ten minutes."

"Where are you going?" Atlas demanded impatiently.

"Civilians' quarters!" she called back. "Don't you *dare* touch it, any of you."

He exhaled harshly, running a hand through his hair and sinking down on the bed.

"I kinda want to, just cause she said not to," Coral mumbled, and Whitsom snickered.

It could have just been eagerness, but it felt as though they waited much longer than ten minutes before Gaiomere reappeared. Jem followed in after her, a satchel slung across her shoulders. "What's crackalackin'?" the freckled-faced girl said, saluting the four boys before plopping down beside Gaiomere in front of the safe.

"Yo, no more *girls*!" Whitsom griped, turning to glare at Atlas. "Man, this is your unit, tell them to beat it —we haven't even played cheat yet—"

"Has anyone ever told you how charming you are?" Jem drawled. Whitsom opened his mouth to retort, but his sister interrupted him.

"Jem can help us figure out which keys have been pressed," Gaiomere explained, shooting Whitsom a glare.

Jem had withdrawn a strange black tube from her bag. She pushed a button and a bright purple light emitted from the end of it. "It's a blacklight," she explained to the rest of them. "It uses ultraviolet light to bring out the fingerprints."

Indeed, even as she spoke, indentations appeared on the keypad where Talikoth's fingers had pressed.

"But...it's purple," Coral pointed out. The rest of them ignored him.

"2-4-5-7-9-0," Gaiomere recited. "Have I got that right?" Jem nodded, clicking off her light and shoving it back in her bag.

"Alright, so what are y'all waiting for?" Whitsom asked, clapping his hands together. "Do the damn thing."

Jem gave Whitsom a look that was half-amused and half-exasperated. "We haven't got the code yet. Those are just the digits that have been punched—now we have to arrange them."

"*What*? Then what was the point of all that?"

"Oh, I'm *sorry*, I think that I'd much rather figure out 90,000 possible number combinations than six *million*—"

"Guys, just shut up a moment," Atlas snapped. He climbed to his feet and paced in front of the bed.

Would the code be arbitrary? Just a series of random numbers that Talikoth had memorized, with no significance or bearing? It was possible, but Atlas didn't think so. Talikoth wasn't sentimental by any means, but there were things that were important to him, and he certainly had a flair for the dramatic.

2-4-5-7-9-0.

He thought first of Talikoth's birthday—the third month of winter, on the twelfth day, in the two hundred and twenty-fourth year since the declared end of the First War. But no, that couldn't be right...

The Obarion clan had officially been formed a hundred and fifty years after the First War, mid-spring —those numbers didn't fit either, though. And Atlas' birthday didn't coordinate—not that Talikoth would have used that anyway.

Atlas had completely forgotten that there was anyone else in the room. His brain was working in overdrive, running through every day, every significant moment Talikoth could have ever had in his life...

He suddenly froze.

They reached the coast early in the spring, and that was when she managed to escape.

I made decisions no one else had the guts to in order to protect my people.

I took my personal life out of the equation.

Atlas looked sharply at Gaiomere, who was already watching him, her brows knitted together. "0-5-0-7-2-4-9," he recounted firmly. "He pushed the zero twice." She nodded, carefully keying in the code. There was a moment of silence, a space in which they all

held their breath, and then—
   Click.

CHAPTER FIVE

The metal door cracked open, and the six of them froze. Atlas was only roused into motion when Coral whispered, "Why are we all just looking at it?"

Atlas dropped down beside Gaiomere, pulling the door the rest of the way open. The safe was empty except for a plain blue folder, which he withdrew and flipped open.

There were only a few pieces of paper inside. The first was a diagram of the water tower that showed where the water pump lines ran, and an attached manual for repairs. The second piece was a long list of dates, most of them with lines struck through them, dating back over a decade. Beneath each date was a number, ranging anywhere from twenty to two hundred. Tucked behind the list of dates was a map, though unlike any map Atlas had ever seen, with long lines running in either direction, at intersecting points.

The final and smallest piece of paper was just a series of numbers, over thirty digits in total, with commas and dashes arbitrarily strewn about.

Atlas let out a frustrated growl, dropping the folder and springing to his feet as he ran a hand through his hair.

Gaiomere pulled the folder onto her lap. "Atlas—"

"This doesn't help us at *all*!" he snapped, before

she could get more than a word out. The other four were staring at him, but he didn't care. "I was certain he would—certain that this would be—"

"Atlas," Gaiomere said again, her tone calm, and determinedly patient. "Look." She got to her feet, spreading the papers out on the bed. "The water tower diagram and manual wouldn't be in here if the rest of this wasn't relevant, too. We just need to figure out *why*." She frowned, carding her fingers through her curls as she chewed pensively on her lip. "These dates go back how far?"

Atlas picked up the list of dates, his eyes skimming down to the bottom. "Fourteen years. To 250. The Obarion clan had only been in the Westland for a year or two."

"And how many dates are there?"

He hastily counted and re-counted the list, just to make sure he was correct. "Fifty-nine. Wait, but—a few of them aren't crossed off." She leaned around him, squinting at the list as well. "Those haven't happened yet," he realized aloud. "Look—" He pointed at the three dates nearest the top. "The third month of spring, on the fifteenth day, 265. And then again in the last month of summer, and once more at the end of the autumn."

Gaiomere glanced up at him nervously. "That first date is less than a moon cycle from now."

He nodded, his brows drawing together. "And what are all these numbers? They seem to coordinate with the dates."

She didn't answer. She was studying the last page in the folder intently. Atlas leaned back against the end table, staring at the little numbers scrawled beneath the dates as though, if he surveyed them long enough, they might reveal their secrets. He tried to recall everything that Talikoth might have ever said about the water —anything that might clue them in to what all this information meant.

But Talikoth had always been suspiciously silent when it came to the water—he had only ever warned them never to drink from any of the rivers or lakes around Headquarters.

"Fifty-six dates crossed off...over fourteen years..." Atlas said slowly. "That's four times a year...quarterly visits—"

"To a location where they could retrieve water," Gaiomere finished, her brown eyes suddenly widening. "Holy honeysuckle!" She reached for the map, spreading it out across the bed, and setting the final piece of paper next to it. "Atlas, these aren't just random numbers—they're coordinates!" He blinked, and she hastily clarified, "The earth's grid system—measuring distance from the equator and prime meridian—I can't remember what you and your clanspeople call it—"

"Latitude and longitude," Atlas breathed, his face lighting up. "They're latitudinal and longitudinal coordinates—Gaiomere, you're a *genius*." He pressed his lips briefly to her forehead, and her cheeks flushed.

"So wait," Bettoni broke in. Atlas started, for he had forgotten anyone else was in the room. Jem was flipping through the water tower manual with vague interest, and Coral and Whitsom were leaning against the wall near the door, both looking rather bored. Bettoni strode over to the bed as well and frowned down at the list of dates. "These demarcate Talikoth's trips to get water, and *these* are coordinates— presumably to some location with a clean water supply

—but that doesn't explain how Talikoth is transporting the water." The two of them stared at him blankly. "I mean, we're talking about three months' worth of water for eight thousand people. You're not going to tell me Talikoth and the Inner Ring were just carting hundreds of thousands of gallons of water back by *hand*."

Atlas and Gaiomere looked at each other. "He must have some sort of—some sort of transport vehicle," Atlas said slowly.

"A plane?" Gaiomere suggested.

He shook his head. "No, it couldn't carry that much weight. This would be something that ran on the ground—some sort of heavy-duty transportation that could lug that much water back and forth between Headquarters and—wherever these coordinates are."

"It must have been a good distance from Headquarters, too, whatever it was," Jem pointed out, "for none of you guys to ever have come across it on patrols."

"Or maybe Talikoth just made sure our patrol routes never took us that way," Coral said as he picked blueberries out of his teeth.

Gaiomere straightened up, her eyes finding Atlas' once more. "There are two different coordinates here," she said.

Atlas frowned, moving closer to her and peering over her shoulder. "What do you mean?"

Her finger traced along the map, and she explained, "The first set of coordinates points *here*—it's got to be at least twenty miles from Headquarters, but I'm almost positive that's where the water tower lines run too, because otherwise—"

"How would they transport it?" Atlas agreed. "So

wait, if that's where the water tower lines run, then—"

"That's where the transport vehicle is," Gaiomere affirmed. "And if we take the transport vehicle to the *second* set of coordinates—"

"We'll find our water."

Gaiomere nodded, beaming at him. "We should take this information to Moonstone—"

"But *not* before we play cheat!" Whitsom burst out. "She's probably asleep, anyway."

Atlas sighed. "Fine."

"YES!" Coral and Whitsom hastily scrambled out of the room and back to the table, divvying up the cards.

Gaiomere rolled her eyes, glancing over at Jem and telling her, "I think this is the part where we're going to be kicked out."

"You don't have to go," Atlas said. "Whitsom can get over it—"

She stood on her tiptoes and kissed him on the cheek. "I probably should. See you tomorrow?"

He started to answer, but was interrupted by Coral's enraged scream, "*ATLAS, GET YOUR ASS IN HERE BEFORE I HAND IT TO YOU!*"

The girls broke into giggles and bid him farewell, disappearing out the door and down the hall.

Atlas let Gaiomere take the folder full of information the night before, since she'd be more likely to be able to get ahold of Moonstone than he would, and she must have been able to pass on the information quickly, for it was only ten in the morning when someone knocked at his unit door.

He had just been getting out of the shower, so he hastily pulled his clothes on, and when he opened the door, his hair was still dripping into his eyes.

Moonstone greeted him with a solemn nod. "Atlas. May I come in?"

He glanced around at his unit. His clothes from the night before lay in the doorway of his room, and there were still dishes in the sink. A giant bowl of popcorn sat on the couch, and there were crumbs littered around where he had been sitting. His cheeks prickled with heat as he held the door open wider. "Oh—uh, sure."

The imposing woman seated herself at the dining room table, and after a moment of hesitation, he sat down across from her. The silence between them hung awkwardly, but Moonstone spared him any further embarrassment by getting straight to the point, "Gaiomere brought me the folder that the two of you found and shared the conclusions you'd drawn."

He nodded. "I didn't even think of looking in his room—it was her idea."

"I've dispatched a squad of soldiers to the coordinates south of the Headquarters—they'll be back this afternoon with their assessments."

Atlas nodded again, unsure, at first, of what else to say. But then guilt bubbled up in him, heavy and putrid, and his cheeks burned. He forced himself to meet Moonstone's eyes. "Uh—General?" He swallowed thickly, forcing out, "I just—I wanted to—to apologize —for my actions, I mean—over the last month. My behavior was disrespectful and reckless and I—I'm sorry. I really do—I really do appreciate everything you've done."

The words had felt sticky in his throat, but once he pushed them out, a huge weight lifted off his chest. Something in her face softened, and her dark eyes looked at him almost fondly—or as close to fond as the formidable woman could get, anyway.

"Thank you for saying that, Atlas." She paused, then added, "I know how frustrating it must be for someone like you to be asked to sit to the side and wait your turn. You have a lot of your father in you—" She must have read his face, because she quickly added, "And your mother—neither of which is necessarily a good or bad thing."

His brows shot up. In any context, how could having *any* of his father in him be a good thing?

"We aren't all just made up of one thing, Atlas," she said quietly. She was giving him that piercing look that he had grown so accustomed to, but it didn't make him uncomfortable as it used to. "Each piece of our souls can manifest a thousand different ways, depending on the path we choose to follow."

She got to her feet. "Thank you very much for the information you shared. It was most helpful."

He jerked a nod, still trying to process her words.

Moonstone was almost out of the door when he sprang to his feet. "General?"

She turned, arching a black brow.

"Could I—I mean—" He took a steadying breath. "I'd like to request an audience with Talikoth, if you—if you'd allow it." She gazed at him inquisitively, and he clarified, "We still don't understand what the numbers beneath the dates mean, and I just—well, I know your interrogators haven't been successful, so I figured I'd just—I'd like to try. One more time, anyway."

Moonstone smiled a little. "I'll consider it. I'll let you know within a couple of days' time. I'm giving you a time frame so that you don't do anything rash, understood?"

He grinned, rubbing the back of his neck. "Yeah, I understand."

"Good. I'll see you soon, Atlas."

The General was true to her word. Approximately thirty hours after their conversation, a note was slipped under Atlas' unit door. He immediately recognized the sharp scrawl as Moonstone's:

Atlas,
I have granted you an audience with Talikoth this evening. Rya will be by your unit at 6 o'clock to escort you to the prison, and you will have one hour to ask whatever questions you need.
General Moonstone

Atlas spent the two hours before the scheduled conference with Gaiomere in the library. She told him some of the theories she'd been working on in the days since they'd discovered the folder—that the numbers represented gallons of water they'd managed to acquire on each given date, in the thousands. "And it makes sense, because the numbers seem to jump significantly as the years go by," she reasoned, drumming her fingers on her notebook as she sat down on the armrest of his chair. "For example, the first trip is only twenty—so potentially twenty thousand gallons, right? If the clan has grown significantly over the past couple of decades, it would explain the jump—"

"The thing is, I'm not sure it has, though," Atlas pointed out, sliding an arm around her waist. "If anything, our clan has only gotten smaller with all our casualties from the trip west and the Long War—"

"Well, I was also thinking those numbers could represent how many of the Inner Ring soldiers Talikoth took with him on those given dates—"

"No, that doesn't fit either," Atlas interrupted. "The Inner Ring has never had more than a hundred soldiers—"

"Well, you come up with something, then!" Gaiomere snapped, turning to glare at him. "I'm the only one trying to think of anything..."

He sniggered, tugging her down off the armrest and onto his lap. "*Or* I could just wait to see what Talikoth says and we could spend the preceding time much more productively."

She arched a brow. "Somehow I doubt your methods for qualifying what is or isn't *productive*—" He silenced her with a kiss, deftly snatching her notebook from her hands and tossing it somewhere on the ground behind him.

Atlas had to sprint back to his unit to meet Rya. The soldier in question was just knocking on Atlas' unit door when he came pelting down the hallway, stumbling to a stop at 5:58.

"Sorry—just—lost track of time," Atlas managed, his breathing heavy.

Rya only scowled, turning on his heel and stalking down the hall. Atlas followed, clutching the folder Gaiomere had returned to him. The bubble of apprehension that had surfaced upon receiving Moonstone's note a couple of hours ago reemerged, swelling rapidly in his stomach, and he contemplated what he would say to Talikoth when he saw him.

There was a good chance that his father wouldn't be any more receptive than last time—but now, at least, Atlas was prepared for his mind games and mockery. If he kept his cool—if he didn't allow his father to get under his skin—Talikoth *might* let something slip...

When they arrived at the little stone shack in the woods, the door had been propped open, and the guards waited inside. As soon as Atlas entered, they wordlessly filed out, and he marveled at how much easier this was with permission—*and* he had an entire hour to work with, rather than stolen minutes.

As soon as the door closed, Talikoth straightened in his chair. His beard had grown thicker, and his dark hair hung over his eyes. Atlas said nothing, but merely held up the blue folder and watched, with unabashed satisfaction, as the smirk slid promptly from his father's face.

"Your dedication to protecting your secrets is admirable, I'll give you that."

Talikoth's face was impassive, but his dark eyes lit up with tangible irritation. "How did you figure it out?"

Atlas shrugged. "Resourcefulness. Deductive reasoning. And an exceptionally good memory—not to brag." It was a good thing the guards had left him alone, for he was enjoying himself quite a bit. Atlas couldn't remember ever having caught Talikoth off-guard, and the power it permitted him was almost intoxicating.

His father tilted his head to the side, his mouth lifting into a smirk. "I see. Well, in that case, I'm impressed."

Just like that, the tables turned again, and Atlas

suddenly felt like a seven-year-old boy vying for a bit of praise and attention from the man who never gave him any.

Atlas cleared his throat, slapping the folder down on the rickety wooden table shoved haphazardly into the corner, and peered at the clipboard, more to give himself a reason to look away from the man cuffed in the chair than anything else. "Moonstone sent a squad to the coordinates twenty miles south of Headquarters —once we determine the second location, we'll be able to solve the water shortage—all without your help."

Talikoth was still smirking, and it unnerved Atlas. He should have been angry, he should have been fighting, or at least trying to push Atlas' buttons, anything to rebalance the power dynamic, to re-establish his own control, unless...

Unless he'd never lost it in the first place.

Atlas picked the folder back up, flipping it open and thumbing through until he'd found the list of dates. "The numbers below the dates—what do they mean?" His father didn't answer, and Atlas continued, almost to himself, "Gaio—one of our researchers theorized that they might represent gallons of water in the thousands, or perhaps the number of Inner Ring soldiers assigned on a given date."

"All respectable theories," Talikoth allowed, giving him a nod of acknowledgement. He said nothing else, and Atlas carefully masked his mounting frustration. After all, that was what Talikoth wanted.

"Who's Gaio?" his father asked suddenly.

Atlas looked up.

"If I'm recalling correctly, no one that works in my lab is named Gaio," Talikoth continued. "Unless

Moonstone has already replaced all of my researchers with whatever morons are under her command."

Atlas refocused his gaze on the paper in front of him. "No one," he said, too quickly.

He chanced a glance up at Talikoth and saw his smirk had widened, and that he was leaning back in his chair, relaxed, as though he were the one outside the prison cell, not Atlas. "Oh, there's something there. I can see it in your face."

Atlas shook his head, straightening and meeting his father's gaze, "I came here to ask you about the numbers—"

"But who are you trying to protect?" Talikoth mused, ignoring him completely. "Perhaps one of your new Vedas comrades—since you did abandon your old friends so readily for new ones—"

"I didn't—"

"Or *maybe*," Talikoth continued, raising his voice ever so slightly, so that he drowned out Atlas' protests, "you're protecting that little Renegade girl who killed off half of my Inner Ring—the one who came so close to having her light snuffed out like a candle—"

Atlas' hand clenched around the folder, and that familiar anger exploded in his chest like a microburst. But Talikoth was only trying to get under his skin— Atlas couldn't allow him to see his effectiveness.

In the end, though, it did not matter, and Atlas should have known that. His father could read his thoughts on his face like a picture book. "Ah," Talikoth said quietly. "So that's it. You're protecting the girl—"

"I don't have to protect her from anything," Atlas snarled, glaring at the older man. "You'll be locked away in this cell until you wither into bone and ash."

He snatched the folder off the table, turning towards the door. "The numbers don't matter—we've got the coordinates. We have everything we need to supply the Obarion with water—we don't need you. Have fun rotting away here for the rest of your pathetic life."

His hand was on the doorknob when Talikoth called, "Just hope they don't kill you."

Atlas wanted to keep walking—surely his father was only goading him, was only trying to keep the fight alive—but his curiosity got the better of him, and he whirled back around. "Hope *who* doesn't kill us?"

Talikoth shrugged, gazing disinterestedly at the ceiling, as though they were discussing a sparring match, rather than the prospective survival of his people. "The ones who provide the water, of course."

Atlas' hand hovered for a moment in the air, and then fell. "The water is traded for?"

His father lazily lifted a shoulder. "In a manner of speaking."

"Then there should be no reason for them to go back on a prearranged agreement," Atlas said. "We'll go back to them on the predetermined date—uphold the vow of protection—"

Talikoth let out a bark of laughter. "They don't give us water in exchange for their safety—they could easily flee east, if that were the case."

Atlas frowned. "Then what?"

Talikoth said nothing, but merely continued to gaze at him unblinking. Atlas flipped through the folder once more, as though he might have missed something, as though there could be another piece of paper tucked away that none of them had noticed, which would give them all the answers they needed.

But no, there would be no solution so simple. Talikoth had made sure of it. "What do you want?" Atlas asked finally.

Even to his own ears, his tone sounded defeated, and indeed, he *felt* it. He had been so certain that this would be it—that this information they had uncovered would be the salvation for the Obarion people, that they would no longer have to rely on Talikoth to reveal secrets that he'd sooner die for.

His father's voice was quiet, but his answer was immediate. "Only my freedom."

Atlas stared at him. "Your freedom?"

"My freedom," Talikoth confirmed, nodding. "The promise of liberation from this wretched cell—and the autonomy to roam, without interference from Moonstone and her...*puppets*." He leered at Atlas, who tapped his fingers against the back of the folder reflectively, his mind working through Talikoth's bargain.

"We can take as many soldiers as we need to," Atlas said finally. "They won't be able to kill us if they're out-gunned—"

"And then how will you get your water?" Talikoth asked, his brows lifting. "I would have thought you would understand, after all of the council meetings you've attended, how few people are inclined to supply provisions on the basis of coercion—"

"Then we'll take the water ourselves!" Atlas snapped.

"You *can't*," Talikoth replied. "If you attack the tribe that supplies the water, you'll only be creating a problem for yourselves in a few months' time, for you'll have no idea where to retrieve the water from, come the time for the next exchange—and before you interrupt, no, you *can't* follow them to the water and retrieve it yourselves, because the source is hidden." He sat back in his chair. "Paint it any way you wish, Atlas, but the fact is: *you need me.*"

Atlas' jaw flexed as he studied his father. He had half a mind to walk away—to disregard his words, and slam the door behind him as he left the dingy stone shack. He could report what Talikoth shared to Moonstone and he might never have to see the man again.

But Atlas knew he could not do that. And what was more...he wasn't even sure he wanted to.

"What do you give them in exchange for the water?" he asked Talikoth quietly.

His father did not answer, but merely continued to stare at him. There was something in his expression that Atlas recognized, though. His eyes held the same sort of provocation they did when the two of them had sparred, or when he gave Atlas a particularly challenging problem to solve.

Prove that you're not the spineless disappointment I've always believed you to be.

Atlas broke his gaze, pacing across the dark stone floor as he thought. What could this mystery tribe possibly seek to gain that Talikoth would be able to provide besides protection? And what did Talikoth have to spare, when he had a clan of eight thousand to provide for?

Food was Atlas' first thought, but Renegades needed little help finding food, and it wasn't as though Talikoth didn't have enough mouths to feed on his own. Could the Obarion be supplying them weapons? No,

Talikoth would never willingly put weapons into the hands of his enemies, no matter what they offered in return. Maybe they traded goods like clothing, or soaps. The clan did have a vast number of skilled laborers, but if it *was* goods they traded, the other officers would have *needed* to know about the exchanges. Artisan goods were tracked and regulated, and it would be nearly impossible to hide such quantities of tradable goods that would pay for nearly a million gallons of water. Why was it that *only* the Inner Ring had been involved in the trafficking?

The rigs were never where you sent the Renegades, were they?

Your Inner Ring would cart them off and slaughter them.

Atlas froze. "Renegades," he whispered. It was as though his heart had stopped in his chest, and the blood in his veins suddenly ran icy cold. He looked at his father, who watched Atlas through narrowed eyes, and said, "You were trading them Renegades."

Something like approval flashed across Talikoth's face, and Atlas realized belatedly that even now, Talikoth was still testing him, still trying to propel him towards some end that he sought, though Atlas wasn't sure what that end might be.

He ran a hand through his hair, shaking his head. "You sell them like slaves," he muttered. He let out a humorless laugh and spat, "I suppose we're damned to repeat history—"

"The Renegades have always been too much of a risk to allow," Talikoth said, shrugging unremorsefully.

Atlas scowled, shaking his head. "What, so this tribe takes the Ren off your hands in exchange for water, then slaughters them in droves? You don't even have the gall to kill them yourself—you just get someone else to do your dirty work for you."

Talikoth arched a brow, and Atlas heard an edge of frustration in his voice as he said, "I—nor anyone in my Inner Ring—have any qualms about slaying traitors. It was how our clan functioned in the early days of our time in the Westland. However, once we discovered our supply tribe, I decided this was more beneficial. For the good of the people."

For the good of the people. It was an expression that Atlas had heard often growing up. It had always struck him as so noble, but now it struck him something like a slap in the face. "Why didn't you just follow them—the supply tribe, I mean?" he demanded. "You could have gotten rid of the Ren yourselves and taken as much water as you pleased."

Talikoth's face twitched. For a moment, he opened his mouth to speak, but then closed it again, as though he'd changed his mind. Finally, he seemed to settle on, "There was no need to. I got what I needed—they got what they wanted. It was a mutually beneficial arrangement—don't look so distraught, boy, I would have killed them just the same."

The door opened behind them, and the two guards filed back in. Talikoth smirked, inclining his head as he remarked, "I presume I'll be seeing you again soon."

Atlas swallowed. "I—yeah. Yeah, you will."

Rya waited outside of the stone shack, and Atlas immediately asked, "Can you contact Moonstone? I need to speak to her immediately."

The sullen man said nothing, but slid the

transmitter off of his belt and pushed the button, "Rya to General Moonstone."

There were a few moments of silence, and then, *"This is Moonstone."*

"General, I'm with the Obarion boy now—" Atlas rolled his eyes. It was rather absurd that he had been working with the Vedas willingly for the better part of a year and they still referred to him as 'the Obarion boy.'

"—he just finished his conference with Talikoth and would like to report. Over."

"Tell him to make his way down to the campsite and I will meet him there. Rya, you may resume dining hall patrol—he won't need an escort. Over."

Atlas blinked, a giddy grin making its way onto his face. She was going to allow him to leave Headquarters—and *without* an escort? He felt like he could sing.

He and Rya parted ways at the edge of the forest, and Atlas made his way down to the gate. The sun had just begun to set, and the woods grew dark, but Atlas was too elated to feel any level of apprehension. He could hear the campsite commotion about a quarter-mile out, and the grin made its way onto his face once more. Worries of the water supply and Talikoth's scheming drifted away as the scent of fire-cooked sausage wafted over to him, and Niko and Luca called out exuberant greetings.

But the sight of Moonstone, sitting near the fire next to Vailhelm, quickly sobered him. She got to her feet as soon as he approached. "Atlas," she greeted. "You have a report?"

"Yes," he replied, unable to repress a grimace. "Yes, I—I have a lot to tell you."

CHAPTER SIX

When Atlas arrived in the meeting room the next morning, Moonstone and Harcliff were already there. Gaiomere sat atop the table, her legs dangling as she briefed the two on the detoxifiers' progress, and Jacoby stood beside her, interjecting occasionally, his glasses dangling precariously at the end of his nose.

Niko wandered in a few minutes later, his bow slung across his back, and he gave Atlas a rugged grin as he plopped down into the adjacent seat. "So, who's ass are we kicking this time?" he asked.

Atlas snorted. "Not sure yet. Some mystery tribe in the mountains, I guess."

"A blind fight? That's my kind of shindig."

Vailhelm, Jaina and Augusto soon joined them, and Colonel Dak filed in after them, along with Major Alekea. Dak gave Atlas a solemn nod as he sat down across the table, and Alekea looked between Atlas and Gaiomere and winked.

Moonstone waved Atlas over, and when he stopped beside her, she said in a low voice, "They're on their way with him. You're sure this is a good idea?"

"Yes," Atlas said firmly. "The only way we're going to accomplish anything is working with him, rather than against him."

No sooner had he spoken did the door open.

Two soldiers walked in, each gripping Talikoth's arms on either side. His wrists were still shackled behind his back, but even in chains, his presence was undeniably imposing. Silence thick and heavy fell across the room the moment he entered, and Gaiomere's hand, almost unconsciously it seemed, twitched toward her throat, before she caught herself.

"Thank you all for coming," Moonstone said finally. If she were at all intimidated by the presence of the Obarion General, her steady voice didn't show it. "I've called this meeting to recount vital new intel that I received yesterday evening."

Atlas only half-listened as Moonstone recounted everything he had shared with her after his meeting with Talikoth, as well as everything from the folder. His eyes affixed on the man in question, who had been forced into a chair by his guards. Talikoth's gaze was on the ceiling, his posture relaxed. He looked almost *bored*, though Atlas didn't buy the act for a second.

"The soldiers I sent to the coordinates south of Obarion Headquarters discovered a train whose tracks run east—"

Niko sat forward, waving a hand in the air. "Sorry, uh—they discovered a what?"

"It's a bunch of big metal cars all connected together," Atlas explained. "According to what I've read, a hundred-car train could carry upwards of four thousand tons."

"How far east do they go?" Vailhelm asked gruffly.

"Our scouts say they overlap another set of tracks in the mountains which continue east," Moonstone said. "We presume the suppliers take this set of tracks to bring the water to and from the source."

"So why don't we just follow *those* tracks to the source?" Niko asked. "Me and my boys can take a couple of cars and scout it out—"

"According to our intel, the source is guarded," Moonstone said. "And either way, I'm disinclined to steal a water source from a population who has claimed it—"

"*Steal* it?" Niko's face flushed red with fury. "General, these goons are trading our folks like barter chips!"

"Niko's right, General," Atlas said quickly. "The suppliers have been taking their people for almost two decades—and they've got no more of a claim to the water than anyone else has."

"Perhaps a negotiation could be reached," Harcliff said in his tranquilizing voice. "The suppliers may be willing to accept some other form of commerce —"

"Oh come *on*," Gaiomere said suddenly, and everyone looked at her. Her cheeks darkened with color.

"Yes, Gaiomere?" Moonstone said bemusedly.

At the sound of her name, Atlas saw Talikoth's head twitch. His gaze dropped from the ceiling and fell on her, before darting over to Atlas. His lips quirked up into the faintest smirk, and he arched an eyebrow.

"Well, it's obvious, isn't it?" Gaiomere said. "What else would some random tribe in the middle of the mountains want with a bunch of people?"

Atlas could have smacked himself. Now that she had pointed it out, it *was* obvious. "They're Flesh Flayers," he said. "Of course they are."

Augusto sat up in his chair, his watery eyes wide as he stammered, "Flesh...Flayers? What—what are

Flesh Flayers?"

"Cannibals," Atlas said. "They eat other people." Augusto's face turned green.

"They normally only travel in packs of two or three," Gaiomere told them. "I've never seen a tribe as large as this one must be, if the numbers are anything to go off."

"They can't live peacefully with one another," Niko added. "They normally just end up fighting so much that they kill each other off, so a tribe this big —that has survived this long—must have some kind of hierarchy. They must be less..." He grimaced as he pressed on, "*savage* than the other Flesh Flayers to have kept from killing each other this long."

"They don't need to kill each other," Atlas remarked, his eyes roving to the ceiling contemplatively. "Why would they, when they've got a guaranteed food haul every three months? Their peace is conditional."

"So maybe they'll kill each other off when the trade ceases?" Jaina suggested hopefully. "And we can take the water source ourselves?"

"Or maybe they'll wander west in search of more food," Atlas said, shaking his head. "No, a problem of that enormity in the Westland—no matter how far from us it is at the present moment—is a problem for all of us." He could feel Talikoth's eyes on him, and it made him uneasy, like he was undergoing an exam and he wasn't sure if he was passing or failing.

Moonstone nodded. "I agree. My scouts saw no activity at the mountaintop, which leads me to believe that the supplier tribe is headquartered at the water source itself and only ventures up the mountain for the exchanges—the next of which is scheduled to take place in a little under three weeks' time."

"So that's when we should strike," Niko said. "We send a squad to follow the tracks and claim the water for ourselves while they're still on top of the mountain —"

"I doubt they leave the entire water source unguarded during the exchange," Atlas pointed out.

Moonstone was frowning. "Yes, Atlas is right. It would be best to send out a team of scouts to give us an idea of what we're up against—we could be facing thirty soldiers, or three hundred—but whatever is out there, we need to be prepared for it." She looked at Niko, saying, "I'd like you to take a recon unit east—to the end of the tracks."

Her face grew very serious, and she looked around at the group of them, her dark eyes narrowed. "Now, the second matter we need to attend to is the origin of our information." Atlas sat up a little straighter. "General Talikoth has provided information pertaining to these exchanges and has requested that this aid be taken into account when considering the length of his imprisonment." She paused, before continuing, "This consideration would be contingent upon the reliability of the information that he has provided, of course. If we find that this intelligence has been fabricated, his indefinite containment in the Obarion prison would still stand—"

"And if it *isn't*?" Niko demanded. "If it is all true— what, we're gonna just let him roam free? General, you saw what he did to Raider—after the rest of his army had surrendered!"

"I propose a reduction of sentence, rather than

outright release," Moonstone said calmly. "I cannot speak for the ways of your people, Niko, nor for yours, Harcliff, but it is not unheard of, in Vedas' customs, to reward a prisoner on account of the assistance they have provided to our people."

"You're speaking of minor crimes, General!" Vailhelm exclaimed. "We've released thieves, and petty vandals—Talikoth is a murderer."

"It is possible," Harcliff interjected slowly, "that a probationary interval might prove to inform our path forward. We need not be in any rush to make decisions." Scattered nods reflected on either side of the table, and Harcliff's dark eyes fell on Atlas. "But what do you say?"

Atlas nearly jumped, his eyes shooting up to meet the older man's. "I—me? I don't think I have much of a say in the matter."

"On the contrary, I think you have as much of a say as any of us," Harcliff told him. He paused, adding, almost as an afterthought, "Perhaps more."

Atlas glanced up at Moonstone, and she gave him an encouraging nod. Beneath the table, Gaiomere's hand squeezed his own. He looked at Talikoth and found his father's glittering eyes already fastened on him, his brows lifted, that taunting smirk already etched upon his lips.

"Well—for starters, anything that came from the folder shouldn't be taken into account," Atlas reasoned. "Since he didn't willingly volunteer that information."

The smirk slipped promptly off Talikoth's mouth, replaced by a scowl, and his nostrils flared. "You ungrateful little—"

"I wasn't done," Atlas said coldly. "Because the folder can't be taken into account, the only information that could be used for his release would be the fact that their water is traded for—which doesn't actually help us, since the trade is morally out of the question —the fact that their transport vehicle and water source are secured—which we could have figured out with a couple of scouts—and that the barter chips in question were, in fact, human beings, which—come to think of it, I figured out on my own, *so...*" He leaned back in his chair, smirking at Talikoth. "At the present moment— the way I see it—his information wouldn't appear to be adequate for reducing his term of imprisonment."

Niko openly sniggered beside him, and Vailhelm chortled, crying, "Here, here!" Atlas even thought the corners of Moonstone's mouth might have twitched.

Talikoth, at first, looked furious. But then, like wax, the expression melted from his face, and the smirk returned. Atlas' gratification vanished, and a wary foreboding bubbled up like vomit.

He cleared his throat, and the atmosphere in the room shifted into a chilling silence. Vailhelm's eyes narrowed, and Gaiomere's hand tightened around Atlas'. "I hate to be the bearer of bad news," Talikoth said, straightening up and tilting his head towards Moonstone. "But I'm afraid you'll find my involvement is...quite inextricable."

Moonstone, to her credit, looked entirely unfazed. "And why is that?"

He did not answer. Instead, his gaze wandered to Niko. "Send your scouts," he said. "Perform all the reconnaissance you please, and when you find—as you inevitably will—that it is not enough..." He leaned back in his chair, grinning dangerously. "Well, you know where to find me."

Dak, Atlas could not help but notice, hid a smile behind his hands, as though Talikoth had told some private joke, which only he understood.

Vailhelm slammed a hand against the table so loudly that Augusto jumped. "He cannot *withhold* information and get away with it, General—"

"So his sentence doesn't get reduced," Niko said, shrugging. "Only hurts him—"

"But if we're walking into a trap..." Jaina started.

"It doesn't matter," Atlas said firmly. "It's our best chance at solving this—possibly our only chance." He looked up at Moonstone. "Niko and his crew can take as many weapons as they can carry, and maybe I'm underestimating them, but I doubt these Flesh Flayers have cars like we do. Even if our guys are outnumbered, they'll be able to get a decent look at things and get out before the Flesh Flayers can do any damage."

Moonstone inclined her head. "Let's get a squadron en route as soon as possible. The track crossover lies a little over a hundred miles from Obarion headquarters—I'd like a report in twenty-four hours, if you can be back by then."

She continued to distribute assignments, and one-by-one the Council members filed out. Atlas had not even noticed the soldiers escort Talikoth from the room, but when he glanced up at the chair his father had occupied, it was empty.

Atlas' mind was working in overdrive as he made his way back to his unit. What, he wondered, were Niko and the rest of them going to find, when they reached the end of the tracks? Would the Flesh Flayers be waiting there, before they were able to get any real bearings on the area or their surroundings? What if the

Flesh Flayers' numbers were unprecedented?

But no, even if the Obarion soldiers did not cooperate, there was no possible way that the Flesh Flayers tribe could exceed the thousand plus troops that Moonstone had at her disposal. Especially not with the numbers he and Gaiomere had seen on the date list—surely two hundred people would not be enough to sustain a thousand Flesh Flayers for three entire months—

He hastily pushed his thoughts in a different direction as his stomach lurched uncomfortably. He didn't particularly want to think about the Flesh Flayers' dining habits, no matter how relevant it was to their problem at hand.

He found Coral, Whitsom, and Bettoni at their usual table in the dining hall and had scarcely sat down before Bettoni asked in a low voice, "How'd the meeting go?"

"Moonstone is sending a crew east for recon," Atlas said, as he piled a couple of baked potatoes onto his plate.

"You're not going with them?"

Atlas shook his head, and hastily regaled them with all the details that had been discussed. "Is Moonstone planning on taking our guys to fight this tribe in the mountains?" Bettoni asked as soon as he'd finished.

"I'm not sure, actually," Atlas said, frowning. "Colonel Dak is pretty convinced of the Obarion soldiers' loyalty but...Moonstone's not sold, and...neither am I, to be honest."

"Why not?" Whitsom asked around a mouthful of corn.

It was Bettoni who answered. "From what I've heard, a lot of the clanspeople thought Talikoth went about things the wrong way—now that they've got the freedom to speak out, they're willing to admit that. But others...well, others think he had the right idea. They really do think that the Ren are savages and that Talikoth was sparing us trouble by having them killed. And they don't regard the Vedas any better."

Coral snorted. "Well, Moonstone didn't do herself any favors by keeping us confined so long."

"How many?" Atlas asked Bettoni, his frown deepening. "How many clanspeople are thinking that way?"

The long-haired boy shrugged. "Hard to say. So many people are afraid to speak against them—they don't know if Moonstone's the sort to have you killed for opening your mouth, you know? But I've heard a lot of talk, and Quandra said she has too. I'd wager at least a third of the clan—and half the soldiers."

"Our loyalty's supposed to be to the clan, not to Talikoth," Coral pointed out, leaning against the table. "We all took the vow—"

"We took the vow to serve the best interests of our clan and heed the orders of our superiors," Atlas said.

"Right, but if they see that Dak is willing to work with Moonstone—"

"But Dak isn't the highest-ranking officer left alive," Atlas reminded him, drumming his fingers against the table. "*Crowley* is—and Crowley's more loyal to Talikoth than anyone."

"Yeah, but no one ever listened to him," Coral said, waving Atlas off. "Crowley's just a puppet—everybody knows it. Dak's the one giving orders now—"

"That's the problem, though, Cor," Bettoni interrupted. "There's a lot of clanspeople—and a lot of soldiers for that matter—who are starting to feel like they might be willing to go against orders." He shot Atlas an apologetic glance. "They saw the General's son do it without getting so much as a slap on the wrist —they're starting to think maybe they can push back, too." He glanced around their table, before informing the other three, "There were eight brawls last night— and a couple of guys—Favio and Hix, remember them? —actually managed to wrestle away some guns from a few Vedas soldiers before one of the officers tased them."

"But I only got away with going against orders because the right side *won*," Atlas argued indignantly. "If Talikoth had won, I would have been executed—"

"*I* know that," Bettoni said calmly, "but a lot of them don't understand that—there's a lot of angry people out there, Atlas, and I just—I hope Moonstone's got a plan for it."

Atlas let out a heavy breath, leaning against the table as he pushed the potatoes around his plate. Fifteen minutes ago, his mind had been consumed by worries about the Flesh Flayer tribe and what threat they could pose to the rest of the population in the Westland. Now he realized their problems were much closer to home.

He had hoped that Whitsom had an accurate read on things—that once the Obarion soldiers got a little bit of freedom, some room to stretch their legs, the tension would dissipate.

But Bettoni was right. Moonstone *had* better have a plan to assuage the resentment festering at the heart of the clan. If she didn't, a water shortage would be the least of their worries.

◆ ◆ ◆

Atlas slept fitfully that night, and the next morning the hours passed so slowly that by nine o'clock in the morning, he was in an exceptionally foul mood.

Whitsom must have sensed his sour spirits from all the way down at the Fringe, for he showed up at Atlas' door a couple of hours before lunch with Bettoni and Coral in tow and declared that Atlas was finally going to teach him bruiseball.

They wrangled together a couple dozen others —mostly Vedas and Renegades—but Ando, Eaton, and three boys who had been two years below Atlas in Academy elected to join them as well. After ten minutes of Atlas' pleading, Whitsom agreed to let Gaiomere play, though only with the sincere promise that they wouldn't disappear into the woods together at any point. The group gathered in a cluster near the front gate, and a couple of Vedas soldiers on the perimeter eyed the crowd suspiciously, but Atlas ignored them.

"Alright, listen up."

The throng of soldiers and tribespeople fell silent around him, and his mouth curled into a smirk. "The rules are simple: your objective is to reach the finish line —in this instance, the water tower—without any of the hunters striking you."

Gaiomere leaned over towards Bettoni, and Atlas heard her whisper, "He takes this very seriously."

Bettoni whispered back, "He *is* the reigning bruiseball champion."

"The hunters will be armed with *these*—" Atlas held up one of the rubbery balls, small enough to fit in his hand, but so dense that their impact felt similar to being punched. "And if any of them manage to strike you, you're out. Got it?" Nods scattered throughout the group. Whitsom bounced excitedly on the balls of his feet.

In the end, Atlas, Whitsom, Bettoni, Zarr, Eaton, and Sitch were elected to be hunters, and the rest of them spread out along the start line they had scratched into the dirt. Gaiomere was the only girl, but she was looking rather self-assured, even beside the much larger and faster boys around her.

"You've got a minute to scatter!" Atlas called over his shoulder as he turned away from them and closed his eyes. "Go!" He heard a smattering of laughter, the hasty retreat of footsteps, and the tell-tale sound of one of Luca's hooks latching onto the branch of a tree.

"Eaton, skirt the ravine," Atlas said, as soon as the minute was up. "I'll bet you anything that's where Niko heads. Zarr, Sitch, you guys wanna make a straight break for the water tower to head off anybody trying to make a dash?"

"Luca will stick to the trees," Whitsom advised as the others took off.

"Then you and me will cover them," Atlas said, nodding.

The two of them half-walked, half-jogged towards the tree line, but they'd only just reached the shade of a tilting catclaw when, from his peripherals, Atlas spotted a figure creeping in the shadows cast by a cluster of mesquites. He caught Whitsom's eye and jerked his head towards where he'd seen the movement.

The older boy smirked.

They tiptoed closer, and a thin strip of sunlight slipping through the canopy of leaves revealed Patz, one of the Obarion boys Atlas had gone to Academy with— olive-skinned, scraggly, and lightning fast.

"Wanna corner him?" Whitsom asked in a whisper.

"Circle around that way—if he runs before we get him, he'll have to go deeper into the trees—they grow closer together the further in you go, and the roots are thick—he won't be able to run as fast."

The two of them closed in on Patz from either side and were within twenty feet before he noticed them. He yelped and took off into the thicket, but Whitsom was on his tail, and Atlas two strides behind him.

The wood around them darkened as the canopy of leaves above their heads grew thicker. Patz stumbled, cursing as his feet caught on thick, gnarled roots that protruded from beneath the earth. There was twenty feet between them—then fifteen—then ten—

"You got that," Atlas huffed, and Whitsom raised an arm and threw—nailing Patz in the dead center of his back. The boy toppled and rolled several times, before he collapsed in a heap on his stomach.

Whitsom and Atlas came to a stop on either side of him, both laughing breathlessly. Atlas rested his hands on his knees, still sucking in lungfuls of air as he managed, "You—looked like a—pill bug."

Whitsom sniggered, clasping Patz's hand and lugging him to his feet. "Them legs can move, though—"

"Never lost a race once," Patz said proudly, and Atlas chuckled, clapping him on the back.

The younger boy took off towards the water tower to wait for the others, and Atlas and Whitsom continued searching through the woods. Atlas guided them at an angle—in the direction of the water tower on the eastern perimeter of the grounds—when Whitsom suddenly veered north, deeper into the woods, and sped up to a jog.

"Hang on, I think I hear voices," he called back.

Atlas took off after him. They'd gone almost a mile now, and apprehension crept into the pit of Atlas' stomach as he recognized where they were.

"I don't think Luca would have come this deep in, Whit, let's head back—"

But Whitsom's feet had stuttered to a halt, fifty feet away from exactly the place Atlas had wanted to avoid.

"What's that?" Whitsom asked, gazing at the little stone building inquisitively.

"That's the prison shack," Atlas said, half-turned, already, back towards the grounds. "That's where they keep Talikoth."

Whitsom glanced sideways at him, his brows flitting up. "In that little thing? That's where he stays all day?"

Atlas nodded. "Yeah, I think he sleeps there, too. It's pretty tight quarters—just a chair, and a latrine in the corner."

Whitsom frowned. "That seems kinda inhumane, doesn't it?"

Atlas stared blankly at him. "It's Talikoth."

The older boy shrugged. "He's still a person. You'd think they could at least give him a bed—"

"That's stupid," Atlas muttered, scowling.

Irritation pulsed through him suddenly, though he wasn't sure where it had come from. "He doesn't need a *bed*—this is justice for all the atrocities he committed—anyway, let's go. It's probably just the guards you heard."

But in another twenty paces it was Atlas that held out a hand to stop Whitsom. The voices sounded closer now, and they were remarkably familiar. "Come on," he whispered to Whitsom.

They edged along beneath the cover of the trees, until they had circled around the stone shack. The door, to Atlas' surprise, hung propped open, and Talikoth leaned against the wall outside, his hands bound behind his back. Dak stood next to him, his dark face somber, and Alvi paced in front of the pair.

After a few moments of searching, Atlas finally spotted the guards posted thirty feet away. They probably thought that their positioning was adequate, but Atlas knew that Talikoth could make a break for it, if he really wanted to. Or had Dak already garnered so much of Moonstone's trust that she believed he'd stop the man, should Talikoth attempt to escape?

"Are they getting ready to take him to the meeting?" Atlas mused, frowning. "Why are they letting him outside?"

Whitsom, however, didn't answer. He was staring at the trio with a strange look on his face. "Who's that woman?" he asked, his voice so quiet that Atlas almost didn't hear him.

"That's Alvi," Atlas replied. "Colonel Dak's wife. They've been good friends with Talikoth since before I was born—"

The older boy only appeared to be half-listening. He crept even closer, positioning himself behind a tall tree, and Atlas hastened to join him. Even with the cover, he felt horribly exposed. There could not have been more than twenty feet between them and Talikoth, and they'd gotten close enough now that bits of conversation drifted over to them.

"—wasn't as though we intended to keep it a secret forever, Al," Dak was saying in a hushed tone.

Alvi's dark brows were knitted agitatedly. "I don't understand why you didn't tell me as soon as you knew —"

"We don't *know*," Talikoth interrupted. His shoulders were taut, and his jaw ticked the way it did whenever he was aggravated. "We don't know for *sure* she's theirs—we were waiting to tell you until we'd confirmed it—"

"Oh, what are you waiting for, a *blood test*?" Alvi snarled. Atlas had never seen the woman upset before. She was normally mild-mannered, but now she glared between Talikoth and her husband with enough ferocity to set a building ablaze. "That girl is my sister's child, as sure as Sutti and Quill are mine. I'm going to speak to her—"

"You can't, Al," Dak said gently, placing a soothing hand on her back. "Not yet. She has no idea her parents were Obarion—"

"*Might* have been Obarion," Talikoth corrected, scowling.

"Oh, don't be a fool, Tal," Alvi snapped, in such a tone that Atlas was quite sure he'd never heard anyone speak to his father. For a moment, he expected his father to lash out at her, but Talikoth didn't even blink. "She's running circles 'round all your boys in the lab, and she looks *just* like Olympion—"

Whitsom went stiff, and Atlas glanced over at him, his brow furrowing. "What is it?" he mouthed, frowning.

"That was my father's name," Whitsom whispered. Atlas opened his mouth to press further, but the older boy held a finger to his lips, his gaze still fixed ahead of them.

"If she doesn't know yet, who better to hear it from than her own flesh and blood?" Alvi reasoned.

"There are things at play here bigger than you, Alvi," Talikoth said firmly.

"Not everything is about your *legacy*, you megalomaniac!" Alvi said shrilly. Dak and Talikoth hushed her, both men shooting wary glances towards the guards, but she looked unconcerned. "I've missed *sixteen years* of her *life*," Alvi hissed, as her eyes filled with angry tears.

Cold dread seeped into Atlas' body. He'd had an inkling of suspicion, just the faintest dawning of conjecture, but now there could be no doubt in his mind exactly who they were talking about.

Something in Talikoth's face seemed to soften. "Give Dak and I the time we need to determine if she really is who we think she is," he said quietly. There was a note of gentleness in his tone that Atlas had previously thought his father incapable of.

"Time to go," one of the guards called suddenly, and Atlas and Whitsom both jumped. "Moonstone is expecting you."

"Let's get out of here," Atlas mumbled, as the guards led the trio away. When Whitsom made no move to follow, he grasped the older boy's shoulder and steered him back towards the Main.

They walked in silence. Atlas' hands clenched and unclenched at his sides, and when he tried to swallow, his throat felt dry and chalky. His brain could not seem to form coherent thoughts.

They had just reached the edge of the woods when he remembered how to string together words. "Whit, did you—did you know?"

Whitsom looked at him, his dark eyes wide. For a moment, he looked much younger than twenty.

"No," he answered. "I had no idea."

CHAPTER SEVEN

A tlas felt vaguely apprehensive about leaving Whitsom alone in such a disoriented state, so he deposited the older boy in Jem's unit and asked her to talk him into playing some card games. When Atlas reached the meeting room, however, he found it empty.

"Moonstone cancelled the meeting about five minutes ago," came Gaiomere's voice from his right. He turned, and saw her striding down the hall, her blue dress rumpled and her hair frizzing around her head. She leaned around him and pasted a note to the door, which depicted Moonstone's sharp script. "Apparently Niko sent one of the cars back to tell her they needed more time."

"Why do they need more time?" Atlas asked, reaching down to pull a leaf out of her hair. "They were just scouting the area, weren't they?"

Gaiomere shrugged. "I guess they didn't find anything. From what I heard they were gonna try to span out further." She tilted her head to look up at him, her brows knitting together. "Where'd you and Whit disappear off to?" she asked curiously. "We waited for y'all at the water tower almost half an hour."

Atlas stiffened. He'd forgotten all about the bruiseball game, with everything that had occurred in its midst.

His eyes raked over Gaiomere's face. He realized, with a jolt, that her nose sloped the same way that Alvi's did. Their faces were both heart-shaped, too. He could have smacked himself for not noticing—but then, why would he have ever had a reason to?

Atlas knew intellectually he should tell her what he'd heard—but how could he, when he didn't understand it himself?

"Oh, Whit tried to climb up a tree to get Luca and fell," Atlas mumbled, rubbing the back of his neck. "We thought maybe he'd broken his wrist, so we went to the infirmary—turned out it was a false alarm." He forced out a laugh, which sounded unnaturally high to his ears, and shoved his hands into his pockets.

"Oh...okay," Gaiomere said, frowning. She looked at him a moment longer, and Atlas got the impression that somehow, she could tell he was lying, before she continued, "Anyway, I've got to run to the lab—"

"We could hang out for a bit—" Atlas suggested, but Gaiomere shook her head.

"Can't, sorry. See you later."

He leaned down to kiss her, but she turned her head to the side at the last second, and his lips brushed her cheek. She spun on her heel and flounced down the hall without another word, her unruly curls bouncing behind her.

Atlas swore, running a hand through his hair as he trudged down the corridor and out of the building toward his unit.

He'd *needed* to lie to her, he reasoned with himself. It wasn't as though it was his news to share —he'd yet to even have a conversation with Whitsom about what they'd heard—and how could they even be sure there *was* news to share in the first place? Even Talikoth and Dak hadn't been certain...

When Atlas pulled open the door to his unit, he was a little disgruntled to see Delurah standing at the sink, rinsing a plate. He did not feel much like company at the moment—most especially company that would be able to tell, in a second's glance, that he was upset.

"You'd think a tornado passed through here," Delurah remarked, without looking up.

"I was going to clean up, honest," Atlas muttered. He slouched over to the sofa and plopped down so hard that its joints groaned. "Soon as we finished playing bruiseball—"

"Mhm, where have I heard *that* before?"

"I'm really not in the mood to be lectured," Atlas snapped. Delurah glanced sideways at him, arching a brow, and he looked down at his boots, mumbling, "Sorry."

She flipped off the faucet and turned to face him, drying her hands on a towel as she gently asked, "Do you...want to talk about it?"

Atlas scowled down at his lap. "Have there—have there been people that have left our clan? To become Renegades, I mean?"

Whatever Delurah had been expecting, it was evidently not that. Her brows flitted up in surprise, and her eyes widened. "Well, of course," she said after a moment. "I'm sure of it. With how many soldiers have gone missing in action, and how many of our people must have gotten lost along the way, on our ventures west—"

"Yeah, but I mean people actually *deserting* the clan, with the intention of becoming Renegades."

Delurah frowned, but Atlas noticed her hands wringing the drying towel rather incessantly. "I couldn't tell you that, sweet boy...how am I to know another person's intentions?"

Atlas straightened in his seat, his hands clenched into fists in his lap. "So after everything, you're still keeping secrets for him, are you?"

"I'm not keeping secrets for anyone, Atlas," Delurah said sharply. "But there are—there are things that we—things that happened—you're too young to understand—"

"No, I get it," Atlas interrupted, pushing to his feet. "Your loyalty is to your clan, before anything else—I forgot that's how it works around here."

"Atlas—" Delurah began, but he had already strode across the room, yanked open the door, and slammed it shut behind him before she could say another word.

He pounded down the hall, anger pulsing in his veins, and shoved through a crowd of people thronging the doorway to get into the civilians' quarters. He was halfway down the corridor that led to Jem's unit when Whitsom appeared at the end of it. The older boy caught sight of Atlas and strode towards him.

"I was just coming to look for you," Whitsom said. "I can't stop thinking about it—"

"Me neither," Atlas said, scooting to the side as a couple of ten-year-old's sprinted down the hallway. He cast Whitsom an apprehensive look. "Did you tell Gaiomere?"

"No. You?"

Atlas shook his head, and Whitsom's harried expression morphed into relief. "Good. I think we should—well, we should probably just keep it to ourselves. For now, anyway." He crossed his arms over his chest, tapping his foot impatiently against the stone floor. "Should we—should we ask somebody—"

"No," Atlas interrupted curtly. "Come on." He turned and took off down the hallway, and after a moment of bewilderment, Whitsom hastened to follow.

"Where are we going?" Whitsom asked.

Atlas pushed open the door that led out of the civilians' quarters. "The only way to get information around here is to take it yourself," he said coldly, his face set with determination. "We're going to the library."

Whitsom groaned, dragging his feet as he lagged behind Atlas. "What good is the *library* gonna do us?"

Atlas pulled open the door to the Main and started up the stairwell to the second floor, calling over his shoulder as he went, "There'll be old newspapers in there. We might find something helpful—"

"*Or* it might be a huge waste of time," Whitsom argued. They'd reached the landing outside of the library, and Atlas whipped around to glare at him.

"What's wrong with you?" he demanded. "Don't you want to know the truth?"

Whitsom shifted his weight between his feet. "I don't know..." He must have caught Atlas' infuriated look, for he hastily amended, "I mean—*yes*, I—of course, I do, I just—" He hesitated, looking away from Atlas to gaze out the window on the landing. "If this is—I mean, if it's true, then I—it's like I didn't know them at all. Like they were strangers or something."

Atlas swallowed thickly. "Well, then you cross that bridge when you come to it. Better to know, isn't it?" Whitsom still looked uncertain, and Atlas decided he needed to take more drastic measures. "Besides, even if it is true, I'm sure they had a very good reason for keeping it from you."

Whitsom straightened up a little taller, his mouth lifting into a smile. "You're right. I'm sure they did."

Guilt squirmed in the pit of Atlas' stomach. It wasn't right to exploit Whitsom's tendency to think the best of everyone—but his guilt was not nearly so strong as his curiosity.

The old newspaper copies were kept at the very back of the library, stacked neatly by date on top of the filing cabinets in several dozen teetering piles that were each about four feet tall.

Whitsom's face blanched when he saw them, but Atlas only gritted his teeth, and reached for a copy at the top of the stack nearest him.

They worked in silence all throughout the afternoon. Around dinnertime, Whitsom went down to the dining hall and returned with two towering plates of food, which he had to sneak past the old, cantankerous librarian, Avanell, who kept walking past their table with a suspicious glare etched upon her face, as though they were using her library for nefarious purposes, rather than its intended ones.

At nine o'clock, she strode over and informed them that the library was closed. Whitsom, who was slung across a couch pressed against the wall, had already drifted off, his head hanging over the armrest and mouth gaping open, but he jerked awake at the sound of Avanell's sharp voice.

Atlas, though, had just come across an article of some interest. He glanced over at Avanell, who was waiting with her arms crossed over her chest, her beady blue eyes narrowed into a glare.

"Just a half an hour longer," he pleaded.

"You've been here long enough, boy," she said, tilting her beaky nose in the air.

He held up the newspaper in front of him, earnestly insisting, "But if we don't learn our history we're doomed to repeat it, aren't we? How many idiots my age are replicating the mistakes of their forefathers? Don't subject me to that fate, ma'am."

The corners of Avanell's mouth twitched upward for half a second, before her scowl reemerged.

"I'll even lock up for you," Atlas continued, giving her his most charming smile. "It's the least I can do, with how hard you work to keep this place so nice for us. I'd hate to think I should never get the opportunity to repay you."

Whitsom sniggered into his arm on the sofa, but Atlas ignored him, his gaze fixed firmly on the old lady opposite him.

She pursed her lips, thinking for a moment, before she said, "Do *not* forget to lock the doors, young man, or I'll be after your head."

As soon as the library doors close behind her, Whitsom burst out laughing. "*Damn.* Teach me your ways, oh wise one."

Atlas, though, had already sat down next to the older boy so that he could see the newspaper too. "Look at this," he said, reading, "*Announcing the marriage of Olympion, only son of Lieutenant General Tempust and his wife, Penela, to Maichell, the eldest daughter of Colonel Garagleen and his wife, Aurelia on this, the fifteenth day of the first month of autumn.*"

Whitsom, though, was staring at the grainy image that accompanied the text. "Those are my parents," he choked out.

Atlas had hardly even glanced at the photo, so swept up in finding the name which he had been searching for, but he looked at it now.

When his eyes first fell on the woman, he thought that he was looking at Alvi. They shared the same almond-brown skin, the same rounded nose, and the same dark, curly hair. But Maichell was perhaps four or five inches shorter than Alvi, and her eyes were russet brown, rather than grey. They upturned at the corners, just as Gaiomere's did, and she smiled like Gaiomere, too—playfully, as though she'd just told a joke.

Both Whitsom and Gaiomere, though, took more after their father. He had hickory brown eyes, and his bone structure was almost aristocratic—high cheekbones, a strong jaw, and a sort of arrogance in the way he held himself. His skin was ebony, several shades darker than either of his children, and he looked as though he might have been around Atlas' height—three or four inches taller than Whitsom.

The couple stood in front of an arbor bestrewn with flowers, a crowd of finely dressed people standing in the background. Alvi stood on Maichell's left. She looked scarcely older than fifteen, though she was already much taller than her sister.

On Olympion's right, two decades younger and clad in a smart black suit, stood Talikoth. His hair was a little longer than it was now, and his mouth curled into a small smile, though it did not reach his eyes. One of his arms wrapped around Olympion's shoulders.

Whitsom and Atlas looked at each other. For a

moment, neither spoke. Then Whitsom leapt to his feet.

"I can't *believe* they didn't tell me!" he burst out, pacing in front of the table. "How could they—how could they keep something like this a secret?"

"Maybe they thought you were too young to explain things to?" Atlas supplied, watching the older boy pace.

"That's bullshit—I was fourteen when dad died— and by the time mom died I was your age. That's—they —*urgh*."

Atlas shifted uncomfortably in his seat. He didn't know what to say. He'd never seen Whitsom so upset— and Atlas didn't blame him. If he found out such a secret had been kept from him...

"The worst part is, they're not even here for me to be properly angry at," Whitsom muttered. He sank back down onto the couch and buried his face in his hands.

Atlas rubbed the back of his neck. "Do you uh—do you want to..."

Whitsom lifted his face from his hands and pulled himself back to his feet. "I just wanna be alone right now," he muttered. He disappeared between the stacks, his angry footsteps echoing against the walls, before the library doors banged open, then slammed shut again.

Not knowing what else to do, Atlas pulled another stack of newspapers towards him and began to flip through them. A part of him wanted to go after Whitsom, but it was better that the older boy have some time to himself. Atlas had felt the same when he'd found out about his mother.

Now that they knew, beyond doubt, that Whitsom and Gaiomere's parents *had* been Obarion, questions flurried in Atlas' mind. It was obvious they'd left the clan, but there was nothing that explained *why*.

From the looks of that photograph, Olympion had even been *close* to Talikoth. Had there been a falling out? Or was it merely a matter of fabrication? Olympion was the son of the Lieutenant General, after all—perhaps he and Talikoth were only keeping up appearances...

Atlas continued to scour through the papers, deep into the night, impatiently blinking away the bleariness that gathered in his eyes. There were other wedding announcements, deaths, praise for developments the Obarion researchers manufactured, but no further mention of either of Whitsom and Gaiomere's parents, nor their choice to sever ties with their clan.

It was as though they had simply vanished, without a trace—like they'd never existed at all.

By the time Atlas had fallen asleep, the sun was creeping over the tops of the distant mountains visible from the eastern-facing windows of the library. He woke later with a jolt, his head jerking off of the table, and he hastily wiped a puddle of drool from the newspaper he'd slumped over.

His heart leapt when he glanced at the big clock at the front of the room. It read 11:56.

Atlas scrambled from his seat, hastily gathering his stack of newspapers and returning them rather messily to their pile, then sprinted out the door. He took the steps downstairs two at a time, flung himself around the corner, and bolted down the hallway.

Atlas reached the meeting room with one minute to spare. By the looks of it, everyone except Niko and his crew had arrived. Moonstone, Harcliff and Vailhelm quietly conversed at the head of the table, and the rest of the Vedas' Council sat interspersed throughout the room. Talikoth was already there too, reclining in his chair, rather like a throne, his guards at either side. Gaiomere sat almost directly across from him, and it looked as though she were trying very hard not to make eye contact, her gaze fixed firmly on the notes in front of her.

Atlas sat down next to her, and just a few moments later, Niko trudged into the meeting room, his brown curls tousled and scarred face weary. Luca slumped in after him, looking uncharacteristically sullen, and a boy with astoundingly pale blond hair that looked vaguely familiar to Atlas took up the rear.

"Well, there's nothing out there," Niko announced, flopping unceremoniously into a chair towards the front. "We searched for hours—a hundred miles in every direction from the end of the tracks. Zilch."

"We found a spout, right where the tracks end," the blond boy supplied. "It looks like it may have been in use within the last few months, based on the buildup around the spigot—but it doesn't work now."

A heavy silence fell across the room. Atlas couldn't help but notice that Talikoth looked decidedly smug. Had he known this was what they would find, when they reached the end of the tracks? He told Atlas he had never had any reason to follow his trade partners

—but that didn't necessarily mean he hadn't done so.

"Well, Talikoth said it was hidden," Atlas pointed out. "Maybe you—"

"We looked, *mi hermano*," Luca insisted. "We checked the desert all around the tracks *y las montañas*, sixty miles southeast—there's nothing."

"Did you get any photos?" Gaiomere asked Niko.

He nodded, withdrawing a bulky camera from his bag and passing it to Moonstone, who took out a cord and connected the camera to the projector at the front of the room. She fiddled with a few buttons, and then the images flickered to life on the screen draped across the front wall.

The tracks ended in the middle of a wasteland more desolate than anything Atlas had ever seen in his entire life. The ground was cracked and dry, as though rain had not touched the earth in years, and he could scarcely see any plant life, save for a cactus or two, few and far between. In the distance, he caught a glimpse of the mountains Luca had referred to.

"Could their water have dried up?" Harcliff mused aloud.

"It's possible," Moonstone murmured. Her eyes were intent upon the nearly indistinguishable images of the desert flashing across the screen cyclically, her brows furrowed with apprehension.

Gaiomere slipped out of her chair and moved to the front of the room. Her gaze was intent upon the projector screen, her teeth chewing at her lip. "Sorry, can I..." Moonstone moved to the side, and Gaiomere reached for the camera, pushing a button to stop the rotation of photos and clicking backwards until she reached the one she was looking for.

The rest of them were looking at the photo on the screen, but Gaiomere's eyes were intent upon the tiny camera, narrowed into slits.

Atlas' lips pulled up into a smirk against his own volition. "You know...it's bigger up there—"

"Shut up, Atlas."

"Sorry."

She looked up sharply at Niko. "These are all the photos you have?" she asked him.

"Well, yeah," he spluttered, a little indignantly. "We took about thirty—"

"No, it's just...there's no output valve."

Atlas leaned forward, peering more closely at the photo. Luca tilted his head, as though some new image might miraculously form at the right angle. "*Chica*, you're *loca*—the valve's right there—"

"That's not the valve—that just controls pressure flow," Gaiomere interrupted impatiently. "That's why it's got the little indicator screen there—it shows you what the water pressure is at."

She hopped up on top of the table, sitting cross-legged behind the projector, and pointed a finger at the image, tapping the base of the long pipe protruding from the ground. "Normally the valve—which is what actually *allows* water flow—would be right here. But it's not."

"What, you think someone stole it?" the blond boy asked.

"There's no signs of damage. No, I think that there isn't a valve because this isn't the right end."

Atlas straightened up very quickly, and from his peripherals, he saw that his father had, too.

"What do you mean, not the right end?" Alekea

asked.

Gaiomere ran a finger along the pipe, explaining, "Some conduits are designed for a direct path downward—if the water source is a well, for example—but these pipes—" She clicked to the next photo, which showed a closer view of the spout. "See the indentations on the tubing—and the hollows *here* and *here*? These pipes are specially designed to channel their contents over long distances—potentially even hundreds of miles—and specially insulated to be able to handle high temperatures and substantial amounts of seismic activity—since they often run parallel to the surface of the ground, just several miles beneath it."

Dak folded his hands in front of him, frowning. "So what you're saying is, wherever those pipes lead—"

Gaiomere nodded grimly. "That's our water source."

Silence followed her words for nearly fifteen seconds, before Niko burst out, "Well how in the *hell* are we going to figure out where they go?"

Nervous murmuring broke out across the table. Dak and Alekea were whispering, Harcliff gazed pensively down at his folded hands, and even Moonstone did not immediately have any solutions to offer. "Quiet please," she said weakly, and it was only after Vailhelm slammed his fist on the table that the commotion ceased.

"We searched a hundred miles in every direction, and there was *nothing*," the blond boy said. "No lakes, no rivers. Plus, we were told the source was guarded—but we didn't see a soul out there, which makes me think we weren't anywhere near it."

Atlas watched Gaiomere, who was fiddling

absentmindedly with the camera between her hands. "The quickest way to find out which direction the pipe runs is to follow the train when it comes," she said quietly, as though she were talking to herself.

Luca shook his head. "No, once you get out of the mountains it's too flat. They'd see us miles off."

Niko let out a heavy exhale. "We could send some cars out to run recon on a wider area—scout two or three hundred miles out, instead?"

"It's possible," Moonstone said slowly. "But we're terribly pressed for time. There's only so much area we could scout in two and a half weeks, and that doesn't account for acquiring the water."

"Perhaps we can storm them at the mountaintop, come the day of the exchange?" Jaina suggested. "They can't possibly have the numbers we do—couldn't we just demand that they take us to the water? Surely they'd oblige, if the alternative is death."

Atlas barely repressed rolling his eyes. "And if they refuse, we kill them all off, and then what? We've got no lead to the water—and we're right back to square one." He frowned, drumming his fingers on the tabletop. "No, they made sure this was the only way."

Twenty pairs of eyes swiveled to look at him, but his eyes were on Moonstone.

"The water source is clearly well-hidden. They're utilizing a conduit that can channel the water hundreds of miles and have disabled the access—the only way anyone can get water out of that spout is with *their* authorization." Atlas looked between Moonstone and Harcliff, willing them to understand, for they were both still gazing at him blankly. He let out a frustrated noise, and strode to the front of the room, taking the camera from Gaiomere and flicking through the pictures until he came to the one that displayed the long stretch of train tracks leading west.

"We can't even *find* the water, let alone figure out how to turn it on. The only conditions under which the Flesh Flayers are willing to turn on the water is if the Obarion provide them with a delivery of Renegades. If the only way they'll provide the Obarion water is by giving them Renegades...then why don't we give them Renegades?"

The silence that fell on the meeting room this time was heavier than any of its antecedents.

"*Gilipollas!*" Luca shouted, his face pink with anger.

Niko glowered at Atlas. "Man, I thought you were alright."

Moonstone, too, looked disturbed. "Atlas, we aren't—"

"No, he's right."

They all looked at Gaiomere, who was gazing sideways at him thoughtfully, her fingers skimming absently along the chain of her necklace.

"Traitor—" the blond boy said loudly, but Gaiomere interrupted him.

"Oh, shut up, Umir," she snapped. "We're not actually going to send Renegades." She turned to Moonstone, who was looking between Gaiomere and Atlas with knitted brows. "As far as we know, the Flesh Flayers have *only* ever interacted with the Inner Ring and—um—him." She jerked her head towards Talikoth as though she were afraid to look at him, or even say his name, and Atlas saw his father's lips twitch into a smirk. "If we send him and whichever Inner

Ring soldiers are left up the mountain to deliver, they won't know the difference between a delivery of *Renegades*...and fully-trained soldiers."

Atlas nodded, leaning against the table next to Gaiomere. "We send in a hit squad to pose as captured Renegades and conduct the exchange, as per usual. The Flesh Flayer's load all the faux-Renegades up on the train, and then they'll lead us to the water source themselves."

As though he couldn't help himself, Atlas' gaze wandered to Talikoth. His father's face was impassive, but there was a glint in his eye Atlas couldn't identify. Was he angry that they had found a way to solve the problem without his input? Or was he still ten steps ahead of them, even now?

"This is all assuming that Talikoth and the Inner Ring are willing to comply," Harcliff pointed out.

"*And,*" Gaiomere piped up, "Just to play the demon advocate—"

Atlas started to correct her, but decided it wasn't worth it.

"This *is* all assuming they don't...you know, just..." she pulled a face and forced out, "eat all our soldiers on the train...you know...*before* they got there." They all stared at her, and she mumbled, "Well...it's a possibility."

"Assuming that they don't travel with their entire tribe," Atlas began contemplatively, "I wouldn't think they would—uh—do that until they got back to wherever they're headquartered." He rubbed the back of his neck awkwardly. "Animals go bad when you kill them—pretty quickly, too, so—if they—you know, slaughtered all of their captives on the train—by the time they got them back to their base, everything might be...you know...spoiled." He forced down the nausea rolling in his stomach, continuing, "The rest of the tribe wouldn't be too happy, and all of that harmony would go right out the door."

Moonstone nodded slowly. "You think that they would take the captives all the way back to their base."

"To the water source. Yeah, I do. Once our soldiers are in, they can get a message to the troops here—Gaiomere has built a booster before, with less to work with, she can do it again—and we send in reinforcements. Then we can take the water for ourselves and put an end to all of the sacrificial bloodshed."

"And what are you thinking of doing," Vailhelm grunted, "if our reinforcements don't get there in time?"

Atlas did not answer him. His eyes lifted to meet Colonel's Dak's. He was sure they were both thinking the same thing, though neither one of them would say it.

Niko spoke up for them. "He's *thinking* that would be a worthwhile sacrifice," he said coldly. When Atlas looked over at him, he realized the older boy was suddenly looking at him very differently.

"I didn't say that—"

"No, but you thought it. What, we *end* the sacrificial bloodshed by allowing more of it?"

"Do you see an alternative?" Atlas snapped, trying to push down his swelling anger.

"What are the lives of a few hundred deserters, huh?" Niko spat, his voice growing louder.

"Niko, it isn't guaranteed they won't make it out, and Atlas didn't say it would *only* be our people—"

Gaiomere said tentatively, but he interrupted her.

"Nah, just another in a long line of figureheads that lets everybody else die first—" Niko was on his feet now, and Atlas had never seen the normally even-tempered boy look so angry.

"*Relájate,* Niko," Luca said quietly.

"Don't think for a second any of us didn't notice that it was Raider's throat he slit, not yours—"

"Guys, cut it out—" Gaiomere said, but they both ignored her.

"Why don't you *ask* him?" Atlas snarled, his hands clenching into fists as he sprang to his feet as well. "The only reason it wasn't me was because Raider was there first—*ask him* how quickly he would have slit my throat, if he had the opportunity—"

"That's *enough*, boys," Moonstone said, before Niko could retort. "Please sit down, both of you." After a moment, they both complied, the two of them glaring in opposite directions, and Moonstone continued, "Understand that I would never send *any* soldiers— Vedas, Obarion, or otherwise—into a situation where there was no egress. However...at the present moment, this looks like this may be our only option."

Niko's jaw was tight, and when he spoke, it was through gritted teeth, "I'm not going to lay my boys out like a buffet platter for the Flesh Flayers." His eyes flickered over to Talikoth. "Especially not for a clan that's been hunting us down like dogs. We're out." He got up, stalking towards the door, and Umir and Luca jumped to their feet to follow after him, the latter of the two glancing back over his shoulder with a remorseful frown.

As soon as the door closed behind them, Harcliff

said, "My tribe will stand behind you, General—but I'm afraid we do not have the numbers that the gangs do."

Moonstone nodded, her eyes flickering over the remaining faces in the room. "We don't need many soldiers—Vailhelm, get together a list of volunteers. Due to the...delicacy...of this undertaking, I won't be mandating any assignments. If any of our captains or majors elect to volunteer, use your best judgement to designate a lead—"

"I'll lead it."

Atlas could feel the weight of his father's stare boring down on him, but he kept his gaze trained on Moonstone. Her mouth twisted into a frown as her shrewd eyes leveled on his face.

"You're sure?" she asked.

His jaw tightened, and for the briefest of moments, his eyes darted towards Gaiomere. Her eyes were crackling with fire. "Yeah, I'm sure," he said firmly, looking back at Moonstone.

She nodded, and proceeded to give Vailhelm and Harcliff instructions for assembling their volunteers, but Atlas was hardly listening anymore. He could feel the anger practically radiating off of Gaiomere's person. Once they returned to their seats, he squeezed her hand in what was supposed to be a comforting gesture, but she dug her nails into his skin.

It was only his father's cold voice that drew his attention back to the meeting room. "—couldn't bring myself to lie convincingly without proper motivation."

"It's not a matter of *lying*—" Vailhelm grumbled.

"Oh, but it is," Talikoth interjected smoothly, smirking. "You see, I promise our suppliers a delivery of unarmed Renegades—anything less or more is indisputable deceit—and integrity is the backbone of any civilized society..."

Atlas couldn't help it; he snorted.

"General, this will *never* work if we can't be one hundred percent certain that Talikoth and the Inner Ring will not betray us," Jaina said.

"It's simple," Vailhelm said gruffly. "If he complies, his sentence is reduced—if he betrays us, he's executed."

"An equitable proposal," Talikoth said, inclining his head towards the bearded man. "I accept."

Atlas stared at him, his eyes narrowing. "Just like that?"

Talikoth's smirk broadened, and he gave Atlas a wink. "Just like that."

If Moonstone was unnerved by the Obarion General's sudden compliance, she did not show it. "Very well. We shall confer with the remaining Inner Ring soldiers at the next meeting to establish procedure. Atlas—" She turned to him. "Colonel Dak, Vailhelm and Harcliff will have their register of volunteers to you within twenty-four hours. Gaiomere, I'd like you to begin working on those boosters as soon as possible." She turned to speak to Dak and Alekea, and Atlas figured that he was probably dismissed, so he pushed himself to his feet and made his way towards the door.

He was only a few paces down the corridor when Gaiomere caught up to him. "I already know what you're going to say—" he began. The five hours of sleep he'd gotten seemed to be catching up to him, and he massaged his temples as he rounded a corner and pushed open the door that led onto the grounds.

"Oh, *do* you?" she hissed. "Good, then I don't have

to waste my breath!"

"Gaiomere—"

"Are you absolutely insane?"

"Gaiomere—"

"One too many blows to the head sparring with Whitsom?"

"Gaiomere, please—"

"Atlas, I—*ugh,* I could just—you just—"

He really didn't know how else to shut her up, so he leaned down and kissed her, but she was fuming, so he was not altogether surprised when she placed her hands firmly on his chest and shoved him backwards. *"You really think I'd want to kiss you right now?"* she shrieked, and he winced, for he was quite sure that, even though they were outside, everyone back in the meeting room would have heard her. "I'd sooner feed you to a pack of *wolves!"*

Despite the gravity of the situation, Atlas' lips twitched. "Wolves, huh?"

Gaiomere's furious expression faltered for a split second before she regained her bearings. "Atlas, why would you *do* that—"

"Because, Gaiomere—"

"It's a suicide mission—"

"Are you just going to shout at me all afternoon or are you going to listen to what I have to say?" he said angrily.

Her mouth snapped shut, though the ferocity in her gaze seemed to magnify. He let out a frustrated exhale, running a hand through his hair. "Now look— I know it's—it's crazy dangerous, and yeah, we could potentially all—all end up Flesh Flayer food, I get it. But we've got the element of surprise on our side, not to mention the fact that however many Flesh Flayers there are, there's no way in hell they're trained half as well as our guys—if at all—"

"But Atlas, if they have weapons and you don't—"

"We won't be able to take machine guns with us, that's true, but there are ways of concealing smaller weapons—knives and handguns—without them being able to tell we have anything on us. If these guys have been trading with Talikoth for that long, they'll already know how he operates. He'd never leave a captive armed, so that's what they'll be expecting. And besides, the Obarion soldiers know to disarm equipped opponents. It's an integral part of our training—that's why they lasted so long during the battle—"

"And how many of the Obarion soldiers are *really* going to be willing to take orders from Moonstone—from the Vedas?"

"Well, luckily they won't be taking orders from Moonstone—not directly, anyway. They'll be taking orders from me." She rolled her eyes, starting to turn away from him, but he grasped her wrist, "Listen, Gaiomere, I wouldn't have volunteered to do this if I didn't believe beyond a shadow of a doubt that I could do a better job than anybody else. You're absolutely right —if anyone else led this mission, it would be suicide— but I won't let it turn out that way."

She shook her head, giving him an exasperated look, but he could see the hint of a smile on the corner of her lips. "Has anyone ever told you that sometimes...you are unbearably arrogant?"

He smirked. "See, the way you said it there, it almost sounded like a compliment."

Gaiomere rolled her eyes. "I just wish you would

have—I don't know—*talked* to me about it, before you decided to do something rash—"

Atlas arched a brow. "How would that have gone over, do you think?"

She let out a little tut of disapproval. "It's not about that."

"Well, you wouldn't have wanted me to," Atlas reasoned, frowning.

"Of course I wouldn't have. But we could have at least *talked* about it."

"It would have just been an argument—"

"Glad we avoided that," Gaiomere interjected dryly.

Atlas' mouth snapped shut, and he shot her an annoyed look, though the impish smile wriggling at the corner of her lips made his irritation difficult to maintain. "Fine. Look, from here on out I'll talk to you about things like that. Even if it means you totally overreact. And get way too emotional. And do that huffy pouty thing that you do for hours on end."

Gaiomere beamed, looping her arms around his middle. "Good. There's no sense in you keeping things from me just because you think they'll upset me."

Atlas glanced down at her sharply, but she'd already buried her face in his chest, and after a moment, he wrapped his arms around her, guilt stabbing at the pit of his stomach. He could tell her now, what he and Whitsom had learned—now that they'd confirmed it, he *owed* her the truth...

Instead, he heard himself saying, "We'll put together a strong squad. It'll be fine. Honest."

She nestled further into his chest, and Atlas absently ran a finger through her dark curls, pushing his thoughts away from his guilt to the issue at hand. His mind was already sifting through which soldiers he might have at his disposal and how they could conceal their weapons. With enough manpower, they would be able to hold their own against the Flesh Flayers, so long as his company was well-prepared for what they might face.

His eyes roved over the grounds. A group of teenage Obarion boys walked towards the Main, laughing and jostling one another. They passed a couple of Vedas soldiers and immediately fell silent, glaring at the passing young men with such hostility that it was almost palpable, and their animosity toward the Vedas did not go unreciprocated.

Atlas frowned, pulling Gaiomere closer to his chest. He could ensure his soldiers stayed up to par on their training—they could memorize how to disarm equipped opponents like the back of their hands—but if the Obarion soldiers could not get along with the Vedas and Renegades—if all of this tension continued—they may not even *make* it to the day of the exchange.

And even if they did, if their troops continued to cooperate poorly...well, the Flesh Flayers would, quite literally, eat them alive.

CHAPTER EIGHT

I t was eleven o'clock in the morning, one week later, when Atlas heard a knock on his door.

He'd already been up for almost six hours, going over Moonstone's notes detailing their tentative plan for the day of exchange ad nauseam. For all her efficiency, the woman did have a tendency towards loquaciousness, and he found himself, several times, dozing off as he perused the document.

At the sound of the knock, however, he jerked awake, and clambered to his feet, trudging over to the door and pulling it open, fully intent on telling Coral to go bother somebody else.

But it was Gaiomere, rather than Coral, that stood at the door, and when she saw him, she beamed brightly. "I know you're super busy," she began, "*But* I brought you a surprise."

Before Atlas could decipher what she meant, two figures popped out from behind her and charged at him.

"ATLAS!"

He stumbled back a few feet, chuckling as two pairs of arms wrapped around him. "Hey, guys. How was the North?"

"I missed you," Rasta mumbled into his shirt. Atlas ruffled his hair affectionately.

"The North is *boring*," Maggi huffed, releasing Atlas and peering around his unit with narrowed eyes.

"Once I built my little army of sycophants, the challenge was gone. I was needing some new turf—"

"Oh, great gooseberries," Gaiomere muttered.

"And then Gai kept us cooped up at the Fringe, and that was even *worse*—"

Atlas was hardly listening. He looked between the two girls with a faint smirk. "Hey Gaiomere...I think Maggi is taller than you now—"

"*Shut up!*" the curly-haired girl shrieked, her cheeks flushing.

"Haha, yes, I *told* you!" Maggi cackled, clapping her hands together delightedly.

"Rasta's going to pass you soon, too," Atlas remarked, his smirk broadening.

Gaiomere snatched her notebook from her bag and disappeared behind it, muttering under her breath.

Maggi and Rasta told Atlas all about their last few months at the Vedas' base, and for the first time since he'd agreed to lead the task force east, Atlas' worries over the upcoming exchange drifted to the back of his mind.

The four of them walked together to the dining hall at lunchtime. Across the room, at their usual table, Bettoni was munching on a plateful of broccoli, watching with distinguishable amusement as Coral and Jem argued rather violently.

"—that's not *true*, it's more than that!" Coral was insisting, his plump face flushed from anger.

"Dude, *literally* all you have to do is go pick up a book in the library!" Jem retorted.

"What are they fighting about?" Atlas asked Bettoni as he sat down next to him.

"How often sloths come down from trees,"

Bettoni informed him.

"Once a week," Atlas said. Gaiomere shot him a befuddled look, and he shrugged. *"Roamers of the Rainforests,* South American edition," he said, by way of explanation.

"You're a nerd," Gaiomere teased.

Atlas' brows shot up. *"You* are calling *me* a nerd?" She stuck her tongue out at him, and he snickered.

Jem had broken into a little victory dance in her seat. "HA!" she shouted, and Coral groaned, slamming his head against the table. Without another word, he shoved his plate of sweet potato towards her, and she promptly snatched it up. "Grovel at my feet, puny dunce!" she declared.

Maggi, who had sat down across from Atlas and Gaiomere, was gazing at Jem with undisguised admiration. "Are you the alpha of this place?" she asked.

Jem arched a brow. "Why yes I am, thank you for noticing."

Atlas snorted into his beans, and the freckle-faced girl shot him a dirty look, before continuing, "It's a heavy burden to bear, but a girl's gotta do what she must."

Maggi nodded officiously. "If you're looking for an apprentice, I'd be happy to take on the mantle."

"I'm really frightened by what's happening right now," Gaiomere whispered to Atlas.

Jem studied the girl, her brows furrowing. "How old are you, kid?"

"I'm twelve, but I usually tack on a few years 'cause I know sixty-seven ways to dismember my enemies," Maggi informed her with a straight face.

Bettoni choked on his broccoli, and Coral lifted

his head up from the table, his face twitching, as though he was not sure whether he should be amused or alarmed.

Maggi continued, "Just as long as you understand that eventually, the apprentice *will* surpass the master, we'll be square." She gave Jem an exaggerated wink. "I'll be the Brutus to your Caesar, if you catch my drift."

Jem's jaw slackened, and she turned to Gaiomere. "Sweet fates, where did you find her? She's an angel."

Atlas buried his face in his arms, his shoulders shaking with silent laughter, and he heard Gaiomere say, "Jem, this is Maggi, and that's Rasta. We all grew up together—they're the ones I was telling you about."

"Oh, pleased to meetcha," Jem said. "I've already got you guys' room set up—"

Atlas emerged from his arm cocoon. "They're staying with you?" he asked, surprised.

"Me and Whitsom are practically never down at the Fringe anymore," Gaiomere explained. "We figured —since she's got two rooms and the place to herself—" Gaiomere broke off very suddenly, as though she had said something wrong, and cast an apprehensive glance at the freckled-faced girl, but Jem looked unperturbed.

"They could have stayed in my unit," Atlas pointed out.

Gaiomere glanced sideways at him, giving him an apologetic grimace and admitting, "I figured they wouldn't want to stay in Talikoth's room."

"Ah. Good point."

"I don't know what you're talking about," Maggi said, as she stabbed rather aggressively at a carrot round. "I'd have loved to sleep in there—can you imagine absorbing all of that power? The indomitable will to conquer siphoning into my body. Yes, please."

Atlas let out a strangled noise that might have been his throat's attempt to stop the laughter from escaping his mouth.

Coral, who had still been staring at Maggi with some level of fear, seemed to shake himself, and he turned to Gaiomere, asking, "If she's twelve...how come she's taller than you?"

Gaiomere dove across the table and had actually managed to grab a fistful of Coral's shirt, before Atlas pulled her back, murmuring, "Alright, come on—down, tiger."

"This place is really cool," Rasta piped up, from where he sat at the end of the table. "It's so big—"

"Wait till I show you the barns," Atlas said, nudging the younger boy. "We've got some horses down there, and a few dozen cows—"

Rasta's freckled face brightened. "Cool! Maybe you could show me after lunch?"

Atlas' mind flitted back briefly to Moonstone's notes, waiting for him on the dining room table in his unit—but Rasta's hazel eyes blinked up at him keenly, and the thought of refusing him made Atlas' stomach turn. "Sure thing," he said.

Rasta beamed. "I'll get that," he told Bettoni, who had just clambered to his feet to refill the water pitcher.

"You two could not be more different," Coral remarked wryly to Maggi, as the little boy shuffled away, empty water pitcher in hand.

Maggi arched a brow. "I know, I'm much more likeable—"

A sudden *boom* split the air. Atlas instinctively yanked Gaiomere under the table, his upper body shielding hers.

Screams reverberated through the dining hall on every side of them. The smell of burnt metal accosted Atlas' nostrils.

He lifted his head, squinting through the haze of smoke and bodies clamoring to get to the door. Maggi peeked her head out from under the table across from him, her dark eyes wide and terrified. Jem had wrapped an arm around the little girl's shoulder. Next to Atlas, Bettoni lugged Coral to his feet.

"Rasta!" Atlas shouted, but he could not spot the boy anywhere. He jumped over the table, pushing through the crowd of bodies, his heart racing in his chest.

He finally spotted the little boy, fifteen feet from the water fountain, sprawled out on the ground. Blood covered the left side of his body, his arm sliced badly and jeans tattered. Bits of scattered shrapnel jutted from his skin, and a long gash ran along his cheek, but his eyes were still open and darted frantically around the dining hall. His chest was rising and falling very quickly, as though he were hyperventilating.

Atlas dropped to his knees next to Rasta, and relief flooded onto the little boy's face, though his breathing scarcely steadied. "Atlas, what's—what's going—what's going on—"

"Later," Atlas said firmly. He reached down and scooped the boy easily into his arms.

Gaiomere reached him a second later. Relief flooded her face when her eyes fell on Rasta. "Let's get out of here, come on," Atlas told her.

Without another word, he began to shove his way through the crowd of panicking people. Gaiomere clasped onto the back of his shirt, and reached behind her to grasp Maggi's hand. Rasta squirmed in Atlas' arms, the little boy's breath coming so quickly that Atlas worried he would pass out.

Outside the dining hall, soldiers and civilians alike—Obarion, Vedas, and Renegade—ran in every direction. Moonstone's soldiers flooded into the Main, towards the dining hall, hardly glancing at Atlas' group as they passed.

As soon as the seven of them filed into Atlas' unit, he slammed the door behind them. Rasta was thrashing now, his fists pounding against Atlas' chest and face screwed up in pain.

"Hey, hey, relax, buddy," Atlas said quietly, as he set Rasta down on the counter. He cast an uncertain look in Gaiomere's direction, but she had disappeared into the bathroom.

A pale pair of hands suddenly pushed Atlas out of the way. Maggi stepped up in front of Rasta, who was clenching his arms so tightly his fingernails drew blood. Maggi grasped Rasta's wrists and yanked his hands back. "Stop that. Look at me."

Rasta's eyes were still wrenched shut, and he shook his head. "It's not—I can't—I have to help them— they're dying—they're dying—"

"Look at me, Ras," Maggi repeated firmly. The little boy finally opened his eyes. "You're here, with me. They're gone. You can't help them. But you're safe, okay?"

Rasta nodded slowly, his lip trembling, and Maggi wrapped her arms around his middle.

Gaiomere returned from the bathroom with a medical kit. "You were so brave, little fox," she said quietly. She moved around Maggi and began to carefully extract the shrapnel from Rasta's arm with a pair of tweezers. Atlas brought over a bowl, and she gave him a grateful smile, depositing the shards of metal into the bowl.

"What was that about?" Atlas asked Maggi, once she'd moved far enough away from Rasta that he wouldn't hear.

Maggi still watched the boy with concern, as though afraid he might start hyperventilating again. "Rasta's parents died in an explosion," she said, out of the corner of her mouth. "Sometimes—when there are really loud noises—sometimes even just when he's sleeping—I think he goes back there. Like he's living it all over again."

Atlas swallowed, glancing over at the boy with a newfound sense of appreciation. He looked back at Maggi, and tentatively began, "Was that how your parents—"

"No," Maggi said sharply. Her black brows furrowed, and she frowned down at her feet. "My mom died giving birth to me. She had a hem—a hemorrhage. Dad caught a bug that he couldn't kick when I was five, and that was that." Atlas started to offer his condolences, but Maggi didn't let him get a word out. "Don't. I don't even remember either of them. Besides, I got off easy." She glanced over at Gaiomere, who was pulling out the last sliver of shrapnel from Rasta's shoulder, and lowered her voice. "I'm the only one out of all of us that didn't have to watch my parents die."

Atlas' throat felt as though it were full of ash, and he tried to swallow again, but found that he couldn't. He looked around the room, more to distract himself than anything.

Coral had sat down at the dining room table, his expression uncharacteristically sober, and Bettoni leaned against the cabinet in the kitchen, his fingers drumming against the countertop. In the living room, Jem had sunk into the armchair next to the bookcase, her legs pulled into her chest.

"What *was* that?" Coral managed finally, after several minutes of tense silence.

"It looked like a pipe bomb," Gaiomere said, in a determinedly calm voice, as she wiped an antiseptic along Rasta's arm. "Not a very powerful one, if I were to guess—hastily constructed, not properly pressurized—otherwise the range might have been three times what it was." She looked up suddenly, her eyes growing wide. "Has anyone seen Whitsom?"

"I'll find him," Atlas said immediately.

He'd scarcely started towards the door when it opened, and the young man in question hurried inside, his uniform rumpled, and his expression harried.

As soon as he saw Gaiomere, the tension in his face eased. "You're here," he mumbled. His eyes shifted over to Rasta, and widened to saucers. "Ras—"

"He's okay," Gaiomere said quickly. "Just a little cut up—were you in the dining hall?"

Whitsom shook his head. "At the main gate." He plopped down into a chair at the table and made to untie his boots. "From what I've heard some idiot set off a pipe bomb—one of the Obarion soldiers, trying to send a message, I guess—"

Gaiomere suddenly let out a disparaging noise, her hands dropping to her sides. "I *saw* Peck and Mirian with a canister of chlorate in the lab earlier this week!

And two days ago, they had a couple of brass caps—I should have *known*—"

"It's not your fault," Atlas said immediately, frowning. "The Vedas guards should have been keeping a closer eye on what they were doing—"

"If I'd reported it, this wouldn't have happened," Gaiomere maintained, shaking her head. She pressed the last bandage over Rasta's cheek, and started towards the door. "I'm sure if Rasta's this cut up, there's tons of other people injured too. The least I can do is help—"

But Atlas grasped her arm and pulled her back again. "Gaiomere, if Peck and Mirian built a bomb, it was to target the Vedas and the Ren. You'll only be putting yourself in danger, going out there—"

"Atlas is right," Whitsom said, as he tossed his boots beside the door. "Moonstone's got her soldiers wrangling up suspects, and medics are in the dining hall making sure everyone gets patched up. The best thing we can do now is stay out of the way."

Atlas glanced over at Whitsom, who leaned back in his chair, his face weary. They'd hardly spoken, since their evening of research in the library, but every time Atlas caught a glimpse of the older boy, that same exhausted expression had been etched on his face. Atlas wondered if he'd been losing sleep over what they'd seen.

Whitsom's transmitter suddenly went off, and they all collectively jumped.

"Dining hall is secured. Currently transporting Obarion soldiers and civilians back to their units," came a voice, through the haze of static.

There were a few seconds of silence before Coral grumbled, "She's gonna put us back under lockdown, isn't she? After only one game of bruiseball—"

"Is that *really* all you care about?" Atlas snapped. "Rasta just got his arm shredded up—who knows how bad of shape everybody else is in?"

Coral's cheeks flushed. "Well, I was just saying—"

"If Moonstone's smart she'll reinstate lockdown indefinitely," Atlas continued, running a hand through his hair as he paced in front of the table. "Clearly the freedom afforded was more than the Obarion could be trusted with—"

"When did you decide you're not one of us anymore?" Bettoni interrupted. His face was impassive, but his dark eyes narrowed as he continued, "The last few weeks—it's been 'the Obarion' this and 'the Obarion' that—I guess I'm just wondering when that stopped including you."

Atlas pointed a finger towards the door that led out of his unit, in the direction of the dining hall. "Maybe around the time you guys decided to start *blowing up* eleven-year-olds—"

"Guys, *enough*," Whitsom said loudly. He ran a tired hand over his face. "*They* didn't do anything, Attie. You can't go lumping all of us together. When I got to the dining hall, General Talikoth's soldiers and civilians were just as frantic as everybody else. I don't think most of them knew that was gonna happen any more than the rest of us." Atlas opened his mouth to argue, but Whitsom did not give him the chance. "We can't start thinking like that. Us versus them. You remember what Raider told us—that's how all this war and bloodshed stays alive."

Atlas sighed, and sank down into the chair next to Whitsom, his gaze wandering pensively to the ceiling. He knew that the older boy was right, but it did not quell the feeling of powerlessness swirling in Atlas' body like a burst of adrenaline with nowhere to go, nor did it squash his desire to blame *someone* for the problem at hand.

He suddenly glanced sharply at Whitsom, who was picking a piece of food out of his teeth. Atlas realized only belatedly what he'd said.

You can't go lumping all of us together.

Not "the Obarion," or Atlas' clanspeople, but *us.* As though it were one in the same. As though he'd already accepted what Atlas was still trying to wrap his brain around.

Gaiomere, at the very least, did not appear to have caught the slip. She hopped up onto the counter next to Rasta, and the little boy leaned against her shoulder, her fingers running soothingly through his hair.

Whitsom was right. The entirety of the Obarion clan couldn't be blamed for what happened today.

General Talikoth's soldiers and civilians were just as frantic as everybody else

Coral hadn't been far off when he'd pointed out how frustrated his fellow clanspeople were, cooped up like caged animals for months at a time. And with what end in sight? The Obarion didn't know whether the Vedas would have them all slaughtered, or turn them out of their homes. They were directionless, without a leader to guide them, and, as far as Atlas knew, had little hope for the future since the day that Colonel Dak had called for a ceasefire.

General Talikoth's soldiers, Whitsom had called them. Despite the fact that the man in question was locked away in a prison cell, and, on paper anyway, had no more authority than an angry toddler.

On paper.

Yes, Atlas, we won. But now comes the hard part.

Atlas got to his feet. "I'm going to handle this," he said quietly.

Bettoni cast him a faintly exasperated look. "What are you talking about, At?"

"Do you want me to come with you?" Whitsom implored, already halfway to his feet.

"No," Atlas said. "But let me take your transmitter. You guys stay here, and lock the doors and windows, just in case the Oba—just in case the instigators try anything else."

Gaiomere gnawed at her lip apprehensively. "Atlas, I'm not sure you should—"

He pressed a kiss to her forehead. "I'll be fine," he assured her. "I'll be back in a couple hours."

The hallways were still chaotic when Atlas emerged from his unit, though the crowd had thinned significantly.

Olli and a handful of other soldiers stood just outside of the civilians' quarters. Cami knelt beside a little Obarion girl, perhaps only five or six, and spoke in a gentle, reassuring voice. "We'll find your mom in no time, sweetheart—you just stay right here with us, nothing will happen to you."

"Have you learned anything else about the attack?" Atlas asked Olli.

"Apparently the cameras recorded a couple of soldiers planting the bomb beneath the food carts at lunch—the soldiers in question have been taken into custody already." Olli shook his head, frowning. "Where they *got* the bomb is another issue entirely."

"Gaiomere said she saw a couple of boys in the lab with the necessary components," Atlas informed him. "Peck and Mirian— I think they both live in the third quadrant of civilians' quarters."

Olli instantly snapped his transmitter off his belt and relayed this information. An unfamiliar voice replied that they'd track down the pair and bring them into custody with the other suspects.

"I just need to check on somebody," Atlas added, and Olli wordlessly stepped aside to let him through.

He reached the second floor in a few moments and half-walked, half-jogged, until he reached the fifteenth door on the left.

Delurah answered just moments after he knocked. Her face was pale, but she looked otherwise unharmed. He hadn't spoken to her since their argument, which suddenly seemed rather stupid, in light of everything that had happened.

Before she could speak, Atlas wrapped her in a tight hug. "I wasn't sure if you were in the dining hall—"

"I was down in the kitchens. I only heard the commotion, but the soldiers got us out quickly enough," Delurah reassured him, squeezing his shoulders. When she pulled back, she gazed up at him earnestly. "Atlas... about the other day—"

"Don't worry about it," he muttered. "Look, I've got to go. Don't leave your unit, okay?"

"Atlas—"

"Just trust me," Atlas said firmly. "Nothing like this is ever going to happen again."

"Atlas, what are you—"

But he had already taken off back down the hallway. He pushed through the crowd, until he reached the door, and then set off across the grounds.

Outside of the Main, Moonstone's medics carried stretchers and laid them down in the grass along the western wall of the building. Atlas counted ten in all. Most of the bodies were covered in sheets, but he spotted a young man, his face so pale it looked unnatural, the skin of his neck gaping and bloodied, just above the collar of his black and red uniform jacket. He could not have been older than fifteen.

The sky was cloudy and dark, as though there were a storm on the horizon, and the forest floor was dim as Atlas wound his way through the trees, deeper and deeper in the woods, until he reached the little stone prison shack.

Talikoth's shape blurred in the periphery of his vision as he entered, but Atlas did not look at him. Only one soldier guarded his father today, and Atlas felt that fate must have been smiling upon him, for it was Yacielle.

"What's been going on?" he demanded, gesturing to his transmitter. "I've only heard bits and pieces—"

"Somebody set off a pipe bomb in the dining hall," Atlas said.

"Is Cami—"

"She's fine. She's helping out at the civilians' quarters." He hesitated, and then divulged, "At least ten people were killed."

Yacielle swore, leaning heavily against the wall outside Talikoth's cell.

"Listen, Yaci, I need to speak with him."

The older man frowned, hitching his gun onto his shoulders. "Moonstone said his visitors have to be approved—"

"I'll talk to Moonstone as soon as I'm done here," Atlas said. He stepped closer, gazing at the older man intently. "She isn't...making decisions that are in the best interest of the people at large. You can see that, can't you?"

Yacielle's eyes narrowed, ever so slightly, but Atlas pressed on, undeterred. "This never should have happened. All the fights, your soldiers who have ended up injured—and now, ten people dead. Moonstone's not going to see reason until she's forced to, so I'm overriding her."

Yacielle's fingers twitched, for a split second, towards his gun, and Atlas vaguely wondered if he was going to attack. "You don't have the authority, Atlas."

"Yaci, when a leader isn't doing what's best for their people, the person that has the authority is the one who takes it," Atlas said. "Nobody else is going to get hurt. Not between our clans, anyway. You have my word."

Another five seconds of tense, uncertain silence passed, and then gradually, Yacielle lowered the hand that reached for his gun. "I'm going to go help at the civilians' quarters." He jerked his head towards the transmitter on his belt, adding, "If you need help, let me know."

Atlas nodded, his gaze finally shifting over to his father.

The door clicked shut behind Yacielle, and Talikoth let out a low whistle. "I'd be applauding if I had use of my hands."

"That wasn't for you," Atlas snapped. There was a chair near the table in the corner, and he pulled it away from the wall, setting it opposite Talikoth, and plopped down into it, leaning his elbows against his thighs. He stared at his father for several moments, choosing his words carefully. "Some of our soldiers were killed too, you know."

Talikoth's face was impassive, but something in his gaze seemed to shift, if only marginally. "How many?"

Atlas shrugged, running a tired hand over his face. "I don't know. But any is too many, isn't it? For something like this?" He scowled, shaking his head. "The morons that planted the bombs—they didn't— I don't think they even cared that our people could get caught in the crossfire. They were too focused on sticking it to Moonstone." Atlas kicked angrily at a loose clod of stone at his feet.

Talikoth's gaze lifted to the ceiling. "They'll be disciplined accordingly—"

"But that's the thing," Atlas interrupted, leaning forward. "It won't matter. They don't respect Moonstone—they're not afraid of her—not the way they fear and respect you. All the brawls—all the pushback, this bombing—it's all because of you."

Talikoth's face flashed with anger. "I never ordered them to—"

"But you never told them *not* to," Atlas argued.

"Colonel Dak called for a ceasefire—"

Atlas sprang to his feet, his voice raising to a shout. "But *you* never stopped fighting! Don't you see? They won't either—not unless *you're* the one to call the ceasefire—not Crowley, not Dak, not anybody else —you. Even if we get the water, unless you implore them to cooperate, they're going to kill each other off and all your effort dragging this clan from the brink of famine—everything you worked for—will have been for *nothing*. Is that really what you want?"

Talikoth leaned towards him, his dark eyes glinting. "I will *not* stand by while Moonstone runs my clan into the ground. That woman is not fit to take the helm of this clan—"

"I agree," Atlas said, in a markedly calmer tone. Talikoth blinked, and Atlas sank back down into his chair, continuing, "I'm not suggesting a merger—just a treaty. And a public statement, from you to our soldiers, and all our civilians, denouncing any further violence between the clans."

Talikoth's eyes narrowed, and his head tilted to the side as he studied Atlas. "And...what would my motivation towards that end be?"

Atlas arched a brow. "Besides, I'm sure you mean, the well-being and safety of your people?"

Talikoth smirked. "Yes, besides that."

Atlas' lips twitched, and he hastily looked away, decidedly uncomfortable with the notion of sharing a smile with his father. "Your freedom," he said.

"I was promised my freedom before—only to have that reward diminished to a *reduced sentence*," Talikoth drawled, sneering. "Certainly preferable to execution, but I digress—"

"I mean it when I say your freedom," Atlas interjected, before his father could continue his tirade in earnest. "Once you issue your public statement— once we obtain the water—you walk free. Stripped of your position as general, of course, but free nonetheless."

Talikoth lifted a dark brow. "And Moonstone has agreed to these terms, has she?"

"She will. One way or another."

"And if she doesn't?"

Atlas held his hands out on either side of him. "You know what happened here today. You see as clearly as I do that Moonstone's control is hanging by a fraying thread. Today was nothing but a small-scale revolt. If she doesn't agree to my terms, she'll have a full-blown insurrection on her hands."

"How can you be sure?" Talikoth asked, though he smirked in such a way that indicated he already knew the answer.

"Because I'll lead it myself."

Talikoth laughed, actually *laughed*, and Atlas was so taken aback by the sound that for a moment, he simply stared at his father, bewildered. Finally, Talikoth said, "I accept your terms."

Atlas nodded, climbing back to his feet. "We'll go speak to Moonstone now." He glanced around, his eyes scanning the little shack for an extra set of keys, before he realized that Moonstone would probably not have those just lying around...

"Summon Colonel Dak," Talikoth said. "He's got a receiver on him." Atlas glanced sideways at him, flabbergasted, but when his father only arched a brow, he complied.

It was ten minutes before Dak reached the prison shack. Without a word, he pulled a key from his pocket, and slid it into the lock. It turned, and the cell door opened with a *click*.

"Oh," Atlas said, rather stupidly. Both the older men looked at him, and his brows furrowed, as he demanded, "What, so you've just been able to get out of here the *entire time*?"

Dak chuckled, and Talikoth let out a snort. "I built this cell myself, Atlas. You think I didn't know there was a chance I'd end up on the other side of these bars? Fate loves irony, after all."

Atlas stared at him. "You're insane," he decided finally, yanking open the door and holding it open.

"It only becomes more evident with time," Dak droned as he strode past Atlas. Talikoth followed after him, chuckling.

The grounds had grown strangely quiet, almost eerily so. The bodies had been moved from in front of the Main, but when Atlas looked closer, he could still see streaks of blood in the grass.

"Moonstone is in her office with a few members of the Vedas' Council," Dak informed them. "That's where I was before you summoned me. She's discussing our routes forward in light of today's events."

Dak opened the door, and the three of them filed inside. The office felt rather cramped, with all the people that had been squeezed inside. Augusto, Vailhelm, Jaina, and the sallow-faced man—Atlas had learned he was named Axe—all sat crammed in front of the General's desk.

Moonstone broke off her sentence at the sight of them, her shrewd eyes narrowing.

"General Talikoth...I was not expecting you."

"Not an unpleasant surprise, I hope," Talikoth quipped, smirking, as he sat down at an empty seat that was pushed up against the wall.

It looked as though Moonstone might have had to refrain from rolling her eyes.

Dak took up a seat next to Talikoth, but Atlas remained on his feet. "General—" he began, quickly adding, "Moonstone," when the two Generals both looked at him. "These attacks have gotten out of control—"

"That is exactly what we were just discussing," Moonstone said. "We've agreed that, until further notice, reinstating unit restrictions would be most beneficial—"

"That's not going to help anything," Atlas interrupted impatiently. "Confining them to their units or restricting their access to weapons—those are just temporary fixes. None of that addresses the root of the issue."

Moonstone arched a brow, but nodded for him to continue.

"Half the clan is trying to cooperate as best they can, and the other half is doing everything in their power to disturb the peace because they believe that's what Talikoth wants. But if Talikoth issues a statement of peace—if we establish a treaty, and the Obarion citizens *see* him denouncing the violence, they'll comply."

"You think that would work? So easily?" Jaina inquired.

"I'm sure of it," Atlas said firmly. "They respect him more than they fear any of you."

"And why would he do such a thing?" Vailhelm asked gruffly.

Atlas took a deep breath. "For his freedom. Not just a reduction of sentence. After all of this is over, he walks free."

"*Absolutely* not," Vailhelm barked.

Atlas shrugged. "He won't agree for anything less."

"His compliance isn't necessary to subdue the Obarion rebels," Axe bit out.

"His compliance is the *only* thing that will subdue the Obarion rebels," Atlas argued. "What are you going to do, really?"

"We've d-discussed shutting down the lab—since that's where the b-bombs were made," Augusto piped up.

"Sure, and then when they run around stabbing people with butter knives in the dining hall, are you going to force them to eat with their hands?" Atlas snapped, rolling his eyes. "How many times do I have to spell it out? The issue isn't the resources they have access to, or the weapons at their disposal! This is a power struggle. Any constituent with respect for the powers that be won't bite the hand that feeds them." He glared around at the group of them. "You don't have any other choice. Do you really want a repeat of today? Soldiers killed on every side—Vedas, Obarion, and Renegade—and for what? Some petty conflict that should have been put to bed ages ago. Especially when we've got the water issue to deal with. Besides, Talikoth's already accepted to terms, so long as you will —"

Vailhelm slammed a fist on the desk. "You did not have the *authority* to offer those terms, you *arrogant* boy —"

"Quiet, Vailhelm," Moonstone said. Her elbows rested on the desk, her hands folded together in front of her, and she gazed at Atlas over the tips of her fingers.

"But General," the bearded man pressed, his round face flushed red with anger. "He *doesn't* have the authority. He can't just go around offering treaty terms

—"

"The rest of you are dismissed," Moonstone interrupted. "Vailhelm." She nodded her head towards Dak, Talikoth, and Atlas. "You three—stay."

Atlas sat down beside Dak, as the rest of the Council filed out. As soon as the door closed behind Axe, Vailhelm burst out, "He's a *soldier*, General! Since when do we let soldiers dictate the terms of war?"

Moonstone had gotten to her feet, and paced behind her desk. "Have you ever tried to stop a natural disaster, Vailhelm? He's not a soldier, he's a hurricane— and a *headache*, too, so you can wipe that smirk off of your face right now, young man—"

Atlas hastily lowered his gaze, though his lips still tugged upwards. "Yes, ma'am."

"You haven't the faintest idea of the inconvenience you cause," she continued without pause. "How many times the Council has recommended I throw you in the prison cell right next to your father —how often I've been advised that your *ego* will be the death of us. All of us." Moonstone stopped her pacing, pressing her hands against the top of her desk and leaning towards them, her dark eyes pinning Atlas to the spot. "If you were Vedas, I'd have dismissed you months ago for your gall." she said candidly.

Atlas glanced up at her, his mouth curling into a smirk against his better judgement. "With all due respect, General, if I were Vedas, I doubt I'd have the gall."

Beside him, Dak let out a bark of laughter, and Talikoth's lips twitched.

"I've told you from the beginning—from the very first day he walked into that first meeting in the North

—that you went too easy on him," Vailhelm griped. "He's arrogant, he's brash, he's reckless, he has *no* regard for authority—"

"Yes, I've long-since learned that I cannot control Atlas, no matter how hard I try," Moonstone remarked, sinking back into her chair behind her desk. Some of the tension seemed to soften from her brows, and she gazed at Atlas the same way she had in his unit, after he'd apologized for his second foray of insubordination —which seemed miniscule, compared to today—almost fondly. "It reminds me of my own son."

Atlas hardly got the chance to deliberate her words, for Vailhelm scoffed, muttering, "Your affection for the boy clouds your judgment—"

Moonstone shook her head. "No, I think it's my judgment that informs my affection. And it's the same reason I trust his conclusions above almost anyone else's."

Atlas looked up sharply. His chest flooded with warmth, and he grinned at the older woman. "I knew I was your favorite," he said cheekily.

This time, Moonstone actually did roll her eyes. She turned to Talikoth, and said, "I accept these terms— with the addendum: should the role of general be filled hierarchically, the role should pass, not to Lieutenant General Crowley, but rather to Colonel Dak."

Atlas glanced nervously between the two men next to him. He had not realized, until the man had arrive with a secret key to Talikoth's cell, that there was every possibility that the Colonel was merely a moving piece directed by Talikoth.

But when the alternative was Crowley...Atlas wasn't sure there was much of a choice in the matter.

Talikoth nodded. "I agree to your addendum."

Moonstone dismissed them and instructed a pair of nearby guards to escort Talikoth back to his cell.

Atlas had already started towards his unit when Talikoth passed by, his guards on either side of him. "Well done," his father called, just loud enough for Atlas to hear.

Atlas stopped walking, and Talikoth did, too. "What are you talking about?" he demanded.

Talikoth shrugged. "Your intercession on my behalf."

Atlas' fists clenched at his sides. "I don't—I'm not —I told you, this isn't for you. None of this is for you."

His father only smirked and turned away from him, his strides confident as walked down the hall and out of the building, and Atlas was left wondering whether, after everything he'd done to separate himself from the man, he was still playing right into his father's hands.

CHAPTER NINE

Moonstone had already passed out notes by the time Atlas arrived to the afternoon meeting three days later, though she spoke quietly to Axe near the front and had yet to address the room at large.

"Where's Gaiomere?" Atlas asked Jacoby, as he slipped into the seat next to him.

The red-haired boy sat stiffly, his hands clenched together atop the table. "She should uh—she should be here any minute—she said she might be a bit late," he mumbled.

Atlas' gaze wandered around the room, and he quickly located the source of Jacoby's anxiety.

They were joined today by several of the remaining Inner Ring soldiers that had survived Gaiomere's explosion. On Talikoth's left sat Zyratier, pale, short, heavy-browed, and scowling. He was in his mid-forties, and had been a part of the Inner Ring for almost fifteen years. To Zyratier's left sat Kordell, the newest induction—he had been accepted into the Inner Ring a month before Atlas was captured by the Vedas —and was widely-agreed to have the most proficient crossbow shot in the entire clan.

At the back of the room, leaning against the table and wearing the haughty expression that Atlas was fairly certain he'd exited the womb with, was Jemahl—

the youngest soldier to ever be inducted into the Inner Ring. Jemahl was three years Atlas' senior and had undergone induction at the same age Atlas was now, only two years out of Academy. He was tall, with deep brown skin and dark, wild eyes, rather like a wolf.

"How are the boosters coming?" Atlas asked Jacoby, more to distract the young man from the Inner Ring soldiers than out of genuine curiosity.

His question, however, seemed only to infuse Jacoby with more unease. "They're uh—well, they're *not* exactly—"

He was saved the trouble of having to explain further, for at that moment, Gaiomere came through the door, practically skipping, her face alight and her smile wide.

"No way," Jacoby said immediately. Some of the nervousness seemed to melt from his face, and Atlas looked between the two of them in befuddlement.

Gaiomere gave the redhead an impish grin as she withdrew a strange black box from her bag, a little smaller than her hand, as well as a long hypodermic needle, and set them at the end of the table. "Told you so. Now you *have* to ask Marbella out—"

Jacoby groaned. "Oh come on, Gai, please don't make me—"

"A bet is a bet, you can't back out now!" Gaiomere scolded.

Atlas, though, was hardly listening. Jemahl, who still stood at the end of the table, had fastened his gaze on Gaiomere. When he spoke, his voice carried across the room, and a hush fell over its occupants. "So, this is the little brat who blew up half our Inner Ring, huh?"

Gaiomere froze on the spot. Atlas half-rose from

his chair, his eyes flickering between the two of them.

Jemahl turned and stepped up beside her, so close her shoulder brushed the side of his ribcage. His hands were cuffed behind him, and his guard stood five feet away, his gun carefully trained at his ward's back, but Jemahl looked unconcerned with any of this.

"They said you were *dangerous*, did you know? *You*. Dangerous." He chuckled darkly. "Tiny little bird like you—funny, isn't it?"

"Funny," Gaiomere echoed. One hand had clenched around the fabric of her bag, and the other tightened around a stapler that sat atop the table. Atlas' heart pounded in his chest, and his muscles grew taut, coiled like a spring in anticipation.

"Jemahl," Dak said from where he sat halfway down the table. There was a hint of warning in his voice, but Jemahl hardly looked at him.

Atlas chanced a glance at the rest of the officers. Moonstone was still speaking to Axe, but her gaze kept flickering over towards Jemahl. Zyratier merely looked bored, but Talikoth observed the exchange curiously, his head tilted to the side, his eyes narrowed, ever so slightly.

"It is funny," Jemahl crooned. "Funny, 'cause I could snap your neck like a twig—"

He moved suddenly, and his guard scrambled forward. Atlas darted to Gaiomere's side, too, but she reacted faster than them both. She turned and slammed the stapler into the center of Jemahl's forehead.

"*ARGH!* Shit!" Jemahl cringed away, groaning.

The guard forced him to his knees and dug his gun into the back of Jemahl's neck. "Try anything like that again and you'll be moved back to confinement," the guard said.

Jemahl glared up at Gaiomere, his eyes watering profusely. "You crazy bitch," he spat scathingly.

Gaiomere's lips lifted into a smile, but it was not her usual, playful smile. It was cold, and calculating. "Don't forget it," she said softly.

Another one of the soldiers helped Jemahl's guard lug the young man to his feet, and they shoved him down into the chair on Talikoth's right.

There was a moment of tense silence, and then Talikoth chuckled. Zyratier joined in soon after, and Dak hid a smile behind his hand.

"It's not *funny*," Jemahl hissed, though Atlas noticed he was careful to direct his words, and his glare, towards the latter two.

"You alright?" Atlas quietly asked Gaiomere as the conversation around them resumed.

"Fine," she said, huffily blowing a curl from her face. "I had it handled."

She continued fiddling with the strange black box, and Atlas leaned against the table next to her, his lips twitching into a smirk. "You know...it's advisable, for your general health and well-being, that you *don't* make a habit of picking a fight with the biggest guy in the room."

"I need a challenge," Gaiomere replied, sniffing. "Otherwise it's no fun. And to be fair, I didn't pick that fight—that was purely self-defense."

"And slingshotting a rock at that dude's head in the lab was *self-defense*, too, was it?" Atlas inquired, his smirk broadening.

"He called Jacoby a milksop! What was I supposed to do, let him get away with it?"

"I *told* you I could have handled it," the redhead piped up from his chair, with a sullen look.

Atlas nodded in agreement. *"Maybe* you should let Jacoby fight his own battles...just an idea—"

"My dad always said that a man dies when he refuses to stand up for what's right," Gaiomere retorted loftily.

At the mention of her father, panic pulsed beneath Atlas' skin. He glanced at her sideways, worried suddenly that perhaps she could see the apprehension written on his face, but thankfully at that moment Moonstone got to her feet at the head of the table and rescued him from any further questioning.

"Gaiomere, what is your progress on the boosters?"

"Oh, I haven't been working on the boosters," Gaiomere informed her. She returned her attention to the black box and missed the searing look the Vedas General gave her.

"May I ask *why*?"

"Because I thought of something better," Gaiomere said simply. She held up the hypodermic needle and suddenly asked, "Jacoby, can I inject this into your neck?"

The redhead's face blanched, "Come again?" he asked, his voice cracking. Kordell made a noise that sounded like a hastily covered snigger.

She waved the needle in front of Jacoby's face, and he looked as though he might be sick. "I just—I um—I don't really like needles," he finished lamely. Gaiomere rolled her eyes, and then turned her gaze on Atlas.

"I'm presuming I shouldn't ask why?"

She only continued to look expectantly at him,

and Atlas sighed, obligingly turning his head.

He felt the sharp stab of the needle pierce his skin and a peculiar rush of pressure before she extracted it.

"Perfect. Now go walk around a bit."

He stared at her blankly, and she let out an exasperated breath. "*Atlas*, come on, just a couple hundred yards."

"Okay, okay," he grumbled. "You're so weird." She shooed him out of the room, and he wandered down the corridor, outside of the building, and to the edge of the forest before he made his way back, wondering what on earth had gotten into her.

When he returned, however, he was baffled to find Dak and Alekea peering over Gaiomere's shoulder at the tiny black box while the rest of the room murmured excitedly.

"You went down the east hall, to the edge of the forest and back, right?" Gaiomere asked excitedly.

Atlas froze, glancing suspiciously around the room, which was completely free of windows. "Yes..." he said slowly, his brow furrowing. "How did you—"

"It's a tracker!" she exclaimed, passing him the box. He peered down at the screen, startled to see a green line demarcating the path he had taken around the building and a blinking green dot that indicated where he stood that very moment.

"Gaiomere, this is...magnificent," Moonstone murmured, as Atlas passed her the box. She looked astounded, which was quite a feat on Gaiomere's part.

The curly-haired girl beamed under the praise. "I found a book in the library all about satellites and everything I read indicated they can stay in orbit for *thousands* of years. And back before the First War, the

Global Positioning System was used by *everyone*, so I figured that if the satellites—or at least some of them—were still in orbit, conceivably, I *should* be able to utilize their signals to track the coordinates of our soldiers, so long as I could hack their systems." She dug through her bag and withdrew another needle, saying, "*These* are microchips. I designed them to be small enough to inject beneath the epidermis..." She shifted uncomfortably, her cheeks darkening with color. "You know, just in case our soldiers are um...disrobed...upon capture."

Atlas' skin prickled uncomfortably. He hadn't thought about that possibility, but given the nature of the Flesh Flayers pursuits, it wasn't entirely out of the question.

Talikoth studied the black box carefully, his dark eyes narrowed. The excited chatter hummed steadily around him, but when he spoke his voice carried over the noise, and the rest of the room quickly silenced. "Have you considered interference?"

Gaiomere did not, at first, seem to realize that he was speaking to her. She was scribbling something into her notebook, and it was not until Jacoby nudged her that she glanced up, her eyes widening.

"Uh...me?"

His lips twitched into a smirk. "Yes, princess."

"Um...I mean..."

He arched a brow, and she straightened up, her brows knitting together. "Well...as far as we've heard, the area in question is barren—which would rule out interference from nearby emissions—"

"But that isn't taking into account natural interference," Talikoth pointed out. "Weather, atmospheric disturbances. Have you considered that?"

Her cheeks flushed. "Well, I—"

"We cannot account for disturbances of that nature," Moonstone said, frowning at Talikoth. "Gaiomere, this is marvelous—you did amazing work. I'd like to get these prototypes to the lab for manufacture as soon as possible."

But Talikoth's interjection had done what it meant to. Gaiomere frowned down at the needle between her hands.

"Don't let him get to you," Atlas told her once the meeting had been dismissed, and the two of them made their way down the hall. "He's just trying to mess with your head—"

"He's right, though!" Gaiomere burst out. "We can't afford to have any kind of signal crossing—"

"You can't control the *weather*, Gaiomere," Atlas reasoned. "Seriously, don't worry about it. The trackers are incredible."

She made a noncommittal noise, slinging her bag over her shoulder. "I'm going to head back to the lab and start working on some modifications."

"Gaiomere, wait—let's go get dinner. Don't worry about it—"

But she was already stretching up onto her toes to give him a fleeting kiss. "Not hungry. I'll see you later."

Atlas sighed as he watched her disappear down the hall, his hands clenching and unclenching at his sides. A steady thrum of anger surged through him, and before he registered what he was doing, his feet carried him back towards the meeting room.

Talikoth emerged, and the two flanking soldiers steered him left down the hall, but Atlas ignored them.

He pounded towards his father, and the older man caught sight of him just as Atlas shoved him firmly backwards.

"What the hell was that?" Atlas demanded. He made to shove Talikoth again, but this time his father was prepared, and he barely swayed. "You play your mind games with me, fine, but if you *ever* speak to her like that again I'll—"

"You'll *what*?" Talikoth sneered, leaning towards him. "Falter again? Freeze like a coward with your finger on the trigger?"

Atlas' fist connected to his face before he even made the conscious decision to swing. He went for a second punch when the soldiers on either side of him finally snapped into action, and pushed him back.

"Get out of here, Atlas," one advised. Atlas realized only belatedly that it was Mabury. "Go on."

Talikoth's nose gushed blood, but he seemed to take no notice of it. He smirked at Atlas as the soldiers pulled him away, disappearing down the hall and out of the door.

Before Atlas knew it, they were only a week out from the scheduled exchange, and tensions were running high at Headquarters. The soldiers who volunteered were noticeably anxious, many of them skipping meals and utilizing the training room late into the evening. Atlas wanted to sit them down and offer some kind of encouragement, just as he'd done in the North, but every time he thought about what to say, his mind drew a blank.

"We're all going to be fitted with concealed knives," Coral reminded him, whenever he voiced his concerns. "And more likely than not, we'll have the numbers on them—they're not going to send two hundred cannibals to pick up two hundred Renegades with a million gallons of water on board—there's no way we'd all fit!"

Whitsom and Bettoni did not match Coral's enthusiasm. The two of them had both been uncharacteristically sullen the past few weeks, though Atlas later discovered that for Whitsom, his sulkiness was not entirely due to their upcoming mission. Not directly, anyway.

"He's feeling a lot of mixed emotions," Gaiomere told Atlas one evening, when he visited her in the lab. "These are the people that took Gwena—as far as we know, anyway. He's not in the best mind-state right now—I'm sort of afraid he'll do something rash."

Gaiomere, though, did not appear to be managing any better than her brother. Atlas hardly saw her the past week, and when he had, she was usually rushing between the lab and Moonstone's interim office. Her normally lucent brown skin looked drawn and ashen, and her eyes seemed perpetually heavy with bags.

Atlas did not find out, until the day before their scheduled departure, exactly what had been keeping her up at night.

"Go again."

The sounds of labored breathing and fists crunching against bone filled the room once more, and Atlas circled the sparring pairs studiously. After dozens of sessions, the volunteers looked decidedly more congruent than they had amidst their first few forays of inter-clan training.

"Nice, Cami, " Atlas called to the blonde girl. She sparred with Trinida, and had just swept his feet from beneath him. The brawny boy shot her a nasty look as he pulled himself up.

Most of the Obarion soldiers had been rather disgruntled when they had found out that they would be training with girls, since Moonstone allowed female soldiers and Talikoth didn't. Atlas was glad for it— it would have looked suspicious to the Flesh Flayers if Talikoth delivered a batch of "Renegades" that was entirely male. Granted, Moonstone only had about a hundred female soldiers, and just a dozen had volunteered—but still, it was more believable than none at all.

Moonstone had set the volunteer cap at two hundred, since that was the largest trade Talikoth had ever made with the Flesh Flayers— any more might have drawn their suspicion—and Atlas had been rather surprised at how many soldiers from every camp had been willing to volunteer. Harcliff submitted a register of about fifty volunteers, which, admirably, was every young man of fighting age at his disposal. Vailhelm brought Atlas two hundred names from the Vedas, and Dak, five hundred from the Obarion.

Whitsom was able to tell him which of Harcliff's warriors would be fit for the task at hand, and they quickly narrowed his list. They recruited Cami, Yacielle and Olli to help them narrow down the Vedas next—the three of them had been in uniform for over a decade and had a good comprehension of the skill levels of most of the soldiers beneath them.

Bettoni and Coral gave Atlas an exhaustive report on the Obarion clan's internal state of affairs—more specifically, the dispositions of their volunteers.

"I heard he and Weckari chatting in the men's a week or two ago—they got real quiet when they saw me come in," Coral told Atlas, as they had come to the name of Lattyris. "Maybe it was nothing, but...well, they know I'm friends with you—"

"Probably better to play it safe," Atlas agreed, crossing his name off the list. This was how most of their selection had gone when it came to Dak's volunteers.

Talikoth's decree had done what it meant to. The brawls ceased practically overnight, but Atlas knew that did not mean the sentiment behind them had vanished. He now assessed the Obarion soldiers based on their attitudes—who were the soldiers eager to extend the proverbial olive branch, and who were those that dragged their feet, that hissed slurs at passing Vedas, that still shared whispers, perhaps even plotted schemes of insurrection. With how precarious this mission was *already* going to be, the last thing they needed was an internal threat.

The process took an entire day, but by the end of it, Atlas had a list that he was satisfied with—a hundred and seventeen Obarion volunteers, sixty-eight Vedas soldiers, twelve of Harcliff's tribesmen, plus Luca, Clancy, and Zarr. They alone, out of all the Ramshackle boys, chose to defy Niko's position, all but demanding that they be added to the list of volunteers.

As Atlas paced around the sparring gym, pausing occasionally to correct a delivery or give instruction, he could not help being pleased with their turnout.

Perhaps a quarter to five o'clock, Moonstone strode into the sparring gym accompanied by Dak and Talikoth, the latter of whom was flanked by a burly pair of guards. Talikoth was finally clean-shaven; Atlas vaguely wondered if this had been his reward for all his compliance over the previous weeks.

Trailing behind them was Capalti, the Obarion clan's lead doctor. He was pale, thin, and white-haired. From what Atlas knew he'd been a practicing medic since Talikoth was a child, before their clan had ever even set off for the Westland.

It was near the end of their session, so Atlas had let most of the soldiers pair off to practice on their own, and he and Whitsom were exchanging blows in a corner near the lockers. Atlas had just gotten Whitsom in a knee bar when Moonstone summoned the two of them over.

He hopped to his feet, holding out a hand to lug the older boy up.

"I was just bringing General Talikoth and Colonel Dak by to witness your success in fusing the Obarion training with my own clan's," Moonstone informed the pair, once they'd reached her. "I would have been here sooner, had it not been for the fact that *someone* planted a stink bomb in my office...."

She gave the two of them a piercing look. Atlas' lips twitched at the corners, but Whitsom slung an arm around his shoulders, remarking, without hesitation, "It was Coral. He's a real rebel, that kid—a whole 'nother month of latrine duty ought to set him straight—"

Moonstone rolled her eyes. "Boys, the cameras—"

Atlas cleared his throat, interjecting, "I just want to say, General, that Whitsom is older than me, and has a large influence on my decision-making, so I have no culpability."

Dak and Talikoth were both studying Whitsom, and when the young man noticed, he unconsciously straightened, a hint of nervousness flitting across his face. Atlas shifted, immensely uncomfortable with what was taking place in front of him: Whitsom was well aware of why Talikoth and Dak were looking at him so probingly, but *they* had no knowledge of his knowing this.

Dak spoke first. "You're Atlas' chosen second. Whitsom, is it?"

"Yes, sir."

"And a Renegade, too?"

"Yes, sir," Whitsom admitted. He seemed to hesitate, and then added, "Though not necessarily by choice."

Talikoth's dark eyes fastened on Whitsom's face, and the corner of his mouth quirked upward. "No, but it's our choices that decide our fate, isn't it?" he said quietly.

A strange look passed over Whitsom's face, and Atlas looked between the two of them with bewilderment. He felt as though he were missing out on a joke. "Yeah, I—I agree," Whitsom said finally.

Atlas wanted to pull Whitsom aside and ask what *that* had been about, but before he got the chance, Capalti stepped forward. "My team successfully administered a dozen rounds of Gaiomere's trackers without any cases of rejections—if she's ready, we could possibly begin distribution today, while all the soldiers are gathered here."

Moonstone glanced down at her watch. "She

should be here any second."

She'd scarcely gotten the words out when the double doors to the sparring gym sprang open, and Gaiomere came bustling inside, her notebook clutched to her chest and her bag half-hanging off of her shoulder. Her curls stuck up in every direction, and her eyes were bloodshot, but her smile was a mile wide.

"Gaiomere, would you be ready for injections this afternoon if Dr. Capalti cleared it?" Moonstone asked.

Gaiomere's smile fell a fraction of an inch. "Oh...uh, no...I'll definitely be ready by tomorrow morning though, before it's time to leave...and it's only because I've made some *minor* adjustments."

Capalti shot the girl an exasperated look, though it was softened by the twinkle of amusement in his eyes. "Ever the perfectionist."

Gaiomere's face was buried in her bag as she dug through it, so her response was partially muffled. "I'm *not* being a perfectionist, I just don't see what the harm is in improving something, if it can be improved—here it is—"

She withdrew one of her tracking devices and extracted a microchip from the needle so small it was barely visible in the palm of her hand. "I did some research and determined that by using a combination of diamagnetic metals in the structure of both the tracker and the chip, we can essentially repel any kind of atmospheric interference."

Atlas' jaw slackened, and before he could stop himself, he turned to glare at his father. It all suddenly made sense—Gaiomere had been driving herself crazy the past week, losing sleep and skipping meals just to jump through the hoops Talikoth had constructed

—*proving* herself on the obstacle course of his twisted mind games, the way Atlas had done for eighteen years before he'd realized that it would never be enough because Talikoth would never be satisfied.

His father did not notice his glare. "It's excellent, in theory," Talikoth said mildly. "But in order to actually confirm the effectiveness, you would need to imitate said atmospheric disturbances—"

"Lightning, yes," Gaiomere interrupted, as if waiting for Talikoth to speak. "And in case you've forgotten, your Headquarters are surrounded by a barrier that effectively mimics high-charge atmospheric disturbances." She slipped the microchip back into the hypodermic needle and held it out to him. "I've tested them twice already—but feel free to test them again, if you feel so inclined."

Talikoth's smirk broadened into an amused grin. "I'm impressed."

Gaiomere hummed disinterestedly, but a smug little smile tugged at the corner of her lips, and Atlas barely repressed a groan.

"I'll be damned if we're ever gifted with a mind like yours again around here, young lady," Capalti said with a chuckle.

"We've thought as much before," Dak muttered. Talikoth shot him a perturbed look, as though he'd said something he shouldn't have, but the dark-skinned man ignored him, glancing between Whitsom and Gaiomere. "Your brother, I presume?"

Gaiomere wrinkled her nose. "Oh, *tell* me we don't look alike."

"You wish you looked like me, funk-face."

"Yeah, about as much as I wish for the plague,"

Gaiomere sneered.

"If Ilquir had known you had a brother, I'm sure he'd have begged you to have him in the lab with you," Capalti piped up, as he wiped a bit of fog from his glasses.

Gaiomere smiled, her voice saccharine sweet as she remarked, "Oh, don't be silly, Dr. Capalti, my brother doesn't even have enough brain cells to string together his own name, let alone anything else."

"Okay, okay—hey, let's go get dinner," Atlas suggested, as he hastily squeezed between the two of them, before they could come to blows. His interjection was two-fold in intent, though, for Dak and Talikoth were looking between the siblings with a dangerous kind of resolution. Atlas feared, for a moment, that the two of them would spoil it all—that they'd let Gaiomere in on the secret that Atlas and Whitsom had already discovered—before either of them had worked up the courage to tell her. It would only be a matter of time before the full truth came out—that Atlas had known all along—and he didn't even want to *think* about how she would look at him if she found that out.

He'd tell her after they'd successfully procured the water from the Flesh Flayers. Once all of this uncertainty had passed, and he had the weight of this mission's success off of his back.

In the meantime, he needed to do a better job keeping her away from Dak and Talikoth.

Thoughts of his father reignited his irritation, but he did not get a chance to bring up the issue with Gaiomere until hours later, for Ilquir called her into the lab just after dinner.

She came plodding wearily into Atlas' unit at a

quarter past nine. "You just finished?" he asked, from where he sat at the dining room table, pouring over his notes for the hundredth time. Gaiomere nodded, tossing her bag on the floor and collapsing onto his couch with an exhausted little grunt.

After a moment, she lifted her head off the couch. "Where is everybody, by the way? Nobody was in Jem's unit."

Atlas lifted her legs and sank down on the couch next to her, before setting them back in his lap. "Apparently Coral and Ando snuck a bunch of booze down to the barns—Coral's calling it the 'We-might-be-cannibal-food-tomorrow-so-let's-destroy-our-livers-tonight palooza.'"

Gaiomere snorted. "Very creative. You didn't go?"

"You know, strangely enough, drunken diablerie is *not* my preferred mode of preparation for lethal missions in which it's imperative I have my wits about me." Atlas gave her a sideways glance. "What were you doing in the lab?"

"Oh, just normal lab stuff, you know," Gaiomere mumbled, shrugging half-heartedly.

Atlas' eyes narrowed, a fraction of an inch.

"Why are you giving me that look?" she asked, without lifting her head from the couch.

He clicked his tongue impatiently. "I was just...*concerned* that maybe you were in there building something *else* to try and stick it to Talikoth."

"I'm not trying to stick it to anyone," she murmured.

"Look, I get that it must be infuriating," Atlas interrupted. "Being called primitive, being treated like you're not as capable—and I know better than anyone that you're smarter than any Obarion they could put you up against—but you can't keep missing meals and skipping out on sleep just to prove yourself. Especially not to him. Talikoth doesn't do things like that because he thinks you're inferior—he does things like that so he can manipulate people into producing *his* desired outcome."

Gaiomere pulled herself up and leaned against the arm of the couch. "I'm *not* trying to prove myself to him. Honestly." She paused, her forehead creasing pensively. "And besides...his outcome *was* better. There will be less fallibility in the trackers. It'll be safer for all of us."

Atlas' jaw unconsciously tightened, and his gaze flickered over to Gaiomere's face. She was already watching him expectantly, as though she *knew* his insides were a tumultuous, molten pool of conflicting emotions, and her brows were already knitted together resolutely, like she expected a fight.

He'd anticipated this, though. He knew her too well—knew that the fact that she hadn't mentioned it didn't mean she hadn't already formed a plan.

"Us?" he repeated, hoping, rather half-heartedly, that she might contradict him. But of course, she didn't.

"Us," she confirmed, sitting up a little taller.

"So, what—were you just going to sneak onto the train?" Atlas asked with a frown.

"If it came to that," Gaiomere returned, arching a brow. "Will it?"

Atlas sighed. "Gaiomere, you know perfectly well that I'd rather you stay here—"

"You don't want to let me go because you think I'm incapable of protecting myself," she snapped, before he could finish. "Because you don't respect me—"

"I do respect you," Atlas interrupted, his voice determinedly calm. "And I know better than to think I *let* you do anything—I learned that the hard way when I tried to make you stay at the Vedas' base during the battle."

Gaiomere's mouth opened, then closed again, and Atlas pressed on, before she could speak. "Look, I get that you have the autonomy to make your own choice—and if you really want to come with us, I can't stop you. But you also can't stop *me* from doing everything in my power to keep you safe—because I *am* stronger and faster and larger than you—so I'm going to protect you ten times better than you can protect yourself."

Gaiomere let out a huff that was something between reluctance and concession. "Fine." Her brows knitted together, and her teeth chewed on her lip the way they always did when she was working through a problem in her head. Atlas pulled her into his lap, carding his fingers through her dark curls as he waited for her to voice what was on her mind.

"You'd kill me before one of them got the chance to eat me—wouldn't you?" she asked suddenly.

Atlas blinked, his hand stilling in her hair. "I'd stop them is what I'd do."

"Right, but if you *couldn't*," Gaiomere pressed. "I just want to know that you'd—I don't know, put me out of my misery, if that's what it came down to."

Atlas' brows furrowed. "If I had the capacity to—to put you out of your misery, as you said—then I'd have the capacity to kill anybody who was trying harm you."

"We have no idea what their numbers are going to be like once we reach the water source," Gaiomere argued. "I just want to know that you could do it, if it came down to that—"

"It's not going to come to that," Atlas said firmly. "I don't care what their numbers are, I won't let it come down to that."

He kissed her, and she kissed him back in a way she had never kissed him before, desperately, as though she really believed it might come to that. Atlas kissed her back just as urgently, his hands gripping her hips, and her arms threaded around his neck, pulling him, if possible, even closer.

But then there was a knock on the door, thunderous and imposing, and they broke apart, ever so slightly. "Ignore it," Atlas murmured against her lips. "It's probably just Coral."

"Coral wouldn't knock," she pointed out. "It could be important."

Atlas let out a frustrated exhale, acknowledging that she was probably right, and clambered to his feet. He took his time making his way to the door, internally cursing whatever halfwit simpleton thought it was appropriate to bother him at nine-thirty in the evening, and already prepared to give the offending party a thorough telling off when he yanked open the door.

"Do you have any idea what time—oh."

Moonstone stood on the other side of the door, accompanied by none other than Talikoth. He was flanked by two soldiers on either side, both toting massive machine guns. "Sorry to bother you so late, Atlas." And indeed, she did look noticeably contrite. Her brows were drawn together, and her mouth was set in a thin line.

"Uh—it's cool."

Talikoth was gazing at the ceiling pensively, but there was a smirk twitching at the corner of his lips, and Atlas rather got the impression that somehow, *somehow* his father just *knew* he was ruining Atlas' evening.

Moonstone sighed heavily, folding her hands behind her back. "Talikoth has requested that—since it is the last evening before your departure—he be allowed the privilege of sleeping in his own bed, rather than spending the night in the prison, with the provision that he remain guarded overnight."

Atlas' jaw slackened. "*Here*? He's sleeping here?"

She nodded. "The Council agreed to allow it."

He barely suppressed his groan as he ran a hand through his hair. "I—fine. Yeah. Okay. Whatever."

Moonstone gave him another apologetic look, explaining, "We'll just um...we'll need to search the unit to ensure that there are no hidden weapons he could utilize during his stay."

Atlas' face flushed, and after a moment of hesitation, he stepped out of the way, waving them inside. The four of them filed in, and a flash of surprise flickered over Moonstone's face. "Oh. Hello, Gaiomere."

"Um...hi." The curly-haired girl looked as though she wanted to sink into the sofa. Her cheeks were dark with color, and her eyes were wide as she watched the soldiers begin to rake through cabinets and drawers.

As soon as he had heard her name, Talikoth's gaze shot across the room. He looked first at Gaiomere, and then glanced back at Atlas, his brows lifting to his hairline. Atlas felt the flush in his cheeks deepen, and he hastily looked away from his father, moving back across the room and dropping unceremoniously down onto the sofa.

"He's uh...he's sleeping here, apparently," he told Gaiomere in a low voice.

"What? She's letting him—what if he tries to kill you in your sleep or something?"

"The guards are staying, too," Atlas said glumly, shooting a glare at their backs as they disappeared into Talikoth's room to search it.

"Tonight of all nights," Gaiomere murmured.

His gaze shot back to her instantaneously. "Why —" The look on her face abruptly ceased his line of questioning. The color in her cheeks had spread, and she shyly avoided his gaze. A dopey grin slowly stretched its way across his lips, and surprise and exhilaration must have momentarily clouded his judgement, for he leaned towards her, laying an arm across the back of the sofa, and started, "You know, we could still—"

"*Atlas.*"

"Sorry. Right. Nevermind."

Her chiding glare was softened by the warmth in her gaze, and her fingers toyed aimlessly with the hem of his shirt as she said, "Maybe tomorrow—if you've got a tent to yourself—"

"Atlas," Moonstone called, and both of them jumped. "If there are any—um...problems, do not hesitate to notify me—both Mars and Atapali have transmitters, and I'll have mine on all night."

"Okay. Uh...thanks."

Moonstone tilted her head towards his father, and one of the guards obliged to remove his handcuffs. Atlas heard Gaiomere's breath hitch, and when he glanced at her, her fingers unconsciously stroked the skin of her throat.

Talikoth flexed his fingers, staring down at his hands as though he had not seen them in many years. After a moment of hesitation, the two guards moved simultaneously—one of them posted up beside the front door, while the other planted himself near the window.

"Very well," Moonstone said, giving Atlas a sharp nod. "I will see the three of you at the morning meeting. Good night."

Gaiomere suddenly sprang to her feet. "Oh uh— actually, I'll um—I'll follow you out. I had something to ask you about—about the um—the trackers." She gave Atlas a tight smile and hurried towards the door, following Moonstone into the hall. Atlas got the feeling that Gaiomere did not have anything to ask the General, but was simply rather frightened at the idea of being in Talikoth's home with the man himself present.

The door closed behind them with a *click* that seemed unnaturally loud, and Talikoth's eyes zeroed in on Atlas. "Since when are you allowed to have girls over?"

Atlas sat up straighter, gaping at him. "Are you serious? You're really going to come in here and act like a father when you tried to kill me a few months ago?"

"You didn't die," Talikoth said dismissively, striding across the room and pouring himself a glass of water.

Neither of them paid any regard to the soldiers posted on either side of the unit, both of whom shifted uncomfortably, as though they would rather be anywhere else in the world at the moment.

Atlas rolled his eyes, huffily flopping back against the sofa. "The only reason I didn't die was because of

Gaiomere's vest—and for the record, I can have her over whenever I like. You aren't in charge of me."

Talikoth leaned against the counter, taking a long sip of water, before he set his glass down. "Are you being safe?" he asked.

Atlas' head whipped towards him, hoping desperately that he'd simply misheard. "What?"

Talikoth shrugged, and Atlas was irritated to note that his father did not look even vaguely uncomfortable. "Since you decided to start inviting girls over—I'm asking if you're being safe."

Atlas' face turned bright red. "I'm not—it's not even any of your business, and I—she and I aren't—I've never even—" He broke off, hastily pushing himself to his feet. "We're not having this conversation," he said firmly, shooting a glare at the guard near the door, who had very obviously hidden his snigger behind a well-timed cough. "I'm going to bed."

"We're going to go over the exchange process once more," Talikoth said.

Atlas froze in the doorway to his room, his hands clenched at his sides. A glance over his shoulder told him that Talikoth had not waited for him to reply—he already settled at the table and withdrew the massive stack of notes that Moonstone had distributed to each of them from his bag.

Atlas seriously considered ignoring him. He could go into his room and close the door and there would be no consequences. Talikoth had no authority over him, after all.

But almost against his own volition, his feet carried him over to the table, and he plunked down across from his father, pulling his own notes towards him once more. "Fine," he muttered. He hesitated, before glancing across the table, asking, "Do you think Moonstone is erroneous in how many soldiers she's taking to pose as the Inner Ring?"

Talikoth glanced up, smirking a little. "You thought so, too, did you?"

"If you've only ever taken ten, it might seem suspicious to double that amount—especially with so many the Flesh Flayers won't recognize."

"Tell her so, in tomorrow's meeting," Talikoth commanded. "You've done a rather admirable job of placing that woman firmly in your back pocket."

Atlas' cheeks warmed, even as his traitorous chest swelled at his father's praise. He glanced nervously at the guard posted beside the door, before insisting in a low voice, "I haven't—she doesn't *always* listen to me. You saw how she reacted when I broke into the prison the second time."

"But she will listen to you in this regard," Talikoth said, as though that settled the matter.

They went over the plan once more, a second time, and then a third and fourth, Atlas asking questions and Talikoth deftly encouraging him to suggest *this* to Moonstone, or to ask her to change *that*. Atlas could recognize that his father was exploiting Moonstone's trust of him, but the matter of fact was, his ideas were *good*. Atlas would be foolish to reject them just because of the mouth that spoke them.

They retired to their respective rooms well after midnight, and for the first time since he had initially proposed the plan, Atlas actually felt good about what they were going to do.

◆ ◆ ◆

Atlas awoke to the smell of bacon. The clock beside his bed informed him that he still had forty-five minutes before he needed to be in the sparring gym, where Capalti's medics would distribute the trackers, so he took his time clambering out of bed. He turned the shower water down as cold as he could bear and submerged himself beneath the glacial cascade until his skin was pink and his mind blissfully clear.

His first glance into the living room gave him pause. Talikoth sat at the table, spearing his eggs with a fork as he flipped through his notes once more, and Delurah shuffled around the kitchen, deftly turning over bacon with one hand while pouring coffee with the other. For a split second, he felt as though he had been launched backwards in time, like he had never been captured by the Vedas and was about to sit down for breakfast before taking off for training, or perhaps to run patrols with his squad.

Atlas slung his bag over his shoulder, and was halfway to the door when Delurah called, "Oh, no you don't, laddie," and stepped directly in his path, wielding her tongs like a weapon.

He let out an impatient noise, "Delurah, come on, I'm not hungry—"

"I don't want to hear it, young man. Sit. Eat."

Atlas rolled his eyes, but compliantly marched back to the table and sat himself down across from Talikoth. She set a plate of bacon and eggs in front of him, and despite his vexation, he groaned delightedly when the flavor of the savory meat hit his taste buds.

"Renegades finally stopped interfering with the hunting grounds, huh?" Atlas remarked wryly, glancing at his father.

Talikoth glanced up at him briefly, his mouth twisting into a frown. "*No.* We suddenly found room in the budget." He started to turn back to his notes, but then did a double take, letting out a disparaging noise. "You look like a vagrant."

It had been Zyratier who pointed out that the Flesh Flayer's leader might recognize Atlas, since he'd interacted so often with Talikoth, so Atlas—much to Delurah's relief—had taken a razor to his head and buzzed his hair. He'd also let the stubble on his chin and jaw grow out, since Talikoth seemed to take personal offense at the idea of donning facial hair.

Atlas shrugged. "I figured I'd really sell the whole the whole 'captured nomad' bit."

"You'd better shave that atrocity off the second you return," Talikoth snapped.

"I think I might leave it," Atlas said, as he snatched up one last piece of bacon and clambered to his feet. "Gaiomere sort of digs it."

Talikoth muttered something mutinously under his breath, and Atlas, barely repressing a snigger, bustled out the door before he could become the target of any more of his father's ire.

When he reached the sparring gym, most of the soldiers had already assembled. The group wore a disarray of clothing and colors—Whitsom had pointed out that it would be suspicious to the Flesh Flayers if any of them came in uniform, so they had needed to find a way to conceal weapons in less-traditional soldiers' garb; loose sweatpants, denim jeans, and oversized hoodies.

Whitsom fell into step with Atlas at the door, and Jacoby joined them moments later. "You guys already got your trackers?" the redhead asked. His face was rather pale and his glasses sat askew on the bridge of his nose.

Whitsom nodded affirmatively, but Atlas said, "I need a new one—Gaiomere gave me mine before she did the modifications." Jacoby nodded, looking a little nauseous, and Atlas held out a hand, "I can do it." Jacoby gave him a grateful grimace, wordlessly passing him the long needle.

As the sting of metal penetrated his skin, Gaiomere came striding across the hall towards them. She pointed a finger at the soldiers lined up in front of Dr. Capalti and said, "That's the last group, and we'll be ready to go."

Atlas nodded, his eyes raking over her. Her wild curls were pushed back from her face with a headband, and she had donned dark clothing that most certainly belonged to Jem, if the fact that her pant legs and sleeves had been rolled up several times over was anything to go by. Cami had suggested she abandon her usual bright, eye-catching clothing, to blend with some of the other soldiers, since she was easily the smallest out of the entire two-hundred soldier company —though Luca was not far off.

As Atlas looked at her now, though, he could not help but think, for perhaps the hundredth time, that he was making a terrible mistake.

"—still haven't gotten mine yet," she was saying to Jacoby, as she withdrew another needle from her bag. "Do you mind?"

Jacoby looked as though he might actually be ill, so Atlas took the needle from her, stepping closer, putting a hand on her shoulder as he pushed the point into her skin. She winced, but Atlas hardly noticed, because she was gazing up at him with the same intensity that she'd worn the night before, prior to Talikoth's interruption.

"It's not too late, you know," he murmured, absently tracing his thumb along the side of her neck. "You could still stay."

Her brow furrowed. "I'm going with you, Atlas," she said firmly. She turned her head and pressed her lips to his knuckles, ever so briefly, before she stepped back and crossed the room to begin collecting the discarded needles. Atlas felt a stab of something foreign, heavy and ebullient all at once—like he was simultaneously floating above the ground, yet being smothered beneath the earth. For one fleeting, desperate moment, he wished that he could renounce his duty.

Atlas had never yearned for normalcy—he had always craved some kind of distinguishment—but he yearned for it now. He craved the freedom to stand back and let others do the fighting, to let someone else take the lead. To go to parties and skip training and laugh in the unburdened sort of way that Coral did. He wished he could spend time with the girl he loved—for he was quite certain he loved her, when his chest was aching so fiercely at the thought that something might happen to her—without having to worry if they'd be dead in the next forty-eight hours.

He took a steadying breath and pushed down the anxiety swelling up to his throat as he latched the knife that Whitsom passed him onto his belt.

But it didn't really matter what he yearned for —not in the end, anyway. Atlas had not been bred for normalcy. He had known that as long as he could remember, and Talikoth made certain that he never forgot it. He couldn't, even when he wanted to.

You're building a legacy.

PART II:

THE BLOOD LENDERS

CHAPTER TEN

The late spring sun bore down as they started their trek south. It might not have felt so warm if they were not laden with so much gear. They elected to leave a day before the scheduled exchange, which would give them ample time to travel south by foot, and a night to camp near the train, ensure the cars were secure, and solidify the last elements of their plan. They'd dump the gear and extra weapons and board the train at dawn—approximately two hours before the Flesh Flayers would expect them at the mountaintop.

Ahead of Atlas, Whitsom regaled some of the Obarion soldiers with a tale of how he'd tricked a couple of Flesh Flayers up north into getting themselves caught in a bear trap. Tetrabathi and Lunes—two of Harcliff's boys that could not have been older than sixteen—argued over whether Flesh Flayers had fangs.

Gaiomere trotted along among a gaggle of Moonstone's female soldiers—Cami, Larky, Joaz, and a couple girls Atlas only knew by sight—chatting cheerfully as her bare feet deftly picked over rocks and broken slabs of concrete.

Journeying east with their team of two hundred might not have felt so different from traveling south with the Vedas soldiers all those months ago, if it were not for the fact that as they trudged through the desert, Atlas watched Obarion soldiers—boys that he had grown up with, who had been raised to hate Vedas and Renegades alike—laughing and talking with those very sorts, as though they were old friends. Yacielle and Martama, a bulky Obarion soldier six years Atlas' senior, cheerfully shared a bag of nuts as they lagged towards the back of the group. Charyzar—a brown-skinned boy a year beneath Atlas in Academy—conversed with Luca rapidly in their native tongue. And even Zyratier and Harcliff had been chatting amiably over the past hour.

Atlas had been surprised to learn that Moonstone, Harcliff, and Colonel Dak would all be joining for the exchange, posing as members of the Inner Ring.

"Normally I prefer to oversee operations from outside of the fray," Moonstone had told him. "But given the intricacy of the task at hand...well, I'd like to be there in the trenches with the rest of you." Moonstone had not, Atlas had noted wryly, volunteered to pose as a captured Renegade.

Halfway through their journey, some of the officers passed out food and extra water bottles. Atlas spotted Gaiomere balancing along a crumbling brick wall and jogged to catch up with her, reaching up to hand her water. "Been here?" he asked curiously.

The past hour, they had been wandering unceasingly through Ramshackles. This particular one looked to be mostly small houses—Atlas hardly saw any of the tall, tipping buildings that dotted the Ramshackle near the Obarion headquarters, and the streets, with massive holes blown right through their centers, were lined with palm trees.

"Yeah," Gaiomere said, taking a long sip, before she passed him the bottle back. "Years ago, though. Back before Dad died."

The second half of their journey took them further inland where the Ramshackles grew denser. The buildings were tall, and the vegetation sparse. Cars sat on every street corner, and every so often, up ahead, Luca or Zarr would dive beneath one of them, ripping off a component and hastily stuffing it into their bag.

"We're near Big Wheel," Gaiomere observed quietly from beside him. They had been walking for over seven hours, and his feet ached inside of his boots. Gaiomere's eyes were droopy, and every so often she drifted sideways into him. He offered to carry her gargantuan bag four different times, but in each instance she narrowed her eyes and huffed in an affronted sort of way.

"Whitsom climbed up the rolling coaster once," she continued. Atlas' lips quirked upwards, and he glanced sideways at her fondly, not bothering to correct her. "I think he was just trying to impress Gwena."

"How's he doing with that, by the way?"

She sighed. "I'm really worried about him, honestly. I know he puts on a brave face all the time, but I just—I'm afraid he's going to do something really reckless, once we—once we get there and see them, you know?"

Atlas frowned. "I trust Whitsom," he said. "I know he wouldn't do anything to endanger the mission."

Gaiomere wasn't looking at him, but there was still tension in her jaw as she said, "I don't know. When Gwena got taken Whitsom just—just totally lost it. I've never seen him like that."

"What happened? The day she got taken, I mean."

It was something that Gaiomere had only talked about a handful of times, and never in detail —presumably because any time she did, Whitsom became uncharacteristically grouchy. Atlas wondered, a number of times, how it could have happened. After all, there had been five of them—she, Whitsom, Gwena, Maggi, and Rasta—and even if the latter two hadn't been able to help much, surely they could not have been *that* outnumbered...

"Gwena was our trapper," Gaiomere explained. "We found her in the far north, all on her own—she had been on her own for a long time, actually. She used her traps to catch animals to eat, and she was really, *really* good at it, but when she joined up with us, she stopped using them to kill the animals—since we didn't eat them, and all. The whole putting paint on the bottom of the traps, so we could follow the animals' tracks? That was all Gwena."

Atlas smirked wryly. "I guess brains run in the tribe."

Gaiomere nodded. "She's the one that taught me how to make trip wires, too, before I taught Maggi." Her teeth caught her lower lip, her eyes dimming, and she pressed on, "Anyway...one night, she and I were out setting traps—about a half mile from our campsite—when a group of Obarion soldiers found us. Gwena had a knife on her, but there were about ten of them in all, and we—we didn't stand a chance. She told me to run and I —" Her voice broke, and she looked away from him, but not before he saw her eyes well with tears. "I did. Like a —like a coward. I ran to get Whitsom, but by the time we made it back, they were gone."

Atlas let out a breath he hadn't realized he'd been

holding. His mind, perhaps selfishly, was not on the horror of their tribe member being ripped away from them so suddenly, but rather how *close* Gaiomere had come to being captured, too. If one of the soldiers had caught her—if one of them fired off a shot—Gaiomere would have gone to the Flesh Flayers, just like Gwena. "If you hadn't run, you would be dead," he reasoned quietly, reaching over and sliding his hand into hers.

She sniffled, but said nothing.

He was trying to think of something to cheer her up when Alekea shouted back, "Alright, let's park it!" Gaiomere blinked, looking up, and Atlas did too.

They were surrounded by short, fat buildings, grey and crumbling, and there was not a train in sight. Up ahead, Moonstone whirled around to look at Talikoth and Kordell, her face stern.

"It's fine," Zyratier grumbled in his deep voice. "It's down there." He pointed towards a low, collapsing wall, and when Atlas moved closer, he realized it was obscuring a stairwell, dark and dingy, leading deep underground.

The other soldiers began to pitch camp. A number of them set up tents, and Yacielle and Olli headed west to try to find firewood amidst the cityscape.

"We should go check it out," Atlas told Whitsom, who had just joined him. "Make sure it's a legitimate— Gaiomere!"

The girl in question had scrambled over the wall, and the top of her riotous curls were only barely visible, for she had already descended a few steps down into the underground.

Jemahl, Kordell, and Talikoth stood near the stairwell, the former two snickering as Gaiomere's head popped out from behind the wall. "What?"

"Fearless little rugrat, isn't she?" Jemahl remarked, swinging himself over the wall and landing in front of her. Atlas saw her eyes dart down towards his unshackled hands, and a flicker of apprehension crossed her face. Jemahl must have noticed, too, for his mouth twisted into a nasty smirk.

"You don't just go wandering into abandoned train stations, dummy," Whitsom grumbled, unslinging his rifle from his back and hitching it onto his shoulder.

"What's there to fear down there?" Gaiomere muttered, pushing past Jemahl as she added, "Can't be anything worse than who we're traveling with." The dark-skinned young man snickered again and followed her. Kordell was on his heels, and Whitsom took up the rear, withdrawing a light from his pocket and shining it down the tunnel.

Talikoth met Atlas' eyes. The guards behind him shifted uncomfortably, both of them casting wary glances down the tunnel. After a moment of hesitation, Atlas said, "Whit and I can handle him. We'll be back up shortly." They nodded, falling back.

Atlas and Talikoth stared at each other for a few seconds longer before they moved simultaneously, both stepping into the stairwell and descending down into the darkness, dank air enveloping them like a blanket.

"Sometimes there are Renegades down here," Jemahl was telling Gaiomere. They walked almost side by side, and Atlas' hand kept twitching towards his handgun, very conscious of the fact that it would take Jemahl only a split second to break Gaiomere's neck.

Jemahl, though, seemed too preoccupied with

boasting. "Most of the time they're just wanderers looking for a place to get out of the heat or rain—but sometimes we get combative folks looking for a fight." He nudged something with his foot, and as Atlas and Talikoth closed in on the group walking ahead of them, he realized it was a decaying body—which explained the putrid stench lingering in the stairwell. "Like this fellow—tried to surprise me." Jemahl glanced sideways at Gaiomere and gave her a leering grin. "Screamed like a little girl when I broke his femur, too."

"Sort of like you did with those staples in your head, huh?"

Jemahl stuttered to a halt, and his eyes narrowed. "You're awfully gutsy for being at a disadvantage—"

"You touch my sister, I'll make you regret it," Whitsom said from behind him.

Jemahl glanced over his shoulder. "You gotta be joking, right? You *do* know who I am, don't you?"

"A douchebag?" Gaiomere murmured. Kordell snorted, and Whitsom let out a guffaw of laughter, but Atlas only watched, his shoulders tense.

Jemahl looked, for a moment, as though he were contemplating hitting her—but then he shook his head, taking the last five steps in a leap.

Gaiomere let out a gasp as they reached the landing, and when she turned back to look at Atlas, her eyes were bright. "Oh, just *look* at it!" she breathed. She seemed to completely forget about the presence of Talikoth or the Inner Ring soldiers, for she giddily bounded towards the train and gripped the edge of one of the cars to slide herself beneath it.

"Yo Gai, hold up!" Whitsom called exasperatedly.

"We're all trained to drive it, but Zyratier's the

most proficient," Kordell told Atlas. "Once it hits top speed, we're looking at about an hour and forty-five minute transport time."

Jemahl moved down the train, peering into each of the cars, and Whitsom followed his lead.

"Fuel?" Atlas asked.

"Diesel—Zyratier is handling our refill now. Freights are efficient on fuel, but it still takes a fair amount—"

"These engines are pretty ancient," came Gaiomere's muffled voice. She dangled from the mouth of a car towards the rear, her head completely concealed behind the engine. "Theoretically, generated power could supplement the fuel to increase the transport range..."

Whitsom popped his head out of a car down the way, calling, "Atlas, you better drag her out—she'll be in here all night."

Atlas snorted. Footfall echoed behind him, and he glanced back to see Moonstone, Dak, and Zyratier descending the stairwell. "How many cars are there?" Moonstone asked, folding her hands behind her back.

"A hundred or so," Jemahl answered. "Each car can carry over a hundred tons—"

There was a sudden clang of metal, and a pounding of footsteps—a figure bolted out of the car Whitsom had just opened and pelted across the platform, darting around Kordell and breaking for the stairwell.

But like lightning, Jemahl sprang into action. He took two massive steps and caught the figure with an arm across the throat. The boy—for Atlas could now see he was little more than a boy—let out a cry of pain and fell to the ground. Jemahl grasped him by the scruff of his shirt and lugged him to his feet.

"Wait!"

Gaiomere scrambled off the car and stumbled towards them with wide eyes. "He didn't—he didn't do anything. Just let him go."

Jemahl had grasped onto either side of the boy's head, and the little boy writhed against him, his face ghostly white.

Atlas' eyes flitted toward Whitsom. He looked as though he were holding his breath. "She's right," Atlas told Jemahl. "He was only seeking shelter. Let him go."

But Jemahl was not looking at Atlas, nor was he looking at Gaiomere, or Whitsom. His eyes were intent upon Talikoth, who watched the situation unfold with an impassive expression.

"Let him go," Atlas repeated firmly. "Jemahl, he doesn't—he's just a kid."

Moonstone looked between the two of them with a frown, but she did not move to interfere, and Atlas realized only belatedly that she would not—this was Atlas' mission, and she would not overstep his authority.

This was why, hours later, the guilt would overwhelm him like a sandstorm, for he should have *known*—he should have done something—because he *knew* how Talikoth trained his soldiers.

Jemahl released the boy, and he scrambled away, looking back over his shoulder as he bumbled towards the stairwell. Talikoth and Dak watched him pass indifferently, and his foot reached the first step when Jemahl whipped his knife from his belt and sent it hurtling towards the boy. The boy was just glancing over his shoulder, so it plunged into the front of his throat, burying itself in his flesh to the hilt. He let out a gurgling cry, collapsing against the wall of the stairwell, hands clutching desperately at his neck.

Gaiomere screamed, and took half a step towards the little boy, but he twitched for a second longer, and then went still.

Kordell rolled his eyes, muttering, "Why do you always play with your food, Jemahl?"

Atlas swallowed thickly, looking first at Moonstone, who was shaking her head, her expression repulsed, and then at Talikoth. But his father's gaze was trained on Gaiomere.

The curly-haired girl trembled, her hands balled into fists and her eyes wet with tears. Before Atlas registered what she was doing, she charged towards Jemahl, reared back, and punched him in the face.

"Gaiomere—"

But she had already pulled her arm back and delivered a second blow. Jemahl stared down at her as though he could not quite process what he was seeing.

Only when she reared back for a third punch did the young man snap into action. He grasped her arm mid-swing and yanked her towards him.

Whitsom vaulted across the room, but Atlas got there faster. He caught Jemahl's wrist in the air, moments before his palm impacted Gaiomere's face. "If you ever," Atlas said quietly, "lay a hand on her again...I'll kill you."

Jemahl yanked his wrist out of Atlas' grip, his dark eyes narrowed. His lips twisted into a sinister smirk. They may have been the same height, but Jemahl's frame was corded with thick muscle, and any envy Atlas fostered for the young man had always been coupled with an undercurrent of intimidation. "You willing to make good on that promise, traitor?"

Whitsom appeared at Atlas' shoulder in an instant.

"Atlas—" Gaiomere began quietly, but he held up a hand to silence her.

"Tonight," Jemahl continued. "Nine o'clock, in the west clearing. Mors Recti."

Moonstone finally stepped forward, her brows furrowed. "Atlas, this is not—"

"It is tradition," Dak interjected. His mouth was turned down, but he pressed on. "Our practices should not be pruned, should they, General?"

"It's tradition," Talikoth agreed, his voice quiet. His eyes met Atlas', and he smirked. "If your aim is not homogenous assimilation, General Moonstone, then prove so."

"Atlas—"

"Tonight, nine o'clock," Atlas confirmed, ignoring Gaiomere. He nudged the young man beside him, adding, "Whitsom is my second. Yours?"

"Favio," Jemahl answered quickly. His eyes flitted over first to Whitsom, and then to Gaiomere, and his sneer widened. "See you there, Attie boy."

"Okay, what the hell was *that* about?" Whitsom asked in a low voice, as soon as they made it out of the stairwell and put some distance between themselves and the others.

Gaiomere glanced back at the entrance with wide eyes, as if she could still see the boy Jemahl had slain, and Atlas slid a hand into hers. "Mors Recti—it's a tradition of our clan," he told Whitsom quietly. "If you can't settle a dispute through words, it can be settled in combat—a fight to the death, to rectify the dispute."

"What's your second do?"

"You're just there to make sure there's no foul play —make sure that he doesn't pull a gun on me if all I'm using is my fists." Atlas shrugged. "More likely than not you won't have to do anything but stand there."

Gaiomere frowned, but said nothing as she snatched her bag from where she'd left it at the top of the stairs and took off towards the tent that Cami and Joaz were setting up for the girls.

Whitsom and Atlas told Coral and Bettoni everything that had happened when they rejoined them near the makeshift fire pit Clancy was building. By the end of it, Bettoni's eyes were wide, and Coral spluttered, "You've gotta tap out, dude."

Atlas shot him a harsh look, plopping down on a concrete slab and pulling off his sweatshirt.

"I'm serious, man. Have you *seen* Jemahl in the training yard? The dude's a machine."

"I think Cor's right, At," Bettoni said slowly, sinking down next to him. "I think you're a really great fighter, but Jemahl is—he's—"

Clancy, who stacked firewood a few feet away from the group, chimed in, "I saw him sparring a couple of days ago—pretty sure he coulda beat Raider—"

"I'm pretty sure Jemahl could beat Talikoth, if he really tried," Coral remarked, in a low voice. He shot the man in question a terrified glance, adding, "Don't—

don't mention I said that."

"I'm not going to back down," Atlas said, scowling.

Coral and Bettoni both looked as if they wanted to continue talking him out of it, but neither of them got a chance, for at that moment a horde of soldiers wandered over, talking loudly, and they weren't able to discuss it further.

It wasn't until after dinner that they got the opportunity to mention it again. "At, man, I'm telling you—*all* you gotta do is walk up to Jemahl and tell him you're sorry," Coral insisted. He was sprawled out across the ground on the opposite side of the fire, balancing a spoon on the tip of his nose.

"There's no shame in it," Bettoni agreed.

Coral nodded, cursing when his spoon plunged to the ground. "Tell him you have no idea what you were thinking—that you were momentarily overtaken by some crazy demon spirit—"

"Y'all still going on?" Whitsom asked, as he sank down next to Atlas. He began sharpening his knife on a stone, his face tense, and his brows drawn together. "Leave him alone—let him do what he wants."

Atlas' eyes wandered over to Talikoth. He was speaking quietly with Dak and Kordell, leaning his elbows against his knees, his jaw flexing in the way it always did when he mulled over something problematic.

"Oh good, Gaiomere—will you *please* talk some sense into your boy before he goes and gets himself killed?" came Coral's petulant voice.

The curly-haired girl had just wandered into the circle of soldiers, her bag slung over her shoulder.

She spared the blond boy a brief glance before sliding into the seat next to Atlas, wedging between him and Whitsom.

When she didn't answer, Coral sat up, fiercely glaring at her in a way atypical of his normally amiable demeanor. "Don't you care at all? Are you seriously going to let him go and get himself killed—"

"Don't you *dare* imply that I don't care about him," Gaiomere snapped. Atlas glanced down at her in surprise, warmth filling his chest like a wave. "I just know better than to think I *let* him do anything."

Coral grumbled under his breath, and Bettoni still looked uneasy, but Atlas ignored the two of them, his eyes affixed on Gaiomere. She picked up a rock and turned it over in her hands. "I—I *hate* this," she admitted quietly, so only he would hear.

"I know you do," he murmured, sliding an arm around her waist. Atlas found himself unconcerned with the rowdy soldiers cavorting around them as she leaned into him, her soft curls brushing the underside of his chin. "It'll be fine."

She looked as though she were going to argue, but broke off when Jemahl ambled over, sitting down on the concrete slab next to Coral. On either side of him were Favio—a lanky young man who had been in Jemahl's year at Academy—and Hix—a blond soldier a year older than Atlas.

"Enjoy your last meal, Attie boy?" Jemahl crooned. His voice was quiet, but it seemed to carry across the circle, and a hush fell over the soldiers surrounding the fire.

Atlas looked up at him, arching a brow, but said nothing. Whitsom's knife sharpening came to a halt, and he watched Jemahl through narrowed eyes.

Jemahl's eyes flickered over to Gaiomere, and his smirk widened. "Maybe later tonight I'll give your girl some comfort—keep her company while the vultures are pickin' at you—"

Atlas was on his feet before he'd made the decision to do so, but Whitsom was right there beside him, his hands on Atlas' shoulders.

"Hour and a half and you can kick his ass," Whitsom promised in a low voice. Atlas' eyes stayed on Jemahl. Hix had leaned over and whispered something, and the two of them sniggered.

"You know what, matter of fact," Jemahl called, "Sweetheart, why don't you just come over here now and—"

"You're disgusting," Gaiomere said scathingly, but her words were drowned out by a sudden scuffle. Whitsom whipped around and lunged towards Jemahl. Bettoni sprang up and grabbed the back of he and Atlas' shirts to drag them backwards. Coral dove to push them back with a hand on both their chests, while Clancy and Luca scrambled over and each grabbed one of their arms.

"That's enough," came Talikoth's cold voice. He was not looking at Atlas, nor Whitsom, but at Jemahl, and as soon as the words left his mouth, the three sniggering boys silenced, looking quickly at the ground.

"Don't make me regret trusting that you were mature enough to handle the rank afforded to you."

"Yes, sir," Jemahl muttered, glancing up at Talikoth.

"You'll have plenty of time to kill each other in the appropriate setting," Talikoth added, smirking wryly.

Kordell snorted.

Jemahl and his cronies wandered away, whispering furiously, and after a moment, Atlas and Whitsom both sank back down onto the concrete, glaring at their retreating backs. "I don't care about Obarion tradition," Whitsom said in a dangerously low voice. "I'm going to kill him myself."

"You can have at him once I'm through with him," Atlas replied, his hands clenching into fists in his lap. "If there's anything left."

"Um, *hi!*" Coral broke in, looking between the two of them, flabbergasted. "Have we forgotten that this is *Jemahl?* He will kill both of you—he could probably kill you *at the same time* if he wanted to—"

"Coral, *shut up!*" Gaiomere burst out. She was sitting between Atlas and Whitsom, and the two of them both looked at her, startled. "You aren't helping anything."

"He's right, though," Bettoni interposed. "And Atlas, you've got to lead this mission. You can't get yourself killed, not over something like this."

"Over something like this?" Whitsom stared at Bettoni with a mixture of anger and pity. "Bet, if a man hasn't got his honor, what else has he got?"

Coral rolled his eyes. "Gee, I don't know, working lungs, an uncracked ribcage, two functioning arms and legs—"

"Shut up, Coral," Atlas said, shaking his head.

"No, I'm serious—"

"No, you're wrong," Whitsom snapped. "Look, our dad used to say that you can spend your entire life building a legacy, but that a hundred years can't repair a moment's loss of honor."

Atlas looked at him quickly, startled to hear Whitsom uttering old Obarion adages. But then, Whitsom probably grew up hearing them as well.

From his peripherals, Talikoth and Dak looked at Whitsom too.

"Look, Whit's right," Atlas hurried to say, frowning at Coral and Bettoni. "I'm not backing out. Whit's already briefed on what we'd do in the event of my death." He felt Gaiomere tense beside him, but he didn't look at her. "I'm going, and that's it, so you two can drop it." Coral opened his mouth to reply, and Atlas gave him a stern look. "That's an order."

Something in his tone must have resonated with the pair, because they finally let it go. After a few minutes, they wandered off to go collect more firewood.

The surrounding conversation had dulled to a muted drone, so when Talikoth spoke, his voice carried easily across the fire. His eyes fastened on Whitsom, and even in the dim light, Atlas could see them glinting shrewdly.

"You sound like your father, when you talk about honor," Talikoth said quietly. "He would have never backed down from a fight."

Atlas stiffened, his heart leaping in his chest. He did not dare look at Gaiomere, but could feel her shoulders tense beside him. Her fingers clenched tightly around the rock in her hands.

Whitsom, however, did not even blink. He met Talikoth's gaze across the fire unwaveringly. "No, sir, he wouldn't have," he said quietly.

Talikoth tilted his head to the side, studying Whitsom. "How long have you known?"

"About a month," Whitsom admitted.

Atlas finally chanced a glance at Gaiomere. Her eyes had narrowed to slits. "Known what?" she asked.

Talikoth's brows lifted. "Ah, but you didn't tell your sister?"

Whitsom shifted uncomfortably in his seat, and Gaiomere looked between he and Talikoth with befuddlement. "Tell me what?" she demanded. "Why would *you* know anything about our father?"

Dak sighed, folding his hands together in front of him. "Olympion was our lead researcher, many years ago. Back before we reached the Westland, he was our most formidable mind."

Gaiomere was so still that Atlas could hardly tell if she were breathing. Talikoth watched her carefully, and it was he that continued, "He's the one that advised me to move west. The one that helped us develop the tanks—the one that made our weapons what they are now." His lips twitched into a smirk as he added, "The Obarion clan would not be what it is today without his contribution."

Gaiomere let out a slow breath and pulled her gaze away from Talikoth. "You're lying. My father didn't belong to either clan. And neither do I."

"He's not lying, Gai," Whitsom said quietly. "I overheard he and Colonel Dak talking about our parents, about a month ago—called our dad by name—"

"It's not so uncommon of a name," Gaiomere snapped. She was trembling, and Atlas put a consolatory hand on her knee, but it did little to placate her. "Our tribe has been nomadic for ages—none of the Obarion abstain from meat—and *both* our parents did —"

"The Obarion clan *was* nomadic, before we settled

in the Westland," Dak said gently.

"And the only reason Olympion and Maichell abstained from meat was because they were part of the Conclave," Talikoth drawled, rolling his eyes as he added, "They were some of the only among our clanspeople who continued the practice, even after the precincts were disbanded—"

"The Conclave?" Whitsom and Gaiomere asked simultaneously.

It was Atlas who explained. "Back in the day, the clan was split into sects dividing the people by class. Like a caste system, of sorts. Talikoth abolished the whole thing as soon as he was elected General."

Dak continued, "The families in the Conclave all abstained from meat—they claimed that by refusing to allow the lifeblood of another creature to pass through their bodies they remained unsullied and *pure*." He and Talikoth shared a wry smile. "Unlike us lowly laborers."

Gaiomere shook her head, pushing herself to her feet and pacing in front of the fire, her fingers flexing around the rock. "My parents didn't kill animals because they believed in doing no harm—"

Talikoth let out a bark of laughter. "Is that what they told you? Your parents didn't kill animals because they were born with silver spoons in their mouths. Just like the rest of the Conclave." Barely detectable, beneath his scorn, was just the faintest hint of bitterness.

Atlas' brows furrowed, and he studied his father with a new sense of intrigue. He always assumed his father had been part of the Conclave—at the helm of that precinct was, after all, the general and his family, followed by their highest-ranking officers...

Gaiomere shook her head again, crossing her

arms. "This is—no—you're lying—"

"Olympion deserted our clan five hundred miles east of where we settled and formed Headquarters —about twenty miles south of the Grand Canyon," Talikoth droned. "He took his wife, Maichell—" Gaiomere flinched. "—and his little boy. The woman was pregnant when they left..." Talikoth's head tilted to the side as his eyes glittered with obvious amusement. "With a little girl."

"*Shut up!*" Gaiomere shouted, whipping around to face him. Several of the soldiers sitting around a nearby campfire glanced up, but she ignored them. "You're *lying* —"

"I told you, Gai, he isn't," Whitsom said gently. "I heard them, in the woods—" His face brightened, and he excitedly recounted, "And I saw—well, Ma's got a sister, back at Headquarters, Gai—she looks *just* like her—and what's more, we saw a picture of Ma *and* Pops, in an old Obarion newspaper clipping—it was from ages ago, at their wedding. General Talikoth was standing right next to Dad—"

But Gaiomere was scarcely listening anymore. Her hands clenched and her face grew tense—Atlas realized Whitsom's mistake a second too late.

"We?" she said, in a dangerously soft voice. "Who is *we*?"

She turned to look at Atlas, who suddenly found himself captivated by a cluster of concrete bits by his feet.

"Oh, I didn't *actually* mean we, when I said 'we'," came Whitsom's hasty reply from beside him. "I was talking about—well, you know, like, the *general* we—"

Gaiomere ignored her brother's rambling. "Atlas,"

she began quietly, "You knew about this?"

From his periphery, Whitsom cast him an apologetic look, but Atlas lifted his gaze to Gaiomere. Thick shame coiled in his stomach and bubbled up in his throat like bile. "Yeah, I did."

Whitsom broke in on Atlas' behalf. "Gai, this is *exactly* why we didn't wanna tell you. We knew you'd freak out. And besides—I mean, does it really matter? It's not as if it changes anything. Even if we *are* Obarion —"

"We aren't!" Gaiomere insisted.

"How could you be anything else?" Talikoth said impatiently. "The things you know—the things you can do—you think any Renegade within a thousand miles of us has *half* your capabilities?"

Gaiomere's face flushed with anger. "I've met plenty of nomads who—"

"Most of them can't even *read*," Talikoth snapped. "Did it ever occur to you how rare you and your brother are? Did it ever cross your clever little mind to wonder *why*, hmm? You're every bit as Obarion as Atlas is— more so, with the legacy incarnated by the bloodline in your veins."

Gaiomere suddenly flung the rock in her hands at Talikoth. He jerked out of the way with a second to spare, and his face flashed with anger, but Gaiomere looked unfazed. She glared unwaveringly at him, her shoulders trembling, and her eyes crackling with fire. "I am *not* Obarion," she hissed.

Without another word, she strode across the clearing, clambering over a toppled light post, and stormed off into the dark.

CHAPTER ELEVEN

There was a moment of silence between the four of them, and then Dak coughed, remarking, with barely concealed amusement, "Objectively...that was a rather good throw." Talikoth's lips twitched, but he only reached back to toss another branch into the fire.

Atlas found himself chewing over Talikoth's words. The idea of Whitsom and Gaiomere being Obarion, when he'd first discovered it, seemed too bizarre to be true. The siblings were wild and strange —brilliant, certainly—but inarguably *weird*. When he'd first met them, he had been enthralled by their understanding of the land, their peculiar way of speaking, and the outlandish, exotic clothing that they —mostly Gaiomere—wore. There had never been a doubt in his mind that they were *different* than him— even if he had found more in common with them than not.

But then...there were always clues that they were not quite so typical as the other "Renegades." No one at the Under, nor any of the tribes they encountered, including anyone in Raider's gangs, subsisted only on a diet of plants and nuts the way Whitsom and Gaiomere had. Stranger still was Whitsom's fascination with war, his unquenchable hunger to be a part of something larger—even from the time Atlas first met him.

If you aren't willing to die for anything...might as well let the wolves take you.

Whitsom's code of ethics was uncompromising, and sometimes...sometimes he *said* things that suggested a wisdom deeper than the fabric of his own lifetime. Things that made sense now that Atlas knew his true origins.

A hundred years can't repair a moment's loss of honor.

Atlas' father said the same thing to him, when he was only a boy. It was the reason why Atlas could not look Gaiomere in the face when Raider had so handily beaten him all those months ago, and it was the same reason that he could not back down now, with Jemahl sneering down his nose at him, even if Atlas most likely would lose. Honor was integral to the identity of the Obarion people—and Atlas had never heard any of the Ramshacklers, nor any of the other Renegades, speak about honor, or integrity, or *truth.* Not the way Whitsom did.

And Gaiomere...well, Atlas had often taken for granted how outstandingly intelligent Gaiomere was, but now that he thought about it, it simply didn't make any *sense.*

We didn't exactly have the luxury of carting around a library of information, Atlas.

But Gaiomere *was* a library of information—and where could she have gotten it? She may have learned some skills from her parents, and some still from Raider and Koda—but that did not explain how she seemed to know how to do *everything.*

Unless...unless she had been raised by an expert—by someone with a deep understanding of reprogramming and engine operation not only from a lifetime of practice, but *also* with access to research from the last library in the Fallen Land.

Whitsom's voice pulled Atlas from his thoughts. "Sorry I got you in trouble," he mumbled.

Atlas sighed, running a hand over his hair. "It's not your fault. I should have told her the moment I found out." He glanced in the direction Gaiomere disappeared. Faintly, he could make out her outline beneath the moon, sitting on a large rock at the edge of the distant east clearing. "I'll be back in a bit."

She sat gazing up at the endless sea of stars, and as Atlas approached, he heard faint sniffling.

"Are you mad at me?" he asked, sitting next to her.

It was a moment before she responded. "I'm not mad," she said softly. "Just disappointed."

Atlas cringed, guilt washing over him anew.

When she turned to face him, her eyes were red-rimmed and wet. "I knew you were lying to me that day, you know—when I asked where you and Whitsom had gone." She let out a little huff of laughter. "You always put your hands in your pockets when you lie—it's just um...it's never been to me, before." She exhaled harshly. "I was worried about it for a little while. I thought maybe you were sneaking off to kiss some other girl in the library, but I told myself it was probably something stupid. Because I was sure, if it was something important, you'd never lie to me about it."

Atlas looked away from her, his cheeks burning. The guilt in his stomach felt something like a fifty-pound weight now. He wished she were yelling at him instead—anything would be better than this. "I won't ever lie to you again," he swore.

She tilted her head to the side, frowning. "Why should I believe that? When you lied to me so easily the first time."

Atlas opened his mouth, his mind scrambling to present a thorough defense of his actions—to list all the reasons why he'd been justified in what he'd done—but then he stopped.

"You don't have any reason to," he said quietly. "And if you chose to, that—well, that would be up to you. Your forgiveness isn't anything I'm entitled to. I'm hoping for it, certainly. I feel like a—like a total idiot, risking this—risking *you* for—well, for anything—but I know ultimately I can't make you believe me. All I can do is show you I mean it." He hesitated, before admitting, "And honestly, it *wasn't* easy. This last month has been hell, keeping that from you."

Gaiomere smiled a little then. "I do believe *that*," she said softly. "You've been awfully twitchy." Atlas chuckled. He tentatively wound an arm around her waist, and relief unfurled in his chest when she did not pull away. "I um—I'll try not to get so upset that you and Whitsom are afraid to tell me things," she added, a little bashfully.

He arched a brow down at her, smirking. "You think I'm afraid of you, flower power?"

"Well, I am pretty intimidating."

"Oh yeah, all five feet of you," Atlas remarked, snickering when she swatted his shoulder. "You're a real tank—" He broke off, for Gaiomere's face suddenly grew serious again, and it did not take him long to determine where her thoughts had gone.

"I can show you the newspaper clipping, when we get back," Atlas offered. "I know it's—it's a lot to process.

Seeing it might help."

"My dad was my hero growing up, you know," she murmured. It looked as though she might have been fighting back tears. "I thought—I mean, my dad just—he *always* did the right thing. Always."

"I'm sure he believed he was doing the right thing, when he helped Talikoth develop all those weapons," Atlas reasoned. "He probably thought they would ensure the clan's protection—"

"Every tribe that was slaughtered on their trek west," Gaiomere pressed on, as though he hadn't spoken, "Every *murder*—that blood is on my dad's hands too, not just Talikoth's." She scowled, adding, "I suppose he'd be proud—his daughter following in his footsteps —"

"Gaiomere, *stop*," Atlas said firmly. "You can't— you can't deliberate over everything your father did or didn't do. For all you know, he believed he was doing the right thing. He's not here to ask, so obsessing over his motivations is just going to drive you crazy. And besides, you were only working with Talikoth to help the people of my—well, our clan—it's not as though you were building tanks for him—"

She shook her head. "That's not—"

"My point is: you can't change it. Any of it. Regardless of what your father's past looked like, he obviously did everything he could to make sure you and Whitsom were taken care of. Isn't that all that matters?"

Atlas shoved down the voice in the back of his mind that said *no*, it was *not* all that mattered. For if it were him, he would *need* to know. If it were him, he'd dig through every newspaper clipping, scour every scrap of information he could get his hands on, until he knew every facet of the truth—the same way he'd coerced Moonstone into giving him the information about his mother.

But it was not him—it was Gaiomere; sweet Gaiomere, who obsessed so much over right and wrong that such details would only cause her undue stress.

Eventually, she relaxed in his arms and buried her head in his chest, though he heard faint sniffles every few moments. His gaze wandered past her, out towards the west clearing, and his mind was brought almost jarringly back to the present, and what was to occur.

Gaiomere seemed to read his thoughts. "How much time do you have left?" she asked, her voice muffled against his shirt

Atlas shrugged. "Not long." He glanced down at her, attempting to school his face into an easygoing expression, and asked, "You're not doubting me, are you?"

"Never for a second," Gaiomere said unhesitatingly. She wrapped her arms around his neck and kissed him. "I meant what I said back in the North—nobody else I love is going to die."

Atlas blinked, his eyes raking over her face, before his mouth split into a grin. He leaned down to kiss her again, pulling her closer against his chest.

"Attie, come on!" Whitsom called.

They broke apart, and Atlas glanced towards the older boy, who was waving him over from where he stood between a couple of tents.

"Must be time," Atlas murmured, nerves surging beneath his skin. He glanced at Gaiomere. "Do you want to—"

"No," she said quickly. "No, I—I'll just wait with

Coral and Bettoni." She pressed her lips to his once again, fleetingly—Atlas wondered briefly if this would be the last time he kissed her—before she pulled back, whispering, "Good luck."

Dak and Talikoth had just gotten to their feet when Atlas came striding back into the campsite. As Atlas passed by his father, the older man stopped him with a hand on his shoulder. His face was impassive, but his eyes glinted. "Zyratier and I will meet you at five o'clock tomorrow morning to ensure that the train is secure and prepared for departure."

Atlas gave him a curt nod. He could not think of anything past this evening's excursion, and scarcely registered what his father said.

Talikoth stood there a moment longer—almost hesitating—and added in a low voice, "Jemahl likes to overcompensate in his strength, but it leaves his lower half vulnerable."

Atlas blinked, staring at him. He opened his mouth, and then closed it again, unsure what he was even going to say, but Talikoth had already walked away, his broad back tense and hands fisted at his sides.

Talikoth had given Atlas counsel on many things throughout his life. He was the one that taught Atlas to fight, long before Academy started. But Atlas couldn't remember a single occasion in which Talikoth had actually tried to *help* him. Atlas hadn't minded—it gave him a sense of responsibility that his peers didn't possess—an autonomy that wasn't afforded to the other boys his age. There had been times, though, decisions he'd had to make, for which he needed his father's wisdom, and Talikoth had not offered any.

So why *now* was he suddenly so willing to offer

his aid? Why, when Atlas would be facing Talikoth's own soldier, a member of the Inner Ring, perhaps his *favorite*, was he unexpectedly so eager to assist?

It had to be a trick. He was trying to lure Atlas into making a mistake, or into fighting in a way that would be advantageous to Jemahl. Talikoth had not gotten the opportunity to finish what he started on the battlefield all those months ago—he had been too heavily guarded to get the chance to kill Atlas, so he would allow Jemahl to do it for him.

Except, Talikoth *was* right. Atlas had watched Jemahl fight for years now. He was used to being the strongest person in the room, and that made him over-reliant on his muscles to win him the fight. He was slower than Bettoni, whom Atlas was used to fighting, and on top of that, he was cocky.

Atlas thought of Raider, and how confident he had been in his ability to incapacitate any opponent. Raider's punches were quick, and he utilized his reach.

Whitsom was only a little stronger than the average soldier, but he moved with such agility that he could easily take down an opponent with years of experience on him.

Atlas could, he decided, heed Talikoth's warning without relying on it too heavily. Jemahl had never fought anyone but highly trained Obarion soldiers and novice Renegades. If Atlas employed the things he'd learned from Raider and the rest of the Ramshacklers, his maneuvers might be unpredictable enough that maybe, *maybe*...he could win.

Whitsom waited impatiently by the fire. "You ready?" he asked, as Atlas reached him. His knees bounced nervously, but his face was set with determination.

Gratitude swelled in Atlas' chest, and he wanted to say something—something to tell Whitsom how much his loyalty meant, how glad Atlas was that the older boy had been assigned his guard, all those months ago, back at the Vedas' base. But when Atlas tried to speak, the words caught in his throat.

They reached the edge of the west clearing, and about a hundred feet away, Jemahl and Favio stood solemnly, their figures strangely magnified under the light of the moon.

"Almost thought you were gonna wuss out, traitor," Jemahl called, when he saw them approaching. "How come your pal didn't bring a body bag for you?"

Atlas arched a brow, stopping ten feet away and asking, "Are you just going to run your mouth all night, or are we going to do this?"

Jemahl snorted, and beside him, Favio sniggered. "This fool acts like he *excited* to die." He pulled off his shirt and tossed it, along with his gun belt, to Favio, who caught them deftly. Atlas did the same, passing his shirt and knife to Whitsom. He and Jemahl turned to face each other, simultaneously stretching their hands out wide on either side of their bodies.

Favio hurried forward and began to pat Atlas down, feeling his pockets and the folds of his pants. Whitsom quickly caught on and did the same to Jemahl. When they were both satisfied, Whitsom and Favio each took up their posts twenty feet away.

Atlas took a steadying breath and turned to step three paces away from Jemahl. His body thrummed with energy, but his mind was surprisingly calm. The brawny boy smirked self-assuredly. His posture was relaxed, as though he were about to play a game of cards rather than engage in a fight to the death.

"Mors Recti," Favio reminded them in a loud voice. "To the death. On my go. Three...two...one...FIGHT!"

Atlas half expected more taunting, but Jemahl instantly drove towards him with a heavy strike, so strong Atlas was sure it would have knocked him out cold if he hadn't ducked out of the way. He kept his weight in the balls of his feet, weaving under Jemahl's outstretched fists, keeping his body just at the end of the stronger boy's reach.

Jemahl was faster than he'd expected—faster than Atlas, certainly—but still not faster than Bettoni or Whitsom, and sparring against the two of them so often had given him the practice he needed.

He kept his eyes on Jemahl's chest. From there, he could see the twitch of the muscles in the older boy's shoulder and the tensing of his leg, just before he threw a punch. From the circumference of his vision, Atlas could see Jemahl's hips twist, just before he attempted to deliver a kick.

Jemahl was not, however, the youngest soldier inducted into the Inner Ring for no reason. Even as they fought, his dark eyes analyzed Atlas' movements. He could only keep dancing around for so long. Atlas' body was not used to fighting like Whitsom—even now, his calves burned, and his breath came in ragged huffs.

But Jemahl did not look unfazed either. He breathed heavily, and his punches were coming more slowly, if only slightly. The thick muscles cording his arms and legs were useful in putting power behind attacks, but they also meant he had more weight to carry than Atlas.

Atlas managed to dance around Jemahl for a solid three minutes before it happened: the brawny boy faked a left hook and his right foot came bulleting through the air, knocking Atlas off-balance. He stumbled sideways, and Jemahl took his chance, planting a foot into Atlas' stomach that propelled him backwards.

Atlas landed hard on his back and gasped for breath. As quick as lightning, Jemahl was on top of him, slamming his fists into Atlas' face. His ribs contracted under the larger boy's weight, and quite suddenly his lungs could not draw breath. It was no longer Jemahl on top of him, but Raider—cold, ruthless hatred etched onto his face as he pummeled Atlas with nothing less than the intent to kill, to end his life right there at the edge of a field of landmines in the middle of nowhere, with only Gaiomere there to watch, helpless, as the life seeped out of him—

But this was not Raider, and Atlas was not stranded in the North. This was the South, his home, and tomorrow he *needed* to lead this mission. He couldn't bear the disparaging look on Talikoth's face, if Whitsom carried his body back to camp, bloodied and lifeless. He could not bear the idea of Gaiomere boarding the train tomorrow, off to face the Flesh Flayers, without him there to protect her.

Atlas blinked the blood from his eyes and wedged his elbows between Jemahl's knees and his own rib cage, hooking a leg over the swarthy boy's foot. Summoning every ounce of strength he had, Atlas bucked his hips upward, and Jemahl fell sideways.

Atlas didn't waste a second—he rolled over top of Jemahl and hammered a fist into his sweating face, adrenaline surging. Jemahl's nose crunched against his knuckles, and the older boy groaned, kicking his legs in an attempt to get Atlas off—but he had made the mistake of keeping his feet together. Atlas got an arm around his ankles and pressed his legs to the side, landing heavily on the boy's stomach, his knee ramming into Jemahl's ribs. They gave a sickening crack, and the older boy let out a wail of pain.

And then Atlas' fists rained down on his face once again, and Jemahl's head slammed back against the ground, over and over, his eyes rolling back in his head, blood dripping down into his teeth, and Atlas could hear Favio screaming something but had no idea what; his ears were filled with a strange buzzing noise, and all Atlas could see was red.

But then Jemahl let out a gurgling noise, and blood dribbled from the corner of his mouth. Atlas' fist froze midair, his chest heaving, his lungs burning and sweat dripping into his eyes. He swallowed thickly, climbing off Jemahl and pulling himself to his feet. The pounding of footsteps approached, and a second later, Whitsom appeared at Atlas' shoulder. "Is he—"

"He's just unconscious," Atlas said, without looking at him. He glanced sideways at Favio. "He'll need a medic," he instructed coldly. "Go." The lanky boy did not hesitate and took off across the clearing in a sprint.

Whitsom's eyes bore into him, but Atlas could not look at him. "I should have stopped sooner," he muttered quietly. "I—I was out of control of myself."

"A lesser man would have killed him, unconscious or not," Whitsom reasoned. Atlas scoffed, shaking his head and kicking at a loose rock. "Don't beat yourself up, Attie. He's the one that challenged you— and he wouldn't have shown you the same mercy."

Whitsom was right, but that didn't stop the shame from bubbling in Atlas' stomach. Jemahl was ruthless, and in many ways, his death may have been a mercy to others. How many Renegades had he handed off to the tribe in the mountains, under Talikoth's orders? How many more had he killed? The Westland might be safer, without a soldier like him treading its ground...Atlas just wasn't sure that was his decision to make.

Favio reappeared moments later with Hix. He grasped Jemahl under the armpits and the blond boy grasped his ankles. Together, the two of them began an awkward shuffle back towards the campsite. Whitsom and Atlas watched them go in silence. The adrenaline was only just beginning to fade from Atlas' body, replaced by a staggering fatigue. Whitsom must have read his mind, for he muttered, "Let's get back to the camp. Your head's bleeding pretty bad."

Atlas had expected most everyone to be asleep by the time he and Jemahl were done, so he was rather surprised to see a crowd still surrounding the fire. Talikoth, Dak, and Kordell were whispering quietly to one another, and Moonstone stood near one of the tents. Coral and Bettoni gaped after Favio and Hix, who were helping Jemahl into the medical tent. When they turned to face Atlas, they both broke into wide smiles.

"*You* did that to Jemahl!" Coral burst out. "I mean, did you *see* his face—"

Despite his exhaustion, a grin tugged at Atlas' lips. "You see why Whitsom's my second? At least he had a little faith in me." Whitsom sniggered, and Coral rolled his eyes.

Atlas could see the tension seep from

Moonstone's shoulders as her eyes fell upon him, and her expression morphed from apprehension to relief. "Atlas. Glad to see you're alright." She glanced sideways at Talikoth and Dak before adding, "As much as I will strive to respect your clan's traditions...I *would* ask that you refrain from engaging in any more fatal duels—at least until the completion of your mission."

He grinned, giving her a salute. "Will do, General."

"You have to tell us what happened," Bettoni said eagerly as Atlas sank down tiredly onto a concrete slab.

"Aw, let him tell you tomorrow, Bet," Whitsom said.

Coral was still reeling, his expression animated as he exclaimed, "His *ribs* were caved in, I mean, did you *see* it?"

"I'm gonna go grab some bandages," Whitsom said, squeezing past Coral, who was bouncing on the balls of his feet, and making his way towards the medical tent.

Atlas' gaze unwittingly darted towards Talikoth. His father was already looking at him, dark eyes glittering. The man's expression was impassive, but when their eyes met, he gave Atlas a nod, and for all Atlas wanted to fight it, his grin broadened.

"Where's Gaiomere?" he asked, snatching up a piece of chicken that one of the soldiers had left near the fire and popping it into his mouth.

Bettoni was not looking at him, but Atlas could practically hear the smirk in his voice as he quietly murmured, "She's uh—she's waiting in your tent."

Atlas had been trying to peel another slice of chicken from the bone when Bettoni's words registered, and he dropped it. "What?"

"She's waiting in your tent." The expression on Bettoni's face was decidedly smug as he glanced sideways at Atlas, adding, "and if you hurry, we can convince Whitsom you just wanted to get some shut-eye."

Atlas sprang to his feet, scooting around Coral and hopping over the barrel that Luca and Clancy had been using as a card table. Whitsom emerged from the medical tent, a bundle of bandages in his hands. "Where are you going?" he demanded, bewildered.

Coral and Bettoni sniggered behind him, but Atlas ignored them. "Got to get some shut eye," he told Whitsom unblushingly. "Big day tonight—um—tomorrow—need my rest."

Whitsom looked between Atlas and the guffawing buffoons behind him suspiciously, but Atlas quickly said, "Night Whit—thanks for backing me and all. See you tomorrow!" He took off across the campsite, glancing over his shoulder to ensure that Whitsom had, in fact, rejoined the others around the fire, before slipping inside his tent.

Gaiomere was pacing anxiously in front of his sleeping bag, tugging at her necklace. As soon as she saw him, she let out a heavy breath. "You're okay," she said softly.

"Yeah," he said, not really knowing what else to say.

Her eyes fell to his bare chest, before darting back up to his face, and her cheeks bloomed with color. "You're bleeding," she observed, hastily scrambling for her bag. She withdrew a couple of bandages and antiseptic wipes. "I figured you would be. I also figured you wouldn't go to the medics..."

She was rambling nervously, and Atlas couldn't help but smile. He crossed the tent, sitting down in front of her, wincing only slightly as she wiped the cut on his forehead. Her other hand rested against his chest, and the feeling of her palm on his bare skin sent a pleasant shiver down his spine.

"I know I said I didn't doubt you, but I—I was so scared you wouldn't come back," she mumbled, carefully pressing a bandage to his forehead. His eyes were intent on her face, and it took him a moment to register what she had said. "Alive, I mean."

"I didn't have a choice," he told her honestly. "I need to be there tomorrow. To keep you safe."

She rolled her eyes, letting out a huff of breath that sounded like a cross between amusement and exasperation. "You don't *need* to keep me safe," she muttered. Her fingers fell from his forehead and brushed over his cheekbone, where he could feel a bruise blooming. "Just like you didn't *need* to step in when Jemahl was being an idiot. You don't have to feel obligated—"

"I don't feel obligated," he said, frowning. His hand had lifted to cover hers, pressing it closer to his chest. He was sure she could feel his heart pounding against her palm. "And it's not because I think you're —you're weak, or helpless, or something, I just—I love you." The words felt strange, coming from his mouth, for he'd never said them to anyone before, but as soon as they'd left his lips, he found that he meant them. "I like keeping you safe. I want to. Won't you let me?"

Gaiomere watched him intently, her brows knitted and teeth agitating her lip, but after a moment, she nodded slowly. He leaned down to kiss her, and when the broke apart, he quietly asked, "Will you stay?" His cheeks burned with heat, and he hastily added, "If—if you want—I mean. It's not like you have to—"

She laughed, pressing her lips against his once more as she climbed into his lap, looping her arms around his neck. "I want to," she whispered against his mouth. He grinned, kissing her more firmly this time, and there were very few words exchanged between the two of them the rest of the night.

CHAPTER TWELVE

A s luck would have it, Whitsom was just passing Atlas' tent when the two of them emerged from behind the flap the next morning. When his gaze fell on them, his eyes widened to saucers, and a strangled noise escaped from the back of his throat.

"Morning, Whit," Gaiomere said pointedly, rolling her eyes.

Whitsom managed to force out a high-pitched, "Morning!" but Atlas did not miss the way the shorter boy carefully avoided his gaze. The three of them walked in silence to get in line for breakfast, and it was not until Gaiomere wandered off to ask Moonstone something that Whitsom leaned over a platter of sausage, looked at him very seriously, and said in a low voice, "Okay, look man—I *love* you. I'd take a bullet for you, dude, but—if we're gonna be tight, we gotta pretend this ain't happening, okay? We don't talk about it, we don't allude to it, *nothing*, you got it?"

Atlas' cheeks flushed, and he nodded hastily, forking a couple of sausage links onto his plate. "Agreed."

"Cool."

The mood around the campsite was solemn. Many of the soldiers looked pale and uneasy, and even Atlas could hardly finish his sausage before it was time to meet up with his father and ensure the train was secured.

Talikoth waited near the stairwell, his two guards posted on either side of him, their guns resting lazily against their shoulders. Zyratier and Kordell were already in their Inner Ring garb—black and red uniforms, identical to the rest of the Obarion soldiers' except for the bright red insignia on their left shoulders.

"You weren't lying, Kordell," Zyratier said, his voice muffled from behind his headgear. "Hardly a scratch on him."

"Is Jemahl recovering alright?" Atlas asked politely.

Kordell snorted. "He'll be hanging back here with the medics—boy can hardly walk."

As the four of them made their way down the stairwell, Zyratier glanced over his shoulder and asked gruffly, "Why didn't you kill him? General Talikoth said you were in perfect position to do so."

Atlas' head whipped towards his father, who was gazing down the tunnel, his face a blank mask. "You were watching?"

Talikoth lifted a shoulder indifferently. "Whitsom didn't grow up in the clan—he isn't well-versed in our traditions. I wanted to ensure there wouldn't be any foul play."

Atlas' eyes narrowed as he watched his father carefully. "You could have asked Zyratier or Kordell to keep an eye out—or any of the soldiers, really—"

Talikoth's brow furrowed, and he shot Atlas an annoyed look. "I was trying to spare you the embarrassment—I was sure Jemahl would make a fool out of you, after all." They reached the landing, and before Atlas could reply, Talikoth strode to the opposite end of the platform. Atlas fought down a smirk and moved to examine the railcar nearest him.

By the time Kordell had finished securing the couplers, the soldiers had begun to file down the stairs. Whitsom passed out handcuffs, and Atlas spotted Gaiomere towards the back of the group, fiddling with one of the tracking devices. She spoke very quickly to one of the Obarion programmers, as well as Moonstone, who looked very out of place in the Inner Ring uniform.

"Twenty to a car!" Kordell called over the soldiers' nervous chatter. "And keep those cuffs close—you'll need to put them on in ninety minutes!"

Though there were a hundred cars, the massive water tanks took up most of the standing room inside them. Each tank was connected to the next by a thick, heavy-duty pipe that ran from car to car. Twenty people cramming into each railcar was a stretch, with how vast the tanks were, but it was essential that they maintain the norm that Talikoth had established in the previous exchanges.

"—since the interference should be negligible, they should only need a reset if the readings become inaccurate," Gaiomere was saying.

The engineer she spoke to nodded patiently, though his expression was rather amused. "Yes, Gaiomere, you've told us five different times—"

"You'd be welcome to stay, to ensure the proper operation of the tracking devices," Moonstone suggested. "After all, nobody knows them better than you."

Gaiomere glared at her, and then turned her narrowed gaze on Atlas. "Did he put you up to this?" He held his hands up in front of his chest, trying to look as innocent as possible, and she rolled her eyes.

Zyratier moved down the platform, pulling the heavy freight doors shut. "We're all set," he announced, once he'd reached them.

"Very well," Moonstone said, nodding. When her eyes met Atlas', her gaze was heavy. "Since I won't have a chance to say so when we get there, good luck." Atlas nodded, shaking her outstretched hand. She climbed into the car next to theirs, and Zyratier shut the door behind her.

Whitsom and Gaiomere were both looking at Atlas expectantly, so he swallowed thickly, climbing into the car behind Talikoth, and the siblings followed. Zyratier slammed the door shut, and the group of them were plunged into darkness.

Weighty silence fell over them, and Atlas finally grasped, like a bolt of lightning, the peril of what they were about to do. Fear like a tidal wave swelled in his chest, and his ribcage tightened, as though constricting his lungs. For a moment, he contemplated shoving his way back to the railcar door, forcing it open, and clawing his way out of this dark, dank, grave they had willingly deposited themselves into—that *he* had foolishly led his friends and comrades towards, without a thought, without even a *shred* of rationality—

But then Luca's voice broke through the dark in a whisper. "*Solo me pregunto,* would this be a good time to tell ghost stories, or *no*?"

Atlas' lips reluctantly tugged up at the corners, and skittish laughter scattered across the railcar. Gaiomere's hand found his in the dark, and he tugged her closer. She tucked her head beneath his chin, and some of the anxiety swelling in his chest shriveled.

The engine kicked on, and after a few minutes, the train lurched forward. Under normal circumstances, Gaiomere would be breathless with excitement, flitting around the train, perhaps even attempting to stick her head out of the car door to observe the way the wheels moved. But she just huddled close to Atlas, her hands clutching the front of his shirt.

"You okay?" he murmured quietly.

She nodded against his chest, mumbling, "I'm just afraid."

The train began to pick up speed, and they must have emerged from the underground, for the dim morning light suddenly filtered through a thin, transparent panel at the top of the car. He could see the soldiers clustered around him. Luca and Zarr sat cross legged on the ground, and were dealing a deck of cards between the pair of them, significantly more at ease than anyone else around them. Cami leaned against Yacielle's shoulder, and Whitsom's eyes were closed as his head rested against the side of the car, his face looking older than Atlas had ever seen it.

Talikoth's jaw was taut, and his eyes stayed fixed on the ceiling of the railcar. Atlas wondered, as he had so many times when he was a boy, what was going through his father's mind.

Whitsom sunk down onto the floor, leaning his back against the cold metal of the railcar, and Gaiomere and Atlas joined him. There was an unspoken affinity between the three of them in that moment, as though they were all thinking the same thing, but none of them needed to say anything at all. Gaiomere's hand grasped Whitsom's, her head resting on Atlas' chest, and his arm wrapped tightly around her.

They had been traveling for at least an hour when Gaiomere's breathing slowed, and Atlas realized she had fallen asleep. He glanced at Whitsom over her head and found the older boy already looking at him.

"Attie, look..." Whitsom began. His voice was thick, and he had to swallow before he continued, "If it comes down to it, if you gotta make a choice between me and her—"

Atlas' jaw tensed. "I know," he said quietly. "But it goes both ways." Whitsom nodded, his expression uncharacteristically serious.

Gaiomere jerked awake when Talikoth called, "Fifteen more minutes. Cuffs on." The oppressive tension that had enveloped them upon boarding the train returned, and the soldiers were morose as they wordlessly cuffed themselves. Gaiomere's fingers trembled as she pressed the cuffs closed around her wrists, and when she looked up at Atlas, her eyes were round and petrified.

"It's not too late, you know," he murmured in a low voice. "You could stay on the train—or pose as one of the Inner Ring soldiers—take the water back with Moonstone and Talikoth—"

But even before he finished speaking, he could feel her resolve between them, firm and unwavering. "I can be afraid and choose to do it anyway." Her lips suddenly quirked upwards into a smirk, and her eyes glittered mischievously. "Besides, what have you and I got to fear?" He arched a questioning brow, and she clarified, "Doesn't fate bend to the will of the Obarion people?"

He stared down at her, a slow, disbelieving smile stretching across his mouth. Atlas leaned down and pressed his lips to hers, uncaring that his father was standing two feet away.

But then the train lurched to a halt. They broke apart, and Gaiomere's eyes shot towards the railcar door. Atlas straightened, his gaze meeting Talikoth's. His father gave him a firm nod, and Atlas, Whitsom, and Gaiomere stepped back against the wall so Talikoth could pass.

Yacielle and Cami both stood stock-still, their cuffed hands hanging limply in front of them, and even Luca and Zarr looked apprehensive.

"On guard—any sign of unnecessary endangerment for any one of us——you know what to do," Atlas told them. The group nodded. He leaned his head near Gaiomere's ear and added lowly, "Stay close to Whitsom and I." She was not looking at him, but her head bobbed jerkily.

And then, quite suddenly, the railcar door slid open, and Talikoth stepped off the train. "Let's go," he called coldly over his shoulder.

They filed out behind him, one by one, and on either side of them Atlas saw the inhabitants of the other cars doing the same. He spotted Moonstone a few cars down, her black hair protruding from the bottom of her helmet, her shrewd eyes flickering over the clearing.

The supplier train had just pulled in as well, and as Atlas watched, a door near the front slid open. A man jumped from the railcar, his boots hitting the ground with a heavy *clunk.*

He was perhaps an inch or two shorter than Talikoth, with inky black hair and ghostly pale skin. He wore black from head to toe, and when he turned his head, Atlas saw that his eyes were a piercing shade of blue. His gaze wandered over their group, which now stood clustered in a pack outside of the train. Moonstone, Dak, and the others posing as Inner Ring soldiers put forth a rather admirable performance—as they shuffled towards the center of the clearing, Atlas saw Harcliff ram the butt of his gun into Clancy's back.

A lazy grin spread across the black-haired man's face, and he stretched his arms wide on either side of him. "Talikoth! You never disappoint me."

To Atlas' surprise, the corners of his father's mouth lifted, and he strode forward to shake the man's offered hand. "I'd be remiss in doing so, I think," he said smoothly. "With all of the provisions your people have granted us."

"Likewise, likewise." His eyes were roving over the cuffed soldiers with a degree of curiosity. "Always fun, scoping out the new stock."

Beside Atlas, Gaiomere made a quiet noise, something between disgust and fury.

The black-haired man seemed to shake himself from a stupor, and he half-turned, snapping a finger towards the figures behind him, whom Atlas had scarcely noticed. "Let's get them hooked up, then. Chop, chop!"

There were around fifty of them in all—mostly large men, much older than Atlas—but he spotted a few women, and even a young boy that looked to be only a year or two older than Rasta.

"They don't *look* like Flesh Flayers," he heard Gaiomere whisper to Whitsom.

From all that Atlas had seen of Flesh Flayers, he couldn't disagree. The Flesh Flayers they had encountered in their travels looked...well, *repulsive.* Gaiomere theorized it was because their bodies weren't designed to consume the elements that their diet consisted of. Their teeth were usually rotting, their hair bedraggled and thinning, and their skin bilious.

As far as Atlas could tell, though, these Flesh Flayers looked relatively normal. Or at least, he didn't *see* any yellowing teeth or blood encrusted in their nails.

There was a sudden, loud churning noise, and Atlas realized belatedly that it was the water pump turning on. The train behind them vibrated as the water flowed from the Flesh Flayers' train to theirs. Atlas felt a small wave of relief then, because if nothing else, the Obarion people back at Headquarters would have water for another three months—even if Atlas and his team failed.

Whitsom made a strange, jerking movement, and Atlas and Gaiomere both looked at him. His gaze was affixed on something across the clearing, his eyes glassy and his mouth hanging open.

"What is it?" Atlas murmured, frowning. Gaiomere, too, was now staring across the clearing.

"Gwen," Whitsom breathed. His throat bobbed as he swallowed thickly.

Atlas' brows furrowed. "Whit, what—what are you saying?"

Gaiomere leaned towards him and whispered, "That's Gwena."

They peered at a gangly redhead girl, with so many freckles that she nearly looked tanned, who was fiddling with one of the connectors on the pipeline, her hands coated with grease.

Talikoth and the Flesh Flayers' leader were

talking quietly, and a few of his men were circling the soldiers now. One of them nudged Ando with a long staff, and the brooding boy shot him a glare.

"What's she doing here?" Atlas asked, looking back at the redhead girl. She had finished with the pipe and was making her way over towards the black-haired man. Neither of the siblings answered him —Gaiomere's eyes were narrowed suspiciously as she watched the older girl cross the clearing, but Whitsom's gaze followed Gwena steadily, as though willing her to make eye contact with him.

"Big, that one," the black-haired man said, jerking his head towards Atlas. "Can't imagine he was an easy catch."

Talikoth spared him a brief, disinterested glance, before snorting, "Big, but stupid."

Atlas scowled.

"Alright, get 'em loaded!" a bearded fellow shouted, slapping a hand against the side of a railcar.

Harcliff and Moonstone ushered the closest group towards the Flesh Flayers' train, their guns aimed at the soldiers' backs, but Atlas' focus was on the black-haired man, who had ambled over and stopped in front of him. His hands were folded behind his back, and even though he stood a few inches shorter than Atlas, he looked at him in such a way that Atlas felt *he* was the one being looked down upon, not the other way around.

"Big and stupid," the man repeated, his lips tilting up into a smirk. His eyes flickered over towards Gaiomere then, partially obscured behind Atlas and Whitsom, and his smirk widened. "And a pretty little thing," he crooned. He reached out a hand, as though he were going to touch her face, and Whitsom and Atlas moved simultaneously, both stepping towards each other, obstructing his path.

The man tilted his head, and his mouth twisted into a sneer, but before he could speak, a voice called from behind him, "We're ready for the next group."

Whitsom's head shot up. It was Gwena who had spoken, and she most certainly had seen her former tribe members now. She stood ten feet behind the black-haired man, her eyes round like saucers, her freckles standing out against her blanched skin.

The black-haired man sighed heavily and took a step back, waving them along. Zyratier jammed his gun into Atlas' back, and Kordell shoved Whitsom forward. The boy beside him stumbled, his eyes still trained on Gwena. She was standing in the same spot, watching Whitsom as though she weren't sure she could trust what she was seeing in front of her.

"Focus, Whit," Atlas said to him, so quietly that his lips were hardly moving. "We can figure that out later, but right now, you've got to focus."

Whitsom nodded slowly, jerking his head forward and clambering onto the train behind Atlas.

The interior of the railcar was nearly identical to the Obarion's train, and Atlas briefly wondered if these trains had been designed once Talikoth struck the agreement with the Flesh Flayers, or if they had been in operation long before that.

"Fifty Flesh Flayers, two hundred of us, two to three Flesh Flayers per railcar," Gaiomere was enumerating in a hushed voice. "I saw at least fifteen machine guns—"

"Closer to twenty, there were a few fellows in the back that had some, too," Atlas corrected quietly.

Patz was the last to climb into the railcar. Atlas, Gaiomere, and Whitsom were pressed against the water tank, towards the front—Atlas wanted to make sure he could respond quickly, should the Flesh Flayers pose an attack. "I would guess they'd want at least one per car—"

But he broke off, for a bulky blond man with a gun strapped over his back clambered into their car, and he watched the group of them through narrowed eyes. A second man started to climb in after him, but a hand appeared on his arm, and a voice said, "I'll take this one, Pinoa. I've got to run some figures by Amarius."

The man stepped back compliantly, and Gwena took his place. He slid the door shut behind them.

It was another ten minutes before the train finally began moving. Gwena was speaking to the blond man quietly, though her eyes flitted over to Whitsom and Gaiomere every few moments. "I've got sixteen finished now, but we'll need more iron if Marathi expects anything else. Maybe Tantabar's feeling generous?"

The blond man shrugged lazily. "With this big of a crop, I'd be surprised if he weren't—although you never know. They're awfully temperamental." The redhead snorted.

Atlas' mind was working very quickly. What iron contraption could Gwena be referring to, that they needed sixteen made? And who were Marathi and Tantabar? From what he'd seen, Flesh Flayers typically did not bother much with manufacturing—but then, Flesh Flayers also normally did not live in groups this large, nor did they facilitate trade with the most powerful clan in the Westland.

The train was gaining speed now, and it felt as

though they might have been going downhill, for the car tipped forward. Gaiomere leaned her head against Atlas' shoulder, and Whitsom stared down at his cuffed hands, though every few moments, he would glance up at Gwena.

They must have been traveling for at least thirty minutes when Gwena suddenly leaned over and whispered something to the blond man. He gave a sharp nod, passing the machine gun to the redhead, and disappeared into what looked like a clumsily constructed gangway, the door closing with a loud *clang* behind him.

"What are you doing here?" Gwena asked immediately.

"What, so you're a *Flesh Flayer* now?" Gaiomere hissed at the same time.

"Course not," the older girl said immediately. "I can't—it's—it's complicated." She cast an anxious glance towards the door, before scrambling across the railcar and enveloping Gaiomere in a hug. She pulled back, peering down at the younger girl with furrowed brows, and brushing a few curls away from her face. "How is it you look about a decade older?"

Despite her trepidation, a reluctant smile pulled at Gaiomere's lips, and she admitted, "We've been through a lot the last six months."

Gwena looked over at Whitsom, and a current passed between them so intense that Atlas had to look away. It felt as though he were intruding on something private and intimate. "Hey, Whit."

"Hey, Gwen," he murmured back, finding her hand and giving it a squeeze.

"Are you going to tell me what you guys are doing

here? You can't have gotten captured by the Obarion."

Whitsom started to answer, but Gaiomere interrupted, arching a brow and intoning mockingly, "It's complicated."

The redhead let out an exasperated huff. "You guys have to get out of here. I can sneak you out when we hit the depot—"

"We can't," Whitsom interrupted. "We've got a mission to complete." Atlas glanced sideways at the older boy, but Whitsom didn't pay him any mind. "Gwen, why are you here? Working for *Flesh Flayers*—"

But the gangplank door started to open, and Gwena's eyes widened. "I'll explain everything when we make camp tonight," she whispered, hastily stepping away from them and resuming her post near the railcar door.

Atlas' mind was whirring the rest of the ride to the depot. He didn't understand what could be so complicated—either Gwena was a Flesh Flayer or she wasn't. And why would she be working with them if she wasn't? Last he heard, she had been captured by the Obarion—he previously thought that meant she would be sent to work on the rigs, but after he had learned what Talikoth *actually* did with the nomads...

Well, by all accounts, she should be dead. She would have been a part of the exchange that had taken place six months ago—why had she been spared, and why for so long?

As the train slowed to a crawl, adrenaline burst in Atlas' veins.

This could be it. There might be a necessity, in the next coming moments, for the soldiers to extract their hidden weapons, cut their cuffs, and fight. So much of their planning had been guesswork—but what more did they have to go off? Atlas presumed that the Flesh Flayers wouldn't have taken the entire tribe for the exchange—they wouldn't risk leaving the water source unguarded—and if this was only *part* of their tribe—well, how could knives fare against even *more* machine guns?

But what if this *was* their entire tribe? What if they began their attacks as soon as they had unloaded their captives from the train? Would they even stand a chance? Atlas knew how to disarm a gunned opponent, and he was confident in his ability to do so, but the others...had they gotten enough training? What if they were mowed down like animals?

Atlas grimaced, glancing down at Gaiomere. This was a terrible plan—and what was worse, he had put Gaiomere in harm's way. He'd worried she might sneak on the train—but could she have, *really*? No, he'd made a rash decision—a decision that might now cost her life.

The train lurched to a halt, and he and Whitsom shared a grim look. "Unload single-file," the blond man told them gruffly. "Anyone tries to make a break for it, I'll shoot. Any one of you gets away—I'll shoot the rest of them, and their blood will be on your hands."

The railcar door slid open, and bright, scorching sunlight came streaming into the car. The air was hot here, and so dry that each inhale felt burdensome. Atlas had expected the barren landscape, but even Niko's pictures could not have prepared him for how desolate it felt. He could scarcely see anything but cracked red earth in every direction, save for a lone cactus some twenty feet away.

"*Mierda,*" Luca muttered, letting out a whistle.

"No wonder they eat people—there's nothing else out here!"

"They could move," Gaiomere snapped. "Travel around like the rest of us do." Gwena was walking a few feet away from her, and Gaiomere shot the older girl a cold look, "There's no excuse for this kind of evil."

Gwena frowned, and opened her mouth to reply, but the black-haired man, who stood near the head of the train, called, "Gwena, darling, I need you."

"Gai, stop being like that," Whitsom said, as soon as she'd walked away. "I'm sure whatever reason she has for being here—"

"There is *no* reason she could give me for being here that would justify it!" Gaiomere hissed.

Whitsom didn't get a chance to answer, for at that moment the blond man began ushering them towards the other side of the train, his gun hitched over his shoulder. When they all were gathered on the south side of the train, the black-haired man moved to stand in front of them, his hands folded behind his back, his smile oddly serene.

"Listen carefully," he called. "My name is Marathi. In a few days' time you will be freed from the miserable confines of your mortal existence."

Atlas glanced sideways at Gaiomere. Despite the gravity of the situation, her lips twitched.

"This dude gotta be playin', right?" Whitsom muttered.

"We will feed you and give you water throughout our journey. In the end, your death will be swift and painless. Look gratefully upon your merciful captors, who deemed you worthy enough to spare your suffering. You will—"

He blinked, his piercing eyes narrowing, and Atlas realized only belatedly why he'd broken off. Zarr was waving his cuffed hands in the air, his brows raised expectantly. "Um...yes?"

"I was just wondering how long you've been practicing this speech—objectively it's pretty subpar—" The Flesh Flayer nearest him slammed the butt of his gun into Zarr's stomach, and the boy doubled over, letting out a cry of pain, but his words had done what they meant to. Scattered titters broke out among the captives, and the Flesh Flayers shifted uncomfortably. They must have been conscious of the fact that, guns or not, they were outnumbered four to one.

"Enough!" Marathi cried, scowling. He jerked his head, and the man who had attacked Zarr tugged the black-haired boy to his feet and dragged him out in front of the rest of the soldiers. "If you're so fond of making jokes, perhaps we shall make an example out of you."

The Flesh Flayer aimed his gun towards Zarr, and for a split second, pure, genuine fear flashed across the boy's face.

"Wait!" Atlas yelled. Marathi's head whipped towards him, and several of the soldiers on either side of him looked at him too. Atlas straightened his back, separating from the rest of them and striding towards Marathi. "You have an agreement with Talikoth, that's clear," he said. Atlas surprised himself, for he sounded self-assured, though inside his heart was pounded against his ribcage. "And I would be willing to bet Talikoth would be very displeased if any of us were to find our way back to his territory."

Marathi's piercing eyes assessed Atlas. "Don't

worry," he said finally. "You won't."

"Oh, but we will—if you proceed." He glanced over his shoulder at Marathi's comrades, and pointed out, "It's simple arithmetic, isn't it? Suppose you *do* make an example out of him—we'll all rush your gunmen—even if forty of us are slaughtered, the other hundred and sixty will be more than capable of overtaking them. And when we do, we'll go running straight back to the coast—and Talikoth, I'm sure, will be very curious as to why the terms of your agreement are being breached."

Marathi's eyes were still narrowed, but Atlas saw a flicker of something like fear in them. "Talikoth needs us just as much as we need him," he pointed out. "If he doesn't bring us barter, we won't provide water—"

Atlas snorted. "Then he'll take it himself."

The black-haired man sneered. "He'd never find it."

"I doubt it would be very challenging for him, with all of the resources at his disposal," Atlas lied smoothly. He arched a brow. "Or perhaps you'd like to find out?"

Marathi gazed at him with trepidation, but there was a sliver of suspicion beneath it now, and Atlas realized too late why. No ordinary Renegade would be willing to threaten their captors with the onslaught of their supposed enemy. He was sure he had blown it— had exposed them all, and Marathi was about to blast a hole through his head before he did the same to the rest of his company, just to show that he had no fear of Talikoth or his army—

But then Marathi stepped back, giving his gunman a solemn nod, and the man lowered his weapon, grasping Zarr's shoulder and shoving him back towards the rest of the group. "Let's move out," he called to his comrades. "We'll need to hit Quagragar by nightfall." Around them, the Flesh Flayers began to jostle the soldiers together, forcing them into groups and directing them southeast. In the far distance, Atlas could see the cluster of mountains he recognized from Niko's pictures, but he couldn't begin to tell how far they were.

Marathi had not moved, and when Atlas turned back, the black-haired man was still looking at him.

"You know what I find peculiar?" he mused aloud, tapping his finger against his chin. "You almost sound like him—the way you speak. You even look a bit like him, too."

Atlas' heart dropped into his stomach, but he kept his face impassive. "I'm not sure who you mean," he said tonelessly.

Marathi was studying him with such intensity that Atlas might have shifted, if he weren't trying so hard to look unfazed. "Big and stupid," he said deliberatively, seemingly more to himself than to Atlas. "Very well, off you go." He tilted his head towards the dispersing groups, and after a moment, Atlas followed them, unsure if he felt relieved, or more uneasy than ever.

CHAPTER THIRTEEN

The Flesh Flayers pushed them thirty miles before they broke to make camp. Night had long since fallen by the time they stopped.

The gunmen hovered at perhaps twenty-foot intervals around the campsite, their weapons hitched over their shoulders as they paced along the periphery of the group, watching the captives with beady eyes. Several of the other Flesh Flayers began to unload scraps of wood from their large packs and worked on making fires.

To Atlas' surprise, Marathi's tribe removed their handcuffs, and for dinner passed around several platters of food to the soldiers. Most hovered nervously around the fires, their apprehension at their proximity to the Flesh Flayers warring with their desire for warmth in the frigid nighttime cold of the desert.

"They're fattening us up," Sitch remarked wisely. "Makin' sure there's enough meat on our bones to go around." This revelation did nothing to damper the enthusiasm with which he bit into his serving of jerky, however.

"Man, is this guy nuts, or what?" Coral remarked as he sat down beside Atlas and popped a couple of walnuts into his mouth. "He's all, '*You will be freed from the miserable confines of your mortal existence.*'" Bettoni and Whitsom, who had sat down across the fire from them, both sniggered at his imitation of Marathi's strange accent. "Like dude, how much herb have you been smoking?"

Gaiomere slipped into the spot next to Atlas, poking suspiciously at a bowl of rice, and Atlas draped his sweater over her shoulders, which were dotted with goosebumps.

"You think they actually make quick work of it?" Bettoni asked. He shifted uncomfortably, before clarifying, "You know, when they—when they eat people, and all."

"Depends how sadistic they are," Gaiomere mumbled grouchily, her gaze fixed on her uneaten rice.

Atlas had been mulling over all he'd overheard on the train, but he voiced his thoughts aloud now. "Maybe...maybe they aren't the cannibals," he mused thoughtfully. Four pairs of eyes looked at him, and he quickly recounted the conversation he'd overheard between Gwena and her comrade in the railcar.

"She's definitely making Marathi animal traps," Gaiomere said, as soon as he'd finished. "She'd melt iron ore into steel—"

"But why would she need to make animal traps, if they're eating—you know—" Coral grimaced, his nose wrinkling as he pressed on, "...people."

"Flesh Flayers can't *only* survive on humans," Gaiomere reasoned. "Think about it—if Talikoth is trading with them four times a year, and the largest batch ever was two hundred...well, they've got to be eating plants and animals too."

Coral looked as though he were going to be sick. "It's fine," he murmured, holding his stomach. "We're just casually talking about humans eating other humans—no big deal at all." As per usual, the rest of them ignored him.

"Maybe they're sharing the trade with this Tantabar dude, and the rest of his tribe," Whitsom offered. "They share the captives in exchange for the water?"

Atlas glanced over his shoulder to where Marathi lazily slouched against a rock. "Well, whatever they're doing, we've got to be prepared to act at a moment's notice. There's no telling how much time we'll have once we reach the water source—"

"Moonstone can send at least a hundred reinforcements on each of her planes, can't she?" Coral reasoned. "There's no *way* they can have bigger numbers than that."

"But that's assuming our reinforcements get here in time," Atlas said frustratedly. He wasn't sure the rest of the soldiers understood the urgency of the task at hand, or even how much peril they truly were in, should things not go according to plan. "We have *no* idea where they're taking us—even if it's only fifty miles—it would take at least an hour to load up the soldiers and get them to us. Marathi's guys could do plenty of damage in that time frame."

"Attie, you're being depressing," Coral said, snatching an apple off Bettoni's plate. "Tell him to cheer up, Whit!"

But Whitsom wasn't listening. His gaze was affixed on Gwena, who was winding her way between fires. She gave Whitsom a meaningful look, before she disappeared behind one of the Flesh Flayers' tents.

"Let's go," Whitsom said, nudging his sister. The pair of siblings wordlessly got to their feet and slipped between a couple of Vedas' soldiers, vanishing behind the tent after her.

"I'll be right back," Atlas muttered.

He found the three of them huddled between two tents, nearly invisible to anyone passing by, whispering furiously. When the redhead spotted him, her hand flew to the knife on her belt, and her eyes narrowed.

"Atlas is alright, Gwen," Whitsom said quickly, placing a hand on her forearm. "He's helped us through a ton these last six months. I'd trust him with my life."

Gwena rolled her eyes and gave Whitsom an exasperated look. "You've always been too trusting, Whit, we all know that—"

"I owe my life to Whitsom and Gaiomere as much as they owe their lives to me," Atlas interrupted quietly. "I can't vouch for my own trustworthiness, but I can promise that I always repay my debts."

Gwena's eyes narrowed even further, and she considered him carefully for a few moments. "He talks like a clansman," she said finally.

Gaiomere glanced between the two boys, before admitting hesitantly, "He's Obarion."

Gwena cursed, shaking her head. "Then why is he here? Why would Talikoth give up one of his own?"

Whitsom started to answer her, but Atlas elbowed him in the stomach, his eyes narrowed on the red-haired girl.

It was Gaiomere, though, who spoke for him. "Why are *you* here? Why are you working with Flesh Flayers?"

Atlas glanced sideways at her, and saw her mouth curled into a frown, and his shoulders loosened in relief. Whitsom, it was clear, had no apprehensions about

Gwena, or where her loyalties lay, but at least one of the siblings was on his side.

The freckled girl sighed, picking absentmindedly at the cuff of her sleeve. "They're not Flesh Flayers," she divulged. "The mountain tribes call them Blood Lenders."

Atlas' own confusion was reflected on Gaiomere's face, and it was she that spoke first. "If they aren't part of the tribe of Flesh Flayers, how come they're taking us to them?"

Gwena shrugged. "It's mutually beneficial. Marathi's not much more than a pawn taking orders—Tantabar's the real man in charge."

"And Tantabar is a Flesh Flayer?" Whitsom asked, and Gwena nodded.

Atlas' frown deepened. "Why didn't this Tantabar fellow facilitate the trade with Talikoth himself?"

The redhead snorted. "How would he have known to? He's never even heard of Talikoth. Most of the local tribespeople around here haven't ventured more than fifty miles from the mountains. Tantabar's tribe has only ever hunted around these parts—they might have even died off, if it weren't for Marathi."

"How did he get the in with Talikoth, then?" Gaiomere asked.

"Marathi's from the coast of the Westland—he led the tribe east almost two decades ago when Talikoth's clan moved in and started rounding up nomads like us." She gave the siblings a wry smile. "He's an opportunist, above anything else. He recognized that he didn't have the numbers or the guns to make a play for the water—not against a tribe as big as Tantabar's—so he capitalized on what he saw happening in the Westland.

Presented himself as the perfect solution to Talikoth's problem...and to Tantabar's."

"Why doesn't the Tantabar dude just make a snack out of Marathi's crew and deal with Talikoth himself?" Whitsom asked. "Sorry," he added, when he saw Gaiomere's disgusted face.

Gwena shook her head. "Look, Marathi may be crazy, but he's also clever. He's never told Tantabar where we get his supply—even if they followed us, they'd have no clue how to operate the train, or when to meet Talikoth for the trades—and Tantabar knows that Marathi would rather let all of us die than give up that information. It's the same reason Marathi doesn't tell Talikoth where the water is. It's his only guarantee that both of them will keep up their end of the deal."

"That still doesn't explain why you're here," Gaiomere pointed out, her brows knitting together.

"When I was captured by the Obarion, Marathi decided to spare me," Gwena said. "I told him what I could do—with the traps, you know? And he gave me a month to prove my worth. After that he just—he kept me on permanently." When Gaiomere's horrified expression did not shift, Gwena turned to face her fully. "Hellcat, they keep me *safe.* They give me food and water and I don't have to fear *anyone.*"

Whitsom's jaw was flexed, and he looked troubled. "What do they do with your traps?"

"We have all sorts of animals for meals—our boys usually take them into the mountains," Gwena said quickly. Atlas did not miss the way that she avoided Whitsom's gaze, and the furrow in his brows deepened.

"Well, we're gonna get you out of here," Whitsom assured her. "Then you won't have to depend on them anymore." She smiled gratefully up at him, but her smile flickered when she saw Gaiomere's glower.

"Hellcat...*you're* the one that taught me that we have to do whatever we need to survive," Gwena said, casting her a frustrated frown. "I don't understand why you're looking at me like that."

Gaiomere shook her head slowly, tearing her eyes away from the taller girl and scowling at the ground instead. "Not at the expense of other people," she said quietly. "Not at the expense of *innocent* people."

"I'm not—"

"Hey, what are you three doing over there?" A tan young man peered around the side of the tent at them, his gun trained at Whitsom's back.

"Sorry, Jacque," Gwena called easily, the tension melting from her face like wax. "I was just giving these three a talking to—they were trying to smuggle food in their pockets." She gave Whitsom a shove, back towards the fires, and grasped Gaiomere by the shoulder, steering her in that direction as well.

Atlas did not get the opportunity to speak to either of the siblings again. A couple of gunmen lingered uncomfortably close to them after the tent incident, and Gwena was careful to stay across the campsite for the rest of the evening.

They lay down on the hard desert floor as the fires died down to a faint crackle. Atlas wasn't sure he'd be able to get any sleep, especially with the armed Blood Lenders prowling the perimeter of the campsite like hungry cougars. Marathi seemed determined to keep his end of the deal, but if the Blood Lenders changed their minds and decided to slaughter the group of them in the middle of the night...

Eventually though, Atlas drifted off, though it must have only been for a few hours, for when he jerked awake at dawn, his eyes felt heavy, and his body moved sluggishly. He gently shook Gaiomere, who had fallen asleep curled into his side.

Around them the Blood Lenders jostled the other soldiers awake, and a brawny brown-haired fellow announced that they would depart in thirty minutes.

The day wore on much like the one before it. The group trudged wearily across the barren wasteland in strained uncertainty. None of them knew what to expect—when they would reach their destination, nor what exactly would await them.

It did appear, from what Atlas could tell, that they were moving towards the mountains. By the end of the second day, they only looked to be a few miles off. Niko insisted they'd scoured the area, but perhaps they'd missed something, nestled among the rugged peaks?

"Hey, I *said* no eyeballs!"

Whitsom's loud voice broke through Atlas' thoughts, and he glanced over to see him batting away a bird that Coral dangled in his face. Luca and Clancy were guffawing merrily beside him.

They'd stopped to make camp for the night. Most of the soldiers had grown significantly more comfortable, the more time had passed without any further occurrence beyond Zarr nearly being made buzzard food. This was largely due to the fact that, for the most part, the Blood Lenders left them alone. They didn't seem at all concerned with how much food the soldiers ate, nor how loud they argued and bantered, so long as none of them tried to make a run for it.

Gaiomere sat cross-legged on the ground beside

another fire, perhaps fifty feet from Atlas, Whitsom, and Coral's. Gwena was seated next to her, and the two of them had their heads bent together as they whispered unintelligibly. Atlas couldn't help the unease that rolled in the pit of his stomach at the sight. Something about Gwena's story didn't sit right with him. She wasn't being completely honest with them, and he worried that Whitsom might allow his affection for her to preclude his judgement.

The two girls suddenly got to their feet and moved away from the fire, and without thinking, Atlas followed. They stopped near the edge of the tents, and Atlas pretended to be refilling his plate at the folding table where the Blood Lenders had laid out a handful of platters.

"—can't be *that* valuable to him," Gaiomere was saying in a low voice. Gwena was much taller than her, so a shadow was cast over her face, but Atlas could still see the furrow in her brows.

The redhead shrugged, taking a long drink from her tankard. "He seems to find the traps valuable. But Marathi's a collector—I'm not the only one he's agreed to spare over the years." She nodded her head towards the brawny brown-haired young man, perhaps five or six years older than Atlas, who seemed to operate as Marathi's second-in-command. "That's Rich. About four years ago, Talikoth handed him over to Marathi, just like the rest of us, but he earned his keep. He can track anything—he's like a bloodhound, better than Whit even. Never seen anything like it. And Malum—" she pointed towards a skinny boy who could not have been much older than Luca or Zarr. "—that kid can slip into any crack or crevice. We call him the Weasel. It's like he doesn't have any bones."

Gaiomere's eyes roved over the Blood Lenders contemplatively. "But Gwena, it's still—can't you see what you're doing is just—it's just *twisted*—"

"Don't you think I could say the same about you, Hellcat?" the red-haired girl interposed. Atlas could not see her face, but he could tell from her voice she was scowling. "Since when are we friends with the Obarion? *More* than friends, by the looks of it..."

Gaiomere's cheeks darkened with color. "Gwena, Obarion or not, I trust Atlas with my life. The clan he comes from doesn't change that. But what you're doing —trading innocent people—trading *children*—"

"The operation would continue with or without me," Gwena said dismissively, shaking her head. "The Blood Lenders were trading with Talikoth long before I joined them—I'm just taking advantage of their protection." Gaiomere started to argue, but Gwena put a hand on her shoulder. "Hellcat, they could protect you —and Whitsom, too. Marathi would kill for a mind like yours on our side, and Whitsom's a damn good fighter —"

Atlas' stomach plummeted as he processed her words. He had never wished anyone dead before, but he wished it at that moment—wished that Gwena had not been spared. For not only was she remorselessly participating in a system so sick that Atlas could scarcely fathom it, but now she was trying to pull Whitsom and Gaiomere, the two people dearest to him in the world, away from his clan—away from their *own* clan—into some repulsive arrangement that benefited a select few at the expense of thousands and thousands of nomads.

Atlas dropped his plate with a clatter, and both girls looked over at him, but he ignored them and strode across the campsite, stopping twenty feet from where the last perimeter guard stood.

He swallowed the bile rising in his throat, his hands clenching into fists at his sides as he stared blankly out across the desert. His mind swirled with rage, and simultaneously, dread, though he could not actually seem to form any concrete thoughts. He wished that they were not so far out in the wilds, with nothing but cacti for company, for he wanted very badly to punch something.

Footsteps sounded behind him. "You okay?" Gaiomere asked quietly, stepping up beside him.

Atlas didn't answer. Instead, he looked down at her and asked, "Do you trust her?"

She bit her lip, tearing her eyes away from his and gazing out towards the mountains. "Yes...and no." She sighed, wrapping her arms around herself. "I trust that she'd never do anything to hurt me or Whitsom—but I don't trust her not to endanger this mission. And I don't think she cares what happens to the rest of you."

Atlas turned to face her fully. "Gaiomere, I need to know that you've got my back—even if that means fighting against her."

"I do," she said without hesitation. She glanced back towards the clusters of soldiers, adding, "But Atlas, I'm not sure Whitsom—" She broke off, her brows knitting together. "I'm just afraid that—that if it came down to it—he'd—he'd choose her. Even over me."

Atlas gave her a bewildered look. "You're his sister!"

Gaiomere shrugged. "I'm just not sure blood

means that much, in the end." He could tell that she was trying to appear unaffected, but there was an evident misery in her expression.

Atlas shook his head. "Gaiomere, it's—he's got to be able to see what she's doing—what she's participating in, it's—it's barbaric."

Gaiomere shot him an annoyed look. "*You* were part of a system like that once too, Atlas," she reminded him.

"Right, and you held it against me," he pointed out, scowling. "You hated me for weeks for no reason other than the fact that I was Obarion. Gwena *knows* what she's participating in—I didn't. I didn't have a clue what was going on behind closed doors."

"Oh, and if you had, you would have just walked out right there?" Gaiomere snapped. "Turned in your badge and kissed daddy goodbye—"

"Well I did, didn't I?"

"Only because you didn't have any other *choice*—you were wanted for treason!"

Atlas opened his mouth to fire back a retort, but froze. Whitsom and Gwena stood just outside the tent line near each other. The two of them had obviously been talking, but now they were watching Atlas and Gaiomere. Whitsom looked concerned, but the redhead's mouth was curled into a self-satisfied smirk.

"I'm sorry," Atlas said suddenly, lowering his voice and running a hand over his buzzed hair. "You're right —it's not fair for me to cast aspersions on anyone. I just think we need to be careful—even if you don't believe she'll hurt you, I want the rest of our soldiers to make it out of this unharmed as well."

Gaiomere blinked, staring up at him suspiciously,

as though not quite sure who she was seeing. "Oh—uh...it's cool. We shouldn't be bringing up things from ages ago anyway. That isn't fair for anyone."

The peculiar way she studied him made Atlas' lips twitch into a reluctant smile. "Do I really concede so rarely that it unnerves you that much?"

Gaiomere smiled, nudging his shoulder as the two of them turned to make their way back towards the fires. "You *are* unreasonably stubborn—"

"*I'm* unreasonably stubborn?"

She opened her mouth to blurt a comeback, but then stopped, her gaze fixing on something behind Atlas. He turned and saw the little Blood Lender boy a few feet away from them, carrying a stack of dirty plates that Atlas presumed he'd been on his way to wash.

"Hello," Gaiomere said, giving the little boy a bright smile.

He half-turned to look at her, stumbling a little, and a few of the plates slid off his stack and onto the ground, landing with a clatter. The little boy let out a squeak of surprise, scrambling to pick them up as he cast a terrified glance over his shoulder, towards where Marathi and a handful of other men sat.

Atlas determined that his initial assessment had been correct: the boy could be no older than twelve, though he looked shorter and skinnier than Rasta. He had a head full of blond curls, and his eyes were amber.

Gaiomere knelt down to help him. "I didn't mean to startle you. Do you want help with those?"

The little boy blinked. She passed him a couple of the plates he'd dropped, and his expression grew even more bewildered. Atlas wondered how awful his life must be out here, that such little acts of kindness befuddled him so.

"I'm Gaiomere," she continued. "What's your name?"

He shot another distressed look towards Marathi, before he timidly murmured, "Azaliah."

Gaiomere nodded her head towards the plates in his arms. "Are you sure you don't want help with those?"

He shook his head, his eyes, almost reflexively it seemed, darting over to his tribesmen once more.

She shrugged. "Well let me know if you change your mind, okay? It was nice to meet you, Azaliah."

His little cheeks pinkened. He started to turn away but stopped, piping up, "It was...nice to meet you, too."

Gaiomere beamed.

As soon as the little boy disappeared behind the tents, Atlas turned and gave her an exasperated look. "Gaiomere..."

"We'll get him out of here, once we've found the water, won't we?"

"How did I *know* that was what you were going to ask?" Atlas drawled.

"Is that a yes?" He opened his mouth to reply, but she pressed on before he could, "I just can't *stand* the idea of that poor thing growing up in a tribe like this—"

"He'll be fine," Atlas grunted, rolling his eyes. "He's survived this long, hasn't he?" She gave him a look, and he sighed. "If it's—*practical*, and it doesn't interfere with the priorities of our mission, we'll *consider* extracting him." Gaiomere smiled, pressing up on her tiptoes to kiss his cheek.

As he lay down that night to fall asleep, Atlas'

mind kept roaming back to the conversation he'd overheard between she and Gwena. The more he thought about it, the more resolutely he concluded that Gwena couldn't *actually* believe Gaiomere would willingly join up with a tribe that traded their own allies to cannibals. But she must've thought that if she could plant enough seeds of doubt in Gaiomere's mind —and probably in Whitsom's too—it might be enough to make them turn on Atlas, or to abandon their mission altogether.

The Blood Lenders were dependent on Tantabar's water. If Atlas divulged the truth to Marathi, would he and his tribe be willing to fight against the Flesh Flayers? They could take over the water source and share it among the clans and tribes—it would be a win-win situation for everyone involved—except the Flesh Flayers, anyway.

But the idea of working *with* the Blood Lenders did not sit well with Atlas. Sure, they weren't the ones actually cannibalizing the tribespeople—but they *were* complicit. And allying themselves with such a tribe wouldn't help dissipate the prejudice with which so many of the Obarion clanspeople regarded the Ren. Half of Atlas' people still believed the Ren were inherently more primitive than they—encountering a clan that embodied that very savagery they'd been warned against would hardly help anything. Atlas certainly wouldn't have garnered any sympathy for the Ren, had Marathi's tribe been the first he encountered.

Meeting Whitsom and Gaiomere, though, had flipped Atlas' entire perspective on its head. The two of them defied everything that Talikoth had taught him, and it had been his first red flag, the first indicator that perhaps he didn't understand as much as he believed.

Atlas stilled, his thoughts coming to a jarring halt.

Gaiomere and Whitsom had been the first to show him that the Ren weren't primitive and savage, as his father had taught—that others outside of the Obarion could offer more than just violence and chaos...

But Whitsom and Gaiomere *were* Obarion...so where did that leave him?

Atlas shook his head, scolding himself for such a thought. He had seen plenty of nomads that were just as intelligent and capable as the Obarion. Harcliff was wiser than two thirds of the Obarion officers, and Raider, Atlas begrudgingly acknowledged, had been smarter than almost anyone he'd ever known.

But then...over the past decade, the gangs had caused little more than chaos. By the time Raider took the mantle, they were a free-for-all attempt at anarchy. Atlas' mother was the one who successfully utilized them to undermine the strongest clan in the West. Without an Obarion in command, though, the gangs were little more than a nuisance.

Even the Vedas, for all their resourcefulness, had cowered pathetically in the North for sixteen years under the shadow of Talikoth's presence. It was not until Atlas had come around that they'd had the courage to take a stand—and without him, their attempts would have surely failed. It would be Moonstone rotting away in that prison cell, not Talikoth.

Not to mention the Blood Lenders—Renegades who *willingly* sold out their own people. And the Flesh Flayers—if that wasn't savagery, he didn't know what was.

Perhaps he should have known from the very

beginning that Gaiomere and Whitsom *couldn't* be Renegades—not when they were so civilized.

He shot a guilty glance at Gaiomere, fast asleep beside him. He didn't want to think about how she would look at him if she could hear his thoughts. But she wouldn't understand, anyway. She had grown up with the Ren—it was what she was used to. If she had been raised in the Obarion clan—if her father and mother had never left—she would appreciate Talikoth's obsession with order.

Atlas' stomach lurched, and he sat up very quickly. What was he *doing*? These people had protected him, fought with and stood beside him—they had defended him against his own *clan*. How quickly he'd turned against them. How ready he had been to cast them into the fire—to side with *Talikoth* of all people...

Atlas scowled, laying back down and rolling onto his side. He pulled Gaiomere closer to his chest, confusion and self-reproach warring like bile beneath his ribcage. The division between the warring clans, and the tribes of the Westland, could only bring about strife. Atlas knew this. It shouldn't matter that Whitsom and Gaiomere were Obarion—or that Marathi's tribe was perpetuating this sick, self-serving cycle—it *shouldn't*. Just because a few dozen Renegades fulfilled every stereotype Talikoth had ever cast upon them—well, that couldn't give the Obarion leave to write them *all* off.

That was what Atlas told himself as he tossed and turned for another hour at least. And when he finally drifted off to sleep, those were the words that colored the backdrop of his dreams—as though their repetition might somehow, eventually, help him to convince himself than he believed them.

CHAPTER FOURTEEN

The following day, they had ascended nearly three thousand feet up the mountain by noon. The higher they climbed, the more vegetation surrounded them—patches of tall pines and shrubs dotted the mountain side, and every now and again, Atlas spotted pools of water, shallow and murky, gathered beneath the shadows of towering trees. Nothing close to being large enough to supply an entire clan, though.

He'd hardly seen Whitsom all morning. The Blood Lenders granted them a brief bathroom break, and it was not long after they had begun traveling again that Atlas found out why.

"I know where the water is," the older boy whispered, sidling up next to Atlas with his gaze trained carefully forward. Rich, Marathi's second-in-command, walked only twenty feet away from them.

Atlas glanced at him quickly, before refocusing his attention towards the front of the group. "How do you know that?" he demanded, his lips barely moving.

"I got the information out of Gwen—I told her what we were doing, and she—"

"Wait, you *what*?" Atlas burst out. He glanced over his shoulder at Rich, who gazed at the two of them suspiciously, before lowering his voice. "Whit, you've jeopardized the safety of everyone here—"

"She isn't going to rat us out," Whitsom insisted. "She wouldn't. You honestly think she wants to be stuck here, making traps for this creep?"

Atlas said nothing. His pulse pounded in his veins, as though his body were already preparing him for an inevitable fight. Would Gwena have reported to Marathi already, what Whitsom had told her? Did they have time to orchestrate a change of plans?

Or was Whitsom right? Was it possible that Gwena actually *could* be trusted?

Atlas' uncertainty did not temper his anger. "I'm —I can't believe you did that, Whit, I—dude, I trusted you to be my second, and you—"

Whitsom frowned, though his face looked a bit abashed. "Attie, if you trusted me then, you gotta trust me now." His mouth twisted in an uncharacteristic scowl, and he mumbled, "I thought you'd be happy that I'd found out about the water—figured it'd be nice to be more help for once, since Gai's always stealing the spotlight..."

Guilt twinged at Atlas' stomach, but it wasn't enough to outweigh his frustration. "Where is it?"

"About five miles down the eastern mountain face—Gwen said that there's a huge cluster of nut pines to the south, and palo blancos to the north. Apparently our water source is smack dab in the middle." He cast another wary glance at the nearby guard, before continuing, "It's a cave—an underground lake, Attie— that's why Niko's boys couldn't spot it. The entrance is only about five feet wide, and concealed, on top of that. Marathi told her that's a big part of the reason he's never tried to fight Tantabar for the water—it would be too hard to launch an ambush."

Atlas' mind raced. Such a small entrance would make any kind of stealth attack difficult, for Tantabar's men could just pick them off, one by one. But Marathi did not have the numbers that the clans did.

He wished, beyond anything, that he had a way to contact Moonstone, if only to share this intel with someone *outside* of his own company, just in case things with Marathi went awry...

"We should send someone ahead, directly to the cave," Atlas murmured, almost to himself. "That way, Moonstone and the others can see the location on the tracker. They can mark coordinates on our maps—we can send in a full battalion—even with such a small entrance, Tantabar and the rest of them wouldn't stand a chance."

Whitsom looked uncertain, but they couldn't discuss it further, for a pair of Blood Lenders fell into step directly behind them, and they quickly silenced.

The group stopped for food perhaps half an hour later, and Atlas sank down onto a rock, peeling impatiently at an orange.

"How do you tell if it's any good?" he heard Coral ask Gaiomere. The curly-haired girl knelt beside one of the murky puddles at the foot of a cedarwood, refilling a water bottle that she had charmed off one of the Blood Lenders.

She dropped a few of the tiny black crystals into the water, explaining, "The detoxifiers have a built-in safety mechanism. If the water is drinkable, it will turn into some variation of blue—if the detoxifiers aren't able to clear out the toxins, the water will keep its natural color."

Bettoni's brows had disappeared beneath his hair.

"That's genius. You came up with that?"

Gaiomere shrugged, her cheeks pinkening as she pushed a wayward curl away from her eyes. "My dad's idea—I just helped develop them."

Coral and Bettoni both looked impressed. Whitsom rolled his eyes, tossing a pinecone at his sister from where he lounged across the ground. "Yeah, yeah, we all know Gai's the little golden child—don't inflate her ego."

"Fascinating," a quiet voice mused from behind them, so softly that Atlas almost didn't hear it over Bettoni and Coral's sniggers. Marathi was standing a few feet away from them, his hands folded behind his back, his pale eyes glittering as he surveyed Gaiomere.

Whitsom instantaneously sat up, and Atlas stiffened, shifting half a step closer to Gaiomere, who had frozen, her eyes wide.

Marathi approached her, peering at the detoxifiers in her hand. "May I?" A couple of gunmen lingered behind him, their postures relaxed, but their eyes were affixed on the group. It would take only a split second, just a signal from Marathi for them to react.

For a moment, it looked as though Gaiomere might refuse—her eyes had narrowed, and her hand momentarily tightened around the crystals—but then her grip slackened, and she wordlessly passed them to Marathi.

"Fascinating," he repeated, clicking his tongue as he held one of them between his thumb and his first finger, peering at it more closely. His mouth quirked into a smirk, and his eyes flitted over to Gaiomere once more. "Not just a pretty face then," he remarked. He reached out a hand, ghosting his fingers along her cheekbone, and she flinched.

Atlas was at her side in an instant. "That's enough," he growled.

Marathi ignored him. "What else can you do, little bird?"

"Nothing," Gaiomere said quickly, edging closer to Atlas. "Nothing, I'm—I'm perfectly ordinary, I promise."

The black-haired man laughed liltingly. "We'll see," he mused. "Maybe I'll keep you." He held out a hand, and after a moment, Gaiomere took the detoxifiers back from him. As her fist closed around the tiny black crystals, his hand wrapped around hers, and he bent his head to brush his lips over her knuckles before whirling on his heel and vanishing into the crowd of soldiers.

As soon as he'd gone, Gaiomere's shoulders sagged, and she let out a heavy exhale. Atlas immediately turned on her, peeling her fingers apart and pulling the rest of the detoxifiers from her grasp. "No more of *this*," he snapped, chucking them into the water. "What did I say, Gaiomere? You need to blend in!"

"I'm sorry," she said in a small voice. Normally, Atlas was sure she might have been angry, but she looked as though she were still frightened from her encounter with the Blood Lender's leader. And he was glad for it—she *should* be frightened. Maybe the fear would knock some sense into her.

"What were you *thinking*?" he demanded. "Gwena *told* you Marathi's a collector—what, you thought broadcasting how brilliant you are was a good idea?"

"I wasn't trying to broadcast anything," Gaiomere insisted. "I really wasn't—I didn't realize he was so close, otherwise I never would have—"

"Well, you should have been more careful!" Atlas said frustratedly. He ran a hand over his hair, turning away from her.

"We all saw her using them, At," Bettoni pointed out quietly.

Coral nodded. "Yeah, man—it's as much our fault as hers—"

"And anyway, no harm done," Whitsom reasoned, lugging himself to his feet. "Marathi's just trying to intimidate us—he didn't actually go and hurt her, and if he tries to, he won't get very far—"

Perhaps it was just that his irritation towards Whitsom had not yet faded, but something in Atlas snapped. "Do you want her stuck here like Gwena, then?" he demanded. "Running trade on human beings like barter?"

"Of course not!" Whitsom said, his dark skin turning blotchy with anger. "I'm just saying, you don't need to flip out on her—"

"Why shouldn't I? She was being reckless! Just because you're okay with that slime bag feeling your girl up in exchange for her safety doesn't mean he can do the same to mine—"

Like lightning, Whitsom was in front of him, his hands on Atlas' chest, shoving him backwards. Atlas stumbled a few steps. "Say that again," Whitsom said in a low, dangerous voice. He looked angrier than Atlas had ever seen him, and his hands were in fists at his sides, as though he actually might swing.

Atlas didn't care though. His throat was parched and his muscles ached and his body—which had been on high alert these past three days, waiting, just *waiting* for the moment they would need to fight for their lives

—sprang into action, coiled and poised, like a jungle cat preparing to strike. He shoved Whitsom back, glaring down at him. "I *said*, just because you're okay—"

"Oh, great gooseberries, *stop it*!" Gaiomere burst out. She managed to wedge herself between them, putting a hand on either of their chests and attempting to shove them both backwards, though she didn't manage to shift either of them so much as an inch. "Come on, guys, cut it out."

Coral and Bettoni looked between the two of them with wide eyes, and Atlas saw a few of the nearby soldiers staring at them, too. He knew he needed to pull it together—it wouldn't do for their leader to begin brawling with his chosen second—but anger was pumping through him faster than a flash flood, and his mind didn't seem to be working as clearly as normal.

Whitsom made the decision for him, though. The shorter boy scowled, pushing his sister's hand away from his chest and shoving past Atlas, striding over to where Yacielle and Olli sat on a couple of rocks.

"Atlas, what's gotten into you?" Gaiomere demanded. "Why would you say that to him?"

"He deserved it," Atlas grumbled, avoiding her gaze. She started to say something else, but he stalked away before she could, towards the edge of the clearing.

One of the perimeter guards, perhaps thirty feet away, eyed him warily, but Atlas ignored the man, pacing angrily between the trees, his breath coming harshly through his nose.

He knew he had been wrong, goading Whitsom, but he just couldn't understand how the rest of the soldiers weren't taking their situation more seriously. They were laughing and joking around every evening by the fires, greedily indulging in Marathi's food—as though this weren't a life-or-death mission that could directly contribute to the demise of the Obarion clan.

It might have been that they just didn't care. Almost half the volunteers were Vedas or Renegades—it wasn't the fate of *their* people that was on the line.

Atlas plunked down onto the ground, pulling his knees against his chest as he glared moodily at a nearby berry bush. He had made a mistake, involving so many soldiers that had nothing to lose. The Vedas and the Ren didn't care about the Obarion—they were hung up on the crimes that Talikoth had committed—crimes committed *years* ago.

The hundred-child slaughtering had been barbaric, certainly—but acts of brutality were par for the course in the game of war. The Westland would never be able to rebuild if most of its population was busy moping over the past—

A branch cracked ten feet away from him and Atlas' attention jerked back to the present. He jumped to his feet, his hand flying to the waist of his pants where his knife was hidden, as he peered into the foliage.

A low branch shifted, and a familiar head poked out from where he crouched behind a bush. Atlas' eyes widened, his mouth falling open. "*Niko?*" He whispered disbelievingly.

The scarred young-man lifted a finger to his lips, glancing towards the gunman near the tree line. The man was looking in the opposite direction, but even as Atlas watched, he peeked back that way to ensure Atlas hadn't ventured further away. A large tangle of shrubbery obscured Niko from the guard's view.

"What're you doin'?" the guard called to Atlas

gruffly.

"Just taking a whiz," Atlas replied easily. He waited until the guard was looking away again, before casually leaning against a tree near where Niko knelt. He kept his gaze trained forward. From his peripherals, he could see Niko's profile, and behind him, Grit and another Renegade Atlas did not know knelt as well, silent and unmoving.

"What are you doing here?" Atlas breathed, his lips hardly moving.

"Wanted to help." Niko glanced sideways at him, his voice bashful as he admitted, "Felt like shit that I bailed on you like that. But we wanted—we wanted to do something now." Atlas looked at him quickly, and saw that he was holding one of Gaiomere's tracking devices. "Moonstone's been following your course day and night, and she's had me and my boys tailing you. We were able to move in closer, once you guys hit the cover of the mountains."

Atlas was only half-listening. "Look, Niko, I need to tell you something."

He hastily recounted everything Whitsom had told him about the water, and as soon as he finished, Niko leaned back on his haunches, his brows furrowed in thought.

"You should send back for reinforcements—you guys could seize the cave before we even reach it," Atlas said.

Niko, though, looked uncertain. It reminded Atlas of the look of doubt on Whitsom's face, less than an hour before their argument, and it sent another pulse of anger coursing through him anew. "I'm not sure Talikoth will want to go straight for the water source before we've gotten more intel," he said slowly.

Atlas glanced at him in surprise. "Talikoth is still working with you?"

"Yeah." Niko hesitated, before adding reluctantly, "He's actually been uh—you know—relatively helpful. For the most part, anyway."

Atlas frowned. He would have thought that Talikoth would have gone back to his predilection for being unaccommodating as soon as the exchange transpired. "We've got the numbers," Atlas reasoned. "What's the sense in waiting?"

"It's not always best to go in guns blazing," Niko remarked, with a wry smirk.

Atlas scowled. He suddenly felt rather like a child, being condescended to.

"Take these," Niko said suddenly. Atlas glanced back to make sure the guard wasn't looking, and Niko stealthily passed him a pair of identical black orbs, smaller than a thimble. "They're earpieces—tiny little transmitters. "Keep an ear out—you'll probably be hearing from us soon—the rest of the reinforcements are waiting at the base of the mountain—"

"They're already *here*?" Atlas exclaimed. He had spoken louder than he'd meant to, and when he glanced over his shoulder, the perimeter guard was peering at him with distrust.

Niko grinned lopsidedly. "Just waiting for your go, boss man."

He started to turn away, but Atlas quickly said, "Wait, one more thing—tell Moonstone...and Talikoth, I suppose...tell them that these ones aren't Flesh Flayers." He quickly told Niko about the Blood Lenders.

"Ay—we're moving out, let's go!" the gunman near

the tree line shouted.

Niko gave Atlas a solemn nod and ducked back into the foliage.

The rest of the soldiers had begun moving by the time Atlas returned to the clearing. Gaiomere, Coral, and Bettoni were lingering towards the back of the group, and when he reached them, he immediately told them everything Niko had shared with him.

"I feel so much better," Gaiomere said, as soon as he'd finished. "Knowing the rest of them are so close, you know?"

"It is a comfort," Bettoni agreed quietly. He shot a glance at Atlas and quickly added, "Though I had complete faith in our soldiers and the plans we had made."

Atlas said nothing, but kept his eyes glued to the dirt shifting beneath his feet.

He felt unfathomably angry. Not the anger from fifteen minutes before, when he and Whitsom had been moments from bloodying each other's noses, but a slow, simmering anger, festering like a wound just beneath the skin.

Why had Niko needed to get himself involved—after the plans had already been made, and each person had been assigned their role? Was he really just that hungry for a bit of glory? And what did Moonstone mean, sending soldiers to tail them so closely? If Marathi or any of his tribespeople had seen them, it could have blown their entire operation.

And Talikoth...

Atlas' hands curled into fists, and his anger bubbled up to a boil.

What did his father think he was *doing*? He had

been involved more than enough—he had done his part convincingly during the exchange. He should have been returned to his cell until the successful completion of Atlas' mission—then released into some dank corner of the Westland to spend the rest of his days wandering the wilderness alone. So why was he *still* working with Moonstone?

Atlas' scowl deepened. Of course, Talikoth did not think Atlas was capable enough to lead this mission. He didn't care about the soldiers, nor did he care about the Obarion water supply—he just wanted one more opportunity to remind Atlas that no matter what he did, it would never be enough.

Atlas wished he had pulled the trigger, all those months ago. He wished he had blasted a hole right through his father's arrogant head, so that he could never again look at Atlas with that condescending sneer. So that he could never again speak to him with that patronizing tone. Never get the opportunity to undermine everything Atlas had worked to build.

Well, Atlas would show him. Moonstone might have already sent reinforcements, but he was still the leader of this mission, and not a single one of them would so much as sneeze without his permission, he'd make sure of that.

They reached the mountaintop late in the afternoon. Great, jagged rock jutted from the earth in every direction. The trees up here were few and far between, but further down the mountainside pines swayed against the brisk wind, and Atlas caught a glimpse of a copse of palos blancos in the distance. Perhaps they were close to the cave entrance.

They started back down the mountainside and

had descended almost a mile when Rich called for them to make camp. Some of the Blood Lenders dispersed to find kindling and logs for firewood, and the others began unpacking the food. Atlas plunked down on an old stump, irritably yanking off his boots and peeling the sweater from his back.

He spotted Gwena and Whitsom across the clearing. The redhead was spreading platters of food on a blanket, but the two of them were clearly talking. Atlas could not help but notice the pair glancing over at him every few moments, and when Atlas caught Whitsom's eye, he glared at the older boy.

Gwena looked decidedly smug—no doubt because she'd spent the rest of the afternoon poisoning Atlas' second against him. Atlas shook his head, looking away from them.

Even a week ago, Whitsom would unhesitatingly have gotten Atlas' vote for the person he trusted most—but Whitsom had been acting differently since discovering Gwena was alive. His priorities had shifted. Atlas understood, to an extent—Coral chaffed him any time Atlas elected to spend time with Gaiomere rather than he and Bettoni—but lately it seemed as though Whitsom would be willing to throw a lot more away for Gwena than a bruiseball game.

A small pair of hands rested on his shoulders, and Atlas glanced back to see Gaiomere behind him. Though he was seated, there was scarcely a few inches of height difference between them. "You're not going to be mad at me just because you're mad at my brother, are you?" she asked, smiling impishly.

Despite his vexation, a smile tugged at his lips. "I suppose that would be rather unfair, wouldn't it?"

She hummed in agreement, her fingers massaging the muscles in his shoulders, and he felt some of the tension melting away from his body as he leaned back against her. His eyes had drifted closed, and he groaned when she reached a particularly large knot in his upper back.

"Have you eaten yet?" he asked.

"I'm not really hungry," she said quietly.

Atlas did not registered her answer, though, for the transmitter that he'd shoved into his ear suddenly gave a great burst of static.

"*Kordell to Atlas.*"

"I'm here," Atlas murmured. He scrambled hastily for the other tiny earbud and worked it into Gaiomere's ear, so she could hear too.

"*We're a half mile out. Prepare for some commotion in the next ten minutes.*"

Atlas' eyes met Gaiomere's. The knit in her brows mirrored his own bewilderment. "You'd be better suited heading straight for the cave—we're fine here."

"*Talikoth believes that Marathi may be useful, given that he's interacted with the cannibals. He wants to interrogate him before we make any hasty moves.*"

"Why?" Atlas demanded. Gaiomere clutched his arm, and he lowered his voice. "We have the numbers—"

A crackle of static interrupted him, and then suddenly, it was his father's voice in his ear. "*Stand by, Atlas. Over.*"

Atlas let out a frustrated noise, and ripped the transmitter from his ear and slamming it against the ground.

Gaiomere sighed, absently carding a hand through her curls. "I hope Moonstone knows what she's doing," she said softly. "I'm worried if they don't go about things the right way, Marathi's gunmen will just start firing at all of us at random—"

"We've all got your vests," Atlas reminded her calmly, though inside he was fuming.

He couldn't understand why suddenly, inexplicably, the modus operandi that his father had utilized for as long as he could remember had suddenly been discarded. Storm in, show your muscles, ensure every dog in the fight knows who the alpha is—that had always been the way Talikoth played the game. So why *now* had that changed?

"Do you think they'll kill them, once we've gotten what we need?" Gaiomere asked suddenly.

Atlas turned his head away from her to hide his frown. He didn't want to admit how much it vexed him, that she had so much confidence in his father's plan. Who was to say what Marathi—or any of his tribespeople—would do? Talikoth couldn't be sure that they would cooperate. Gwena seemed certain that Marathi would rather let his entire tribe die than give Tantabar more information than he needed—why wouldn't he behave the same with Talikoth?

"Most likely," he answered finally. "They've played too big a role in all this."

"All of them...do you think?"

Gaiomere's tone was nonchalant, but when he glanced sideways at her, he could tell that her interest was not, in the way she carefully avoided his gaze. "You told me that you didn't trust her."

"I don't!" she said quickly. "I just—I don't know that it means she deserves to be killed. I mean—Atlas, she *was* just trying to survive—and she *did* tell Whitsom where the water is." He made a disparaging noise, pushing to his feet, and her arms slid away from his shoulders. "I'm not saying it wasn't *horrible*, I just—"

"You and your brother's loyalty isn't worth much, is it?" he said coldly. "Not when its stolen away from me so easily—"

He started to walk away, but she grabbed his hand. "Atlas—" He yanked his hand out of her grip, and started off again, but this time she clutched the back of his shirt.

"Let *go!*" he snapped.

"I won't!" When he turned back to face her, her eyes were blazing, and her face was contorted into a venomous glare. For a moment she looked like some avenging goddess, the kind he'd seen in ancient mythology books. Fiercely beautiful and deadly all at once. "I don't care if you think I'm being childish—you aren't just going to stomp off and pout every time we have a disagreement. That isn't how this is going to work."

Her words gave him pause, and he turned to face her fully. "You said you loved me," she pressed on. "Were you lying?"

His brows furrowed, and he stared down at her, bewildered. "No. Of course I wasn't."

"Then you have to trust me." He blinked, his head tilting to the side as he studied her. "I've got your back— I told you that. And I wouldn't say that if I didn't mean it."

She stood on her tiptoes, pressing her lips against his, and he wrapped his arms around her waist, wholly indifferent to the fact that there were soldiers and Blood Lenders on every side of them, uncaring, suddenly, if

Gwena *was* over there distorting Whitsom's mind to her whims. It didn't matter, for at least he had one sure bet, one person he could count on in his corner.

A loud *bang* ripped across the clearing, and the two of them broke apart.

The campsite suddenly grew deathly quiet. Marathi's gunmen all stood at attention, and the man himself had half-risen from his seat, his piercing eyes narrowed shrewdly in the direction from which the sound had come.

There was another *bang*, and then a tank came pummeling up the hillside, plowing down trees in its wake. Atlas' soldiers let out a clamor of cheers as they hastily scrambled out of the way. Their captors were in disordered havoc, and Marathi screamed orders at the top of his lungs.

Another shell ripped from the tank gun, hurtling towards a group of Marathi's men. Most of the Blood Lenders were focused on the tank, and Atlas wasted no time. He ripped his knife from where it had been attached at his hip, and around him, he saw his soldiers doing the same.

The gunman nearest him—Pinoa—had his back turned. Atlas closed the distance between them in three loping strides, slamming his foot into the back of Pinoa's legs. He was still gripping his gun, so it was nearly too easy for Atlas to knock him to the ground, bringing his knees down onto the Blood Lender's back. He grasped the man's head and swiftly swiped the knife across his throat. He hardly even registered the thud of the man's body hitting the ground before he wrenched the gun from his still-warm fingers.

Atlas shoved his knife into his pocket and moved

towards the next gunman.

This one had just turned towards him, and Atlas' torrent of bullets caught him in the side of his face. He grabbed the blood-drenched gun from where it fell on top of the man's corpse. "Here!" he called, tossing it to Joaz.

A glance across the clearing showed him that the Blood Lenders still had ten guns on their side. The tank was rounding towards a pair of Marathi's gunmen. On the other edge of the clearing, Atlas spotted Gwena, hiding behind a tree, her eyes wide and freckled face blanched. Whitsom was posted up behind a boulder ten feet from her, exchanging rounds with another Blood Lender, but Atlas could hear him shouting, "Come *on*, Gwen, *move!* You gotta run for it!"

Atlas scowled, shaking his head and turning away from them. He was about to start towards Rich—who had managed to land several shots on a handful of Atlas' soldiers—when a movement in his periphery caught his eye.

Gaiomere was darting between trees, skirting the clearing, her gaze focused on something ahead of her.

He turned and spotted what she was running towards. The little boy—Azaliah—was crouched in the foliage fifty feet behind the gunmen, his dirty face streaked with tears. Directly in the tank's firing path.

"Gaiomere, *don't!*" Atlas shouted, already sprinting towards her—but even as his legs moved, the eruption of the cannon sounded again. She had just reached the little boy, and was tugging him to his feet. The shell blasted the cluster of Blood Lenders in front of them backwards—and Gaiomere turned, wrapping her body around the little boy like a shield. The explosion sent the two of them careening into a tree, smoke momentarily shielding them from view.

Atlas couldn't think. His feet carried him across the clearing, but he felt as though he were watching himself from outside his own body. Every sound around him suddenly grew faint.

The smoke began to clear, and Atlas found her sprawled beside the tree they'd collided with. The little boy knelt beside her, eyes wide and frightened, but he was not there alone—Gwena had reached Gaiomere first, and she had her fingers pressed against the younger girl's pulse.

"Get away from her," Atlas snarled.

Gwena spared him a brief look, scowling. "Oh, get a grip, Obarion. You're not the only one that cares about her."

He fell to his knees beside her, and Gwena muttered, "She's breathing...but she's unconscious."

Atlas said nothing, and the redhead glanced up at the little boy. He had a deep gash across his arm, and his lip was bleeding, but otherwise, he looked unharmed. "You alright, Az?" He nodded. "Go find Damia, okay?" He nodded again, disappearing into the trees. Atlas wondered vaguely if they'd sent the members of their tribe that weren't fighting to hide—he had no idea— he'd scarcely noticed anything beyond the gunmen, and the sudden, hammering need to eliminate as many of them as he could.

Atlas glanced over his shoulder and saw that Marathi's men were dropping their weapons. A couple of Obarion soldiers were climbing out of the tank, and —Atlas' stomach dropped—Talikoth strode across the clearing, Moonstone and Harcliff on either side of him.

Gaiomere suddenly jerked awake, her mouth opening in a blood-curdling scream. "Hey, hey, little Hellcat," Gwena said soothingly, stroking a hand across her face. "*Shh*, it's going to be okay." Atlas was suddenly very glad the older girl was there. He had never seen that look on Gaiomere's face before—as though her insides were being burned—and he felt a desperate cloying to make it stop, but had no idea how.

"Help me roll her over," Gwena said. "Gently, now."

The red-haired girl grasped her legs, and Atlas set a hand on her shoulder, and another on her hip, revolving her until she was lying flat on her back. Gwena gasped, and Atlas immediately realized why.

Gaiomere's side was shredded. The skin of her stomach was bloody and tattered, bits of metal lodged into her flesh. The shrapnel had torn straight through her vest, as though it were flimsy paper. And there was blood—so much blood. Coating her clothes, glistening on her ashen brown skin, bubbling from the wound. Her hands were clawing at her side, and Gwena grasped her wrists, trying to keep her from touching the mangled skin.

"Hang on, Hellcat, we'll—we'll fix it." Gwena glanced up at Atlas, her expression helpless, and for a split second, he felt a stab of pity.

"Go get one of our medics," he told her firmly. Her eyes flashed with alarm. "Hold your hands above your head, and they won't hurt you," he assured her. Still, she hesitated. "Gwena, *now*. She needs help."

She swallowed, nodding, and sprang to her feet, taking off across the clearing with her arms raised.

Gaiomere was still sobbing, and when she drew breath, it was raw and ragged. Atlas stared down at her numbly, unsure of what to do, unable, even, to think. She looked frighteningly pale.

Whitsom rushed into the thicket, his face bloodless as he dropped beside Atlas. "What happened?" he mumbled.

When they looked at each other, Atlas knew in an instant that all the animosity between them had been completely forgotten.

"She got in the tank's line of fire," Atlas told him. "The little Blood Lender boy would have been killed— Gaiomere, she—she saved him."

Whitsom made a noise from the back of his throat that Atlas interpreted immediately. He was furious too, but he could not focus on that—not when he was unsure whether she would live or die—

He shook his head, pushing his mind in a different direction.

Dr. Capalti appeared moments later, with Quandra —Bettoni's girl, who worked in the hospital—hastening after him. She gave Atlas a tight smile, crouching beside Gaiomere and checking her pulse.

"Do you want us to move her?" Whitsom offered. His voice was choked, and when Atlas glanced at him, it looked as though he were trembling.

Dr. Capalti shook his head. "We'll set up a medical tent around her—no one else alive has injuries as severe as hers."

Atlas and Whitsom's eyes met once more, and he knew they were both thinking the same thing. *No one else alive...*

Several other doctors hurried over, and with them, the injured soldiers. One of Harcliff's boys was sporting a bullet wound in his shoulder, which he had pressed a piece of fabric over. Luca was holding his wrist in the opposite hand. When Atlas looked closer he realized the boy's arm was bent at a sickening angle.

"*Dios mío,*" Luca whispered when his eyes fell on Gaiomere.

"We're gonna have to cut some of this out—it's deep," one of the doctors—blond and wiry—muttered to Capalti. The old man nodded distractedly—he had taken out a pair of thin tweezers and was carefully extracting shards of metal from Gaiomere's mangled flesh. "You two should go," the blond man added. Whitsom and Atlas both glared at him, and his expression turned stern. "Go on now, boys. We'll take care of her."

Still Atlas did not move, until Whitsom let out a heavy sigh, tugging on his sleeve and murmuring, "Come on, let's go see if the others need help."

When they returned to the clearing, the soldiers had rounded up Marathi's men and were cuffing them. Even as they watched, more soldiers were ushering tribespeople from the trees. Azaliah clutched the arm of a black-haired woman, his eyes wide and terrified. Lined in a row near where the tank had been parked were four bodies, unnaturally still, and Atlas' stomach lurched when he realized they were dead. Two Vedas soldiers that Atlas had sparred with a handful of times, one of Harcliff's boys, and Patz. In death, his scraggly frame looked even smaller.

Harcliff greeted the two of them with a solemn nod as they approached the quartet still speaking at the center of the clearing. "—can't be expected to comply when you so readily violated our agreement," Marathi was saying in his oily voice.

Talikoth's eyes met Atlas', and he wanted very

badly to give his father a taunting smirk. He had *known* that securing Marathi's acquiescence would not be nearly so easy, but his father had been rash, and his determination to make Atlas look a fool had clouded his judgement.

But then Talikoth's dark eyes slid back to Marathi, and he arched a brow. "The terms of our agreement were nullified prior to this point. You informed me that you kept the captives on to serve as thralls..."

Atlas' brows flitted up in surprise, but before he could think any further on his father's words, the man tilted his head towards the group of Blood Lenders, clustered near the edge of the clearing, and continued, "However, I see only a handful of faces that I recognize from our exchanges throughout the years. And you never mentioned the cannibals." His lips twisted into a sinister smile. "Or did you think I wouldn't find out?"

Marathi's face whitened, and the smirk slid promptly off Atlas' lips.

Talikoth took a step closer to Marathi, and said quietly, "Now...since *you* have contravened on the terms of our agreement, the penalty for your treason is death —for you, and the rest of your tribe."

Moonstone opened her mouth, as though she wanted to object, but then she closed it again. Harcliff frowned, his black eyes flickering between the two men.

"The alternative," Talikoth continued mildly, as though he were not discussing the annihilation of an entire tribe, "is to impart any knowledge you have of the cave housing the water source, as well as the tribe guarding it."

Atlas glowered down at his feet, his ears filling with a strange galvanic buzzing. He did not even listen to the rest of their conversation—he already knew how it would go from here. Talikoth had said and done all he'd needed too—and Atlas was left feeling every part the fool that his father had made him out to be.

CHAPTER FIFTEEN

Capalti would let neither Atlas nor Whitsom back into the medical tent, so the two of them sat outside in a glum silence. Despite the late hour, the rest of the soldiers seemed to have forgotten their tiredness. Talikoth's reinforcements had brought plenty of food with them—they hadn't known whether the captives would have eaten since the exchange—so many were helping themselves to a second dinner.

Moonstone had come by an hour before and informed Atlas that they would be interrogating Marathi and asked if he would like to participate.

"It's fine," Atlas had grunted, without looking at her. "I'm sure my father has got it handled magnificently."

She had looked at him strangely, but obligingly left him alone after that, and he was grateful for it. He didn't want to see her disappointment, nor Harcliff's, and he certainly didn't want to listen to the interrogation with Talikoth's smug face staring him down.

He didn't understand what he'd done wrong. Moonstone had clearly had enough faith in him to put him in charge of this mission—what had made her revoke that confidence so quickly? Was Talikoth already influencing her that strongly? But how could he— Moonstone *knew* what sort of person Talikoth was.

Perhaps she had never had any faith in Atlas in

the first place—maybe this had been the plan from the beginning, but he just hadn't been made aware of it. Perhaps she had believed from the start that Atlas was leading the volunteers to their deaths—and in a way, she hadn't been wrong. How close had Gaiomere come to dying?

His stomach clenched as his thoughts wandered back to the curly-haired girl. He had never felt a fear like that, not in his entire life, when he had seen her lying unconscious on the ground. He and Whitsom had agreed—they had been working *so hard* to protect her, and still, *still* it wasn't enough.

Atlas' gaze roved over to the young man sitting opposite him. Of course, Whitsom hadn't been concerned with protecting his sister—he was too busy trying to protect his snake of a girlfriend.

But then, Atlas hadn't done any better. The second that tank had come pummeling over that hill, bloodlust had seeped into Atlas' veins like a drug—not unlike what he'd felt during his fight with Jemahl—and all he'd been focused on was making the Blood Lenders *suffer.*

"Hey, guys."

Atlas glanced up and saw Jacoby shuffling towards them, his hands wringing in front of him, and his expression agitated. "How's she doing?"

Whitsom shrugged. "We don't really know. Know she's alive—they won't tell us much else."

Niko, Zarr, and Clancy visited the medical tent three times to inquire after Gaiomere, and Cami and Joaz had stopped by to inform Atlas and Whitsom them that they were keeping a few plates of food saved for her, so the rest of the boys didn't eat it all. Dak and Alekea had come over as well, both looking rather concerned as Atlas told them what had happened.

An hour passed. Whitsom and Jacoby were talking quietly, but Atlas wasn't listening to their conversation. Every so often, he would glance up towards the clearing, where he could just make out Moonstone and Harcliff sitting on a log across from Marathi. Talikoth was on his feet, his hands tucked into the pockets of his leather jacket, gazing contemplatively towards the treetops.

Dr. Capalti came out of the medical tent, and Atlas and Whitsom sprang to their feet. Before either of them could fire off a barrage of questions, he held up a hand preemptively, tiredly massaging his temples with the other. "She's stable," he told them. "She lost a lot of blood, but she was very lucky—none of the shrapnel penetrated to any of her organs. I believe I have it under control—"

"What do you mean, you *believe* you have it under control?" Atlas interrupted sharply. "Either you have it under control or you don't."

The old man sighed. "We've been able to patch up the damage easy enough, but we have to keep an eye on her for a while—ensure that there isn't any infection or hemorrhaging—"

"That isn't likely, is it?" Whitsom asked nervously.

Capalti shrugged. "It's not unheard of, but it certainly isn't a guarantee. She should awake from surgery any moment now, at which time we can do a thorough assessment—"

The blond medic popped his head out of the tent. "She's awake," he announced.

Atlas didn't bother waiting for Capalti's okay. He shoved past the old man and ripped aside the tent flap, Whitsom hot on his heels.

Luca's cot was nearest the door, and he waved brightly at them as they entered, his injured arm swathed in a blue cast. Midway across the tent, Harcliff's boy was fast asleep on his cot.

Gaiomere lay at the opposite end of the tent, and as they approached, she pushed herself up to a seat. Her skin was still ashen, but her smile was wide.

"Don't you go smiling at us, you punk!" Whitsom snapped, smacking her lightly on the side of the head once they'd reached her. "What the hell were you thinking?" Gaiomere opened her mouth to reply, but Whitsom didn't let her. "That was totally reckless and —*stupid* and just...just..." He trailed off, as though he'd run out of words to describe his sister's unintelligence, and turned to give Atlas an admonishing frown. "Why you ain't backing me up? Tell her how stupid she was being!"

Atlas' brows furrowed as he gazed pensively at the bedridden girl. She was looking up at him apprehensively, as though she were waiting for him to explode, to scream at her and tell her that she had indeed been foolish. But Atlas didn't feel angry. He felt very little at all, except perhaps relief.

"I'm just glad you're okay," he said quietly.

Whitsom made an indignant noise in the back of his throat.

The tent flap was pushed aside once again, and Talikoth and Moonstone came striding into the tent. Dak and Alekea trailed behind, with a handcuffed Marathi between them, and taking up the rear were

Zyratier, Kordell, and, to Atlas' surprise, Jemahl, who, he could not help but notice, carefully avoided his gaze.

Dak and Alekea forced Marathi into a nearby chair, and Kordell kept a crossbow aimed at his back. "You know, if you had an academic interest in testing the tank's blasting power, we could have run a simulation in the lab," Dak remarked wryly.

Gaiomere gave him a furtive grin. Atlas vaguely wondered if she'd garnered some level of affection for the man, now that she knew he was technically her uncle. "Well, there's nothing quite like the real thing."

"Your actions were very noble, Gaiomere," Moonstone said quietly.

"Or very stupid," Talikoth muttered. He shot the girl a vexed look. "You think your father would want you diving in front of tanks?"

"No, but only because he'd be doing it first," Gaiomere fired back, without missing a beat.

Talikoth's lips twitched upwards, for just a split second, before he shook his head. "How long would it take you to craft me some new explosives?"

Gaiomere's eyes narrowed. "Why?" she asked suspiciously.

It was Zyratier who answered. "We discussed the possibility of launching a bomb in through the entrance of the cannibals' cave—take a good number of them out —drive the rest of them from hiding, at the very least—"

Moonstone looked between the two of them with a frown. "Can't we perhaps bring the idea to one of Ilquir's other researchers—Gaiomere was very close to being killed, I'm sure she needs to take some time to recuperate." She glanced at Capalti for backup, and Talikoth looked at him, too.

The doctor shifted uncomfortably under Talikoth's gaze. "General...with all due respect, the girl *has* been through significant trauma."

"She should rest, Talikoth," Moonstone agreed. She turned to look at Atlas, asking, "Don't you think?"

"He forfeited the right to think when he elected not to participate in the interrogation," Talikoth said. His eyes flickered between Atlas and Whitsom, and he continued scornfully, "Glad to see the first and second in command have been taking their responsibility seriously and making themselves useful."

Whitsom, at least, had the decency to look properly reprimanded. He looked down at his boots and mumbled, "Sorry, sir."

But Atlas just shrugged, and surprise flashed through his father's eyes, though the next second, it was gone.

"It depends on what kind of bomb you want," Gaiomere said, sitting up straighter in her cot. Despite both Moonstone and Capalti's insistence that she needed rest, Atlas could already see the cogs in her brain turning. "But honestly, I'm not sure that would work. I mean, think about it. It's a small, confined area. I could make a blaster—that would be fast—but I'm worried the explosion could trigger some kind of cave-in—then we wouldn't have any access to the water at all. And if we went with something chemical, we could risk contaminating the water source." Her brows suddenly furrowed, and she looked very quickly at Moonstone. "How is it that this water source isn't contaminated already?"

"According to what Marathi has told us, it's because of its positioning underground. The water itself is pristine—none of the radiation from the bombings could reach it," Moonstone said, nodding her head towards the black-haired man, who was gazing at the roof of the tent with a bored expression. "There are no traces of any of the toxins present in our water above ground."

"Fascinating," Gaiomere murmured. "Normally mercury and lead transfer quite easily through soil—especially in high-moisture environments—"

"The caverns are almost entirely composed of carbonate and sulfate rocks," Marathi supplied in a drawl. "Not even cadmium or arsenic can penetrate them."

"Why don't we just storm the entrance?" Kordell piped up, frowning. "We don't need a bomb to drive them out if we trap them in."

Jemahl shot Kordell an impatient look. "We're not just gonna storm the entrance when we haven't got any idea what their numbers are like, how many weapons they've got, what the layout of the caves are. For all we know, the cave could be a hundred miles—and they got the lay of the land when we don't. It'd be like walking into a crypt."

Atlas shifted uncomfortably. He'd been thinking along the same lines as Kordell only a couple of hours before—but all Jemahl's points made the error in such thinking seem rather obvious.

"But you must have *some* idea about their numbers," Gaiomere pointed out, frowning at Marathi. "I mean, don't they at least come out during the exchanges?"

"Tantabar usually has about a hundred men with him, on the day of exchange," Marathi informed them, in a weary drone. "All armed, obviously. Whether or not that is his entire tribe remains to be seen."

"Not to mention the fact that they've probably got the water access concealed," Alekea pointed out, from where he leaned against one of the tent supports. "That's their failsafe, in the event Marathi's tribe betrays them, isn't it?"

Talikoth was gazing towards the sloping canvas above them meditatively.

"Let's send a recon team early tomorrow morning," Moonstone began. She continued to issue directives, but Atlas' attention drifted away from the conversation. He sat down on the cot next to Gaiomere, and leaned his head back against the tent, letting his eyes drift closed.

He should, his brain reminded him practically, be paying attention, but he could hardly bring himself to care. In fact, now that he knew Gaiomere wasn't in danger of dying, Atlas could not bring himself to care about *anything*. What did it matter, if they couldn't recover the water? Let Talikoth deal with the problem —he was obviously better equipped to—certainly better equipped than Atlas, who couldn't seem to do *anything* right...

He vaguely registered Moonstone calling his name, and Gaiomere sent a swift elbow into his stomach.

"What's up?" he asked, yawning and stretching an arm behind his head.

Moonstone eyed him with a rather concerned expression. "Um...I was asking if you or any of your soldiers had any information to offer from your time with the Blood Lenders—anything else that Marathi might not have told us," she repeated.

Atlas shrugged, glancing over at Whitsom. "You got anything, buddy?" Whitsom gave him a bewildered look, and slowly shook his head. Atlas nodded, tilting his head towards Gaiomere. "What about you, flower power? Anything? No?"

Gaiomere stared at him with a mixture of amusement and mystification. "Well, I guess that settles it," Atlas said indifferently. "Can I go to bed now?"

Talikoth had been massaging the bridge of his nose, but his head snapped up in an instant. "Are you serious right now?"

Atlas lifted a brow. "Did that sound rhetorical to you?"

"I think it's best we all get some rest," Moonstone interposed quickly. Dak and Alekea were looking between Talikoth and Atlas nervously. "You and your soldiers have had a trying few days. We'll meet in the morning for a full report on the recon."

One by one they trooped out, until only Talikoth and Whitsom were left, both staring at Atlas, albeit with very different expressions. "You uh...you alright, Attie?" Whitsom asked.

Atlas had already slid down onto the cot, rolling over to his stomach and burying his face in Gaiomere's pillow as he slung an arm across her lap. "Fine," he mumbled, his voice muffled by the pillow. "Why wouldn't I be?"

"Oh for the love of..." his father muttered. "Whitsom, go back to the campsite and grab a couple of handguns. Find Jemahl and instruct him to meet us here in five minutes. Am I understood?"

Atlas wasn't looking at him, but the confusion in Whitsom's voice was audible as he answered, "Uh...yes, sir." His footsteps trailed out of the tent.

"Get up, Atlas," Talikoth said coldly.

"Nah."

Gaiomere was trying to wriggle away from him, so he wrapped his arm around her tighter. "I um...I have to use the bathroom."

Atlas immediately knew what she was trying to do. "No you don't," he argued.

"How do you know?" Gaiomere replied indignantly. "I was in surgery for hours."

Atlas grumbled into the pillow. He was fairly certain she *didn't* need to use the bathroom, but there was little he could do to prove his theory, so he let her go.

"*Atlas*," came his father's warning tone.

He groaned, burrowing further into the cot and pulling the pillow over his head. His father made a scathing noise, his footsteps pounding towards him, and before Atlas could do anything to stop it, Talikoth had grasped the sides of the cot and flipped it over, depositing him on the densely packed dirt of the forest floor.

Atlas was so shocked that, for a moment, he didn't move. But then he bounded to his feet, whirling around to glare at his father. "What do you *want*?" he snapped.

Talikoth rolled his eyes, leaning against the tent support as he strapped his gun to his arm. "Moonstone doesn't want to send recon till the morning, but I'd prefer to get an idea of what we're up against sooner rather than later."

Atlas scowled, dusting the dirt from his sweater. "Well, *you* always know what's best. So send a squad."

"Don't be stupid. You and I will go. Whitsom and Jemahl, as well." Atlas opened his mouth to argue, but Talikoth had already turned to address Gaiomere, who had just reentered the tent. "Keep an eye on our trackers the next two hours, princess."

Gaiomere's eyes were bloodshot and droopy from exhaustion, and it looked as though every movement caused her pain, but she only nodded, pulling her bag towards her and digging around until she found one of the tracking devices.

Whitsom returned with Jemahl close behind him. The shorter of the two wordlessly passed Atlas a gun, sliding his own into the holster at his waist.

"Well, as much as I'd *love* a moonlit stroll, it looks like the three of you have got this covered."

Talikoth stared at Atlas, his face stoic. "Are you finished with your jokes?" he asked tersely.

Atlas shrugged, dryly remarking, "I live to entertain." Behind him, he heard Gaiomere giggle, but when Talikoth glared at her, her cheeks darkened with color, and she hastily redirected her gaze.

"Let's go," his father snapped, before any of them could say another word. He stalked out of the tent, and the three of them followed after him.

The moon was so large in the sky that the woodland around them looked bright. Most of the soldiers had gone to sleep for the night, but they still had to venture about a quarter mile before the sounds of the campsite faded completely, replaced by the creaking of crickets and the skittish patter of whatever nocturnal creatures roamed the mountainside.

Atlas trudged along at the rear of the group, glowering at the back of his father's head—not that the man in question took any notice. Talikoth was razor focused tonight. Atlas recognized this kind of intensity, for he had seen his father employ it many times. When he needed to focus, he didn't eat. When he needed time, he didn't sleep. Atlas had always envied this ability, but witnessing it during a mission was rather unnerving.

Jemahl and Whitsom must have found Talikoth's intensity disconcerting as well, for they had been largely silent. After walking for nearly an hour, though, Whitsom said, "Cool gun, man."

Jemahl glanced back at him, smirking a little as he spun his bright red revolver in his hand. "It is, isn't it? A gift from my father, the day I was inducted—he said I needed something distinguished."

Behind them, Atlas rolled his eyes, but if Whitsom was fazed by the older boy's haughty tone, he didn't show it. "He the one that taught you how to fight?" he asked.

Jemahl nodded, slashing at a low-hanging branch with his knife. "Him and my big brother." He snickered and added, "Calihl was pissed when I made it in to the Inner Ring and he didn't—he's too small though. Five years older and scrawny as hell." Whitsom snorted.

Atlas had always admired Whitsom's ability to get along with just about anyone, but at that moment he resented it. He felt the sudden childish urge to remind Whitsom about the lewd comments Jemahl had made towards his sister, or the fact that, just a few evenings ago, he had been trying to kill Atlas.

"What's your deal with that redhead in Marathi's

tribe?" Jemahl was asking Whitsom. "How do you know her?"

"That's my girl. She got captured by the Obarion up north six months ago—thought she was dead, until now."

Jemahl glanced over his shoulder, giving Whitsom a wry smirk, and remarked, "She's cute. If you ever get bored with her—" He broke off, sniggering as he hastily dodged the branch Whitsom had hurled at his back.

"Hey, I can sic Atlas on you again if I need to," Whitsom said.

Jemahl glanced back suddenly, as though he'd forgotten Atlas was there.

"I been wondering, Attie boy," he said, after a moment, "how come you didn't kill me."

Atlas looked away from him, his brows furrowing as he gazed down the sloping mountainside. For a split second, he considered telling the truth—but then he just lifted a shoulder lazily and droned, "You know, as fascinating as I find the inner-workings of your mind, Jemahl...I don't."

He didn't even care that Jemahl could very well decide to turn around and attack him—he wasn't even sure he'd try to defend himself.

But Jemahl didn't rise to the bait. He rolled his eyes and turned back around to continue after Talikoth. Whitsom fell into step with Atlas, nudging his shoulder and asking, "You okay?"

"I told you I'm fine, Whit."

"You just—you haven't seemed like yourself..." But he trailed off, his brows drawing together as he lurched to a stop. "Hold up, y'all," he called ahead, and

Jemahl and Talikoth stopped too. "You smell that?"

Both Atlas and Jemahl shook their heads, but Talikoth wrinkled his nose, and tilted his head east. "Fire," he muttered. He pushed through the foliage, and the three boys followed. As they drew closer, Atlas began to smell it—he could even see smoke spiraling into the night sky, and as they came to the sheer cliff rock face, they spotted it. Perhaps three hundred feet below them rose a tower of flames, and around the firepit were at least fifty men, firearms strapped across their backs.

"Well done, Whitsom," Talikoth said quietly. Jemahl withdrew a pair of binoculars from his bag and passed them to him.

"How come that Niko dude couldn't spot all that?" Jemahl muttered, frowning.

"I'll bet you they only come out certain times of day," Whitsom pointed out. "Lots of nomads work that way. Plus, if Niko's cars were making a whole bunch of noise, they probably knew better than to come above ground..."

Atlas leaned back against a nearby tree, and his eyes drifted shut. He could hear Jemahl, Whitsom, and Talikoth speaking quietly, but he couldn't be bothered with trying to listen to what they were saying. Perhaps Talikoth would be satisfied with what information they had gathered—maybe Atlas could even slip off now, before any of them noticed—before he had to suffer another second taking orders from his father. As if he hadn't been humiliated enough.

As though he'd read Atlas' mind, Talikoth suddenly called his name. Atlas grunted in response, without opening his eyes. "Come with me. Jemahl,

Whitsom, you two keep watch. Take note if there are any changes in their numbers or if you see anyone go in or out. If we aren't back in an hour, head back to the campsite."

Jemahl looked rather offended. "Don't you think I should—"

"Yeah, I think Jemahl would be better suited," Atlas drawled at the same time.

"The next person to argue with me gets a bullet to the balls," Talikoth snapped.

Atlas scowled, pushing himself off the tree and trailing after his father, who had disappeared into the thicket.

When Atlas finally caught up, Talikoth angled their path to skirt the mountainside. Atlas noted it would dump them around two hundred feet east of the Flesh Flayers' bivouac, and well within range of their firearms.

Talikoth continued to lead them circuitously down the mountain, and they were almost halfway to the valley, before Atlas finally muttered, "Let's cut north and double back down. I'm sure they've got eyes on the mountain."

His father shot an amused glance over his shoulder, and Atlas, at first, thought Talikoth was going to ignore him. But then the older man altered his path and amenably started north up the mountain.

Nearly a half an hour later they made it down into the valley, and the sounds from around the Flesh Flayers' fire were little more than distant murmurs.

If Atlas hadn't known how near to the underground lake they were, he would never have suspected its existence. The foliage here was dense, and he couldn't spot any signs of the carbonate or sulfate rocks Marathi had referenced—not that he had much of an idea what they looked like.

Talikoth peered through the thicket in the opposite direction, his dark eyes narrowed. "We can more likely than not find the opposite end of the caverns if we keep east."

Atlas felt a flicker of annoyance. "That's stupid—you're assuming that the caverns run continuously in one direction—that's not accounting for any variance. And it's like Jemahl said, for all we know, they could be hundreds of miles."

Talikoth's lips were twitching now. Atlas didn't understand what could possibly be funny about this situation. "Well, what do you think we should do, then?" his father asked.

The words spilled from Atlas' mouth before he could stop them. "Right now? Go to bed. Although if you felt like drowning yourself in the lake first, I wouldn't stop you."

For the second time that night, he saw his father's mouth lift into a smile, and in spite of his exhaustion, and his vexation towards the man opposite him, Atlas felt the corners of his own mouth tugging upwards, too. He didn't wanted to help his father. He didn't want to participate in the plan designed to undermine his own—but he couldn't help the fact that his brain had started to churn.

"If the rock near the entrance had distinct greenery—lichen and the likes—we could keep an eye out for the same patterns across the bank. If there's another entrance to be found, we're sure to come across it."

He wasn't even sure Talikoth had been listening. His father was already moving away from him, his gun clenched in one hand and eyes scouring the hillside. Atlas let out a huff of annoyance and took off after him.

He had planned to follow along in silence, to complete whatever probing Talikoth had his mind set on with as little complaint as possible, so as not to spend any more time with the man than absolutely necessary. But something about his father's blatant dismissal lit a fire in Atlas' insensate heart.

"*Or* we just do things Talikoth's way, since that's *always* infinitely better," Atlas intoned. "In fact, why don't we just storm into the Flesh Flayers' camp right now, like you did earlier this evening—tank fired up and guns blazing."

His father glanced over his shoulder, arching a brow. "Once you informed us of the location, there was no sense in following through with the mission as planned—"

"Yeah, but you could have—I don't know, I mean —well, who said anything about leading with the *tank*? Gaiomere almost died—"

"Your inability to control your soldiers is nobody's problem but your own," his father said. Talikoth was not looking at him, but his words made something in Atlas snap.

Inability.

Your inability.

Your inability to control.

"How long were you planning this?"

Atlas had stopped walking, his hands clenched into fists at his sides, and his heart suddenly pounded in his chest. It took Talikoth a few moments to realize he was no longer following. When his father turned around, his expression was exasperated.

"Atlas, I'm not—"

"Was this your plan from the beginning? You and Moonstone thought it would be fun to—what—*fool* me into thinking you thought I was ready for this sort of responsibility? Give me the reins just so you could yank them away again—make me look like the idiot, right?"

The exasperation melted from Talikoth's face. His expression was impassive, but his eyes were glinting. He opened his mouth, but Atlas did not give him an opportunity to speak.

"I thought at least Moonstone had a little bit of faith in me—or have you always had her wrapped around your finger? I thought she at least might give me an opportunity to prove myself, even if you never do."

His father opened his mouth again, but Atlas was really going now, and wasn't going to let him get a word in. Atlas turned away, running a hand over his hair as he paced in front of Talikoth. "I mean, I don't even understand what I *did*. I followed the plan. I kept any serious harm from coming to any of our soldiers —Marathi was going to kill Zarr, you know, and *I* negotiated him down, without you, or anyone else's input. We had it handled before you decided to barge in just because you *could*."

His feet had carried him towards Talikoth, and before he'd even realized it he had stopped in front of his father, so that they were eye-to-eye. "So what, is this your revenge?" he spat, his mouth curling into a sneer. "The penalty for treason is death—but you couldn't kill me, so now what? You'll make me out to be some incapable child instead. Was that your plan? Was it?"

His father was staring at him, his lips tilted into a smirk, his dark brows arched. "Are you...finished?" he asked.

Atlas scowled, shoving past him and continuing around the hillside. Talikoth followed soon after, and when he spoke, he almost sounded amused. "I'd wondered how long it would take to get you to admit what was bothering you. You're just like your mother—heart on your sleeve, you can never keep your *feelings* in for long." Atlas said nothing, but continued to follow the path of lichen—up ahead, bathed in moonlight, he could make out a massive rock covered in the foamy green moss. He had just begun to clamber over a felled tree when Talikoth continued, "How highly must you think of yourself."

Atlas whirled around, his eyes narrowing. "What did you just say to me?"

His father gave him a patronizing look. "Atlas, do you have any idea how many times Dak or Zyratier have altered my plans in the midst of a mission? How many objectives have been reconfigured, or scrapped altogether? Do you have any *semblance* of a clue how many times I've had to swallow my pride and admit that someone else's way may be better?"

Atlas blinked, staring at Talikoth. He was waiting for the smirk to reappear, waiting for the dark chuckle, or perhaps for him to roll his eyes. But none of that happened. Talikoth only continued to stare right back at Atlas, as though he were actually waiting for an answer. "I—I've never seen you do that," Atlas said quietly.

Talikoth rolled his eyes. "Of course you haven't. That doesn't mean it doesn't happen. My officers know better than to question me in public—that's the quickest way to lose the trust of your civilians. They need to see that their general knows what's best for them."

Atlas frowned. "I think they need to see that their general is human."

Something strange flickered over Talikoth's face. "I think they've seen enough of my humanity," he murmured, so quietly that Atlas wondered if he were talking to himself, but before Atlas could probe further, his father continued, "Two hundred soldiers volunteered to pose as captives. Two hundred lives that could become little more than cannibal feed— Atlas, even for a *moment*, did you consider that my interference was bigger than you? That perhaps my involvement had more to do with sparing their lives than making you look like a fool? Hmm?"

Atlas' face flushed as a burning shame enveloped his body. He had thought of little else the past twenty-four hours, besides how irritated he was at Whitsom, for so readily trusting Gwena, his vexation at Niko for what Atlas had seen as his last-ditch effort for a share of the glory, and his anger towards Talikoth, for usurping his opportunity to lead, to prove that he could do more than what anyone expected of him. He had been so certain that Talikoth was out to make him look like an idiot—but he had done that to himself.

His father continued around the bank. They had veered fully south now, and the smoke spiraling up from the Flesh Flayers' campfire looked like little more than a haze of clouds from here.

Atlas suddenly froze. Talikoth was right—he *had* been acting like a child. But that was, in reality, only half the equation—and Atlas was rather sure that his father was hoping it would be enough to distract him from the other half.

"You don't care about the lives of the Vedas, or any of Harcliff's warriors," Atlas said slowly. "You're doing this to win back the favor of the Obarion people." Talikoth stopped as well, and turned to face him. "You've still got a third of the tribe in your corner, but you know that if you help with this mission—if you play this large of a role in recovering the water permanently—the other two thirds will elect to vote you back in as well."

And there, *there* was the chuckle. Talikoth held his hands out on either side of him as he asked, "Must I always have an ulterior motive?" Atlas arched a brow, and Talikoth shook his head, still chuckling as he continued around the massive boulder. "How is it that you came back from the North more my son, rather than less?"

Atlas wasn't sure whether or not he should be offended, so instead of answering, he asked the question that had burning in the back of his throat since Talikoth let the words slip. "Why do you think our clan has seen too much of your humanity?" Since the time Atlas was young, his father had almost always seemed more machine than man—there was no one he could think of more dependable, when it came to leading their clan—nor more dangerous.

Talikoth grew quiet then, for quite some time. The ground beneath them had grown rockier and the foliage thinned. Both of them carefully watched the tree line in the distance, lest any of the Flesh Flayers emerge to attack.

Atlas was just beginning to think that his father was not going to answer, when Talikoth said softly, without turning to look at him, "The punishment for treason is death—do you really think if I wanted you dead, you'd be standing here alive right now? How easy would it have been for me to lift the gun to your head?"

Atlas gaped at his father's back, bewildered. "You tried to kill me. Even if you failed, you still tried."

"I did. And I may not have been able to kill you while I was imprisoned in that cell, or while I was guarded that night in our unit—but I am very much unbound now, Atlas—and there is no Moonstone here to protect you."

"Moonstone would know, though," Atlas said. "And then you'd lose your support from the rest of the Obarion." He was only speaking as a matter of fact. Strangely, Atlas did not feel afraid, even as his father turned to face him, his gun hanging loosely from his arm.

"I could make it look like an accident. There are a hundred armed cannibals just a few miles from us—it wouldn't be a challenge."

Atlas tilted his head defiantly. "You would have done it by now."

"Maybe I wanted to be as far from the campsite as possible." An amused smirk was playing around his father's lips.

Atlas shook his head stubbornly. "You're not going to kill me."

"I tried to kill you," Talikoth reminded him. "Even if I failed, I still tried." His fingers were tightening and untightening loosely around the trigger, and as Atlas watched, his father tapped twice against the barrel of his gun, paused, and then tapped thrice more.

Atlas stared at him a moment longer, before he shrugged. He found himself repeating Whitsom's words, from all those months ago—though he hadn't believed them at the time. "Maybe you were angry at first—because I'd betrayed you. Maybe at first, you wanted me dead, but—but not enough to lift the gun to my head, when it came down to it. And I certainly don't think you want me dead anymore."

Talikoth said nothing as Atlas stepped closer to him, but the muscles in his jaw were tense. "I think you see as clearly as I do that we were both meant to survive. It's the same reason that I was captured by the Vedas and imprisoned with the same nomads that just *happened* to be the children of your late lead researcher. It's why I ran into Raider, who just *happened* to be the son of a man who had learned to plant gangs from my mother. It's the same reason you were imprisoned, when most of the Vedas Council wanted to have you executed."

His father stood very still, and his eyes looked so black that Atlas could see the reflection of the woodland behind him—and the faintest shifting, among the brambles at his back. "Both of us can see that the hands of fate are at play here—this is something larger than either of us, and even you, with the trail of blood you spilled across a thousand miles, aren't willing to interfere with fate."

Talikoth's eyes narrowed, and his smirk grew even wider. "Haven't you learned, Atlas? Fate bends to *my* will—not the other way around."

He moved so quickly that Atlas could scarcely trace his movements. His arm lifted in a flash, leveling his gun, and he pulled the trigger.

PART III:

THE FLESH FLAYERS

CHAPTER SIXTEEN

Atlas didn't even think—instinct took over as he flung himself sideways against the large rock. Pain should have burst at his neck—where Talikoth had aimed—but then, if Talikoth's intent had been to shoot *him*, he'd have had no time to dodge, and his father certainly wouldn't miss.

He ripped his own gun from its holster and took aim. Talikoth's shot had struck the first Flesh Flayer in the center of his face, and his comrade was still fumbling for his firearm when Atlas sank a bullet between his eyes.

"You trying to show me up?" Talikoth muttered out of the corner of his mouth. He was already moving towards the fallen gunmen, his dark eyes flitting across the distant stretches of the valley.

Atlas reloaded his gun, watching the foliage shift fifty feet from them—but it was only an animal. "You deserve it, coming that close to shooting me."

"I thought you saw my signal!"

"I *did* see your signal, that didn't mean you had to fire that close—I felt the bullet pass me—"

"Oh, don't be such a baby."

His father nudged one of the Flesh Flayers with his foot. Atlas knelt next to his comrade and began to unstrap the gun from the dead man's back. Blood was oozing steadily from the wound on his face. "Do you think the others heard the commotion?" Atlas asked.

Talikoth had already slung the other man's gun over his shoulder and was making his way back across the jagged rocks. He shrugged, and replied, "Perhaps —but even if they did, they won't send too many to check. They wouldn't risk leaving the main entrance weakened—"

"Assuming that *is* the main entrance," Atlas reminded him as he fell into step beside him. "Still, it might not be a bad idea to hide those bodies on our way back—we don't need to alert them to our presence —although it'd be a miracle if the tank didn't do that already."

Talikoth shot him an amused glance from the corner of his eye. "Good to see you're not sulking around pretending not to care anymore. It wasn't a good look for you."

Atlas scowled, kicking at a loose pebble, but said nothing.

"I thought for a while that it might have been about the girl," his father continued. "I'm glad that it wasn't—I would have been disappointed."

Atlas' brows furrowed. "What's wrong with Gaiomere? She's brilliant."

"She's certainly her father's daughter," Talikoth agreed. "No, I meant no offense against the girl. Only that I would have been rather disappointed if you'd gotten so out of sorts because of her recklessness." He paused, and then continued, almost contemplatively, "Olympion would do things like that all the time."

Atlas snorted. "I'll bet you thought he was an idiot."

"I thought he was the best of us," Talikoth said

without hesitation.

Atlas stared at his father bemusedly. "Why do you—why do you talk about him that way?" Atlas asked. "You speak about him like he's a hero—like you respected him—or like you *still* respect him, but he—he betrayed you. Committed treason."

"The penalty for treason is death," Talikoth said quietly. "Justice came for him—he received his penance, so I see no reason to disrespect his memory. Besides..." He gave Atlas a wry smirk. "His children are now assisting me dutifully—whether they realize it or not. They pay his toll, even in his death. Funny, how destiny unfolds, isn't it?"

"Funny," Atlas echoed distractedly. His mind was racing, but he was hesitant to voice the thoughts in his head.

Still, the worst that Talikoth could do was get angry with him, and Atlas was quite used to his father's anger. "If Olympion's name was cleared in death—if you don't bear him any ill will—why don't you speak of my mother that way?"

If he hadn't been watching Talikoth so closely, he might have missed him flinch. His shoulders stiffened, and when he spoke, his tone was icy, "That's very different."

"But how come? Olympion betrayed you based on his own principles—my mother did the same."

"Your mother wasn't the saint that Delurah led you to believe, you know," Talikoth said coldly. "Besides, her case cannot be compared to his."

Atlas let out a frustrated exhale. "But *why*? Olympion did some awful stuff, too, didn't he? So isn't it —"

"Enough."

His father's voice was like the crack of a whip, and his mouth snapped shut, seemingly of its own volition. The air between them was suddenly thick with tension, and Talikoth's face slipped once again into a solemn mask of concentration.

Despite the swift end to their conversation, Atlas couldn't help but feel a sense of satisfaction. For perhaps the first time in his life, he had seen something beyond the composed, unflappable exterior that Talikoth presented to the rest of the world. For just a few minutes, the facade had come down. And Atlas had known he was taking a risk, asking such questions, but he didn't regret it, even now, when his father had carefully reassembled the barbed walls he kept around himself—Atlas didn't regret it a bit, because for the first time, he had actually felt as though he were talking to his *father*, and not just the feared Obarion General from the South.

"You knew the vest was there, didn't you?" Atlas realized aloud. "That's why—that's why you didn't lift the gun to my head."

Talikoth's jaw flexed, but he said nothing.

"The penalty for treason is death," Atlas repeated, undiscouraged. "You're just as bound to uphold the Obarion customs as the rest of us—if you hadn't put up the appearance of settling the score with me, I'll bet those old windbags on the Obarion council would have been after your head. You didn't *actually* want me dead." His conclusion was accompanied by a smug smirk, and the look Talikoth gave him was scathing.

"I'm reevaluating that sentiment at the present moment."

Atlas pressed on as though he hadn't heard him. "You felt it, didn't you? When we were brawling." He cast his father an affronted glance, and pointed out, "It might not have worked, for all you knew—"

Talikoth scoffed. "Please. I got a look at it when I had you on the ground—vanadium steel—you think any bullet of mine could have gone through that?"

Atlas' brows furrowed. "How do you...know that?"

Talikoth's lips twitched, but he only shook his head, refocusing his gaze in front of him. "Your time in the North has made you very bold," he observed, ignoring Atlas' question. "You never would have spoken to me this way before you were captured. You would have sacrificed every one of your insipid little friends rather than displease me."

Atlas' face flushed. "That's not true!" he insisted. "And besides, even if it were, that was what you wanted: mindless drones to do your bidding. That's how you like your soldiers, and that's all I ever was to you."

"Or *maybe*..." Talikoth mused. "I wanted you to prove that you could think for yourself—that you were meant for more." Atlas opened his mouth to argue, but Talikoth cut him off. "Soldiers are good for the mindless tasks—follow orders and don't ask questions—"

"You *told* me not to ask questions!" Atlas protested furiously.

"And you *listened*. Like a sheep." Talikoth sneered. "Do you know how I came to be general, Atlas?"

Atlas shook his head, a little embarrassed. He knew that Talikoth was the youngest general ever appointed in their clan's history—knew he succeeded his wife's father, Anakhletus, and that he had led the clan west soon after, but beyond that...

"I was appointed general because I wouldn't stop asking questions—because I had ideas that I wouldn't shut up about—"

"But *you* would never tolerate that, even if my grandfather did," Atlas reasoned frustratedly.

"How do you know?"

"Because you weren't—because you just—I mean —I just *know*."

Talikoth let out a breath through his nose that might have been laughter. "You know less than you think you do, Atlas."

"So do you," he snapped petulantly.

His father lifted a brow. "Explain," he commanded, in an aggravatingly calm voice.

Atlas sighed, shoving aside a thorny branch, ignoring the beads of blood that bubbled on his palm. "Look, I just—I just think maybe I wouldn't have been so obsequious if you ever just—just—"

"Coddled you?" Talikoth proposed mockingly.

"*No*, I didn't want to be coddled," Atlas snapped. "I just wanted—I mean, would a 'good job' every now and then have been too much to ask?" He could feel the redness in his cheeks spreading to his neck, but now that his mouth was moving, he couldn't seem to stop it. "I mean, I got top of my year in Academy four years straight—"

"I expected nothing less of you," Talikoth said coldly. "I wasn't going to congratulate you for meeting expectations."

"And I *shredded* everyone that I came up against when I petitioned to be inducted into the Inner Ring— the only reason I didn't get in was because the Council voted against me—"

"As I advised them to," Talikoth said. "You understand now why I did, after seeing the tasks the Inner Ring are ordered to oversee. You would have been miserable—"

"This is exactly what I mean," Atlas said, exasperatedly rubbing his temples, where he could feel the beginnings of a headache forming. "Doesn't matter what I did, you were never impressed."

"Maybe if you had spent less time trying to impress *me* and more time forming your own place in the world, I might have been."

Atlas' head whipped towards his father, but Talikoth was not looking at him. "The best thing that ever happened to you was getting captured by Moonstone," Talikoth said quietly. He snorted, adding, "It damned me, certainly, but...you came back to the South a man, not a little boy trying to make everyone else happy. Least of all, me."

The muscle in Talikoth's jaw was tense, and Atlas got the impression that paying forward such a compliment was actually causing his father physical pain. After a moment, Atlas shrugged, running his fingers along the cold metal shell of his gun pensively. "I guess it's just that I'm not so afraid of you anymore. Actually, it's not that—I'm not so afraid of disappointing you anymore."

Talikoth stopped walking again, and was looking at him oddly. "Is that so?"

Atlas couldn't tell if his father was angry or not, and it unnerved him. He kicked at another loose pebble and watched as it bounced across the rugged bank and collided with a lichen-covered rock wedged beneath a jagged overhang of limestone. "Yeah. I already betrayed our entire clan—just like my mother did. Can't really disappoint you anymore than I have, can I?"

Talikoth studied him, and Atlas looked away, suddenly immensely uncomfortable with the level of vulnerability he had just shown—and in front of his father, of all people. Atlas had just opened his mouth to suggest that they double back for the night—more to change the subject than anything—when he stilled, his eyes intent on the rocky hillside ten feet away from them.

"What is it?" Talikoth asked immediately, following his gaze.

"Does that rock—does it look a little strange to you?"

The longer that Atlas stared at it, the more he was sure he was not imagining things. The lichen-covered rock had a faint blue-ish outline—so muted that he surely would have missed it, if he hadn't been staring in that direction.

"There's light coming from the other side," he murmured.

Talikoth knelt next to the rock, a hand tracing along its surface. "Help me move this."

Atlas immediately positioned himself opposite of his father. The two crouched simultaneously and grasped the underside of the rock. "On three," Talikoth said. "One, two, *three.*"

Atlas grunted under the weight, his fingers sliding down the mossy surface with his awkward grip. The two of them had to wriggle the rock back and forth to free it from beneath the limestone, and when they finally managed to extract it fully, they let it fall with a thud, both breathing heavy.

A passageway led deep into the hillside, lit faintly by the same blue-ish glow that surrounded the rock. "Do you think it—" Atlas began, but Talikoth held a hand up to silence him. He leaned his head towards the opening, and Atlas did the same. In the distance, ever so faintly, like the playing of a far-off river, he could hear voices—little more than whispers to his ears, but distinguishable nonetheless.

"This is our way in," Talikoth murmured

Atlas' jaw slackened, and he looked between Talikoth and the passageway with a flabbergasted expression. "Are you out of your mind? This tunnel is too narrow—only a child could fit in there—" Talikoth gave him a look, and Atlas' eyes grew as wide as saucers. "No—no *way* we're sending Marathi's little boy in—"

Talikoth shrugged. "Fine, then we'll send that chatty little Ren boy—the one in the medical tent—"

"Luca? His *arm* is broken—"

His father waved him off. "He can crawl fine with one arm. No matter—we'll organize the details later—the important thing is that we've found our way in. Help me move this rock back."

Atlas continued to gape at him, before his father snapped a finger impatiently. He grumbled as he knelt to help move the rock back into place.

Their journey back to the campsite passed largely in silence; Atlas spent most of the trek trying to come up with an argument against his father's plan that the man in question might actually find convincing. But even as he thought about it, he knew the likelihood of changing Talikoth's mind was slim.

The sun was beginning to creep up over the

mountainside when they trudged up the slope and into the clearing where the soldiers had set up camp. One of the perimeter guards—a Vedas soldier with whom Atlas had sparred a couple of times—gave Talikoth a somber nod, and Atlas wondered, for perhaps the dozenth time, how many of their volunteers would turn on Moonstone in an instant, if his father asked them to.

When they pulled open the flap to the medic's tent, the first thing Atlas saw was Gaiomere, slumped over a table, an oil lamp flickering weakly near where she had spread a large piece of paper out in front of her. Her dark curls fell into her face, and one of the tracking devices hung limply from her fingers.

They drew closer, and Atlas realized that Gaiomere had been sketching a detailed map as they had moved down the mountainside. She had even inserted mile demarcations, and the margins of the map were filled with notes.

Sudden eastern veer—Flesh Flayer territory? She had written, in her neat scrawl, with an arrow pointing towards where they had begun to descend into the valley, and *Possible water source location—encircling region*, along their path they'd taken beside the gradient.

Talikoth let out a low whistle, tugging the map from beneath Gaiomere's arms and holding it up to the light. Her head flopped sideways onto the wood of the table, and Talikoth's eyes raked over the map fervently. "Good girl," he muttered.

Atlas knelt beside her and slipped an arm beneath her knees, and another around her back. "Maybe now you'll stop being so hard on her," he said quietly, lifting her out of the chair. She made a little noise in her sleep and curled into his chest.

Talikoth was not looking at him, but he must have been listening, because he snorted. "Not likely," he muttered, as he traced a finger around the perimeter of the underground lake.

"Oh? And why won't you?" Atlas asked grumpily. He managed to lay Gaiomere down without waking her, and after a moment of hesitation, he pulled off his boots and sank down onto the cot next to her.

"Because she's like you," Talikoth said. He was rolling up the map neatly, but he spared Atlas a brief, reprimanding glance. "You need to sleep in your own tent, Atlas."

Atlas ignored the latter part of his statement, demanding, "What do you mean, she's like me?" His father was still gazing at him expectantly, and he rolled his eyes. "Come on, just let me crash here—I'm just going to sleep, honest." Talikoth's brows lifted so high that they disappeared into his hairline, and Atlas decided that he needed to bring in the big guns. "You know, I've helped you *tons* tonight—if you think about it, it's really the least you could do."

Talikoth stared at him for a full five seconds, before he shook his head, the corners of his mouth inching upwards.

Atlas, though, would not be distracted. "What did you mean when you said she's like me?"

His father gazed contemplatively at him. "In both of your cases, your excellence manifests most prominently when you have something to prove."

He wanted to pick his father's brain further, but even as he lay there, he felt his body beginning to drift between wake and sleep, his eyes blearily blinking closed.

Atlas heard Talikoth say something else, but his sleep-addled brain could not pick apart the words well enough to distinguish them. Within seconds, he was fast asleep.

◆ ◆ ◆

When Atlas awoke the next day, the air was sticky and warm, and he could tell by the sunlight beating through the canvas above that it was already afternoon. The medical tent was empty, though outside he could hear the clamor of voices and laughter.

He wondered, at first, if the previous night had merely been a very strange dream. But even as he lay there, he could feel the scratches on his arms from where the thorns had snagged his skin, and when he sat up, he saw the gun taken from the Flesh Flayer he'd slain leaning against the side of the tent.

When Atlas ambled into the clearing, he spotted Whitsom, Bettoni, and Coral at the edge of the tree line tossing a leather-skinned ball between the three of them, and Gaiomere and Jacoby sat side by side on a log near the firepit, talking quietly. Moonstone was hunched over a folding table, her brows furrowed as she perused a large piece of paper spread atop the table in front of her. When she saw Atlas, she quickly waved him over.

"Our recon team arrived back an hour ago, and we were able to update the map that Gaiomere started last night," she informed him. "Our team found no other entry points, besides the passageway that you and your father discovered."

"Just two total, then," Atlas confirmed, nodding. "I take it Talikoth filled you in on the information we were able to gather?"

Moonstone glanced sideways at him, her mouth curving into a wry smile. "He did. I see where you get it from—the inability to follow orders, I mean."

"Talikoth certainly likes to do things his own way," Atlas murmured distractedly, his fingers tapping against the table as his eyes flitted over the updated map. He hesitated, glancing back at Moonstone, and asking, "General, why—why are you still working with him? I mean...after everything he's done, I would think—I guess I just assumed after the exchange you wouldn't trust him so easily."

Moonstone stared at him in that penetrating way, and if Atlas wasn't so used to it, he might have looked away. "Your father has made himself quite indispensable," she said slowly. "But understand, Atlas, that not for a moment does that mean I trust him." She tapped her pen against her temple. "Not to mention the fact that I'm still keeping my promises."

His cheeks prickled with heat, and he gave her a reproving frown. "I'm not sure if you've noticed, General, but I don't exactly need protection anymore."

Moonstone chuckled, shaking her head and turning back towards the map. "Maternal instincts don't shut themselves off, no matter how many moons have waxed and waned since I gave my vow to your mother. Perhaps you'll understand someday.

Perhaps you'll understand someday. An image suddenly thrust itself inadvertently into his mind's eye: a toddling youngster, brown-skinned, curly-haired, and grey-eyed. He hastily shook his head, directing his thoughts away from the image, and the strange, although not altogether unpleasant emotions that surfaced along with it.

He suddenly remembered what Moonstone had mentioned back in the meeting room, several weeks before. "Your son, is he—is he a soldier?"

He was rather embarrassed to admit the fact that he had never actually thought about Moonstone outside of the context of being a general—it was just bizarre to imagine her going home and kissing her husband goodnight, or cuddling an infant.

But then, he might not have believed that Talikoth had a son if his existence wasn't irrefutable evidence.

Moonstone hummed, grasping the edges of the map and rolling it up. "My eldest was. He would be —" She broke off, letting out a heavy exhale. "Twenty-five now. He was killed seven years ago. My youngest is just a little older than you—he will have just turned nineteen."

She was shuffling through her notes, and Atlas affixed his eyes on the papers clasped between her hands, rather than on her face. "Is he uh—is he still—"

"He's still alive, yes," Moonstone said quietly. "He went east two years ago." She smiled a little. "To 'find out what was out there,' he said." Moonstone suddenly looked unaccountably sad. "Searching the depths of his soul, I think—not anything he could find outside of himself."

Atlas frowned, wondering exactly what *that* meant. It was not the first time that Moonstone had confounded him—he remembered so vividly that day, in his unit, when she had spoken to him about how similar he was to his parents. He liked Moonstone well enough—respected her, certainly—but all her talk of *souls* made him uneasy. He didn't understand it.

Fate, he could understand. From the time that he was young, he could see the significance of his own destiny—and now, he could see how intertwined it was —how each choice he made wound itself into the fabric of his reality. His destiny, as he had always understood it, could be crushed like an insect beneath the foot of a mightier foe if he did not train hard enough, think smart enough. There was no victory he would ever be entitled to—the only prosperity that fate would ever grant him would come by the sweat of his brow and the blood of his flesh.

But all Moonstone's talk of *souls*—it did not fit into that worldview.

He glanced over at Gaiomere, who was pulling her wild curls up into a bun as Jacoby rambled to her. How was it that *she* could be so averse to the idea of fate, when her own father had been Obarion? Had her father abandoned his old beliefs, when he had deserted his tribe? Or had her ideas been formed after she had seen her parents slain before her eyes?

But even so—Gaiomere *acted* as though she believed in fate. She readily sacrificed herself for the little Blood Lender boy—had been willing to build her solar energy system to protect the North, and now, she was helping the Obarion when she had no real reason to.

It couldn't be because she found out about her heritage—no, for she had been helping Ilquir in the lab long before that, without ever even having been asked to. It seemed as though she had a genuine desire to aid, but why? She had *hated* Atlas because of the tribe he had hailed from, when they first met. And she had certainly been reluctant to help the Vedas, in the beginning. What had changed?

He was interrupted from his thoughts when Moonstone summoned he, Gaiomere and Whitsom to follow her towards the center of the clearing, where Talikoth, Dak, Harcliff, and a handful of other soldiers and officers had gathered. An argument had already unfolded amongst them

"It's only a matter of getting a visual," Zyratier was saying in his gruff voice. "We don't have a way to drive them out without potentially damaging the water source or our access to it, so this is the best course of action—it's not as though the boy will have to fight off the cannibals himself—"

"His arm is broken," Harcliff said firmly, his voice uncharacteristically aggravated. "It's quite a request, asking him to crawl down a passageway and pull himself back out without full use of his limbs."

"It isn't a request—he'll follow orders, as sure as any of the rest of the soldiers," Talikoth said coldly.

"What about making one of Marathi's boys do it?" Dak suggested. "That skinny one—he's got to be around the same size—"

"He was killed in the scuffle," Talikoth interjected dispassionately.

"What about the child?" Zyratier suggested.

There was a thoughtful sort of silence for a few seconds, before Gaiomere burst out, "Oh, you *can't*. He's just a kid!"

Talikoth snorted. "It would certainly be adequate recompense—him having almost gotten my best brain killed—"

"He doesn't owe us recompense!" Gaiomere argued.

"How many *kids* did the Blood Lenders deliver to the Flesh Flayers?" Niko pointed out, as he leaned against a log. "Compared to that, this is nothing—"

"Oh yeah, let's just sink down to their level," Gaiomere snapped, rolling her eyes. "Look, if you need someone to get a visual, I'll do it. I'm smaller than Luca, I can fit in there just as well as he could."

Silence fell over the group a second time, thicker this time. Whitsom was glaring at his sister, and Moonstone, too, looked apprehensive. Dak cast Talikoth a disapproving frown, but Talikoth ignored him, his eyes fastened on Gaiomere.

A cold knot of dread formed in Atlas' stomach, reminiscent to his realization that he could not stop her from coming on the train. She'd made up her mind...and it wasn't as though he could control her...

But if he could out*think* her...

Atlas suddenly straightened where he stood near the perimeter of the circle. "Maybe nobody has to," he said quietly. Several pairs of eyes swiveled to look at him, but Atlas' gaze found Zarr, who was leaning back against a log with a bored expression. "When we first met Raider, he had a big old stash of drones in his trunk. Did you guys have any more of those back at your Hideout?"

Zarr shrugged. "Sure, dozens. We moved all our gear and tech down to Harcliff's camp, though—soon as Niko decided we were gonna be all chummy-chummy with you southerners."

Atlas turned very quickly to Moonstone. "How

long until the exchange is scheduled to occur?"

She glanced down at her watch. "About eighteen hours. Marathi says they always meet the Flesh Flayers at dawn—"

Atlas nodded, turning back to Niko. "Let's get a car en route back to the coast to collect the drones—and any other gear that Gaiomere might need. We can potentially kill two birds with one stone."

The curly-haired girl looked up at him with knitted brows. "Why are we killing birds?"

"It's—never mind. Listen. If we attach a couple of cameras to a drone and fly it in through the passageway, we can get a full count on their numbers. That way, when we go in to seize the water, we don't have to worry about anybody springing out from any crannies or crevices, or hiding away and picking off our soldiers one by one—"

"But there's no guarantee that the camera will pick up every person in the cave," Alekea reasoned. "Especially if it's dark—"

"Exactly," Atlas replied. "Which is where the second bird comes into the equation. *They're* not expecting anybody until dawn tomorrow. We'll attach smoke bombs—maybe we can odor them with some kind of gas that smells poisonous but won't actually sully the water—and drive the Flesh Flayers out. They'll think they've been gassed and take off out of the main entrance—where our troops will be waiting."

There was a five second pause, and then Niko let out a guffaw of laughter. "Man, I like the way your mind works, Attie." Dak and Zyratier both gave him a nod of approval, and Gaiomere beamed.

Atlas found his gaze, though, inevitably drawn to

Talikoth. His father's face was impassive, but there was a rare glint in his eyes—the same glint he'd worn in the meeting room when Atlas and Gaiomere had come up with the plan to send the Flesh Flayers a batch of soldiers posing as Renegades—and Atlas had the sudden realization that his father might have actually been impressed with him.

"Niko, I want a car on the road in twenty minutes," Moonstone said. "It's six hours round trip so we don't have a second to spare."

Whitsom suddenly sat up, his expression a strange mixture of guilt and excitement. "Hey, uh— if y'all are swinging by so close to Headquarters...and you were already planning on stinking up the smoke bombs...I *may* have an entire case of stink bombs hidden under the loose floorboard in the sparring gym, for...classified purposes."

Moonstone looked, for a moment, as though she could not decide whether she should reprimand him, before she settled on, "Very well. Thank you, Whitsom."

Gaiomere sidled up beside Atlas and sank down onto the log next to him. "You're kind of smart, you know," she teased.

"Well, I have to be," he replied, with a cocky grin. "People count on me. It's a heavy burden, always being the biggest brain in the room—"

"I don't know how you bear it."

"Inhumanly strong shoulders," he informed her, with a conspicuous wink. She laughed, and he pulled her against his side gingerly, mindful of the injuries she'd sustained the evening before.

"Are we going to talk about yesterday?" he asked her quietly.

She sighed, her fingers curling absently around her necklace. "What's there to talk about? Didn't you say you're just glad I'm okay?"

"Well, of course I'm glad you're okay, I just—" Atlas sighed, running a hand over his hair. "I—I'm just— Gaiomere, if something happened to you, I—"

"I know," she interrupted. "But he—he's a twelve-year-old boy. He should never have been caught in the middle of all that." Gaiomere glanced across the clearing, towards where the Blood Lenders were all clustered. The child in question knelt in front of his mother—a dark-haired woman named Damia—who was meticulously wiping his grubby face with her cuffed hands.

"He reminds me of Rasta," Gaiomere said quietly. "I couldn't just let him die."

"But you also just can't throw yourself in harm's way like that," Atlas told her, frowning. "Do you have any idea how close *you* were to dying?"

She opened her mouth to reply, but then she closed it again, her brows knitting together.

"What is it?"

"I just think that it's the least I can do," Gaiomere said. "After—after everything that happened."

His brow furrowed, and he looked at her blankly. She glanced up at him, her shoulders hunched, and Atlas could tell that she was desperately fighting back tears. "Do you know how many people I killed, that—that day at Headquarters?"

Whatever he had been expecting, it hadn't been that. He racked his brain. "I don't know. I mean, there was the grenades—"

"The grenades, and the missile launcher," she

reminded him. She let out a slow, shuddering breath. "Seventy-four. I killed seventy-four people."

He stared at her, the muscles in his jaw clenching as he contemplated what he could say. Tears fell freely down her face now, and her fingers had stilled around her pendant.

"I saw the death count in the infirmary, a couple of days after the battle. Have you ever killed seventy-four people, Atlas?" She shook her head, swiping hastily at the tears tracking down her cheeks. "I have nightmares every single night. I have for—for months now, and I just feel like maybe if I—if I can…" She snorted, lifting a shoulder half-heartedly. "…rebalance my karma, I guess, maybe I'll feel less—less…wicked."

"You were just doing what you thought was right at the time," Atlas reasoned. He started to day something else, but Gaiomere interrupted him.

"Do you know who Gabriel is? I work with him in the lab, he said he was in your year." Atlas nodded, vaguely recalling the uncoordinated young man that had nearly always been in the library whenever Atlas visited. "I killed his father. He was in the Inner Ring, and I—I killed him. He doesn't know, of course—probably wouldn't be so nice to me if he did, but I—I had to go in there every day and look him in the face, knowing that he doesn't have a father anymore because of me."

Atlas swallowed thickly. "His father knew what he was signing up for when he was inducted," he said distractedly. "And besides, I threw plenty of those grenades too—and I told you where to aim the missile. You can't just blame yourself…"

Gaiomere only gave a miserable little hiccup, but said nothing more. Atlas was grateful for the silence as he mulled over her words.

He'd had nightmares, too, for weeks on end—but *his* nightmares had only ever been violent flashes of all he'd seen. *He* had never once, for a moment, considered what the families of the soldiers he'd killed might be going through. It had never crossed his mind to feel guilt, for what he'd done—it was justified, wasn't it?

Except...every Obarion soldier who had slain one of Moonstone's soldiers, or any of the Ren—they had also believed they were justified.

And Gaiomere...well, he couldn't think of anyone who was so inherently *good*—and she'd been wrestling for months with remorse that had never even crossed Atlas' mind. What did that make him?

He had been so egocentric, most especially over the past few days—but now he could see that his self-absorption ran much further back than that. He'd believed he was just fighting for the right cause, when he'd betrayed the Obarion, but what if he'd only been lying to himself? From the beginning, maybe deep down all he'd ever cared about was his own share of glory. He'd seen that easily enough with how insulted he'd been by Moonstone relegating him to the role of mere soldier. As though he were *better* than his comrades—as though he were entitled to more.

He was no better than his father, really. Perhaps that was just it, though—perhaps that was his fate, that the evil inside of him was too intrinsic to ever really overcome.

Gaiomere shifted closer to him, and he glanced sideways at her. He wondered if she'd thought the same, after learning everything her father had done. To Atlas, the idea was ridiculous. The very essence of who she was revolved around doing what was right.

Atlas leaned down and pressed his lips against her forehead. "You're not wicked," he said firmly. "No matter what you've done, you could never be wicked. You care too much about doing the right thing."

Gaiomere sniffled, and Atlas' lips quirked up into a smirk as he continued, "But um...next time you feel like *rebalancing* your karma...how about you just stick to volunteering in the sick hall, or knitting socks for orphans or something?"

She let out a watery little laugh, and Atlas, for the moment at least, felt a little less wicked himself.

Niko, Luca, and Clancy returned that evening a quarter after six with the drones. Atlas' company had spent the afternoon organizing themselves into squadrons and scouting the area to determine the best location for their soldiers to station themselves in just a matter of hours for their attack, but even amidst the day's activity, Atlas' attention kept wandering to the Blood Lenders.

They'd been strangely subdued since Talikoth's reinforcements had arrived—though perhaps that should have been expected, since they were shackled, and had no real idea whether Talikoth and Moonstone had any plans to let them live. Still, it set Atlas' nerves on edge. Even the eccentric Marathi had been sitting taciturn atop a log, staring broodingly down at his cuffed hands.

By seven o'clock, restlessness had descended

amongst the soldiers. Many had already drifted off to their tents to get as much sleep as they could before their two A.M. wake-up call, but a few dozen disappeared into the woods to play capture the flag. Umir had produced several gallons of whiskey seemingly out of nowhere, and some soldiers still lingered around the fire, laughing and talking noisily. Every so often, Gaiomere, who was working diligently perhaps a hundred feet away, shot the rowdy group a seething glare.

Atlas and Zarr were cleaning their guns on the eastern perimeter of their camp when the younger boy remarked, "What *I* want to know is where the Flesh Flayers got all these weapons. They can't have just found them lying around—especially not out here."

"Maybe they travel every few months to trade," Atlas suggested.

Zarr snorted. "Flesh Flayers don't usually trade. They're not generally friendly with other nomads— maybe you noticed, with the eating people and all..."

"Well, yeah, but they also don't normally live in tribes this big."

The black-haired boy shrugged. "I think they're being supplied." His tone was nonchalant, but Atlas did not miss the accusatory glare he shot towards Talikoth.

"Look, I know he's done some shady stuff, but Talikoth wouldn't do that. He'd never supply weapons to his enemies—"

"Enemies?" Zarr gave Atlas a patronizing look. "They've been getting rid of us pesky *Renegades* for nearly two decades, doing all his dirty work for him—he owes them an awful lot, don't you think?"

Atlas' thoughts flitted back to what Talikoth had

said to Marathi following the tank scuffle. "Talikoth's never even met Tantabar. And anyway...I think Marathi told Talikoth he was keeping the Renegades as slaves." He hesitated, and then pressed on, "In his own twisted way, I think Talikoth sort of convinced himself he was choosing the lesser of two evils—in his mind subjecting them to slavery was better than death."

"Death that *he* pledged them to," Zarr said, scowling. "And anyway, I'd rather die than be anyone's slave."

Frustration surged beneath Atlas' skin, though he wasn't sure why. "Either way, my point stands—it's stupid to supply weapons to anyone outside of your own clan—"

"It's also *stupid* to sell human beings like barter chips, but here we are," Zarr snapped, his pale cheeks flushing red with anger.

"Nobody's debating that," Atlas said persistently. "I'm just saying I don't think it makes sense to jump so quickly to pointing fingers—"

Zarr's head whipped sideways to glare at him, his gun dropping to his feet. "You know what I don't think makes sense, At? You defending someone that tried to kill you. And your girlfriend. Pretty much every one of us, actually."

Atlas opened his mouth to fire off a retort, but black-haired boy did not give him a chance. He snatched up his gun and stormed off, disappearing into the foliage.

Atlas stared after him, anger and defensiveness bubbling in his stomach. Besides Whitsom, Gaiomere, and perhaps Bettoni, there wasn't anyone that he trusted more than Zarr, and he would hate for the

Ramshackler boy to think that he was loyal to Talikoth. Because he wasn't. He *wasn't.*

He got to his feet, intent on tracking Zarr down and informing the little twerp exactly how much he'd done to prove his loyalty to their cause, when he stopped, his attention caught by something across the clearing.

Marathi and Gwena were standing very close to one another, whispering urgently. His eyes narrowed as he tried to make out what they were saying.

Atlas had been trying, since the tank incident, to give Gwena the benefit of the doubt—she hadn't betrayed them to Marathi after all, despite Whitsom's blunder, and she *had* retrieved the medics for Gaiomere —not to mention the fact that they'd have no clue where the water was without the information she'd slipped to Whitsom. But her behavior naturally gave way to his suspicion. She had been hovering near Whitsom almost unceasingly, and there was a sort of desperation on her face whenever she spoke to him. Atlas wondered if she sensed, as he did, that her influence over her former beau was waning.

Something metal glinted against the late afternoon sun as it passed between Gwena and Marathi's cuffed hands, and all of Atlas' resolve to give Gwena a chance dissipated like vapor.

He snatched up his gun and pounded towards them. "What are you doing?" he called to the pair. Gwena jumped, but Marathi merely glanced over his shoulder, lifting a brow and shrugging his shoulders lazily.

"We aren't allowed to speak now?" the redhead snapped.

"No, it's the concealment I'm more concerned about," Atlas said coldly, glancing down pointedly at her hands, which were clenched into fists. "Hand it over." She made no move to comply, and Atlas swung the gun around to his front, shoving the barrel under her jaw and hovering his finger over the trigger. Gwena froze, her eyes widening. Marathi looked between the two of them with little more than mild interest.

"You wouldn't," she snarled, her eyes narrowing to slits. She glanced sideways towards where Gaiomere sat by Jacoby, and Atlas followed her gaze. "She'd never forgive you."

"Want to bet?" Atlas muttered, shoving the barrel deeper into her skin. "Because I think she would, and I —"

"What's going on?"

Whitsom emerged from the tree line, and was looking between the three of them with furrowed brows.

"I saw them whispering over here—they're concealing something," Atlas told him, lowering his gun.

"You didn't need to get so aggressive about it," Gwena grumbled, unclenching her fists. She was holding a scrap of foil, and Whitsom took it from her and unfolded it. "It was the last of our chocolate Damia made a few weeks ago—so I didn't want to share it."

Atlas stared at the foil. He was almost certain that had not been what he'd seen the two of them passing back and forth. It was the wrong size, and the color was all wrong too, but Gwena's hands were otherwise empty.

"Yeah, you know, I'm gonna have to confiscate

this," Whitsom told her, grinning wryly, and Gwena rolled her eyes. The dark-skinned boy punched Atlas' shoulder, remarking, "Ease up, Attie. Tomorrow we'll be headed back to Headquarters, everything squared away."

Gwena and Marathi hastened back over to where the other Blood Lenders were clustered, and Whitsom ambled to the campfire to make himself a plate of food. Atlas watched each of them go, his mind still churning.

"What are you brooding about now?"

Talikoth stepped up beside him, diligently dusting the dirt from his leather jacket, but his gaze was intent on Atlas' face.

"I think they're planning something," Atlas said lowly, his eyes affixed on the back of Marathi's head. "Whitsom thinks I'm being paranoid."

"Paranoia is useful," Talikoth said unhesitatingly, shrugging his arms through his sleeves. "I'll have Jemahl and Kordell keep an ear out the rest of the evening. Don't give any of them any idea that you're suspicious from here on out, understood?"

"Yes, sir."

The words had left his mouth instinctively, like an impulse almost, but the moment they had fallen from his lips, Atlas wished he could wrangle them back. Talikoth smirked, but said nothing, and Atlas' mind flashed back to his argument with Zarr. A scowl unwittingly made its way onto his face.

Gaiomere came flouncing over to pair of them, a couple of drones cradled in her arms.

"The smoke bombs need to harden for an hour before I add the fuses, but otherwise they're finished."

Atlas eyed the drones curiously. Two tiny

cameras were fixed on each of their fronts, and on the bottom of either, a pair of clamps extended perhaps four inches past the drone's base.

"That's where the smoke and stink bombs will go, respectively," Gaiomere explained. "Jacoby set each of them to be released manually—we figured a timing system would be too risky, what with the potential of interference in the passageway—"

"You are planning on testing these, aren't you?" Talikoth interrupted, as he took the drones from her arms to inspected them.

Gaiomere rolled her eyes, blowing a curl from her face and huffily replying, "Of course I'm going to test them. Who do you think I am?"

"Little more than a coffin-filler, if you continue speaking to me in that tone, princess," Talikoth drawled, without looking at her.

Gaiomere crossed her arms over her chest. "Excuse *you*. The only words out of your mouth should be 'thank you,' you prick."

Atlas choked on his saliva, and let out a violent, spluttering cough. Talikoth's eyes jerked away from the drones to fasten onto the curly-haired girl, who was glaring up at him with a rather impressive amount of ferocity, considering he was twice her size and could kill her with very little effort.

"What did you just say to me?"

"You heard me," Gaiomere muttered, though with markedly less confidence than moments before. Her weight shifted between her feet, and her fingers were twitching in the way they did whenever she was nervous, as though she were preparing for a fight.

Talikoth tilted his head to the side and studied

her silently. After a few moments, during which Atlas wondered whether or not he would have to jump between his father and his girlfriend, the ghost of a smile flickered around the corners of Talikoth's mouth. "You know," he mused, as his eyes returned to the drones, "I'm glad I didn't kill you."

He strode off without another word, and Gaiomere blinked, surprise flitting over her face, before her expression became unabashedly pleased.

Atlas looked between she and his father's retreating back, utterly flabbergasted. "Can I just uh—can I just jump in here to remind you that, regardless of whether or not he's *glad* he didn't, he did, in fact, *try to kill you*?"

Gaiomere gave an embarrassed little shrug. "I know, it's just—it's—it's probably silly, but...he *is* your dad, so...there's a part of me that actually...you know...really wants him to like me." The last segment of her sentence was uttered in little more than a whisper, and Atlas rolled his eyes, despite the smile tugging at his lips.

"Okay, one: that's ridiculous. It wouldn't matter to me one bit if he didn't like you—"

"Well, it would matter to me—" Gaiomere huffed, but Atlas continued as though she hadn't spoken.

"And two: ninety-nine percent sure he likes you better than he likes me...Whitsom, too, for that matter."

The two of them went to sit by the fire, listening mildly as Niko played a small, holey instrument that Gaiomere said was called a harmonica, and Luca warbled a tune in his native tongue.

After a couple of songs, though, Gaiomere nudged him, her eyes glinting coyly. "Firewood's looking sorta low," she murmured, tilting her head towards the thicket of trees behind them. Atlas immediately lugged himself to his feet, pulling Gaiomere up with him, and the two of them wandered over past the tree line, beneath the heavy canopy of the tall, tilting pines and cypresses.

They'd only walked a couple hundred feet when Atlas stopped and gently pushed Gaiomere against a nearby tree, pressing his lips against hers. She looped her arms around his neck, kissing him back with a frantic kind of desperation. After a while, he pulled back, frowning. "Are you okay?"

"Fine," she said, too quickly. "Why wouldn't I be?"

The frown on his face deepened, and she shook her head. "I'm just nervous about tomorrow," she said quietly. "I know we've gone over the plan loads and we've got lots of reinforcements, but I'm just—I'm afraid something will go wrong."

"There's no reason for Tantabar or his tribe to be up in arms hours before the trade's scheduled to take place," Atlas said quietly. She said nothing, but knelt to grab a few branches from the ground near the base of a rotting tree. "And we've got the numbers on them—that's not to say things *can't* go wrong, but I'm confident in my father's plan."

She glanced sideways at him. "When did you start doing that?"

He didn't hear what she'd said at first. The bushes a dozen feet to his left had shifted marginally. "Doing what?" he muttered distractedly, his gaze narrowed— but it was only a rabbit.

"Calling him your father. You never did that before. It was always 'Talikoth.'" She was gazing at him with undisguised intrigue, but Atlas suddenly found that he couldn't meet her eyes.

"Uh...not sure," he mumbled, shrugging, as though it were a matter of little importance. "That's what he is, though, isn't he? It only makes sense."

Gaiomere was still studying him intently. "I think he likes you too, you know. And respects you. In his weird sort of way."

Atlas let out a huff of annoyance. "Gaiomere, not you, as well. This is what he does—this is how he controls people. Don't let the act fool you, you're smarter than that. The only reason he's here—the only reason he's helping us, at all, is to save his own skin."

Gaiomere looked as though she wanted to argue but seemed to decide against it. The two of them finished collecting firewood in silence before heading back towards the campsite. They had almost reached the tree line when Atlas heard a sudden *crack* in the foliage, not ten feet away.

Both of them froze, and Atlas' hand flew to the knife in his pocket. There was a beat of stillness, and then Azaliah emerged from the bushes, his amber eyes wide, and his blond curls mussed.

"Oh, it's just you, Az," Gaiomere said softly, her shoulders visibly sagging. "What are you doing out here all by yourself?"

His little cheeks turned bright pink, and he clenched his cuffed hands together in front of him, shivering a little. Atlas noticed his fingers were blackened, as though he had been digging in soot. "Mama said she was gonna help me find some wildberries, just near where the guards were posted, over there," he mumbled, pointing a skinny finger towards the western perimeter of the camp, where Atlas could just make out Olli and Yacielle through the trees, their guns hitched high on their shoulders. "But Marathi called her away, and I—I got a little lost."

Gaiomere shrugged out of her sweater and draped it around Azaliah's shoulders. "I spotted her near Gwena before Atlas and I left," she told him. "We'll take you to her."

By the time they made it back to the clearing, Luca and Niko—who sounded quite off pitch, and rather drunk—were merrily belting a tune that sounded vaguely like a parody of the Obarion clan's anthem. Most of Atlas' clansmen were laughing good-naturedly, even when Luca loudly warbled something in Spanish that Atlas was fairly certain, when translated, would have been considered highly insulting.

Gaiomere returned Azaliah to his mother, and Atlas retired to his tent, but he had scarcely been lying in his sleeping bag for five minutes when Gaiomere slipped in through the flap, swathed in Whitsom's sweater, her feet bare against the forest floor. He scooted over, and she squeezed into the sleeping bag beside him. He opened his mouth to ask her to wake him when she left with Talikoth and the Inner Ring soldiers, but she was already kissing him again, her fingers tangling into his hair.

But while her lips on his normally filled his mind with a pleasant sort of emptiness, he could not seem to push down the nagging sense of worry—for all around her, he could still sense it. The same distressed energy that she carried with her when they had been collecting firewood in the forest.

He pulled back, stroking her hair back from her

face. "It's going to be fine," Atlas assured her.

Gaiomere tried to smile, but her lower lip trembled. "I'll just feel better when all of this is over," she mumbled.

"It'll be over soon. And then we can go climb up Big Wheel. And you can show me the Devil's Abyss."

Gaiomere laughed. "That's hundreds of miles from here."

Atlas shrugged. "What's it matter? We've got all the time in the world."

An odd expression appeared on her Gaiomere's face, like traces of joy tainted with the sting of a bad memory. For a fleeting moment, it looked as though she was going to cry. "I mean it," he said quietly, absently ghosting a finger over the sharp angle of her cheekbone. "I'm not going anywhere."

She kissed him once more, harder this time, and Atlas finally allowed himself to be distracted as Gaiomere pushed him back onto his sleeping bag, and his worries became little more than a faint murmur at the back of his mind.

CHAPTER
SEVENTEEN

The woods were largely silent as Atlas and his company moved through them. Silent almost to the point of peculiarity—he could not even hear the rustle of leaves or the scuffle of creatures on the ground, though that perhaps could have been because his blood was pounding so loudly in his ears.

Just ahead of him, Marathi wound between the trees, his face uncharacteristically tense. Talikoth had instructed Atlas to place the Blood Lender's leader near the front of their company. Should things go south, it seemed only fair that the first one to pay was the man who had facilitated the Flesh Flayers' exploits for the last decade. Whitsom was at Marathi's back, his gun hitched over his shoulder in such a way that Atlas knew, in a moment's notice, he could swing the barrel round and bury a bullet directly in the back of Marathi's head.

The rest of the Blood Lenders walked interspersed among Atlas' soldiers, their cuffed hands hanging limply in front of them as they trudged down the mountainside, unabashed fear written on many of their faces. A niggling of guilt bubbled in Atlas' stomach when he glanced back and saw Azaliah shuffling among them, his amber eyes wide.

"About a quarter mile," Whitsom called quietly.

As they came over the last hill, the dim moonlight revealed the valley below, still bathed in darkness.

"Where are we at, flower power?" Atlas murmured, his lips hardly moving as he spoke.

Gaiomere's voice sounded through the transmitter in his ear. *"First drone is almost through."*

Atlas glanced west, in the direction Niko's company would be making their way through the woodland. "We're in position, Niko."

"Almost there, At," came the older boy's reply. *"Maybe another five hundred feet."*

"Coral?"

"Tank's on standby," the blond boy assured him, presumably from where he and the tank crew were posted a mile back, waiting with guns loaded.

"I've got a visual, Atlas—" Gaiomere began, but a sudden explosion to the west drowned out her voice.

It was *loud*, so loud that the mountainside seemed to tremble. Atlas whipped around, and many of the other soldiers did, too. A massive plume of smoke erupted from beneath the canopy of trees, not a quarter mile away. Even at that distance, Atlas could hear shouting, and could see flames licking at the trees and foliage in the distance.

"That's the footpath Niko's company was taking!" Whitsom whispered urgently.

Terror pooled in the pit of Atlas' stomach. What had happened? Had a weapon backfired—or had Niko's company run into another foe?

Down in the valley, there was a sudden scraping of rock, and the echo of voices against the mountainside —a handful of Flesh Flayers were emerging from the underground—drawn, no doubt, by the sudden explosion.

Atlas glanced at Marathi. The Blood Lender's leader, unlike the soldiers on every side of him, looked entirely unfazed. Almost as though he'd expected this. And suddenly, everything fell into place.

"We've been betrayed," Atlas said shortly to Whitsom. He jerked his gun off his shoulder, levelled the barrel, and blasted a bullet directly through Marathi's temple. The black-haired man tipped forward and his dead body hit the ground with a pronounced *thud*, blood pouring from his head in a steady stream.

The rest of the Blood Lenders started to scramble, but Joaz and Olli hastily rounded them up and forced them into a huddle near a large oak. "Keep a barrel trained on them," Atlas commanded.

"*Atlas?*" Gaiomere's frantic voice crackled through. "*Atlas, what was that?*"

"The Blood Lenders set off some kind of explosion, to alert the Flesh Flayers that something was awry," Atlas said quickly. "Have you got a count?"

"*Maybe two hundred—but I'm not positive, a handful of them left when the explosion went off. All armed with automatics—*"

"Drive them out now, Gaiomere. We'll see if we can pick them off as they come out. Once the cave is clear, see if you can get a visual on the water valve."

Whitsom echoed directives to the rest of their company, and they started down the slope into the valley.

The ground beneath them had begun to level, and they'd drawn close enough now that the Flesh Flayers spotted them. Atlas dove behind a tree as the cannibals turned their guns on the approaching soldiers, and around him, his comrades scrambled to take cover too.

"Bombs away," came Gaiomere's nervous murmur.

Scarcely a minute passed before a second gaggle of Flesh Flayers came clamoring from the entrance. Atlas peered out from behind his tree, and took aim, successfully landing six consecutive shots before he had to whip behind the tree once more.

"What are *those?"* came Whitsom's voice, from somewhere to Atlas' left.

He glanced out from behind the tree again. Ten new Flesh Flayers had emerged from the entrance, each sporting a tall, metal shield, six feet tall, and four feet wide, like something Atlas had seen in old history books.

Yacielle fired a series of rounds at one of the Flesh Flayers, but the bullets ricocheted off his metal shield, as though they were only pebbles, in every direction.

"Be careful with those," Atlas warned. "Let's move to higher ground—we've got a better chance at getting around those things."

A proper flood of Flesh Flayers was emerging from the entrance now—but Atlas' company was making a dent in their numbers. They had not expected the assault upon emerging from their cave. As one Flesh Flayer scrambled from inside the rock, Atlas landed a shot through his cheekbone, and he promptly collapsed back inside the hole again.

Footsteps pounded behind them, and when Atlas turned, he spotted Ando and Zarr, followed by a dozen other soldiers. Both boys were covered in soot, and a gash ran across Zarr's cheek.

Atlas' brows shot up to his hairline. "What, this—this can't be all of you?" When Atlas and Niko had split up, there'd been a hundred soldiers assigned to each of them.

Ando grimaced. "The explosion did a lot of damage. Capalti already has a team of medics there to help who they can."

Zarr's eyes met Atlas'. "Niko's dead," he said quietly.

Atlas swallowed thickly, his eyes wandering towards the throng of Flesh Flayers. "Gaiomere," he said suddenly. "How's the cave looking?"

"*Almost empty,*" she replied. "*I see three stragglers.*"

Atlas nodded to himself. "Coral—I want you to come overload the tank at the entrance."

The blond sounded apprehensive. "*You don't think the shells will cause a cave in, Attie?*"

"You don't need to release any shells," Atlas returned calmly. "Bring the tank all the way down and mow them over."

"*Copy that.*"

"*Zyratier and I are circling with a squadron to ambush from the southeast,*" came Talikoth's voice suddenly.

Atlas glanced sideways to look for Whitsom—but the older boy was nowhere to be seen. "Where's—"

"The Blood Lenders were giving Olli trouble," Yacielle called, from where he crouched behind a rock, exchanging rounds with a Flesh Flayer who had pale, mealy skin. "Whitsom went to help."

Atlas turned instead to Zarr. "When the tank rolls through, let's you and I make a push for the cave."

They hardly had to wait two minutes before the tank came pelting down the hillside. Some of the Flesh Flayers spotted it a ways off—a few even scrambled back into the cave, apparently more off-put by the idea of being steamrolled than by choking on poisonous gas— but others were not so fortunate. They tried to dive out of the way too late, and a series of revolting cracks split through the air as the tank tracks crushed them.

"Let's go," Atlas told Zarr, and the two of them took off, weaving around soldiers and darting in and out of cover as they caught the attention of the Flesh Flayers that remained.

"Here!" Atlas called, ripping one of the shields from a dead Flesh Flayer's arm and tossing it to Zarr. "Watch your head."

Atlas had scarcely grabbed a shield of his own before a couple Flesh Flayers that had clambered over an outcropping of rock to get out of the tank's path sent a stream of bullets towards them. He lifted the shield clumsily in front of his face—it was bulky and difficult to maneuver, so heavy that he could barely manage more than a jog.

Zarr reached the entrance first. "Gaiomere, I need your eyes," Atlas said. He yanked Zarr down just as a pug-faced cannibal unloaded a shot in their direction.

"There's two by the entrance—right below the hole," Gaiomere informed him. *"The others are clustered around the southernmost corner of the cave—Atlas, I think that might be where the valve is located."*

"Copy that." He took a steadying breath. "Here goes nothing." Before Zarr could ask what he meant, he dropped into the hole.

Atlas didn't wait to see if Zarr had followed him, or even to gather his bearings. A flash of color and movement from his peripherals was all Atlas needed, and he swung his gun around, slamming the barrel into the first Flesh Flayer's head. The man groaned and slid to the ground. The second had not even lifted his gun before Atlas fired a shot through his heart.

The cave was disarmingly dark—he and Zarr stood in a dim window of light seeping in through the entrance, but outside of their little haven of visibility, it was only glimpses of smoke and shadow.

"How can you see in here?" Atlas murmured, as he passed Zarr the other earpiece.

He could almost hear the smile in Gaiomere's voice as she replied, "*I've got night vision—they don't.*"

"Can you see me?"

"*I've got you.*" Atlas could hear the faint whir of propellers further into the cave. "*Don't worry. I won't let you fall.*"

Atlas' lips quirked upwards, and he started across the slick rock, Zarr right on his heels. Gaiomere guided them deeper into the cave, and with every step they took, the dark seemed to grow denser. The silence was suffocating—the noises from the battle above ground slowly faded, and then vanished altogether, until all Atlas could hear was the sound of his and Zarr's breath, and the distant *drip, drip, drip* of water, coming from somewhere in the cave.

Atlas skin crawled, and his heartbeat felt as though it were pounding in his throat. "Gaiomere, we— haven't we got to be close?" he muttered.

Gunfire ripped through the air, and Atlas and Zarr both dropped to the ground. The echo reverberated off the walls of the cave, like some strange, haunting melody, and in the distance, Atlas heard the quiet murmur of voices, though he could not tell from which direction they came.

"*They can still hear you, even if they can't see you,*" Gaiomere chided.

Panic swelled in Atlas' chest, pulsing and fluttering violently, as though it threatened to overtake the beating of his own heart.

He could not think—not when the blood in his veins thrummed so loudly. He needed to get back to the entrance—back to the light, where he could rely on his own eyes, his own ears, his own feet—he needed to get out of this dark, dank *hell*, where he could not even trust himself, where he had *no control no control no control*—

"*Atlas,*" came Gaiomere's voice in his ear, further away at first, and then louder, until it was as though she were standing right next to him. "*Atlas, can you hear me?*" She seemed to sense he was panicking.

He swallowed, clearing his throat, before he managed to force out, in as quiet a voice he could, "Yes."

"*You've got to trust me, okay? Completely. Do you?*"

Atlas swallowed again and bobbed his head. "*Good. You've got four Flesh Flayers two hundred feet from you. Lift your gun at a fifty-degree angle towards your two o'clock. Then fire.*"

He did as she said, his breath catching in his throat as he pulled the trigger. There was a split second of silence, and then a sudden cry of pain followed by a pronounced thud. Atlas' lips lifted into a grin, and Gaiomere praised, "*Well done, Captain.*"

"They're probably checking his pulse," Zarr murmured at Atlas' side. He lifted his own gun—lower this time—and fired off two shots. The first seemed to miss, but the second hit its target, for one of the Flesh Flayers let out a groan.

"*Duck.*"

Atlas and Zarr pressed themselves flat against the cold stone slab of rock at their feet as an indiscriminate rain of gunfire burst over their heads.

"*Ten and twelve at sixty degrees as soon as they let up*," Gaiomere said.

They waited fifteen seconds until the gunfire ceased, before they sprang to their feet, and followed her directives. Two more *thuds* followed, and Gaiomere's voice hitched with excitement as she said, "*Your path forward is clear, a hundred steps southeast— careful twelve paces directly in front of you, unless you feel like going for a swim.*"

Atlas half-walked, half-jogged over the slippery rock, carefully skirting the lakes' edge, and clambering over the fallen Flesh Flayers' bodies. His hands clumsily skimmed the cave wall until he found it—a thin, flat, metal slab unmistakably shaped like a handle attached to a long pipe that plunged deep into the rock.

Zarr had evidently knelt beside the lake. Atlas could hear him splashing his face, and greedily sucking down great gulps of water. "This tastes like paradise," the black-haired boy declared. Atlas grinned. It was only then that he registered a faint blue light glowing in his peripherals, and too late.

"*Atlas!*" Gaiomere screamed. But she was too late, too.

The blue light emanated from a lantern, which Atlas did not realize until it swung towards him and collided against his forehead with a *crack*. Atlas groaned, his vision blurring, and his legs growing wobbly. His gun slipped from his hands and fell, clattering against the cave floor before it skidded into the lake.

He blinked away the haze in his eyes, peering at the Flesh Flayer. He was about as large as Grit, with shoulders as broad as a doorway, and legs like the trunks of small trees. His hair was long and matted, nearly reaching his elbows, and the lower half of his face was almost entirely obscured by a thick beard that brushed his sternum. This, undoubtedly, must have been Tantabar.

"Folks usually don't sneak *into* our cave," Tantabar remarked, leering. His voice reminded Atlas of the growl of a wild dog. "I won't complain."

He lunged for Atlas, and Atlas dove out of the way, stumbling a little on the edge of the water.

Zarr had taken advantage of the distraction and fired off a shot, which sank into Tantabar's shoulder. He let out a pained hiss, but the bullet seemed little more than a minor inconvenience, for he turned and knocked the gun from Zarr's hands. He grasped one of the boy's arms and flung him into the cave wall.

Atlas surged forward, ducking beneath the cannibal's outstretched arms and delivering several swift blows to Tantabar's stomach. The massive man grunted, and sent a meaty fist swinging towards Atlas' head, slamming him sideways into the rock face.

Tantabar reached for Zarr's gun, two feet from where he stood, but Atlas pushed himself off the wall and slammed into the larger man, wrapping his arms around one of Tantabar's massive thighs and driving him backwards.

Tantabar smacked his hands down so forcefully on the back of Atlas' head that his grip slackened, and the large man flung him sideways. Atlas collided with a jagged rock jutting from the cave wall, which scraped along the flesh of his back as he slid to the ground. Tantabar started towards him again, but Atlas swiped his leg low, knocking the Flesh Flayer's feet out from beneath him, and Tantabar stumbled to the ground.

In the dim blue light, Zarr looked as though he were flitting in and out of consciousness, his eyes darting rapidly beneath closed lids, but Atlas could not help him now. He sprang to his feet, diving on top of Tantabar and slamming a fist into his face as hard as he could. One of Tantabar's hands reached for the gun once more, and Atlas grasped blindly for a rock, slamming it down on Tantabar's nose.

The giant man roared, but his pain only seemed to fuel him, for he bucked his hips and sent Atlas sprawling sideways. He tried to stand, but Tantabar kicked him in the ribs, the heel of his boot digging so deep into Atlas' stomach that it knocked the breath from his lungs. Tantabar kicked again and a sharp pain burst on Atlas' side as a rib cracked. One of the giant's beefy hands reached down and clasped the collar of Atlas' shirt, dragging him to his feet and off the ground.

"Don't know why you fought so hard," Tantabar grunted, spitting blood from his mouth as he slammed Atlas into the rocky cave wall. "Your life means nothing."

His fingers tightened around Atlas' throat, until he could not draw breath. Atlas clawed desperately at Tantabar's hands, his eyes watering profusely. His chest burned—like someone held a match to his lungs and they caught fire, burning and building, the flames crawling up into his throat, and down into his stomach, consuming him entirely.

"*Atlas—hang on, Atlas!*" came Gaiomere's

desperate plea. She dropped another set of bombs, filling the cave with smoke—Atlas couldn't even smell the putrid stench—but Tantabar only leered wider, his fingers tightening around Atlas' throat. The drone veered down towards the large man, ramming into the side of his face—but he merely batted it away like an irksome insect, and the drone collided violently with the cave wall, and crumbled into a heap of useless scraps on the floor.

Atlas' skin prickled, as though tiny needles pierced every inch of his flesh, and he opened his mouth to yell, but couldn't. His legs flailed hopelessly, trying to find purchase on Tantabar's body, but the massive man pinned down both of Atlas' legs with one of his.

Tantabar sneered. His lips had pulled back over black rotted teeth, stale breath pluming between them, and Atlas realized that this was how he was going to die, thrashing like a fish out of water, pathetic, forgotten, insignificant—

His eyes had begun to blink shut, but they snapped back open when he heard a loud *clunk.* Tantabar groaned, sliding sideways, his grip on Atlas' throat slackening, and then releasing altogether.

Atlas fell to the floor, gasping for breath, massaging the skin of his throat as he looked up.

Talikoth stood over Tantabar, his face cast in eerie, blue light. Blood dripped from the butt of his gun, where he'd stricken Tantabar.

"I've killed *dozens* of these soldiers," Tantabar rasped, glaring up at him, even as the barrel of the gun pressed into the skin of his face. "What's one more?"

Talikoth's eyes flickered over to Atlas for the briefest moment, before he drawled, "That's not a soldier. That's my son." He pulled the trigger, and Tantabar sagged onto the ground, his dark eyes glassy and unblinking.

Talikoth offered him a hand, and Atlas gratefully took it, clambering to his feet, grasping at his stomach as pain shot through his ribs. "Uh...thanks," he mumbled.

His father was looking at him strangely, but after a moment, he asked, "You alright?" Atlas nodded, and Talikoth inclined his head. He looked, for a moment, as though he were going to say something else, but then he just reached over and gave Atlas' shoulder a squeeze. "Come on. Let's finish this."

Atlas picked up the gun lying near Tantabar's corpse and slung it over his back. He cast a glance at Zarr, who had fallen unconscious near the edge of the lake.

"We'll send a medic down for him," Talikoth assured him.

Atlas nodded, reaching for Tantabar's lantern, and the two of them hastily made their way back across the rock, until they reached the sliver of light slipping through the entrance hole.

Above ground, their soldiers had the last of the Flesh Flayers backed against the rockface, their weapons surrendered at their feet. Moonstone was striding across the clearing.

"We'll need to acquire some flashlights and send a squad to locate the water valve," Moonstone was saying to Yacielle, who walked beside her.

"There's no need," Talikoth called. "Atlas has already secured it."

Moonstone arched a brow. "Well done, Atlas."

Atlas' gaze, though, had already moved past her, as he surveyed the battlefield. Some of the Blood Lenders must have tried to escape, for he spotted bodies he recognized strewn about the ground. Malum, Amarius, and Damia.

Whitsom was still nowhere to be seen. A helpless sort of consternation welled up in Atlas' chest, until Talikoth leaned over and muttered, "He's up there." Atlas followed his father's extended finger and let out a breath of relief. Whitsom knelt atop the hill, his shoulders hunched and head bent.

"His treacherous little wench tried to make a run for it," Talikoth said, as he wiped the blood from his gun. He glanced sideways at Atlas, asking, "Do you believe he knew? And don't lie to me. I'll be able to tell if you're lying."

"He didn't know," Atlas said quickly. And as he said the words, he realized that he believed them. Whatever suspicions he might have had about Whitsom's loyalty, Atlas knew he would have never willingly sacrificed so many of his comrades.

Further west, smoke still spiraled towards the sky, which grew brighter by the second. The tank had parked about fifty feet from where they descended the mountain, and next to it sat Coral, hunched over a figure...a disarmingly familiar figure...bronze skinned and gangly...

Atlas' feet moved before he told them to. As he drew nearer, though, his steps slowed, his breath catching in his chest.

Bettoni lay sprawled out on the ground, unnaturally still, his head resting in a pool of blood. His dark eyes, which were normally bright, looked dull, and his skin was abnormally pale. Coral's hands gripped the blood-splattered fabric of Bettoni's shirt, his shoulders wracking with silent tears.

Atlas crouched down next to Coral. The blond boy had only just noticed him, but he let out a pained sob, like a wounded animal. Atlas wrapped an arm around his neck and pulled the shorter boy against his shoulder. "It's alright," Atlas muttered, sniffling, as his own eyes prickled and his nostrils burned. "It's alright."

Two of the medics soon came over to collect the body. Atlas and Coral got to their feet, stepping back and watching as the medics carried Bettoni away, his long frame drooping awkwardly between them.

"What happened?" Atlas asked quietly, tearing his gaze away from Bettoni's head, lolling beneath one of the medic's arms. "The explosion—"

"Ando said there was a tripwire that set off the explosives," Coral told him. "There were tons of them—he was one of the only ones that wasn't injured since he was near the back. I don't know how the Blood Lenders would have had an opportunity to set them up though..."

A pair of small, sooty hands flashed through Atlas' mind, and suddenly it clicked.

"Azaliah," he said. Coral looked at him. "The little boy that was with the Blood Lenders. Gaiomere and I saw him in the woods last night with soot all over his hands. I'll bet you anything Gwena taught him how to do it—she's the one that taught Gaiomere to set up trip wires." Atlas shook his head, spitting into the dirt. "I *saw* Gwena showing Marathi the wire—I just didn't realize what it was at the time—I was so—so *stupid*—"

"It wasn't just you," Coral interjected. "None of us

watched him close enough. No one thought a kid could do that kind of harm."

"Well, he *couldn't* have on his own," Atlas muttered, scowling. "Gwena showed him all he needed to know—Gaiomere warned me, in a way—"

He broke off suddenly, his eyes darting around the battlefield, but Coral cut him off before his panicking could start in earnest. "She's up there, with Whit."

Atlas peered up the incline and spotted them. After a moment of hesitation, he made his way towards them.

Whitsom was still kneeling, just where Atlas had seen him before, but now his sister had joined him. His body shook with sobs, and Gaiomere had an arm wrapped around him. Relief flooded across her face when she spotted Atlas, but when Whitsom saw him, he only let out a pained noise. His dark face was wet with tears.

Gwena lie in front of them, her skin pallid beneath her freckles, her eyes vacant and expressionless. There was a gaping, bloody hole right through the side of her forehead, and another in her neck.

"She was just trying to stay safe," Whitsom said, his voice raw. "She was just trying to survive, just like the rest of us."

Atlas and Gaiomere looked at each other, and he was quite sure they were thinking the same thing. Atlas wanted to yell at him, to tell him how many lives Gwena had sacrificed, in her selfishness. He wanted to tell him how she'd turned an twelve-year-old boy into a mass murderer, how he never should have trusted Gwena in the first place.

But instead, Atlas sank down beside him, placing a hand on Whitsom's shoulder, and the older boy sagged against him, fresh tears tumbling down his face, great gasping breaths wrenching from his throat. Gaiomere curled into her brother's side, her fingers delicately rubbing circles on his back, and the three of them sat there, none of them speaking, until the sun had risen far past the mountain crest, basking the valley in a warm, golden glow.

CHAPTER EIGHTEEN

I t had been three weeks since they'd returned from the caverns when Atlas knocked on Dak and Alvi's door. There was a faint shuffling of papers, the scratch of a chair against floorboard, and then the soft thud of footsteps, before the door swung open. "Atlas," Colonel Dak greeted, with a small smile.

"Hey, Colonel. Is Gaiomere here, by chance?"

Dak held the door open wider. "She is not. She and Alvi took the twins down to feed the ducks by the pond —but while you're here, I wanted to speak with you. Come in, won't you?"

Atlas stepped inside the unit, nervousness tingling under the surface of his skin. "Sir, I just wanted to say—if this is about last weekend—the um—*couch* situation—Gaiomere and I were watching the twins the whole time, honest—they had just fallen asleep, and we uh—we just got a bit carried away—she was terrified you guys would never let her watch Sutti and Quill again—"

Dak held up a hand, chuckling heartily. "This is *not* about that, Atlas. From what I heard your father gave you enough of an earful to last you a lifetime."

Atlas' cheeks flushed, and rubbed the back of his neck. "Yes, sir, he did."

"No, this is about the aftermath of our excursions three weeks ago," Dak continued, pulling out a chair and gesturing for Atlas to sit, before he settled in a seat across the table.

"Has there been word from the lake?" Atlas asked.

Two and a half weeks ago, Talikoth had sent Kordell with a team of five hundred soldiers to serve as a permanent patrol for the caverns, but their first task had been to locate Azaliah—he alone had escaped execution, while the remaining Blood Lenders that had not been killed in the conflict were lined up against the cavern wall and mown down like little more than pawns on a chessboard. Moonstone was furious when she found out that Talikoth had taken such actions without consulting her, and Atlas couldn't say he blamed her. How many of the Blood Lenders might have been like Gwena or Rich—only taking advantage of protections that kept them alive? How many of them might have turned away from their practices—even elected to begin contributing to the rebuilding of the Westland, as so many of the Ramshacklers had—were they given a chance?

But instead they'd been killed before they'd ever been given the opportunity. And Azaliah had fled into the mountains.

Dak shook his head. "No, no sign of the boy. I've told Talikoth he'd be better served disbanding his search—the boy's likely dead by now, without any water...." Dak gave Atlas a wry smile. "But, you know your father. He is nothing if not determined."

Atlas doubted that Azaliah was dead. The tribespeople knew how to survive in the wilderness—more likely than not, this was Talikoth's thinking, too.

Still, Atlas thought it better that they didn't find the boy. Everyone who had shepherded his path was dead, and he'd have to come to terms with what he'd done when he was older, one way or another.

"I didn't see you at the secondary trial," Dak observed, leaning back in his chair and folding his hands in front of him.

"Yeah, well, I didn't think I'd have much to contribute to this one," Atlas said dryly. "Besides, I already knew what the outcome would be."

Dak nodded, his dark brows furrowing. "Moonstone considers herself to be at a great impasse," he murmured softly. "The Obarion clan has voted to reinstate Talikoth as General—overwhelmingly so. 5,917 to 1,975."

"I'm not surprised," Atlas said, scowling. "This was his plan from the beginning—he knew his wrongs would be forgotten as long as he recovered the water and cast himself as the hero. And we all played right into his hands." He cast an accusatory glance across the table. "You knew all along what he was doing, and you—you *let* him do it. You stood by and watched."

"I did," Dak agreed. "I'm under no delusions that your father had led our clan perfectly these last twenty years, Atlas. But the mistakes he has made do not outweigh the tireless effort he's put into ensuring our people's prosperity." He leaned forward, resting his elbows on the table. "And on a personal level—I owe your father a lifetime of debts. No amount of riches could persuade me to betray him."

Atlas' eyes raked over the older man's face. He wanted to ask a thousand questions. But some, he knew, were more pertinent than others. "Moonstone doesn't want Talikoth elected back," Atlas concluded, and Dak's nod confirmed this. "So is she ignoring the vote and giving the post to you, like she mentioned in her addendum?"

Dak sighed, setting his glasses on the table and massaging the bridge of his nose. "There is considerable risk in either path she chooses, moving forward. *She* believes that if she does concede to elect him back, we may see an end to every other tribe in the Westland."

Atlas nodded. "Talikoth knows their numbers now—their strengths, and weaknesses. He knows the location of the base in the North, and the landmines aren't there to stop him. The Vedas wouldn't stand a chance if he chose to turn against them again."

"And if Moonstone *doesn't* adhere to the vote, she may face revolt," Dak said. "She will have essentially made a mockery of our people's democratic process. And we may not all be armed, but she knows very well that we have numbers she cannot contend with." He sighed heavily. "Even if I took up the post, I fear that would not stay our people's fury, and, to be perfectly honest...I have no real desire to serve as general." He gave Atlas a wry smile. "Alvi and I have toddlers. They are...quite a handful. I'd rather not take on the helm of the clan in *this* particular season of life."

Atlas let out a huff of laughter. He tipped back in his chair, gazing contemplatively at the ceiling. "She's got to elect him back, doesn't she?" The front legs of his chair hit the ground with a pronounced *thud*. "The only way the Westland will rebuild is by unifying the clans —we know for certain that if we don't elect him back, there will be nothing but discord. Electing him back runs the risk of discord still, but if I've got the choice, I'd rather go the route of potential mass destruction, rather than guaranteed—wouldn't you? Besides, the

Obarion people know what he's done. The good and the bad. They made their choice."

Dak inclined his head, drumming his fingers pensively against the tabletop. "For what it's worth," he began, "I do not think that Talikoth will turn on Moonstone, or our allies among the Renegades, so long as its mutually-beneficial. Your father likes to do things his way, but...he also learns from his mistakes."

He seemed to hesitate for a moment, before he said, "There was an...amended option, that I mentioned to Moonstone following the trial. I suggested that it would be in the best interest of *all* of the inhabitants of the Westland, to place a figure at Talikoth's side who might serve as something of a preventative force—a voice of reason, if you will—to his more...nefarious...leanings. It certainly may have spared some lives at the caverns."

Dak's eyes fixed on Atlas' face. "Moonstone trusts you—as do the Renegades—and from what I've observed, this trust has not been won from deceit. You *genuinely* care for their well-being."

Atlas shifted uncomfortably. "Well, of course I do," he mumbled, rubbing the back of his neck. "They're my friends—fellow soldiers that I've fought beside—"

"Which is why Moonstone agreed that it would be beneficial for every party involved, if you were to take up the mantle of Lieutenant General."

Atlas blinked, staring at Colonel Dak for a full fifteen seconds. He waited for him to crack a smile, or perhaps for Talikoth to poke his head through the door and declare that this was all just a prank he had put his old friend up to. But when Dak merely continued to look back at him, Atlas started to get the sense that he wasn't joking.

"Me?" Atlas spluttered, his cheeks flushing. "No, you—come on, be serious."

Dak arched a brow. "I assure you my proposal was quite earnest." Atlas opened his mouth, closed it, and then opened it once more, but before he could say a word, Dak held up a hand. "I don't want your answer just yet. Think about it a day or two, will you?"

Atlas swallowed thickly. After a few seconds, he bobbed his head. "Good," Dak said, pushing himself to his feet. "Alvi and Gaiomere are probably on their way back from the pond—you'll more likely than not run into her, if you head in that direction."

Atlas nodded again, though he'd scarcely registered the older man's words. He numbly clambered to his feet, and had almost made it to the door when he stopped, a photograph that hung beside the entrance catching his eye.

He hadn't seen it before—or perhaps he had, years and years ago, but it hadn't meant anything to him back then. He recognized Maichell in the photograph, that familiar impish smile curled around her lips, and Olympion stood next to her. Alvi sat cross-legged on a stone wall beside her sister, beaming at the camera, and off to the side, looking rather regal and standoffish, were Alvi and Maichell's parents, whom Atlas had met a handful of times, when Talikoth had forced him to attend dinners in their unit.

Atlas' eyes, though, had fastened on Olympion. The sight of him had stirred a memory Atlas' mind.

Your mother wasn't the saint that Delurah led you to believe. Her case cannot be compared to his.

What had been so special about Olympion that

his sins could be so easily forgiven, when Talikoth could not look past his own wife's misdeeds?

Or perhaps the better question was: what had Caterra done so terrible that Talikoth's resentment lived on, even beyond her death?

Another memory stirred in Atlas' mind, more distant than the first, and it was only Dak's voice that pulled him from his thoughts.

"Atlas? Is something wrong?"

He realized belatedly that he still stood in the doorway of the Colonel's unit. But instead of continuing out into the hall, he turned back to face Dak.

"I need to ask you something," Atlas said. "About my mother."

Dak's brows flitted up, and surprise flashed through his dark eyes. "Your mother?" he repeated.

Atlas nodded. "What did you mean—what you said to me, three months ago? About how I didn't 'know her like you did?'" Before Dak could answer, Atlas' eyes narrowed, and he added, "And don't tell me that it's complicated, or that I'm too young to understand. Don't —don't tell me anything but the truth."

The older man watched him for a few moments. It looked as though he warred with himself, and Atlas had the sudden apprehension that Dak would not tell him. Talikoth had not given him express permission to do so—and who was he but another person in Talikoth's pocket?

But then he sighed. "Your mother coordinated an attack on Obarion headquarters in union with the Vedas. She gave them the intel on where and how to strike." Dak looked away from Atlas, the muscle in his jaw tightening, and continued, "They launched explosives in a mangonel over the southern perimeter of our wall, and struck a—" His voice broke, and he rubbed at the bridge of his nose, pressing on, "And struck a crèche, where fifty or so children were being looked after." He hesitated, before adding, "Alvi and I had a—a son—he'd be about Gaiomere's age, now..." He trailed off, but it was not difficult to discern the rest.

Atlas stared at the Colonel, sickness pooling in his stomach, so strong that he worried, for a moment, that all the contents of his lunch would end up on Dak's kitchen floor. "When was this?" he asked, his voice scarcely louder than a whisper.

"Sixteen years ago, this autumn."

Atlas frowned. "Sixteen—but that—that would have put her attack right around the time of the hundred-child slaughtering."

Dak arched a brow and gave Atlas a dubious look. "Well, of course—do you think your father would have let such an atrocity go unpunished? He promised Alvi that whatever harm the Vedas had caused, he would double it. And Talikoth always keeps his promises."

Atlas realized that he was trembling, and he dug his fingernails into his palms to stop it. "Was Moonstone...was she the one that—"

Dak shook his head. "The Vedas General at the time was a fellow named Mamotek. He was killed some two weeks after the hundred-child slaughtering, after which Moonstone was elected in. She wrote to Talikoth and requested they meet on neutral ground, and they came to the agreement that no more children would be killed in the conflict between their clans." Dak smirked wryly, inclining his head as he admitted, "I'm sure, in Talikoth's mind, he was upholding their agreement, in his trades to the Blood Lenders. That's the only reason he didn't come North for you, last winter—he trusted Moonstone to keep her word."

Atlas couldn't decide what to address first. The fact that the hundred-child slaughtering had been retaliation—or perhaps the fact that his father had not merely left him for dead, as he'd suspected for so long, when he was captured by the Vedas.

But then a sudden realization struck him. "Moonstone, she—she knew. About the attack at Headquarters, about what my mother had done—she knew everything?"

Dak lifted a shoulder. "I presume so."

Atlas swallowed thickly, nodding his head. "I —okay, I—thank you. I'll um—I'll think about your proposal, I've just—I've got to...." He didn't bother finishing his sentence, but bolted out of the room.

He stalked down the corridor, out of the officers' lodgings, and across the grounds, yanking open the door to the Main, blood pounding in his ears.

When he reached her office, he didn't knock. He flung open the door so hard that it slammed into the wall behind it.

Moonstone, who sat behind her desk with a stack of notes, jumped, though she quickly regained her composure. "Can I help you with something, Atlas?"

He didn't waste a second. "You didn't mention that the hundred-child slaughtering was retributive. On the transmitter in the North, when I warned you about the Obarion soldiers near your base. You didn't mention it."

Moonstone blinked, sitting back in her chair. Only the faintest hint of surprise crossed her face before it quickly returned to an impassive expression. "No, I did not," she said mildly.

She still looked calm, and for some reason, this infuriated Atlas. He wanted to see her fumble, he wanted to watch her scramble for an excuse or stutter out lies, but instead, she just gazed back at him, her dark eyes watching him shrewdly.

"Why?" Atlas blurted out, before he could stop himself. "How could you—I mean—"

Moonstone leaned forward, folding her hands together atop her desk. "I meant what I said, Atlas. I trust your conclusions above almost anyone else—I like you, I truly do—"

"Then how could you lie to me?" he growled out.

"This is war, Atlas," Moonstone snapped, a hint of impatience seeping into her tone. "Would you have been nearly so malleable to our cause if I hadn't withheld *some* information?"

Atlas jerked back, staring numbly at the woman across the desk.

"I saw in you a boy—a young man—with remarkable talent, arrogance that superseded the caution that a more seasoned soldier might employ— more charisma than you knew what to do with. I knew that if you honed those gifts, the people of the Westland would follow you wherever you saw fit to lead them." She got to her feet, pacing behind her desk. "I *also* knew that if I wasn't careful, I might create, in you, a very powerful enemy. It was why I had to tread so carefully, why I protected you when half my council wanted to have you exiled. I feared, were you to go, that a thousand Renegades might follow you. And their alliance is very useful to my clan."

Atlas scowled, pushing aside a chair and snarling, "That's the reason you're so keen on Dak's proposal, isn't it? You want me at Talikoth's side because you think you can use me—"

"It's never been about using you, Atlas," Moonstone said with a sigh, as she sank back into her chair. "You've got innovative ideas, your mind chews through problems like vapor—I just needed to steer you in the right direction—for the good of the people."

For the good of the people.

Atlas shook his head quickly, his eyes raking over Moonstone's face, wondering how, *how* he had not seen it before—for what were she and Talikoth, but two sides of the same coin?

"If you'll only work with me, you'll see that I want nothing more than what's best for the Westland at large —"

"Why would I want to work with you?" Atlas said, his hands clenched at his sides. "All you've ever done is manipulate me—just like him."

"Atlas," Moonstone began. Her voice sounded almost pleading, and when Atlas glanced at her, he thought, for a split second, that her eyes were wet with tears, but when he blinked, the illusion was gone. "I'm sorry that you feel betrayed. That was never my intention."

"No need to apologize," Atlas said coolly. He grasped blindly behind him for the doorknob, adding, "That's what soldiers are good for, right? Being used. I'm happy to be of service." He gave her a mock salute, yanked the door open, and stormed from the room.

Atlas' mind was a torrent of emotions as he pounded through the halls back to his unit. When he'd discovered the truth about his mother's death all those months ago, he'd been upset, but if he were honest with himself, he couldn't be *that* surprised. The Obarion clan was consistent in its practices—treason was not something taken lightly. Then when he'd learned that it was his father who'd done the deed, he'd been angry. But now...

Now he felt *hurt*. It was as though a rug had been ripped from beneath his feet, and he was scrambling for purchase, trying to orient himself amongst an indistinguishable blur of shape and color. Moonstone had been his one constant—she'd protected him, back in the North—and even a few months ago, when she'd confined him at Headquarters—after all of his indignation had subsided, he'd recognized that she was only allowing him to undergo the natural consequences of his actions. Almost like a parent would.

Had any of it been genuine? Her affection, her respect—or was it all just means to an end?

Atlas wound his way through the hall and out onto the grounds, his feet carrying him back towards the officers' lodgings.

At least with Talikoth, he'd operated under no delusions that his father *liked* him—even before he'd been captured by the Vedas. Atlas didn't take it personally. Talikoth was always just so razor focused on his work that he seemed to take little enjoyment from *anyone's* company.

But Moonstone, he'd known, had a soft spot for him. He'd even taken advantage of it.

Or at least—he'd *thought* she did. Was even this just a fabrication to keep him serving her interests?

Talikoth sat at the dining room table in their unit,

but he did not even glance up from his notes when the door opened. Atlas crossed the room in silence and disappeared into his bedroom, slamming the door shut behind him.

He sank down onto the edge of his bed and pulled off his boots, staring unseeingly at the blank stretch above his desk. For the first time since he'd found out about his mother's attack, Atlas allowed his mind to wander to Dak's proposal.

A year ago, Atlas would have given his right arm for such an opportunity—to be the youngest lieutenant general ever appointed in their clan's history. The boy he was before being captured by the Vedas would have taken Dak up on the offer without hesitation.

But then, that boy also would have killed Moonstone without a second thought, if he'd needed to. That boy had seen Gaiomere as a useful vessel for information to be utilized and, if necessary, discarded. That boy would have bent over backwards to please his father.

Atlas leaned back on his bed, folding his hands behind his head. He contemplated hunting down Whitsom and asking him what he thought about it, but Whitsom would only encourage him. For all the boy's wisdom, Whitsom had more faith in him than Atlas thought he deserved.

Coral would be no help, of course. He would be flabbergasted that Atlas would even consider refusing Dak's offer.

No, the advice that Atlas really needed right now was Bettoni's.

Yesterday was the first morning he hadn't woken up feeling like an ox was sitting on his chest. The first few days after they had returned, every time the door to his unit opened he half-expected Coral and Bettoni to come trouncing in together with some crazy story to share or a stupid joke to tell.

Besides his mother, Atlas had never lost someone close to him—and even in her case, he had been far too young to remember her. Raider's death had been jarring in a different way. Atlas respected Raider, but he had really only just begun to like him as a person, and not nearly enough to make his death truly painful. Atlas had mourned the loss of potential, certainly, for Raider had been a formidable fighter, brilliant and gifted, and would have made his clan an exceptional ally.

But with Bettoni, Atlas had so many *memories*. They had known each other for years—had gone through Academy together, trained together, fought together, pranked together, played hundreds of games of bruiseball together...only to have him ripped away in the blink of an eye, as though suddenly, all of that meant nothing. A person was missing from their clan—from the world—a heart that wasn't beating anymore, blood that wasn't flowing, neurons and synapses that weren't firing—and still the earth kept spinning. It was almost insulting. Even infuriating.

Most days Atlas could distract himself. But every now and again a wave of anger swelled up, so fierce and intense that it felt as though it might consume him.

Quandra—Bettoni's girl—had, unsurprisingly taken his death harder than any of them. Gaiomere went to visit her often, bringing baskets teeming over with muffins and sweets she'd traded for at the Hole, or sometimes just keeping her company, despite the fact that the two of them had only ever exchanged a handful of words. It was one of the things Atlas admired most about Gaiomere.

He scowled, rolling over onto his stomach. Even Gaiomere, with all her aversion to war, would be better suited as lieutenant general than he. Atlas was too selfish. He would not hesitate to sacrifice any number of lives, if it meant saving Gaiomere's, or Whitsom's.

But Gaiomere embodied the sort of unreserved compassion that a leader should have, to serve their people. Atlas hadn't thought to bring Quandra flowers, like she had, or to drive with Zarr and Luca up to Niko's Ramshackle to give he and Clancy a proper burial. He most certainly would not have spent an entire day crafting Jemahl a brand new pistol to cheer him up after he'd found out Favio and Hix had both been slain in the scuffle with the Flesh Flayers the way that she had.

Still, Atlas doubted that Dak would have proposed the role if he did not think Atlas suited for it. Moonstone's motivations were questionable, but what did Dak have to gain?

What had he done, Atlas wondered, that demonstrated to the Colonel—to *anyone*—that he could take on such a position—and only months after he'd betrayed his entire clan? He'd been hungry, just weeks ago, for more responsibility, but now he wondered if this would be too much.

Never had Atlas yearned so badly for a parental figure that he felt close to—someone he could actually talk to, without feeling foolish. His first instinct was usually Delurah, but he could not speak to her about this. She, like Whitsom, thought too highly of him.

No, he needed someone painstakingly rational, someone objective. Someone capable of compartmentalizing their emotions almost to the point of machinery...

Atlas sat up slowly on his mattress, eyeing the closed door that led out to the main room. After a moment of hesitation, he swung his legs over the edge of his bed and pushed himself to his feet.

Talikoth's chin was resting on his fist as he flipped rather disinterestedly through his thick stack of notes. It looked as though his eyes might have been drooping, but he snapped up very quickly when Atlas opened his bedroom door.

"If I had been an adversary, you'd have a bullet lodged in your skull right now," Atlas said, plopping down into the seat across from his father.

"If you were an adversary, that door would have been locked," Talikoth retorted, blearily rubbing his eyes.

"The front door was unlocked when I came in," Atlas pointed out, leaning back in his seat. "Split second —boom—arrow through the temple—"

"Have you shot many arrows that go 'boom'?" Talikoth asked wryly.

"I like to make my own sound effects, actually," Atlas fired back. "Makes everything a little more high stakes—"

"You're absurd," his father snapped, though the corners of his mouth twitched suspiciously.

Atlas drummed his fingers against the wooden tabletop for a few seconds before he managed to force out, "Can I uh—can I talk to you about something?"

Talikoth blinked, straightening up in his seat. The only distinguishable indication of his surprise was the faintest tilt in his eyebrow. He leaned back in his chair, mirroring Atlas' position, and mildly asked, "Did you get the girl pregnant?"

The front legs of Atlas' chair slammed down onto the ground with a bang. "What?" he spluttered, his cheeks flushing bright pink. "Did I—no!"

"Damn," Talikoth muttered. When he caught Atlas' astonished expression, he explained, "Dak was going to owe me an entire week's worth of cigars. Ah well, the year is young."

The flush in Atlas' cheeks had deepened to crimson red. "You two bet that I'd get her pregnant, and you—you bet against me?" Atlas demanded. "What, do you think I'm irresponsible or something?"

Talikoth made a noncommittal noise, pushing himself up from his seat and moving around the table to rummage through the pantry, oblivious to Atlas' seething glare. He returned moments later with a large strip of jerky. "I presume this isn't about the girl, then?"

"No," Atlas said quickly. His father arched a brow in question, and suddenly, the words were gushing out of him rather like a dam had been loosed.

Talikoth listened silently, his face impassive. By the time Atlas finished, he was breathless, and angry all over again.

"I was wondering when they'd present you with their little proposition," was the first thing his father said.

"You knew about it?" Atlas asked.

"I encouraged Dak to coax Moonstone in that direction," Talikoth said, lifting a shoulder lazily.

Atlas stared at him for a few moments, his mind working at an irritatingly sluggish pace. "You—*you're* the one that wanted me as your lieutenant general?"

"Dak made me aware that he had no desire for the role," Talikoth confirmed. He leaned his elbows against the table, folding his hands together, and continued, "I considered it a favorable alternative to any other dolt Moonstone might elect in his place."

Atlas hesitated, running a hand through his hair. "I'm not....ready to be lieutenant general," he said, unsure if he was trying to cement the fact in his own mind, or merely conveying the information to Talikoth. Even to his own ears, his words sounded less like a statement, and more like a question.

"None of us are ever ready," Talikoth remarked cryptically. He smirked, adding, "Besides, you're much more reasonable than some of the fools you surround yourself with."

"You would only allow me to take the position because you believe I would be a puppet," Atlas guessed, frowning. His glower was steely as he maintained, "I wouldn't be."

"No, you've proven yourself to be much more than a puppet," Talikoth agreed.

He said nothing else, and Atlas let out a sound of frustration. "But you—you can't honestly want me as your lieutenant general. I mean, I—I disagree with you on tons of things."

His father shrugged. "So does Dak. A good leader surrounds themselves with different perspectives, to maintain balance. You know that. You've seen it."

Atlas let out a heavy breath. He wanted very much to walk back into his room and slam the door behind him, to forcibly put an end to this conversation, but these thoughts had been weighing on his mind now, too long.

"Did you ever regret it?" he asked. "What you did to my mother?"

For a moment, Atlas thought his father would lash out again, like he had back on the mountainside. Or perhaps he'd shut down all together. Maybe he would leave the unit and ensure Atlas never got the opportunity to raise such questions again.

But Talikoth did something strange, then. He absently reached for his pencil atop the table, turning it over between his fingers.

"Sometimes," he murmured, so softly Atlas nearly didn't hear him. "Sometimes I wish I hadn't chosen the way that I had—though probably not for the reasons you're thinking." Talikoth swallowed so hard that Atlas saw his throat bob. It was such a human movement that it looked strange on his father.

"I had scarcely been General for two years when Caterra betrayed us," Talikoth told him in a low voice. "The climate in our clan was already...tense. I needed to cement my people's loyalty. I needed to ensure that they knew I was willing to do whatever was necessary for the sake of our people. That I could protect our clan against anyone—rivals, foes, or even our own."

"But—but how come you needed to cement their loyalty?" Atlas asked, bewildered. "Wouldn't you have already done that, after bringing our clan back from the brink of famine?"

"No. I was already on thin ice with the Council. They were...deliberating whether or not I was fit to lead this clan. Just a year before, our clan's lead researcher betrayed us, and I let he, his pregnant wife, and their four-year-old son walk free against the Council's wishes."

Atlas' mouth opened, and then closed again. He pushed to his feet, paced a few steps, and then sat back down. "You let—you let Gaiomere's parents go? But—but why? If Olympion really did contribute so much to our clan's success, wouldn't you have wanted to make him stay?"

Talikoth smirked a little, then. "Olympion and I disagreed on our...managerial approach. Eventually he started to denounce my leadership publically. The Council wanted to have him executed. I disagreed, but eventually, they grew impatient. When I discovered that they had decided to carry out their plans behind my back, Dak and I organized an escape for Olympion and his family."

Atlas' mind churned as he tried to digest this new information. "Why—why would you do that for him? Especially if he was publically denouncing your actions? Wouldn't an execution have served to make an example out of him?"

Talikoth's face twitched, and he set his gaze somewhere above Atlas' head. When he spoke again, his voice was scarcely more than a whisper. "I wasn't referring only to you when I mentioned that this clan has seen too much of my humanity, you know." He shook his head, scowling. "An unfortunate byproduct of my friendship with Olympion was an inability to watch the man hang for his crimes."

It was perhaps the most emotion Atlas had ever gotten out of his father—apart from anger—but he could not even take a moment to appreciate it, too quickly was his mind moving.

"But why did Olympion get that benefit, and not my mother?" he demanded. "Even if you were on thin ice with the Council, she was still your wife."

It an instant, irritation furrowed his father's brows. "Not by choice," Talikoth said coldly. "I didn't regret killing her because I loved her, Atlas. I regretted killing her because I knew someday, inevitably, you would find out the truth. And when you did, I knew I would run the risk of losing your loyalty—perhaps forever."

Atlas' mind was reeling. He wasn't sure what he wanted to address first—the fact that his father had just admitted he never loved Atlas' mother, or perhaps that Atlas' loyalty meant more to him than he ever realized —that was, if his father was telling the truth. "What do you mean, it wasn't by choice?" he asked finally.

"It was an arranged marriage," Talikoth said, waving a dismissive hand in the air. "It was quite common within the Conclave, back before I assumed my rank—I abolished the whole practice within the first year of being General."

"An arranged..." Atlas wrinkled his nose, appalled, bewildered, and mortified all at once. He had known, of course, that such things had existed, from all the books he had read, but he had always thought the practice was archaic. He never would have suspected that his own people would partake in such customs— and so recently, too.

"So, you didn't—you and my mother didn't even like each other? Not even a little?" Atlas rather felt as though he'd been dropped in the middle of the sea with no sense of direction. He felt tainted. As though his birth—his very existence—was less meaningful, being the result of a union that neither party wanted. An obligatory merger of mutual benefit.

"We tolerated one another, Atlas. The union was necessary to secure my position as general. Anakhletus didn't want any of the other laborers to think their own ascension to power could be so feasible without the Conclave's hand of favor." Talikoth shot him a wry smirk, adding sardonically, "If you're waiting to hear me tell you tales of all the sonnets I sang to her, dangling from the balcony of her bedroom window, you'll be sorely disappointed."

Atlas' brows furrowed. "Look, regardless of how you felt about her—even if my mother *wasn't* a saint—you've slaughtered hundreds of tribespeople—civilians—*children*—"

"Do you think I'm alone?" Talikoth interjected impatiently. "All the history books you've read, and you're still operating under the delusion that every season of mankind hasn't looked the same? I did what was necessary to secure our place in the Westland. It was the choice between their wellbeing, and ours. There was never going to be a question of which I'd choose." His father leaned forward and gave Atlas a piercing look.

"Tell me honestly, Atlas. Did you ever want for anything?" Atlas said nothing, and Talikoth continued. "In my day, laborers might go a week without seeing a meal. I worked until my hands bled, for scraps, and watched my father simper at the feet of men who were not fit to lick the ground he walked on, so I'll ask you again, did you *ever* want for anything?"

Atlas shook his head numbly, and mumbled, "No, sir."

"Of course you didn't. You can air out all the atrocities I've committed and whine and gripe about how I didn't tell you 'good job' as much as you'd have liked, but you've never had to struggle the way I did —I made sure of it." Talikoth scowled, continuing, "I never claimed to be perfect, Atlas. I see now that there are areas where I could have done better. I'm not going to apologize for the past, but—I do think we have an opportunity moving forward to reshape the future." He raised an eyebrow, his dark eyes glittering, and asked, "Join me?"

A jittery sort of nervousness bubbled up in Atlas' stomach, not unlike the excitement before a fight or a game of bruiseball.

Dak had offered him the world, but Atlas hardly stopped to consider his proposition. Until, that was, he'd learned that it had come from Talikoth, and then —well, that changed everything. Suddenly, everything he'd ever wanted—a place at his father's side, and at the recommendation of the man himself—had been thrust out before him, on a shining silver platter. All he had to do was reach out and take it.

Maybe if you had spent less time trying to impress me and more time forming your own place in the world, I might have been.

Atlas pushed himself out of his seat to stand. "No. I'm not going to be lieutenant general."

Talikoth blinked. "No?" he repeated, as though perhaps he thought he might have heard Atlas wrong.

"No," Atlas replied calmly.

The best thing that ever happened to you was getting captured by Moonstone.

"What do you mean 'no?'" Talikoth snapped, standing up as well and straightening to his full height. "Have you got any idea—"

"I'm grateful for everything you sacrificed," Atlas said earnestly. "And I want to pay it back tenfold, but...I don't want to be lieutenant general. I know that's what you want, but it's not the path I choose."

Talikoth looked unquestionably flabbergasted as he stared at Atlas. He started to speak several times, before his mouth snapped shut, and he seemed to reevaluate. "Atlas," his father ground out through gritted teeth. "Do you have any idea what you're refusing—"

"I know exactly what I'm refusing," Atlas said firmly. He stood his ground, even as his father rounded the table and stopped directly in front of him, his glower so venomous that it could have curdled milk.

"Look, I spent my whole life trying to make you happy—trying to give you a reason to be proud of me, and I know my becoming lieutenant general would make you proud, but I just—I can't do it."

"Atlas, don't be absurd," Talikoth growled, slamming his hand against the tabletop beside them. "You said it yourself—you and I are a part of something larger. You've already seen what we can do together if we're willing to strike a balance—"

"I *do* think we're part of something larger. And I know we both have a role to play in restoring the Westland," Atlas said. "I just know my role isn't here right now."

You came back to the South a man, not a little boy trying to make everyone else happy.

Talikoth scoffed, angrily turning to pace in the entryway. He shoved over a chair, and it fell to the floor with a clatter, but they both ignored it. "Oh, and what will your role be then?" his father asked sneeringly. "I suppose you'll fill your days with meaningless patrols and games and drivel, like Coral and the rest of the soldiers—spend your nights drowning in pints of beer and squandering away your potential like a pathetic scrounge, will you?"

Atlas registered all of the condescension in his father's tone and gaze, but it didn't seem to punch him in the gut the way it once had. He shrugged his shoulders. "Gaiomere likes the North. Maybe we'll go help out in the Ramshackles up there for a bit. Or, if she wants, maybe we'll go east. Find out what's out there, I suppose."

His father's eyes had thinned to slits now, and a triumphant smirk suddenly flitted across his face. "Dak and Alvi will never let her go," he said lowly.

"They aren't in charge of her. If she wants to go, she can go. Besides, if we're in the North, she'll be close enough to visit whenever she wants—"

"Who's to say she'll even want to go?" Talikoth snarled, his lip curling scornfully. "Her entire family's here—it would be selfish of you to ask her to leave all of that, when she's just reconnected with her aunt, and her grandparents."

Atlas was not so naive as to think his father didn't know exactly what he was doing. Talikoth would needle at every doubt, every insecurity that wriggled in the back of Atlas' mind to get what he wanted. If there was a snowball's chance in hell at convincing him to stay, it would be through Gaiomere.

"If she really didn't want to leave, we'd figure it out," Atlas said, crossing his arms over his chest. "But there's nothing left here for me." His father started to argue once more, and Atlas continued, "There's tons of untapped potential in the Westland—just think how much more there could be in the East. The rest of the Ren have been doing it already for ages—"

Talikoth had stilled, his expression morphing from angry to murderous in a split second. "You are *not* a Renegade," he said in a low, dangerous voice.

Atlas shrugged. "In a way, I sort of am."

Talikoth let out a growl. "I refuse to allow you to go tramping all around the Fallen Land like some transient. You have responsibilities here—"

"No, Dad, *you* have responsibilities here."

Only belatedly did Atlas realize what he'd said, and he only realized it because Talikoth's head jerked back, as though Atlas had slapped him, his expression shuddering down almost in an instant.

Atlas sighed, turning away and starting towards his room, but he stopped in the doorway, glancing over his shoulder at his father, who was still standing in the same spot. "And for the record," he said quietly. "You've still got my loyalty."

CHAPTER NINETEEN

A tlas had scarcely been lying in bed for five minutes when there was a soft knock on his window. He lifted his head off the pillow, and spotted Gaiomere on the other side of the pane, waving.

Hastily padding across the room, he pulled open the window and helped her to climb inside. "I figured your dad wouldn't let me come over this late," Gaiomere explained in a whisper. She glanced up at him, frowning. "My Uncle Dak said you were sort of distraught when you left his unit earlier. Are you okay?"

Atlas sighed. "I am now. It's—I've got a lot to tell you."

He sank down onto his bed, tugging her into his lap and burying his face in the side of her neck as he contemplated, for several moments, where to begin. Finally, his lifted his head, and said, "Talikoth wants me to be his lieutenant general."

Gaiomere did not look particularly surprised. Atlas wasn't sure whether he found that fact angering, or flattering. He sighed, shaking his head. "It's funny—a year ago, it would have been all I'd ever wanted."

"But now it's not," she concluded. She hummed, before remarking, almost to herself, "Dad always used to say that fate loves irony."

Atlas blinked, studying her intently, but before he could ask the question on his mind, Gaiomere continued, "Is it just that you don't want to work with Talikoth?"

"Well no, it's not just that," Atlas said, frowning. "I just don't think—I'm not sure that a role like that—something that comes with so much—so much...power...would be good for me."

Gaiomere gave him an impish little smile. "Are you worried that you might turn into a power-hungry genocidal maniac?"

"Well, maybe!" Atlas spluttered indignantly, his cheeks prickling with heat. "What's so funny about that?"

Gaiomere giggled. "I'm not making fun of you, Atlas. It's just...the idea of you being like that is—it's laughable."

Atlas shifted uncomfortably. "I don't think it's much of a stretch," he muttered, scowling. "Not with the legacy I'm carrying."

Gaiomere rolled her eyes. "Your father's choices don't dictate yours, Atlas—"

"It's not just him," Atlas interrupted sharply. He hesitated, then asked, "Did you know that Dak and Alvi had another child? Sutti and Quill—they would have had an older brother."

"I know," Gaiomere said quietly. "Alvi told me."

"Did she tell you that it was my mother that coordinated the attack that killed him?" Atlas demanded. Gaiomere's eyes widened, and she shook her head. Atlas let out a humorless laugh. "Oh yeah—your cousin is dead because of her. I'm real proud of that one —"

"But Atlas, that's not—that's not you," Gaiomere insisted. He only shook his head, glaring down at the quilt atop his bed, but she cupped his cheek and turned his face towards her. "None of their choices have any bearing on who you are. Just like my dad's choices don't have any bearing on me. *You're* the one that showed me that."

Atlas sighed, leaning his head back against the wall. "It's different. Every day you make up for any evil your parents could have ever committed. The way you care about other people, it's—it's easy for you. Your first instinct is always to do the right thing, no matter what it will cost you., but I'm—I'm not like that. You don't hear the things that go on in my head. Every crime either of my parents have ever committed...all the violence staining my bloodline...all I ever seem to do is perpetuate it."

Gaiomere let out a little huff of laughter. "Atlas, you're judging your own thoughts against my actions," she pointed out. "You don't know what goes on in my head either. I've thought awful things, but it's what we choose to act on that matters. Both of us have done awful things."

She looped her arms around his neck and wriggled even closer to him. "I'm not trying to convince you to take the position—I just want to make sure this isn't a decision you're making out of fear, or because you're...I don't know...running from everything you've done."

"It's not," Atlas said quickly. "I just know myself. It's better for the clan this way. And everybody else, too." He sighed. "My whole life, I thought I was destined to take my father's place—but I don't think that was ever supposed to be my path."

"I imagine that would be rather freeing,"

Gaiomere muttered, with a little huff of laughter. "Otherwise it's like ruining the end of a story."

Atlas glanced down at her sharply. "Yeah, I—I suppose it is." He drummed his fingers absently against her thigh, his brows furrowing as he thought. "But your father believed in fate, didn't he? Even though you—you mocked me for it, back in the North."

Gaiomere's cheeks pinkened. "It wasn't personal," she said. "I just—my dad always acted as though his path was directed by fate—so naturally, when he died, it sort of became the thing that took him away from me." She absently traced patterns on his shoulder, and her voice was little more than a murmur as she added, "I think—I think I might believe in it now, though."

Atlas had been carding his fingers through her wild curls, but he promptly froze. "I thought you didn't," he said, his tone almost accusatory.

Gaiomere glanced up at him, arching a quizzical brow. "I didn't."

He stared at her for several seconds before persisting, "But now you do?"

"I suppose I do."

Atlas gaped at her, befuddled, and irritated at her lack of forthcomingness. "Well, how come?" he demanded. "What changed your mind?" Gaiomere shrugged, but did not open her mouth to offer any further explanation, and Atlas let out a frustrated breath. "Well, something must have changed your mind," he reasoned.

"It doesn't matter what changed my mind," she said firmly, shooting him a vexed look.

"Well of course it matters," Atlas insisted stubbornly. "Given how hard it is to change your mind about anything—"

"Atlas, just forget it—"

"No, I want to know," he said rather petulantly.

"It's none of your business, it doesn't matter—" Gaiomere rambled, straightening up taller.

"Well if it doesn't matter, why won't you tell me?" he snapped.

"Ugh, fine!" she burst out, glowering at him. "Fine, if you just—just promise to drop it afterwards, and promise—promise you won't be weird about it." Atlas gave her a bewildered look, and her eyes narrowed to slits. "Promise, Atlas," she said in a fierce voice.

"Okay, yeah, fine. I promise," Atlas agreed, frowning.

Gaiomere nodded slowly. "Okay, well I just—I just think it's a little...a little weird that your dad used to be best friends with my dad, and even though my dad left the Obarion clan sixteen years ago, me and my brother still ended up trapped at the Vedas base at the exact same time that you were. It's just like..." She let out a heavy exhale. "It's just a little too freaky to be a coincidence, you know?" She looked up at him, her eyes searching his face as she said, in a timid voice, "It's almost like—like—"

She's like you.

Your excellence manifests most prominently when you have something to prove.

"Like fate brought us together," Atlas finished for her.

As soon as the words left his mouth, all the pieces seemed to click into place. Talikoth had seen it long before Atlas, and the truth had been evident long before he'd ever been looking for it.

Atlas had recognized, all of those months ago, when he'd first met her at the Vedas' base, how dangerous Gaiomere could be. Had recognized what she was—a threat to the Obarion. Not only because of her mind, but because of her strength. He had recognized that strength in her almost immediately, but he never would have guessed that that strength would become his own. That this thread between them would not serve to weaken him, but rather to bolster him.

"It sounds sort of stupid said aloud," Gaiomere mumbled, looking away.

Atlas shrugged. "I think it's true," he said quietly. He watched her carefully, his face very serious. "If I went east, would you—would you go with me? I know it's—it's asking a lot and everything, with your whole family being here—I'm sure Whitsom wouldn't come, he loves it here—and I know how important it is for you to keep your tribe safe—"

Gaiomere interrupted him, stretching up to press her mouth against his. "That includes you now too, you know," she said softly, as soon as they'd broken apart. "I know that my family's safe here at headquarters— especially with how terrified all the Obarion soldiers are of your dad—but how can I make sure you're safe if you're traipsing all over the Fallen Land?"

Atlas' brow arched. "Oh, you're keeping me safe, now, are you?"

Gaiomere swatted his shoulder. "Excuse *you*. Does the name Jereis ring any bells? Or Raider?" Atlas pulled a face, and she laughed. "We keep *each other* safe."

"Okay, but if we were keeping track, I think the scale would be tipping significantly in one direction over the other," he drawled. Gaiomere laughed again, pressing her lips to his once more. He'd just cast a glance towards the blinds, with half a mind to get up and close them, when an imposing knock sounded against his bedroom door.

"Last time I checked," came Talikoth's irritated drone, "Your laugh wasn't that high-pitched, Atlas."

Atlas glanced sideways at Gaiomere, who had frozen on his lap. "I don't know what you're talking about," he said, in a rather pathetic attempt at a falsetto. She burst out laughing once more, and Talikoth yanked open the door. He evidently was still grouchy from their previous discussion, for his glare was even more cutting than usual.

"How did you get in here?" he demanded, frowning at Gaiomere.

She looked up at him innocently, her brown eyes wide, and his gaze flickered over to the window. "You sneaky, *conniving* little—"

"I was just leaving!" Gaiomere said hastily. She gave Atlas a fleeting kiss on the cheek and hopped off the bed, shuffling by Talikoth. When his back was to her, she caught Atlas' eye and mouthed, *"I'll sneak back in later."*

As soon as she'd left, Talikoth turned to give the window a contemplative once-over. "I'm bolting that," he said decisively.

"Wouldn't be the first time she'd gotten around that," Atlas muttered.

Talikoth was already halfway back to the dining room table, but he whipped around. "What did you just say?"

Atlas hastily flipped off his lamp and yanked his covers over his head. "I said 'goodnight, Dad!'"

◆ ◆ ◆

Atlas and Gaiomere decided, over the course of the next few days, that they'd leave in a month's time. That would give them ample opportunity to scour the maps in the Obarion library and ask the older members of the clan—the ones who remembered details of the East—for as much information as they could obtain.

Whitsom, by all accounts, took the news rather well. He did not seem even remotely perturbed by the idea of his little sister traipsing all over the Fallen Land.

"She's a little fighter, that one," he'd told Alvi one night at dinner, around a mouthful of chicken. Alvi and Dak did not seem nearly so keen on the idea, but Whitsom had been quick to take Atlas and Gaiomere's side. "She's survived this long, hasn't she? And besides—she's got Atlas."

Maggi, however, threw a proper fit. "You don't even know what's out there!" the little girl exclaimed, pacing in front of the sofa in Atlas' unit. She ticked off on her fingers, "There could be tribes of Flesh Flayers ten times the size of the one by the caverns. There could be all sorts of animals we've never encountered. There could be radioactive fumes from all the bombings—"

"Maggi, we'll be fine," Atlas attempted to appease her from where he leaned against the kitchen counter.

Maggi whirled on him like some wild creature bent on vengeance. "And you—you honestly think you've got a chance surviving out there?" Atlas' mouth opened to argue, but she didn't give him the chance. "You spoilt, pompous, mollycoddled little *clansman*."

"*Ooh*, she said clansman like a diss, though," Whitsom whispered. He sat on the couch beside Coral where the two of them watched the argument unfold in front of them with no small degree of amusement as they passed a plate of Delurah's cookies between them.

"Five extra points for using the word mollycoddled," Coral piped up. "I give extra points anytime someone uses a word I don't know—"

"You're probably giving away a lot of extra points," Whitsom said, snickering.

"And another thing!" Maggi continued, as though there hadn't been an interruption, "What happens when you two inevitably break up?" She turned towards Whitsom and censoriously snarled, "He's gonna ditch her in the middle of the jungle and she'll get eaten by a bear!"

"Are there even jungles in North America?" Atlas asked to no one in particular.

"North ah-whatica?" Whitsom said around a mouthful of cookie.

"If there are, they certainly wouldn't have bears," Gaiomere pointed out reasonably.

"That's not the point!" Maggi shrieked.

"Maggi, we aren't going to break up," Atlas told her matter-of-factly.

"Pfft, okay," Maggi said, snorting. "You guys fight like three times a day—I give it another year, tops."

"Ooh, I'll get in on that bet!" Coral called, a handful of cookie crumbs spilling from his mouth. "I say six months—seven, if Gaiomere's really desperate and lonely..."

Rasta, who was sitting in an armchair near the bookcase, had been largely silent, but at that moment, he piped up, "Can I come, too?"

A tense quiet fell over the room. Atlas and Whitsom looked at each other, and Atlas was quite certain they were both thinking the same thing.

"I'm worried it could be too dangerous for you, little fox," Gaiomere began tentatively. "And I wouldn't want you to—"

"Maggi just said it was too dangerous for you to go, and Atlas said it'd be fine!" Rasta argued, his little brows furrowing. "You can't tell me I can't go for all the same reasons Whitsom said you could!"

"Oh no, you guys are *not* taking Rasta!" Maggi snapped. "That's not fair!"

"You could come, too," Rasta said.

"I don't want to come!" Maggi yelled. Atlas was surprised to see tears in her eyes, and her voice quivered when she spoke. "I like it here! I like sleeping in the same place every night, and always knowing I'll have food, and having friends my age! I just don't understand why we can't stay in one place for a while!"

"Hey, Mags, I'm not going anywhere," Whitsom reassured her. "And it's not like they'll be gone forever—"

"It should only take us a few months to reach the Atlantic," Atlas reasoned. "And we're not even heading east straight away—Zarr wants to wrap up some of Raider's loose ends in the North, so we'll be close enough to visit whenever you want, for a little bit anyway—"

Maggi rolled her eyes, tossing her black hair over her shoulder. "Fine, whatever. But you aren't taking Rasta."

"You're not the boss of me, Maggi!" Rasta shouted, springing to his feet. His little cheeks were flushed red with anger. Atlas exchanged a surprised glance with Gaiomere, for he'd never seen Rasta so much as raise his voice, but now he stood with his hands clenched and eyes narrowed into a frosty glare. "I want to go and if Gaiomere gets to, so do I!"

Whitsom rested his elbows on his knees and folded his hands in front of him. "I think it'd be good for him," he said slowly. "Maggi's always doing things for him—it'd be good for him to get out on his own. So long as Gai isn't babying him out there, too."

"I don't baby him," Gaiomere insisted, but both the older boys ignored her.

Atlas was scrutinizing Rasta. The little boy glared right back at him, his gaze unwavering. "I won't let her baby him," Atlas said quietly. "You have to learn to fend for yourself though, understood?"

Rasta nodded, his face splitting into a bright smile.

"So *unfair!*" Maggi bellowed, storming out of the living room. She shoved several chairs over on her way and slammed the unit door behind her so hard that it rattled in the frame.

Gaiomere sighed, hopping off the counter. "Damage control," she muttered, kissing Atlas on the cheek and trudging out the door after Maggi.

Delurah had unsurprisingly been distraught, and spent forty-five minutes trying to talk Atlas out of their plans. Gaiomere said that her grandparents, Alvi's mother and father, who resided in the first quadrant of the civilians' quarters, hadn't responded any better.

"She told me that only *harlots* go tramping around the country with their boyfriends before they're married—can you believe that?" Gaiomere railed one afternoon, a week before their departure date.

"Garagleen and Aurelia are just old-fashioned," Atlas had assured her, but Gaiomere had continued as though he hadn't spoken.

"She said I was a hussy! *Me!* Oh, the temper on that woman! And she's *so* self-righteous all the time—"

Atlas smirked wryly. "It's an awfully good thing none of those attributes got passed down the line."

The day before they were bound to leave, Atlas knocked on Moonstone's office door with his arms wrapped around a giant, brightly decorated basket, painted hot pink.

When she glanced up from her paperwork, she blinked in surprise. Atlas had not spoken to her since he'd stormed from her office several weeks before. For a moment, the two of them just looked at each other.

Finally, she said, "All this time I didn't realize you were hiding such remarkable decorating skills from us, Atlas."

"Gaiomere did all the bows and stuff," he told her. "But I take full credit for the paint job." He set the basket on her desk, and she peered inside.

Moonstone arched a dark brow, glancing back up at him. "Are those—"

"Stink bombs," Atlas confirmed, his lips twitching upwards. "About thirty of them in all. So you can get Whitsom and Coral back for all the times they've hit your office."

"And I'm to believe you weren't involved in any of those incidents," Moonstone droned, smirking wryly.

"Me? No way, I'm just a humble messenger."

She smiled, shaking her head. "Thank you, Atlas."

Silence filled the room once more, before

Moonstone said, "I suppose it's wishful thinking on my part to believe that you're here to tell me you've changed your mind."

Atlas rubbed the back of his neck, gazing absently at a silver picture frame that sat atop her desk—the same frame that adorned her desk back at the Vedas' base.

"I'm afraid so," he said. "But I am here to say that —well—" He broke off, frowning. "My father did some awful things—for the good of the people, he said. I don't —I don't agree with a lot of what he's done, and I'm not unaware of all the pain and suffering he's caused, but I can at least see that—well, his role in the Westland, everything he's done, it's—it's not quite so black and white as I might have believed."

He took a deep breath, lifting his gaze to meet Moonstone's. "And I just figure—well, I figure if I can give him that impartiality, maybe I can do the same for you."

Moonstone smiled—a genuine smile, not her barely-there twitch of the lips. "That means more than you know," she said quietly.

Atlas nodded. He hesitated, and then reached over her desk and grabbed the silver picture frame. "What's your son's name?" he asked, as he studied the young man in the photo. He must have been only fifteen or sixteen at the time the photo had been taken, but he looked to be almost as tall as Atlas. His skin was almond brown, and his hair was braided tightly to his scalp. He had Moonstone's dark, shrewd eyes.

"Diggory," she said quietly. She seemed to sense what was on Atlas' mind, for she continued, "It's a big country, Atlas. There's no guarantee you'll run into him."

He shrugged, setting down the frame and sliding his hands into his pockets, his gaze roving absently towards the ceiling. "It's a smaller world than you'd think," he replied. "Besides, fate always tends to work to my advantage. It's a gift, really."

Moonstone rolled her eyes. "There's no telling whether or not he's alive," she argued determinedly.

Atlas arched a brow, snatching one of the stink bombs from her basket and absently tossing it between his hands. "You said I reminded you of him," he said reasonably. She nodded, and he continued, "Well, if there's one thing I know, it's that guys like me are notoriously hard to get rid of."

Moonstone laughed—actually laughed, which Atlas had never seen her do before. It made her face look decades younger, and for a moment, he saw the same woman he'd seen in the photograph with his mother.

"I'm gonna borrow this," he said, tapping the stink bomb against the back of the chair. "Not for me to use, of course."

"Of course," Moonstone allowed.

Atlas smiled. "I'll see you around, General."

She inclined her head. "Goodbye, Atlas."

The morning of their departure was bright, warm, and dry. The sky was cloudless, and there was the faintest breeze playing through the trees.

When Atlas passed through the front gates, Zarr already had the car parked and waiting for them. "The others coming soon?" the black-haired boy asked.

"Should be here any minute, I told them nine o'clock," Atlas replied.

Even as he spoke, Jacoby, Rasta and Gaiomere

came plodding down the sloping lawn. "I was saying goodbye to my grandparents," Gaiomere explained. Atlas took her bag from her and heaved it into the trunk as she continued, "Aurelia was surprisingly collected—she didn't lecture me again or anything—what?"

Atlas had been trying very hard to hide his smirk, but Gaiomere was rather adept at reading his expressions. "I may have spoken to her last night, to ease her concerns," he said nonchalantly, as he swung Rasta's bag into the trunk.

Gaiomere's eyes narrowed, and she crossed her arms over her chest, edging out of the way as Jacoby shoved his monstrous backpack in after Rasta's bag. "Oh? And what is it you said exactly?" she demanded, tapping her foot rather impatiently.

Atlas slammed the trunk shut, leaning against the back of the car and drawing Gaiomere into his arms. "I may have implied—and by implied, I mean outright stated—that if she let you go I'd marry you as soon as we returned to Headquarters."

Gaiomere's eyes narrowed, and her nostrils flared. "Oh, you did, did you?" Atlas nodded, and she huffed, muttering, "That was a rather presumptuous thing to tell her—"

"Well, I figured I had at least a couple years to talk you into it," Atlas said, smirking. Gaiomere's lips quirked up into a smile, despite her irritation, and she allowed him to pull her closer, draping her arms around his neck. "I'm pretty persuasive—a flower crown every day for the rest of your life would be a pretty hard offer to turn down—"

"I'm pretty sure that's bribery, not persuasion," Gaiomere remarked, laughing.

Atlas spotted Whitsom, Maggi, and Jem making their way down the slope, and just past the gate, Dak and Alvi were corralling Sutti and Quill towards them as well.

The crowd had scarcely reached them when Jem walked up behind Gaiomere, grasped her around the middle, and yanked her out of Atlas' arms with a surprising amount of strength. "Stop hogging her, you're already taking her away from me," the freckled girl said fiercely.

"Yeah, and *I'm* the uncivilized one," Whitsom muttered. Rasta had already gotten into the car, but he hastily clambered out and flung his arms around Whitsom's middle. "Aww, hey little buddy—I'm gonna miss you. You gotta promise to make Attie play lots of card games with you, keep him from brooding too much, you hear?"

Maggi was hovering a ways away from the rest of them, her arms crossed over her chest and her face set into a scowl. Gaiomere had gone over to her, and was speaking in a soothing tone, an arm wrapped around her shoulders.

Atlas' attention was drawn away when Whitsom yanked him into a headlock. "You better take care of my sister, you punk," Whitsom said, ruffling Atlas' hair before he released him. "Otherwise I'm gonna have to hunt you down."

"I'm sure you'd find me, too, Wolfman," Atlas taunted. Whitsom smacked him in the side of the head.

"Especially with how bad he smells," Zarr crooned from where he sat in the driver's seat.

"You!" Whitsom said suddenly, extending a finger towards the black-haired boy, who leaned his head out of the car. "Don't corrupt Rasta...or Atlas for that matter."

"I'm just a little boy," Zarr said, his eyes widening innocently.

Alvi had wrapped Gaiomere in a tight hug, and Sutti clung to one of her legs, while Quill had somehow managed to scramble halfway up her back. "Atlas," Dak said quietly, holding out a hand to shake. "Hope you don't stay away too long."

"Knowing Gaiomere, she'll probably get bored within a couple of months without a lab to blow things up in," Atlas said with a snort, as he shook Dak's hand. He cast a quick glance over the older man's shoulder, and hesitantly asked, "Is uh—is Talikoth—"

"He's not really one for heartfelt goodbyes," Dak said. He hesitated, and then admitted, "I think perhaps he is under the impression that refusing to watch you go will give him some level of deniability." He put a hand on Atlas shoulder. "Take care of yourself, will you?"

Atlas nodded. "Will do, sir." He climbed into the backseat and intertwined a hand with Gaiomere's, giving her a small smile. They were just about to pull away when Whitsom gestured for Atlas to roll down the window.

"Don't you get my sister pregnant, Attie, " Whitsom warned. Zarr burst out laughing.

"Not any of your business, Whit—" Gaiomere said indignantly.

Dak interrupted her, adding, "Or if you are going to, do it after the last week of winter—I'd really like those cigars."

"I'm sitting right here!" Gaiomere spluttered. "I'm

not some breeding cow!"

Zarr was still sniggering as he slammed on the gas, and Atlas watched the familiar gates that towered in front of the grounds shrink in the distance, until they vanished altogether.

◆ ◆ ◆

Talikoth stepped up beside Dak, who still stood at the foot of the slope outside the gate, just as Atlas' car caught a glint of sunlight, and winked out of sight.

Whitsom and the rest of Atlas' little cronies ambled back up onto the grounds, talking loudly. Alvi was watching the twins collect pinecones near the tree line, but Talikoth's attention was drawn away from her when Dak spoke.

"The boy was disappointed that you weren't down here to say goodbye," he said quietly.

Talikoth let out a harsh breath. "Well, I'm *disappointed* that he's leaving," he snapped, aggravation leeching into his tone before he could stop it. "Fleeing his fate like some kind of—"

"You should know better than anyone that no man can *flee* their fate," Dak scolded. "If his path is more circuitous it will only make him better prepared to face it."

"He's only going because he's afraid to fail," Talikoth argued.

Dak snorted. "Of course he is. There is nothing quite so terrifying as the potential for one's own greatness."

Talikoth scowled, but said nothing.

"Chin up, old friend," Dak remarked, as Alvi led Sutti and Quill past them, and back up towards the main gate. "When he inevitably returns, this will only make his biddability all the sweeter."

The corner of Talikoth's lips twitched, and Dak strode away to join his family. Talikoth stood there for a few minutes longer alone, and then heaved a sigh, turning and making his way up the slope towards Headquarters, dread already knotting in his stomach at the thought of Moonstone's obnoxiously loquacious report that sat waiting on his desk.

Still, he supposed, it could be worse. The danger, for the present moment, had passed.

The acquisition of the Vedas' alliance gave Talikoth the time he needed to adjust his plans. Atlas' refusal to assume the rank offered him was a minor setback, but Dak was right. It was only a matter of time that the boy came to his senses. Talikoth was patient. And when the time came, Atlas would return to the Westland, and take his place at his father's side.

Just as fate had written for him.

BOOKS IN THIS SERIES

The Fallen Land Chronicles

Obarion

Renegade

Made in the USA
Middletown, DE
05 November 2022

14129863R00239